5

D1601144

TRINI! COME!

TRINI! COME!

GERONIMO'S CAPTIVITY OF TRINIDAD VERDÍN

A Novel

W. MICHAEL FARMER

FIVE STAR
A part of Gale, a Cengage Company

LIBRARY OF CONGRESS CATALOGING-IN-PUBLICATION DATA

Names: Farmer, W. Michael, 1944– author.
Title: Trini! Come! : Geronimo's captivity of Trinidad Verdín : a novel / W. Michael Farmer.
Other titles: Geronimo's captivity of Trinidad Verdín
Description: First edition. | Waterville, Maine : Five Star, 2022. | Series: Five Star frontier fiction | Identifiers: LCCN 2022012579 | ISBN 9781432895785 (hardcover)
Subjects: LCSH: Geronimo, 1829–1909—Fiction. | Naiche, approximately 1857–1921—Fiction. | Apache Indians—Wars, 1883–1886—Fiction. | BISAC: FICTION / Biographical | FICTION / Westerns | LCGFT: Biographical fiction. | Western fiction. | Novels.
Classification: LCC PS3606.A725 T75 2022 | DDC 813/.6—dc23/eng/20220606
LC record available at https://lccn.loc.gov/2022012579

First Edition. First Printing: November 2022
Find us on Facebook—https://www.facebook.com/FiveStarCengage
Visit our website—http://www.gale.cengage.com/fivestar
Contact Five Star Publishing at FiveStar@cengage.com

Printed in Mexico
Print Number : 1   Print Year : 2023

For Corky, my best friend and wife,
the wind beneath my wings.

TABLE OF CONTENTS

ACKNOWLEDGMENTS

There have been many friends and professionals who have supported me in this work, to whom I owe a special debt of gratitude for their help and many kindnesses.

Lynda Sánchez's insights into Apache culture and their voices are a major point of reference in understanding the times and personalities covered in this work.

Audra Gerber provided excellent editorial support that contributed to this work's clarity.

Good friends are a rare and a true gift. Pat Fraley and Mike Alexander opened their home to me during numerous visits to New Mexico. Their generosity allowed me time and a place from which to do research that otherwise would not have been possible.

The patience, encouragement, and support of my wife, Carolyn, through long days of research and writing made this work possible and it is to her this work is dedicated.

The histories listed in Additional Reading that I found particularly helpful were those by Angie Debo; Eve Ball, Nora Henn, and Lynda A. Sánchez; Alicia Delgadillo and Miriam A. Perrett; Lynda Sánchez; Sherry Robinson; Edwin Sweeney; and Robert Utley.

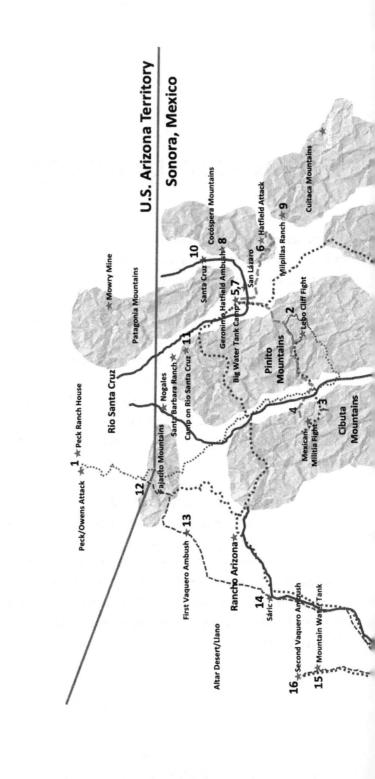

U.S. Arizona Territory

Sonora, Mexico

Peck/Owens Attack ★ 1 ★ Peck Ranch House

Mowry Mine ★

Patagonia Mountains

Rio Santa Cruz

Cocóspera Mountains

Santa Cruz ★ 10

Geronimo Hatfield Ambush ★ 8

★ 5,7

Hatfield Attack

San Lázaro

6 ★ Milpillas Ranch ★ 9

Cuitaca Mountains

Nogales ★

Santa Barbara Ranch ★

Camp on Rio Santa Cruz ★ 11

Big Water Tank Camp

Lebo Cliff Fight

★ 2

Pinito Mountains

Fajarito Mountains

4 ★ 3

Mexican
Militia Fight ★

Cibuta
Mountains

★ 12

First Vaquero Ambush ★ 13

Rancho Arizona ★

Altar Desert/Llano

14 ★ Sáric

16 ★ Second Vaquero Ambush

15 ★ Mountain Water Tank

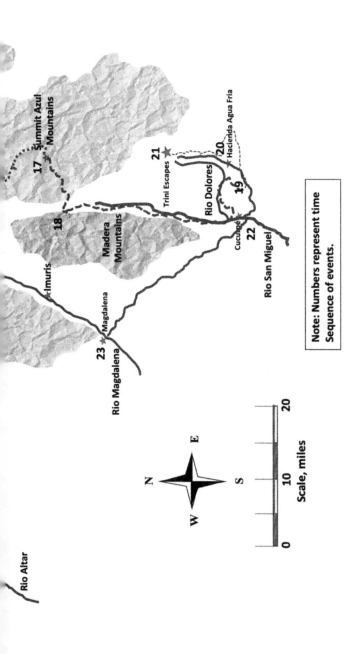

Map of the Assumed Naiche–Geronimo Band Trails and Story Locations in Sonora during Trinidad Verdín's Captivity

FICTIONAL AND
HISTORICAL CHARACTERS

FICTIONAL

Blood Ear (also known as Badger)—scalp-hunting vaquero

Francisca—servant for Don Valenzuela

Gritto—hacendado with land bordering that of Don Valenzuela

Jose—lead vaquero for Don Valenzuela

Juanita—wife of Natculbaye

Old One—scalp-hunting vaquero

Paco—vaquero for Don Valenzuela

Rosa—servant for Don Valenzuela

Young One—scalp-hunting vaquero

HISTORICAL

Americans and Mexicans

Artisan Peck—owner of Peck Ranch and husband to Petra

Captain Lawton—field commander of American soldiers pursuing Geronimo

Don Patricio Valenzuela—owner of the Agua Fría Hacienda and comandante of the Mexican militia that helped free Trinidad Verdín

Gabriel Sinohui—treasurer and leader of the militia for the village of Cucurpé

Lieutenant Dr. Leonard Wood—logistics officer and doctor for Captain Lawton

Lieutenant Finley—second in command and executive officer for Captain Lawton

María Cuen—Trinidad Verdín aunt

Petra Peck—Trinidad Verdín aunt

Trinidad Verdín—niece to Petra Peck and María Cuen

Apaches

Ahnandia—warrior in his early twenties who speaks English

Atelnietze—prime warrior, close friends with Naiche

Beshe—father-in-law to Naiche

Chappo—warrior in late teens, son of Geronimo

Garditha—orphaned boy about the age of Trinidad

Geronimo—war leader and medicine man for the Apaches

Haozinne—wife of Naiche

Hunlona—warrior in late teens who travels with Geronimo and Natculbaye

Kanseah—teenaged novitiate warrior

Leosanni—girl about age six

Naiche—chief of the Chokonen Apaches

Natculbaye—warrior, segundo (number two) for Geronimo

She-gha—wife of Geronimo

Tah-das-te—wife of Ahnandia

Yahechul—warrior in his early twenties who nearly kills Trinidad

SPANISH WORDS AND PHRASES

Alcalde—mayor
Ataque—attack
Ayúdame—help me
Bosque—forest
Buenas tardes—good afternoon
Cállate—be quiet or shut up
Capitan—captain
Casa—house
Cautiva—captive
Cena—supper
Comandante—commander
Comida—lunch
Comprende—understand
Cortinas—drapes
Desayuno—breakfast
Dispare—shoot
Dueña—guardian (female)
Espere—hold on
Gallo—rooster
Guerrerocito—Little Warrior
Habla español?—Do you speak Spanish?
Hacendado—wealthy landowner
Hija—daughter or dear child
El jefe—the chief or leader
Jacal—a small hut or house made of adobe or reeds

Limonada—lemonade
Llano—dry prairie
Malditca—damn
Mija—mi hija—my dear child or my daughter
Mujer—woman
Mujercita—little woman
No dispares—don't shoot
Puta—whore
Puta jovencita—whore, young and small
Reata—thin rawhide rope
Río Bavispe—Bavispe River
Río Dolores—Dolores River
Río Grande—Great River
Río Altar—Altar River
Río Magdalena—Magdalena River
Río San Miguel—San Miguel River
Rojo—red
Sí, muy bien, gracias—Yes, very well, thank you
Tía—aunt
Soldados—soldiers
Teniente—lieutenant

APACHE WORDS AND PHRASES

Ch'ik'eh doleel—all right; let it be so
Dahndáh—start
Di-yen—medicine woman or man
Doo dat'éé da—it's okay; it doesn't matter
Enjuh—good
Gonit'éé—it's fine; a good place; okay; clear weather
Nakai-yes—Mexicans
Nakai-yi—Mexican
Nantan—big chief
Nish'ii'—I see you
Nit'ééhi—that which is good
Nt'ah—wait
Pindah-lickoyee—white-eyed enemy/enemies
Pesh—iron
Pesh klitso—yellow iron (gold)
Tsach—cradleboard
Ussen—the Apache god of creation and life

APACHE RECKONING OF TIME AND SEASONS

Harvest—used in the context of time, means a year

Hand width (against the horizon sky)—about an hour

Season of little eagles—early spring

Season of many leaves—late spring, early summer

Season of large leaves—midsummer

Season of large fruit—late summer, early fall

Season of earth is reddish brown—late fall

Season of ghost face—lifeless winter

Time of shortest shadows—noon

FOREWORD

On March 27, 1886, Geronimo, Chief Naiche, and other leaders with one hundred fifteen Chiricahua Apache men, women, and children surrendered to General George Crook in Canyon de los Embudos about twelve miles southeast of the San Bernardino ranch on the United States–Mexico border. That night, the Naiche-Geronimo band got roaring drunk, and a whiskey peddler, who wanted the Apache war to continue for its lucrative army supply contracts, convinced Geronimo that as soon as he and Naiche crossed the border, the army would turn them over to civilian authorities for hanging. Although told as a lie, it was in fact what President Grover Cleveland wanted to do. Deep in the night of March 29, within three miles of the border, and camped on the way to Fort Bowie, Arizona, Geronimo and Naiche with eighteen men, fourteen women, and six children broke away from the main group of surrendering Chiricahuas and headed for parts unknown.

Army Apache scouts who had trailed the Chiricahuas since their May 17, 1885, breakout from the Fort Apache Reservation expected the Naiche–Geronimo band to run east into their favored haunts in the rugged Sierra Madre Mountains near the origin of the north-flowing fork of the Bavispe River. Instead, the band ran west, deep into northern Sonora, and after numerous raids for horses and supplies, they established a base camp around April 12, 1886, on the highest peak in the Azul Mountains about forty-five miles southeast of Nogales, Arizona.

There, they rested for about a week.

The entire band then began raiding to the west and, from the town of Imuris, moved north down the Magdalena River toward Nogales. Within twenty miles of Nogales, they turned east into the Pinito Mountains and left their women and children hidden for later pickup at a long-abandoned ruin before heading north to cross the border and raid American ranches, businesses, and villages.

On the morning of April 27, the Chiricahuas boldly stole horses off the street in the little village of Calabasas, Arizona, about eight miles north of Nogales, and then rode southwest down Agua Fría Canyon to the ranch of Artisan and Petra Peck. They arrived at about 9:00 a.m.

Trini! Come! is the story of the Chiricahua raid on the Artisan and Petra Peck ranch and what followed. Its heroine is the twelve-year-old niece of Petra Peck, Trinidad Verdín, who lived with the Pecks to help her pregnant aunt—who already had a two-year-old son—with her chores. Based on true events during the raid and the following two months, it is a story of survival by a young girl in a rugged wilderness, who lived with an unknown culture widely known for torturing to death captives and whose warriors killed nearly all who crossed their paths.

Most of what is known about the Naiche–Geronimo band during Trinidad's two months of captivity comes from reports to the American and Mexican militaries that Trinidad gave them in interviews within a week after she had escaped the Apaches. From the battles she knew about between the Apaches, American cavalry, and Mexican militia, we know she lived as the Apaches lived while under the supervision of Geronimo and his wife, She-gha, and traveled hundreds of miles in the rugged mountain and desert country of northwestern Sonora.

The stories and reports of the Peck raid from others who did not directly witness what happened, such as the story by then-

Lieutenant Dr. Leonard Wood, future army general, make the
raid, while horrific and heartbreaking even as Trinidad told it,
sound much worse than it was. There are many blanks in time
and questions relevant to the story. Among them are why
Geronimo took a small group west into the desert and *llano*
north of the village of Altar and what they did there while Naiche took a much larger group into Arizona.

I've taken a storyteller's license to fill in those blank records
with what might have happened, knowing Geronimo's inclina-
tions from his history in raiding and war. Also, no records exist
about the actual trails the Apaches traveled to their different
camps. Hence, the map of their travels and camp locations is
my best guess based on study of stereo imagery from Google
Earth of the land over which they roamed, a knowledge of how
they preferred to travel, and the general areas where they
established their camps or made attacks on travelers.

During her time in captivity, Trinidad spoke her natural
tongue, Spanish, a little English, and what must have been a
pidgin Apache she had to have learned fast to survive two
months as a captive of Geronimo. To give the reader some sense
of Trinidad's world with the Apaches I have used a few Spanish
and Apache words consistently throughout the text. The meaning of these words is listed in the vocabulary list in the front
pages of this work.

Although only twelve years old, Trinidad Verdín was no child.
She had a woman's heart in a girl's body. Her courage and
determination to survive and escape were admired by the
Apaches who took her and the Mexicans who rescued her.

W. Michael Farmer
Smithfield, Virginia
October 2020

PROLOGUE

Nogales, Arizona, September 1939

It had been a big funeral for Dad Peck, an old man long loved by his community who, in his earlier years, had suffered a staggering tragedy he rarely spoke of. A grandmother, alone with her thoughts, sat gently squeezing a smooth, marble-size pebble in her well-manicured hand. She watched from the shade of a graveside tent as men shoveled dirt onto the coffin in the dark hole where it rested.

Tall and willowy, a girl in her mid-teens left the crowd drifting out the cemetery gate and went to sit with her. "Everyone's leaving now. Are you coming?"

"Tell your momma I want to sit here awhile."

"Yes, ma'am." The girl left the tent and disappeared into the crowd, but she soon returned.

"Momma said she'd be back in an hour or two and said that I should sit with you if that's all right."

The gray-haired lady nodded, still staring at the dark place reclaiming the earth, listening to the grunts of the men shoveling it there, and rolling the pebble against her fingers.

The girl silently watched the gravediggers at their labor as their shovels slid against the sandy soil and the sun painted the evening clouds blood red, oranges, and deep purples. She said softy, trying not to disturb the solitude of the moment, "Momma says that when you were a girl, Dad Peck saved you from Geronimo."

"That's what they say. Do you want the true story?"

The girl's eyes grew wide. "The true story? Please, Grandma, I've wanted to hear your story since I learned you were a Geronimo captive, but no one wanted to talk about it because it might upset Dad Peck."

Trinidad nodded and looked again at the filling grave. "Well . . ."

Chapter 1
The Raid

I was twelve, orphaned at an early age, and didn't remember my mother and father at all. I lived with one of my aunts, María Cuen, until another aunt, Petra Peck, asked if I'd come live at the ranch that she and her husband, Artisan, had started a year or so earlier, about eight miles, as the crow flies, northwest of Nogales. They already had Andy, a two-year-old son. Petra was pregnant again and needed help managing Andy and taking care of the house while she got ready for her next baby. She wanted more children, but not so quickly. I guess things work out that way sometimes.

One morning, Artisan and Charlie Owens, a neighbor he hired to help him, left the ranch house just as the sun was coming up to catch and mark a couple of wild bulls they had recently found. By the time the pendulum clock hanging on the wall showed nine, I was sweeping the rooms in the adobe ranch house and the day was already growing hot in brilliant yellow light, the air filled with the sweet scent of blooming yucca, and the sky a soft blue like polished turquoise.

The chickens out by the barn started squawking, and the horses in the adjacent corral suddenly seemed restless, snorting and moving around a lot. Aunt Petra, her belly swelling with her second child, sat rocking Andy in the cool gloom of the big room used for everything from sitting by the fireplace with her husband on winter evenings, to cooking and eating, to mending clothes, to visiting with passersby. The big, opened door let a

27

cool breeze pass through as the sun rose higher and the myriad insect chorus praised the day. Petra patted the child's back and listened for his breathing to show the beginnings of an early nap after lying at her breast.

I hummed "Camptown Races" like it was a fast jig sung along with a banjo and fiddle and folks dancing. My broom made the short, rapid chops a good sweeping required to gather the dust collecting across Petra's big room on the oxblood floor. I had swept the floor nearly to the edge of the doorway framed by the sun's glare.

Old Blue, with long floppy ears and gray around the muzzle, Artisan's favorite hound, was taking his usual nap in the middle of the porch. He suddenly stood, tail wagging slowly, and stared at the corral. Lifting his ears, he paused a moment, whined, and leapt from the cool porch shade into the morning heat as he ran for the corral. I smiled. He must have heard or smelled some critter out near the coop that made the chickens nervous. I pushed the dust out the door, eager to finish and find out what Old Blue was after. I had a feeling this was going to be a fun day.

Just as Aunt Petra's little son relaxed into dreamland in the nest of her comforting arm and body, Old Blue's barking and occasional howl woke him up. She frowned and said, "What's the matter with that old hound? Maybe the coyote we saw yesterday is after the chickens again. No matter. Whatever it is, he'll have it gone soon enough."

But if anything, Old Blue got louder and more frantic with his barking and howling as a couple of minutes ticked by.

After I finished sweeping the dust off the porch, Aunt Petra said, "Trini, please go see what's making that hound howl and help him run off whatever's out there. His noise is waking up the baby. I have some sewing to do, or Artisan is going to have some mighty breezy pants. If it's a coyote, a few rocks will run

28

him off. If it's a snake or a skunk, just leave it alone. They'll eventually leave, but hold Old Blue so he doesn't try to go after them."

I leaned the broom against the doorframe. "Yes'm. I'll be right back. Old Blue and me, we'll run it off."

I jumped off the porch, pretending it was a high cliff, landed on both feet in a squat, and walked across the dusty ground starving for water that Uncle Artisan called a "yard." I tried not to make a sound, hoping to surprise and see a new varmint, but not if it was a skunk. A fox or Gila monster would do just fine. Old Blue glanced my way as I approached but never missed a beat with his barks and howls.

Pretending I was an Indian, I crept up to the plank corral gate I usually used when I went to collect eggs and feed the chickens, and leaned forward, one eye in a squint, to peer through a crack between the planks. My breath caught in my throat, nearly making me cough. I saw an Apache squatting by the chicken coop holding a gleaming new repeating rifle while he studied the horses, mules, and steers milling about in the corral. Uncle Artisan and Charlie Owens had penned them up there before they went to look for the bulls.

The Apache wore a long-tailed shirt, long white breechcloth, moccasins that reached to his knees, and a blue bandana tied across his forehead to keep his shoulder-length hair out of his eyes. I guessed he was in his mid-to-late teens, in his own way a nice-looking young man—for an Apache—and he was all business, studying the livestock and ignoring Old Blue's barks and howls. My heart pounding, I swallowed my fear and took care not to make noise or raise dust as I backed up, watching the corral gate as if it were the gate to hell.

When I was halfway back to the house, I turned and ran for the door and was inside just as the baby had settled back into a nap, ignoring the ruckus Old Blue made.

Petra raised her brows as she held a finger over her lips for me to keep my voice down. She whispered, "What is it?"

Nearly out of breath, I whispered, "There's an Apache squatting in the dirt out by the chicken coop. He's looking over the stock."

Petra's eyes grew wide and her jaw dropped. With the baby still in her arms, she went to the window and pulled the curtain to open a crack so she could see the corral gate and the barking hound.

"Trini, bring me Artisan's pistol off the dresser. He didn't take any guns this morning. Wouldn't you know he thought it was too much weight to haul around taking care of cattle and horses?"

The pistol was heavy, cold iron shining with a light coat of oil and a smell of kerosene. Artisan had just cleaned it the night before. I checked for cartridges loaded in the cylinder. Loaded. I handed it to Petra, who paced by the window with the baby still cradled in her left arm. She cocked the pistol and, heading for the door, ready for business, said over her shoulder, "Stay inside, Trini! Don't let him see you if he comes to the house. Don't worry, we'll be all right. He's probably just looking for some corn to make *tizwin*. Those Apaches are awful drunks, you know."

Petra crossed the porch shade from the roof overhang and took two steps across the yard toward the corral. I peeked out from the edge of the curtains against the windowsill, my heart pulsating from a strange mixture of fear that something awful might happen and the excitement that I might see my aunt capture an Apache.

Old Blue was gone, no longer barking, and nowhere in sight. The plank gate flew open, pushed by the Apache I'd seen, heading for the ranch house.

Petra yelled, "Stop, you bloodthirsty mongrel. Get away from here before we kill you."

The Apache paused for an instant and, seeing Petra raise her pistol, threw his rifle to his shoulder and fired before she could even think of pulling the trigger.

The snapping roll of thunder from the rifle roared in my ears as I saw blood explode in a spray from a big hole torn between Petra's shoulder blades. Clutching the baby to her chest, which was turning bright blood red, she stumbled back half a step and then fell backward, landing hard, her eyes and mouth frozen open in surprise. I knew she was dead before she hit the ground. The rifle's boom and the hard bump against his mother when she landed on the hard ground, raising a puff of dust, made the baby start screaming.

My eyes were about to bulge out of their sockets as I threw a hand over my mouth to keep from screaming and then swallowed hard to hold down the vomit. I watched the Apache through the crack in the curtains. He walked up to Petra, calmly snatched the screaming baby out of her arms by his feet, swung him in a swooping arc to smash his head against a post, and then tossed his body back onto Petra. He saw the pistol in her fingers, jerked it away, and pushed it under the cartridge belt around his waist.

By the time he reached the porch, I was trembling and praying, stretched out under Petra and Artisan's bed. The soft shuffle of his moccasins filled the room as he glided through the doorway. I held my breath, barely breathing. The sound of crashing drawers jerked from cabinets and their contents hitting the floor filled the room. To keep from screaming, I chewed so hard on my lower lip that I tasted blood and remembered stories the women told at quilting bees and covered-dish suppers about Apache raiders ruthlessly violating women and then scalping them. I wasn't even a woman yet, nor was I even sure what "violate" meant. Would they do that to me? I prayed silently over and over, *Help me, God. Help me.*

I heard the pounding hooves of many horses galloping up to the door and then voices of men speaking in a language that sounded like a series of clicks, short and melodic grunts, and soft groans. Some came in the house, and others headed toward the corral. Horses neighed, mules brayed, and cattle bellowed as gate bars across one side of the corral dropped. Sounds of furniture smashed and overturned came quickly. Glass broke, and pans and Petra's big skillet rang against the floor amid laughs and yells.

Three pairs of moccasins with silver dollar-sized leather buttons on the toes appeared on the floor near the bed. Drawers came out of the armoire, their contents hitting the floor, and moccasins dragged through them as they looked for special prizes hidden away. Clothes from hangers began hitting the floor, Petra's marrying dress and Artisan's suit among them. There were long comments in the strange language and then laughing as the armoire crashed over. The big mirror hanging on the wall shattered amid much laughing, the silvered pieces crashing against the floor and scattering across the room. Suddenly, the room grew still. A piece of the broken mirror had landed on its edge and tilted back against the dresser. In its reflection, I saw two Apache men staring at me.

Help me, God. Help me.

Faster than a striking rattlesnake, a pair of rough, calloused hands reached under the bed, grabbed my ankles, and began dragging me out. Bits of gravel in the smooth oxblood floor, like sharp, tiny knives, stabbed me in the back and hips. I grabbed hold of the ropes supporting the straw-tick mattress and kicked hard against the hands and laughs pulling me out of my hiding place. I knew my fighting only delayed the inevitable, and inch by painful inch, it didn't take long before they pulled me free of the bed. The man who had my ankles looked about as old as the one I had seen in the corral. He wasn't big, but had muscles of iron on thin arms unhidden by a shirt, a long red scar across his chest, and a cur's snarl of a grin.

He took both my feet with one hand and my hair with the other and, in one smooth motion, flipped me over on my belly, let my feet go, and yanked me to my feet, his fingers curling into and pulling my hair. My scalp felt like it was on fire. I knew he was going to scalp me, and I swung my fists at him, but they only made arcs in the air, hitting nothing as he held me out at arm's length.

The other two laughed and shook their heads as he shoved my head, first toward one and then toward the other. He jerked me back, grabbed my wrists, and slammed them up behind my back. My arms were in agony from the pain shooting up them. I clenched my teeth, vowing to give these killers no pleasure in my pain. The man who had me felt both sides of my chest, where my breasts were just beginning to grow, and shook his head.

He mumbled and shook his head when he forced me to my knees and let my arms go. They were so numb they fell to my sides like useless weights. He grabbed my hair again, pulled my head back, and reached around for a knife stuck in a scabbard behind him in his ammunition belt. The sunlight streaming through the broken window reflected off the blade's shiny edge, and I knew I was about to die as he brought his hand holding the knife to the other side of my head to slash my throat.

My tingling arms were fast gaining strength and began to rise in order to grab the wrist holding his knife. A voice, different from any I'd heard among the men, low and whispery, old and commanding, said, *"Nt'ah!"* (Wait!) A short exchange of words followed between the old man with the voice of authority, whom I could barely see out of the corner of my eye, and the warrior ready to cut my throat. The warrior sheathed his knife and, while still holding my hair, yanked me to my feet. We walked out to the porch, where warriors on their ponies waited. The men inside followed.

The warrior motioned to a young man on a brown-and-white pinto pony and then pushed me off the porch. The young man on the pony made a face of disgust. I stumbled but didn't fall as I saw Petra and the baby lifeless, their blackening blood watering the thirsty dust.

My mind screamed, *It isn't fair! Petra and Artisan don't deserve this. They worked hard for months and years to start this ranch and a family. Now these murderers take it all away like it was nothing. It isn't fair!* My need to scream and cry for Petra and the baby was almost overpowering, but no sound left my lips. I knew that showing any emotion would encourage them to torture me for fun.

The young man walked his pinto over to me. I felt naked and afraid, like all the men were staring at me, but thank God and the whispery old man, I was still alive. Then the Apache who had murdered Petra and the baby came out of the house, pointed at the young man on the pinto, and said in English, "Leader say you live. Ride behind son, Chappo. We go."

Chappo, frowning, stuck an arm down. I grabbed it although my arms still were sore and weak. He swung me up behind him on his saddle. Three men came out of the house. One had a sack of cartridges Artisan kept in the armoire with his new lever-action Winchester one of the other men had taken. Another had the shotgun, Artisan's second pistol, and a sack of shells. The third was pouring oil from a lantern all over the floor and walls. He pulled a match and, like I had seen cowboys do, used the flick of his thumbnail to strike a flame and toss it on the oil. In an instant, blue flames spread across the great room. Over by the barn, flames burst out of the sides of Artisan's blacksmith shop as three men ran out the barn door. The old man who had spared me effortlessly grabbed his saddle horn and leaped into his saddle. He pointed toward the foothills and, with a flip of his arm, motioned toward the range where I knew Artisan and Charlie Owens had gone looking for the bulls they had planned to mark.

CHAPTER 2
MANGAS COLORADAS

The Apaches took all the cattle, horses, and mules in the corrals around the barn and rode toward the foothills. I had ridden horses often at Artisan's ranch, but never without a saddle or behind some man, splayed out unladylike behind the cantle. My thighs, growing tight and sore from riding behind the young Apache warrior, added to my misery as my mind played over and over the images of Petra and the baby lying murdered in the dust, and the humiliation I felt in being dragged from under the bed to face the laughs and sneers of the Apaches who had me. The Apache I rode behind and a few other young men herded the livestock to keep dust down and make them less easy to see. Even so, the dust quickly made us look like ghosts. I even felt grit crunching between my teeth. Other warriors rode behind us and off to each side. I thought I heard them call their leader out in front "Geronimo."

I had heard of Geronimo since I was old enough to understand what the words "heathen," "thief," and "bloody murderer" meant. Now I understood why the ranching people hated and wanted to hang him. Here in the middle of a beautiful hot morning, I was captive to the leader of these despised men, who had smashed Andy's head against a post and murdered Petra, leaving their bleeding bodies sprawled in the dust for the flies, vultures, and coyotes.

The Apaches had destroyed everything in the house, set it and the workshop ablaze, and almost killed me. I expected torture and death from these awful monsters who had appeared out of nowhere only to disappear again until their next murder. Now they rode in the direction of Artisan and Charlie Owens. I prayed the Apaches wouldn't find them.

I thought, *If the Apaches find Artisan and Charlie Owens, they'll surprise and kill those good men too. Most of my family wiped out in a morning. Why? Why? Why are they doing this? It's not right. We haven't done anything to them. Please, please, God, don't let them take Artisan and Charlie.* I started sobbing and couldn't stop as the tears streaked across my face, making rivulets in the dust like water roaring through an arroyo after a summer storm.

Chappo said over his shoulder, in good Spanish just loud enough for me to hear, *"Cállate!"* (You be quiet!)

I swallowed sorrow's ball of thorns and tried to snuffle back tears and wipe the mucus running from my nose. I held my grief in check for a little while until I saw Geronimo and two or three other leaders rein to a stop on top of a low rise in front of us. They studied the land sloping down in front of them. Geronimo waved to men on his right to move downslope and to men on his left to come toward his position. Chappo and the others, leaving two teenage boys to keep the cattle and horses below the rise, rode up to Geronimo, stretched, and leaned around each other to see where he pointed. Then they dismounted with their rifles, and—creeping like cats stalking a mouse—moved down toward Artisan and Charlie, who had dismounted after roping a bull.

I wanted to scream, "Run!" But I hesitated, knowing if I made a sound I would die. I saw the Apaches creeping downhill pause to wait for a signal. I looked over both sides and downslope, trying to understand what they were up to. I hesitated an instant too long. Struggling to get the bull under control, Charlie heard or saw something unusual.

He lifted his head to look up the hill and, seeing Geronimo

and others, yelled, "For God's sake, Artisan, run! Apaches!"

The air was suddenly filled with the snap and roar of rifles. Artisan's and Charlie's hats, as though swatted by some giant hand, flew off in crazy tumbling spirals. Bullets whined past them, punching holes in their shirts and pants and raising little geysers of dust and sand around their boots but miraculously missing their bodies as they ran to swing up on the already-running horses.

I watched their getaway with hopeful eyes and was about to thank God for their escape when rifles began firing from a hidden ravine downslope of the hill much closer to them. Charlie's head jerked back and then flopped forward. He sailed from his horse and into sand and gravel, raising a cloud of dust. Blood streamed from his throat, and he didn't move when he hit the ground. Artisan's horse went down in a hailstorm of bullets, but Artisan managed to clear the saddle, jumping just in time from his falling horse. He landed on his back and was still. Tears began to flood my face. I tried to stop crying but couldn't, and kept saying over and over, "They killed you too, Artisan. They killed you too."

Warriors on the right side of Geronimo rode over to Charlie Owens. They didn't dismount as they circled their horses around him and yelled in wild screams like wolves after a kill and shook their rifles in victory. Then they galloped the short distance to where Artisan was lying, unmoving, not far from his dead horse.

The Apaches walked their horses around Artisan, studying him. Three dismounted and, holding the ends of their rifle barrels, jabbed and punched him with the butts of their stocks. Soon he stirred, sat up, and shook his head, his face scratched and bruised, his bright-red long-handle sleeves showing from the wrists to the elbows of his rolled-up shirtsleeves. The canvas pants and calico shirt he wore were torn in a place or two, but he didn't seem wounded. Two Apaches grabbed him by his shirt, jerked him to his feet, and pushed him up the little rise where Geronimo watched from his horse.

Sick with fear, I felt acid in my throat but managed to keep my stomach down. I expected that they would find some horrible way to torture Artisan and I'd be next. Artisan was a good man who had shown me every kindness. He didn't deserve to die this way.

Pushed and pulled, Artisan reached the top of the rise to face Geronimo, the warriors circling their prisoner. The young Apache who had shot Petra and spoken English stepped into the circle, his rifle cocked and ready, while Chappo swung up on his pony in front of me to watch the show. The sounds of silence encompassed the group as they waited for Geronimo's instructions on how to destroy the *pindah-lickoyee* (white-eyed enemy). He studied the rancher standing straight and proud, raising his chin in defiance, expecting to endure a hard death.

The young Apache said, swinging his arm toward Geronimo, "White Eye, Geronimo, great *di-yen* (shaman) of the Chiricahuas."

Artisan nodded. "Yeah. Ever'body 'round here thinks he's in Mexico. Reckon he ain't."

Geronimo smiled and pointed his rifle at the red long-handle sleeves showing at the end of Artisan's rolled-up shirtsleeves and said, "Mangas Coloradas. Red sleeves. No gun, Mangas?"

"I left it with my woman to purtect herself and the children. Ain't got no need for it up here workin' strays."

The English-speaking Apache interpreted Artisan's words, and Geronimo nodded he understood. Watching and listening from behind Chappo as Geronimo made small talk with my uncle, all the while knowing that Petra and the baby had been murdered, I sobbed and screamed in rage, "Artisan! They killed Petra and the baby and took me."

His face turned red and he clenched his teeth. His eyes

scanned the Apaches, stopping when he saw my dress sleeves wrapped around the middle of Chappo. He opened his mouth to call to me, but the young Apache who spoke English was quick to hold up his hand. "Stop! Speak to her—you die!" Artisan looked at the ground and shook his head.

Geronimo spoke through the young English-speaking warrior. "Geronimo say, Mangas Coloradas, you a good man. No carry gun. You brave. Today you lose family. I lose my family in one day—wife, three little ones, my mother—many harvests ago. Today you live. Go far away, *pindah*. Start again. You stay, maybe I come again. You not so lucky next time." He nodded at the men surrounding Artisan. "I have no more to say. We go."

The men threw Artisan to the ground, jerked off his boots, and stripped him down to his red long johns. He looked around, trying to catch a glimpse of me, but I don't think he saw me. The Apache who spoke English stood watching him with his rifle cocked and pointed at Artisan's middle. One of the other Apaches handed him his pony's reins. Like a pronghorn, he leaped in the saddle, his rifle still pointed at Artisan, who stood shakily to his feet and saw, behind the nearby hills, smoke rising in a long plume straight up from where his wrecked ranch house and his dead family awaited him.

The Apache pointing toward the smoke said, "Go back there—we kill you," and then rode off to join the others. I twisted to look over my left shoulder, hoping to see Artisan. In the red long johns, he was easy to spot trudging barefoot, east toward his ranch house. I began crying again when I thought of what he would find there.

Hearing Chappo warn, *"Cállate!"* I snuffled back my tears and wondered if I would live to see the sunset as the Apaches rode south, driving the livestock along a narrow wash at the bottom of a deep canyon.

CHAPTER 3
THROUGH THE PAJARITO MOUNTAINS

Scattered junipers clinging to the steep canyon walls gave us a few shady spots down in the canyon bottom, but the bare grassy and weed-covered places put out heat like a woodstove in the middle of winter. After picking our way down the narrow canyon wash for two or three miles, the trail made a hard turn toward the east. The curve filled with piñons and a few junipers made a shady area large enough for the band to stop for a little rest.

Chappo threw a leg over his saddle horn, slid off his pony, motioned for me to jump down, and then nodded toward an old twisted piñon for me to sit under. Geronimo and a tall, thin young man sat down together, made a cigarette, smoked it using some kind of ritual puffing, and then began talking. Geronimo used a short stick to draw in the dirt while he talked. The tall man would nod, wave a hand, and shrug his shoulders as if to say, "Who knows?" or he would look away in disgust while Geronimo brushed aside what he had drawn and made more scratches in the dirt. It seemed odd that Geronimo, who looked old, scarred, and experienced, was trying to convince the younger man what to do next.

I saw men disappearing for a short time into the brush on the other side of the wash. I was terrifically thirsty, and my tongue could feel my cracked lips. Even more than my thirst, I wished for a private place to relieve myself. But I didn't dare go in the brush until they told me.

The Apache who spoke English motioned me to him. He sat

41

in some shade with his back against a large boulder, shaped like a giant egg standing on its big end, tipped against an old piñon. He studied me for a moment, his flint-black, narrow-lidded eyes unblinking, tapped on his chest, and said, "Ahnandia."

I nodded, and tapping on my chest, I said, "Trinidad." I chewed the inside of my cheek to keep from crying in rage and attacking the man who had murdered Petra and Andy.

He tilted his head toward the brush against the canyon wall behind us, the side opposite from where the men had disappeared. "You go there. Make water. Watch for snake. You see snake, no kill or yell. You say words I tell you. Snake go away." He spoke the words and then made me say them back. They made a short and simple command, not hard to remember. I said the words back to him in one try. Nodding, he said, "You have light behind your eyes. Come back, I give water and food."

I nodded, thinking, *These Indians are crazy. He kills my aunt and baby cousin but won't kill a snake. You always kill snakes.*

I found a place back in the brush against the canyon wall, where I made my water without exposure to the stares of the men and boys. Contrary to my expectations of them killing or molesting me, they seemed to have little interest. My spirits rose as I thought, *Maybe all they want is a slave. Maybe close to some town or village, when they're not looking, I can get away.*

I stood, straightening my dress, when a loud rattle filled the still, quiet air. I froze. Prickles of fear raced up my spine. What the Apaches called a big grandfather snake—its colors and bands blending almost perfectly into the colors of the wash rocks, its head the size of my open hand with fingers closed and shaped like an arrow point, its tongue rapidly flicking toward me and its vertical-pupil eyes looking evil—was coiled not five feet from where I had squatted. I felt a sudden urge to make water again. I knew the snake was warning me I had disturbed him, but he wasn't angry enough yet to strike. Heads of men and boys rose about the tops of the piñons and looked in my direction.

In the shimmering heat, I felt faint and could barely breathe. I saw the end of a piece of wood caught in the brush from a previous flood within reach, and I thought to grab it and bring it down hard on the snake. Artisan had taught me how, and I had practiced a time or two on snakes I found in Petra's garden, after knocking them senseless with a hoe handle, to grab them by their tails and snap their bodies like a whip to break their backs. But this snake was a big, heavy animal, and I doubted I had the strength to kill it by snapping it to break its back.

I knew what Ahnandia had told me to say to the snake was just Apache superstition. Even so, I decided to repeat the words he gave me. Keeping an eye on the piece of wood in the brush just in case the snake didn't listen, I spoke up and said the Apache words in a loud, commanding voice. "My mother's father, don't bother me. I'm just a child. Go where I can't see you. Keep out of my path."

To my surprise, the rattling stopped in the space of a couple of breaths and the grandfather rattler glided away over the hot rocks and into the brush against the canyon wall. I saw Geronimo among the heads poking above the brush watching me. He was smiling and said for all to hear, *"Enjuh!"* (It is good!), before returning to his talk with the tall young man.

Ready to collapse, I walked back to Ahnandia, who had returned to his seat against the boulder. He smiled and nodded. "You do well. Listen to my words. You brave." He tossed me an army canteen. "Snake bad. Even no touch, can make skin bad. No good. Moon grows whole, Geronimo sing, make smoke for you. Snake no make you sick."

I wondered what Ahnandia was talking about, but he didn't stop me from drinking all I wanted. The water trickling down my throat, even if it was warm, had never felt so good, and I

43

sighed with relief after the last swallow. He smiled and offered me a brown, green, and white mixture of ground-up stuff he was eating from a leather bag he carried. "Eat, brave girl. Make you strong. No hunger. We go far this sun."

I held out my hand. "Give me a little. I'll try it." The mixture wasn't bad. I could taste the bitter chocolate-like taste of roasted piñon nuts, some sticky sweet stuff that tasted like molasses, bits of meat, maybe venison, some dried, waxy sweet things (I learned later were juniper berries), and a few other nuts and pieces I couldn't identify. I said, "Good!" He grinned and poured me a handful, which filled me up, and I felt stronger, ready to ride.

While I nibbled on pinches of his trail food, Ahnandia walked over and spoke to Geronimo, who nodded, and then spoke to an adolescent boy who waited on him. The boy nodded and disappeared into the brush around the bend, where the stolen horses, mules, and cattle grazed.

Ahnandia returned to sit by the egg-shaped boulder and eat a pinch more from the leather food bag.

I decided to learn all I could about these men, thinking I might learn something I could use when I escaped. "Who is that man Geronimo talks to?"

Ahnandia glanced over his shoulder at the two talking and said, "Geronimo talk to Naiche, chief Chokonen Apache. Geronimo his di-yen and war leader."

"Naiche looks too young to be a chief."

"Second son great Cochise. Only son living. The People want him chief."

I remembered hearing stories from Artisan and cowhands about the Cochise war, how bloody it was, and how Cochise finally settled on a reservation after some old white friend agreed to be his agent. I had heard a little talk about Naiche, but mostly it was about Geronimo.

The resting time didn't last long. Geronimo and three men rode up a low ridge and off down the west fork of the canyon toward the midafternoon sun. Ahnandia tied off his food bag and disappeared into the brush, toward the horses. Naiche swung up on his pony, made an arm motion to the men, and said, *"Dahndáh!"* (Start!)

Chappo mounted and headed down the canyon without me. I almost yelled with joy, thinking, *Chappo's forgot me. Now I can get away. They don't care nothin' about me anyway.* I looked for some brush where I could stay out of sight until they had all left, but just as I saw the perfect spot, the young boy who served Geronimo, followed by Ahnandia, came running up with a brown-and-white pinto pony with a fine Mexican saddle. The boy, his hair long and tied back like a man, grinned and handed me the pony's reins. I took the reins but frowned, not understanding what I was to do.

Ahnandia said, "Grandfather snake show us you do as we tell you. Geronimo say you ride own pony. This pony and saddle he gives you. You stay with us. Do what we say, you live. You run away, we find and kill you." I looked in his eyes and remembered how he killed Petra and her baby. I knew he meant business. I nodded thinking, *You wait. When I get away, you murderers will never catch me.*

I had been around horses all my life, and I had watched expert wranglers handle them. While Ahnandia adjusted the stirrup leathers' lengths so I could use the stirrups, I let the pony smell me and my breath as I checked and adjusted the bridle, scratched behind his ears, and spoke softly to him. When Ahnandia finished with the stirrups, unlike a lady, but I didn't care, I pulled my dress up between my legs and mounted as though I wore pants. My thigh muscles burned, tight and sore from riding behind Chappo, but sitting in my own saddle on my own pony, they didn't hurt as bad as when I got off Chappo's saddle. Ahnandia mounted and said, "Stay with me," and we were off down the canyon.

Naiche led us up a steadily rising trail in the sand and rocks of the canyon bottom until it ended at a ridge that we climbed over, as it lay covered in long shadows from junipers catching the last sunlight. The ridge was so steep we had to dismount and lead the ponies up the last hundred yards. On the ridgetop, we stopped for a short rest as the light in the valley below us faded to deep-purple evening twilight, but the white caliche path down the hill in the deepening darkness stood out bright and clear and was easy to see. My pony understood how to move down the steep hill path and never slipped or frightened me. Soon our horses were picking their way along the white, sandy bottom trail that twisted through the brush around another tall hill.

A quarter moon didn't give much light on the mountain trail, but it was enough for us to find our way. We had to push our animals hard to stay up with Naiche. Not used to such long, hard rides, my legs trembled with exhaustion. I began to wonder how much longer I could stay in the saddle, when the animals suddenly charged forward and stopped at a shiny black surface just off the trail. It was water, a big pool filled by a spring burbling out of the rocks.

The horses drank a few big gulps, but then we pulled them back to wait a little while so they wouldn't founder before they drank more. The Apaches and I drank next and threw water on our faces, and some dunked their heads. I started to think I might live after all. The horses drank again before the same young boy led them to a little box canyon nearby, where he watched them while the men made small fires and cooked.

I unsaddled my pony and left it with the other horses. My

pony was an easy-to-ride mare, and she held up well during the long afternoon and early-evening ride to water. At home, I rarely rode more than an hour or two at a time, and that was on Sunday afternoons. After this long ride down mountain canyons and over ridges, part of the time riding behind Chappo, I was so sore, I could barely flex my legs without screaming in pain. I carried my saddle to a place near where Ahnandia had put his and sat down, intending only to rest and not eat, too tired to find and cook anything even if they gave it to me.

The day had seemed to last years rather than hours. A lifetime had passed since Petra and the baby were killed, rough hands dragged me from under the bed and grabbed my hair to jerk my head back with a shiny blade flashing for my throat, and then unexpected salvation came from the whispery commands of some old Apache I had never seen before. Tears filled the edges of my eyes and I choked back a sob as I remembered the deaths of Petra and Andy, and Artisan thrown on the ground to have his boots ripped off and his clothes taken, leaving him only in his red long handles to walk barefoot across two miles of hot desert to find his wife and baby murdered.

The grief filling my guts gave way to fire. I wanted to kill every one of the raiders who had murdered Petra and Andy and left my uncle nearly naked to walk barefoot across a burning desert. These weren't human beings. They were wild animals ready to rip the life from anyone they came across. I thought about killing as many as I could before they killed me, but I knew, after watching them all day, that they were tough, hard men and boys. I had no chance of killing even one of them.

I thought, *Patience. I have to wait for an opportunity to get away and bring the soldiers down on them. That's my only chance to stay alive and make 'em pay for what they've done to Petra's family and me. I don't care what Ahnandia thinks about me, I'm not staying and they're not gonna catch me when I leave neither.*

47

The young men cooking had slaughtered a beef and slid cuts of meat onto sticks tilted to cook over their little fires. The overpowering smell of the roasting meat, its juices sparking into a quick blaze and then smoke as it dripped into the flames, changed my mind about eating, but I didn't know how to get any of the meat to cook.

Ahnandia returned to his saddle and flopped down to rest against it after talking with Naiche.

"How do I get a piece of meat to cook?"

"Young warriors cook for older men. Geronimo leaves you with me. You eat with me. They bring meat soon now."

I leaned back on my elbows and looked at the bright points of light in the black velvet sky and then at the fires around the camp and the men cooking. Apaches were strong, tough fighters, yet they had their young men cooking meals for older men at an age when young Anglo boys and men rarely cooked even for themselves. I tried to forget Petra's and Andy's killings, and what they'd done to Artisan, but the memories smoldered in my brain like smoke from a fresh cow brand.

"Can I ask you a question?"

Ahnandia raised his brows but nodded. "Speak, I answer."

"Why'd you shoot my Aunt Petra and then bash the baby's head against the house? They didn't do anything to you."

Ahnandia shrugged his shoulders. "She run out of house with gun. Time of war. I shoot before she shoot. She fall with baby. Baby no live without mother. Better to kill baby than let suffer. They go to Happy Place, and she no tell soldiers about us."

"Then why didn't Geronimo let the warrior with the big scar across his chest kill me?"

"Geronimo great di-yen. See future. Maybe trades you to Mexicans for wife they take three harvests past. Maybe wife with him now needs slave to help her. Maybe you make good Apache after your woman time come. Maybe one day warrior here makes you his wife." He shrugged again and nodded toward Naiche's fire. "You ask Geronimo. He tell you."

"Geronimo's not here now. Where did he go?"

"Go west. Big horse *rancho.* Maybe takes many ponies. Bring here. Meet tomorrow before we cross iron road into what *Nakai-yes* (Mexicans) call Pinito Mountains."

"Why the Pinito Mountains?"

"We hide families there while we raid across the border. Get families, then go big camp on top of Azul Mountains. Nakai-yes and Bluecoats no find there."

"How many days to get to the Pinito Mountains?"

"Maybe three days if Geronimo come quick."

I shut up for a while, listening to the night birds and watching the stars. I swatted a bug flying near my face and felt the grit that I knew must cover my body.

"I'm filthy from the day's ride. Can I wash before I eat?"

"Boys and men no wash until after meal. Go wash. None bother you."

The water in the pool was still warm from the day's sun and pleasant to my grit-coated skin. I swirled my hair in the water and washed as much of my body in dark moon shadows as I dared if someone was watching. No one disturbed me before I finished, and I felt better than I had since morning. I returned to the flickering orange and yellow light as a boy brought Ahnandia a stick covered with roasted meat, which he shared with me.

I watched the men and boys eat. They used their knives and fingers with a kind of etiquette that didn't leave grease stains on their clothes or around their mouths. Having no knife, I pulled strips of beef off the stick with my fingers and ate them, trying not to let the meat juices from the strips fall on my dress. All the men I watched got nothing on their clothes and, when they finished eating, wiped off their mouths with their fingers and then ran their hands over their legs and soft leather of their moccasins. I imitated them and felt like I might survive living like an Apache until I remembered they got their supplies by stealing and killing anyone in their path.

Men gathered at Naiche's fire, and Ahnandia joined them. They made a cigarette to smoke in the same kind of ceremony I had seen between Naiche and Geronimo. I learned later that the ceremony meant they smoked to the four directions because they were discussing serious business.

I saw the boys gathering brush to pile nearby for their morning fires and cooking and decided I ought to do the same for Ahnandia. I quickly found enough loose brush for making a small fire that should last long enough to cook over, but just in case not, I gathered a couple of more armloads, getting dirty and sweaty again even in the cool night. Returning to the pool, I saw no one there and rinsed the sweat and dirt from my face and arms again. Back at my saddle, I wrapped the blanket Ahnandia had given me around my body and lay back to look at the stars as grief and emotional numbness brought me rest with the thought, *Somehow, I'll get away. Just open the door a crack and I'll be gone.*

CHAPTER 4
INTO THE PINITO MOUNTAINS

I jerked awake, sucking in cold air, feeling like I was under water. I looked around the camp, wide-eyed, startled, and confused, before remembering where I was. Coyotes yipped in the distance as Ahnandia, grinning, shook my shoulder. Night was fading into dawn's gray light from a low white glow in the eastern sky, but the up-high stars still glowed in black velvet.

"You bring much brush for fire. Trinidad works like good Apache woman. Go wash, make water. Soon now, we ride."

The trail leading away from the water pool was wide enough to ride side by side on the slight downgrade. Riding was much more comfortable than yesterday, but soon the trail began to climb until it ended on the top of a low ridge, where we had to climb a steep switchback trail to get to the top. Unlike yesterday, we didn't have to dismount to get to the top of this ridge, but from the ridgetop down to another wide canyon trail far below was much steeper than the one yesterday. The steepness and height of the trail down scared me, but I was determined never to show it. Keeping the reins loose and letting the mare find her footing, as Artisan had taught me on his horses when we rode across the ridges close by the ranch, we were soon safe on the canyon trail below the ridgetop.

Ahnandia, with a grin, watched me ride down the ridge and said as I reached him on the trail, "You ride good. You strong, brave, not afraid like child. You like little woman. Nakai-yes, they call you *'mujercita'* (Little Woman), good name for you like

51

names they give warriors they fear."

Naiche, leading the band, continued out of the mountains on a fast trail ride until the trail began crossing ugly red and brown dirt and rocks heading toward the east and spreading south. Naiche paused to let us rest and slid off his pony.

I saw columns of dark, slate-colored smoke to the northeast rising high above the brown hills dotted with the green of junipers and the browns and tans of stretches of barren sand in front of us. The men rarely used their fingers to point. They seemed to always use their noses or head tilts to indicate direction. Sitting in the midmorning shade of junipers with Ahnandia and nodding toward the smoke plumes, I said. "Where's that smoke from?"

He grinned as if teasing me. "Nogales. Maybe you go to Nogales?"

Nogales was about a half day's ride from Petra and Artisan's ranch. I thought, *If I can just get to Nogales, I'm certain I can find my way to my Aunt María Cuen, who took me to the ranch the first time.* My mind filled with ideas for escape. Yesterday, Ahnandia had said they would kill me if I tried to escape. There was no room for error and much to learn about the country if I aimed to get away. I ignored his question.

"When are we gonna meet up with Geronimo again?"

Ahnandia glanced at the sun, shrugged his shoulders, and said, "Maybe by time of shortest shadows (noon). He moves fast but maybe not move as he likes with many horses to drive."

As if by some unseen signal, the men were suddenly standing on their feet and tightening their cinches. Ahnandia tightened my cinch and jerked his head up for me to mount. We rode northeast in a slow trot that ate up the miles across the red and brown land, where little or nothing grew except creosote bushes, prickly pear, and cholla cactus. Near midday, I glanced over my shoulder and saw a small dust cloud on the trail behind us.

"Is that dust cloud behind us from Geronimo with his horses?"

Ahnandia watched the dust cloud for a moment and nodded. "Geronimo comes."

Within an hour, Geronimo and his men came rumbling down the trail. Naiche saw them coming and slowed his pony to a walk. They drove their stolen horses among the other horses, mules, and cattle herded by the boy and a couple of experienced men. Geronimo, with his four men in a line streaming behind him, galloped up to Naiche. Ahnandia and I were close enough to hear them exchange greetings.

Ahnandia told me Geronimo said we should ride on to the next water, rest until dark, and then follow the iron road south. I nodded but didn't understand what "iron road" meant. "How far to water?"

"Maybe two hands."

When I frowned, Ahnandia smiled. Pressing his fingers together with his palm out, he held his hand against the edge of the sun and moved across it. "Same as one circle on box you call clock."

I nodded. A hand must be about an hour.

We rode at a gallop into the middle of the afternoon and found a water tank some rancher had made by blocking and backing up water trickling out of the trees back in a small canyon running into the north side of the wide canyon in which we rode. It had been a long, dusty trail. I felt the crunch of grit between my teeth when I closed my mouth and dirt in every wrinkle of my body. I swung off my pony on legs so stiff they barely flexed. After letting the horses drink, I tottered away to drink and wash on the other side of the tank, away from the men doing the same. The water was warm and green with plants and algae, but

I didn't care as long as my raw, burning thirst went away. The boys let the livestock graze on the nearby grass between the trail and tank while the men went into council.

I looked toward where I had seen the Nogales smoke plumes at midday but now saw nothing. The council broke up after meeting a short time. Ahnandia came to me and said, "Moon come, we ride." He opened his leather food bag, gave me a handful of the mix to eat, and then ate a handful, closed the bag, and eased down in the shade of a big juniper tree. I found a grassy spot nearby and lay down, exhausted. Watching a great black bird, wings spread wide, soaring and wheeling on the high air currents above, I wondered if the buzzard could see No-gales. I thought, *Wish I was a bird. I'd fly away and lead the soldiers back to wipe out these people.* The buzz of dragonflies and other insects around the water tank mixed with the warm afternoon solitude and men sleeping, one or two softly snoring, led me to my own sleep.

Ahnandia tapped the bottom of my shoe with his rifle barrel. I sat up, slow and creaky like an old woman. Frogs and insects around the tank croaked out their songs. The night had come, but no fires drove away the darkness. Ahnandia said, "Moon come quick now. We ride."

From the light of the half-moon rising above the mountains to the northeast, I saw the boy who helped Geronimo in leading our horses from the place where the stolen herd had been graz-ing. I walked over to the tank and, kneeling by the dark water reflecting the bright stars, spread the surface and drank many swallows before splashing water on my face to wake up. Ahnan-dia and the boy were saddling the horses when I returned and said, "We ride all night?"

Ahnandia nodded. "Ride all night. When sun come in Pinito Mountains, we far away from iron road. Now you ride with me.

In Pinito camps, you stay with Geronimo and his wife. *Comprende?*" (Understand?)

Nodding, I took my pony's reins and waited with Ahnandia to mount. "I see many more horses than we had before Geronimo came. Was it a good raid?"

"Good raid. Geronimo and men take fifty horses. Kill two vaqueros they find. Good raid. Now plenty horses."

Geronimo and Naiche swung into their saddles, and everyone followed. Soon we galloped down the steadily widening canyon that turned a little northeast into a much bigger canyon running north to south with a river on one side and railroad tracks on the other.

I saw the narrow ribbons of rail steel shining in the moonlight and disappearing in the distance and thought, *Of course, the "iron road."* Looking back toward the north, I saw a golden glow on the horizon from town lights—Nogales. *If I can get away, all I have to do is follow the iron road north to reach Nogales.* But discretion spoke loud and clear in my ears. *One mistake in a country you don't know and the Apaches will find and kill you. Patience, patience. Wait for the best time.*

We watered the animals at a pool on what I later learned was the Río Magdalena, and then Naiche led us south at a gallop.

The horses were tiring even in the cold, crisp air when we stopped for water and rest by the river. The iron road, easy to see through the river's bosque, ran past a wide canyon, its high ridge sides covered in deep, black shadows from junipers and rough brush, and disappeared due east into the darkness. Naiche studied the sky and then sat for a while with Geronimo to roll and smoke a cigarette.

In the blackness, I washed what I could of my body while still keeping my modesty. In the cold night air, the shock of the water on my grit-covered skin awakened and made me much more alert. Vigorous rubbing brought warmth back to my arms and legs, bringing me hope I might yet escape. The men still seemed to ignore me, and I grew more comfortable, acting myself and not always on guard around them. I began to understand what Artisan once told me: "The Apaches have their code about women and girls." Glancing toward Geronimo and Naiche, I saw them stand and move toward their ponies. Time to ride.

Naiche led us across the iron road toward the wide, dark canyon and then up a narrow trail along its north wall to the ridgetop forming the canyon's rim. With the white sand and caliche trail easy to see in the moonlight, Naiche still moved slowly so no stock or riders would step off its edge and into the black air to fall to their death below. From the rim of the canyon, the trail wound across the tops of ridges, down into another canyon, and back up another steep side trail with a long drop-off on one side and vertical rise on the other before it began to climb up and across ridges that rose higher and higher.

I couldn't tell if my teeth chattered from the cold night air or the thought that my pony's next step on that narrow trail in the dark might be her last. We lost three or four of the stolen ponies on steep parts of the trail. It was sad to see ponies slip and fall screaming off the trail's edge, and it made me want to cry.

And then, as if a wick raised in an oil lantern, a golden light drove away the shadows on the west side of the hills and ridges, while the eastern sides hidden from the sun's light stayed in dark shadows. Rounding a curve, I saw Naiche and Geronimo stop at a small pool of water and dismount. Time to take a little rest. Thirsty and covered with trail dust, I had wanted another drink of water soon after we crossed the iron road.

I let my pony drink. The fading stars above the brightening horizon and the golden light beginning to glow in patches on the mountains and ridges below us brought the morning.

Ahnandia came up to stand beside me while our horses drank. "We rest here for two or three hands while our families come to us. Then we ride all day. Rest, mujercita."

Nodding, too tired to even speak, I led my pony to a place where it could nibble on the brush and I would have some shade when the sun climbed across the sky. I loosened the saddle cinch and then sat down, watching the others do the same. Ahnandia offered me a handful of his trail food, and I drank again. I felt a flicker of life stir in my body, but I couldn't remember a time when I had been so weary.

It seemed I had barely closed my eyes before a stir of activity around the water awakened me. Something strange was happening. I didn't understand what it was until I saw women and children appearing on the narrow trail above us, running toward the men. I'd never seen family reunions like these. When men on ranches returned from being away for a time, their womenfolk were happy and ran to hug and kiss them, and the men held their children high. The Apache women and children smiled and nodded at their men, but there were no hugs or kissing. Later, when I asked Ahnandia about this, he laughed and said, "Our people say man and his women no show affection in front of others. In wickiups away from other eyes, man and his women show much happiness finding each other again."

All had chores to do before moving on. Women loaded and rearranged sacks of supplies they had brought with them on pack mules and horses. The young boys slaughtered another beef for the women to cook over hot coals that gave off little smoke, making the gathering impossible to see from other mountains and canyons. The men checked their saddles and rifles, knowing a long ride was in front of us.

Ahnandia showed me to his woman, and after some talk back and forth, he nodded toward me and said, "Trinidad," and then nodded toward her and said, "Tah-das-te."

I liked Tah-das-te's kind eyes. I thought she was a pretty woman. She smiled at me, studied my hair and features for a moment, and then asked in perfect Spanish, *"Habla español?"* (Do you speak Spanish?)

Ahnandia's jaw dropped and Tah-das-te laughed when I answered, *"Sí, muy bien, gracias."* (Yes, very well, thank you.)

Ahnandia smiled and said in Spanish, "You spoke the White Eye tongue. I didn't think to use Spanish. This is a good thing. Geronimo also speaks Spanish well. From now on, we'll speak Spanish with you unless we need to do otherwise. Come. We have your saddle and bridle. I take you to Geronimo."

Long shadows began to grow on the mountains. I saw Geronimo smoking and sitting with his woman beside their little fire while she cooked. His hard, narrow eyes set in an old man's face, smooth but sculptured by deep lines defining his cheeks, followed us as we came to his fire.

Ahnandia said in Spanish as I put down the saddle, "Geronimo, I bring you the girl you saved at the ranch of Mangas. I have learned with the help of Tah-das-te that the child speaks español (Spanish) well and the tongue of the Americans, but knows nothing of the Apache tongue. Is there more I can do for you?"

Geronimo flipped the remains of his cigarette into the fire and smiled. "She speaks the tongue of the Nakai-yes? *Nit'ééhi!* (That is good). I learned it from my mother when I was still on the *tsach* (cradleboard). What is the child's name?"

"Trinidad. I heard the woman with the baby at the rancho of Mangas call her 'Trini.' She answers to either one."

Geronimo looked at me, tapped his chest, and said, "Geronimo." He nose pointed to the woman cooking at the fire and said in good Spanish, "My woman's name is She-gha, daughter of the great chief, Cochise. You help her. Do as she says. If you disrespect or disobey her, she will use a stick on you. Comprende?"

I nodded and said, *"Sí, comprendo."*

He nodded toward Ahnandia, who walked back to Tah-das-te's fire, and Geronimo motioned with a flip of his wrist for me to move over to the side where She-gha worked. I squatted beside her and watched her. She was a nice-looking woman, with wide, eagle-like eyes and well-groomed hair, but for reasons I didn't and still don't understand, she seemed frail, almost sickly.

She glanced over her shoulder at me and said in good Spanish, "Get busy, Trinidad. Gather a pile of wood and brush for the fire. I tell you when you can eat. Hurry. Soon we will go on down the trail. The longer we have light, the better off we are. I think we lose many ponies riding tonight. The trail is very bad in places. Hurry."

I worked fast and gathered brush that burned without much smoke. I kept adding to the piles of brush and twigs as I saw She-gha serve Geronimo his meal. Then she motioned for me to come to the fire, where we waited until Geronimo nodded and waved his hand that we should eat. She filled two gourds with meat, steamed yucca tips, and a slice of sweet molasses-tasting stuff I later learned was steamed, dried baked mescal. I watched her eat from the gourd with her fingers and tried to imitate her. She watched me for a moment, smiled, and then showed me how to manage the things in the gourd without letting them slide through my fingers and how to fill my mouth without making a mess all over my dress.

After we ate, she straightened up the area so it looked unused, poured Geronimo a cup of coffee, collected the gourds and her cooking tools, and we walked to the pool. Other children and women were there and stared at me while we waited for our turn to get some wash water.

When we returned, Geronimo had taken his coffee and joined other men who sat with Naiche. They were going through their ritual smoking before a council. She-gha waved me to sit down and be still. I flopped on my blanket, too tired to move, hoping for a nap before the trail ride began. Before my eyes closed, I remember She-gha sitting on the other side of the fire with her head cocked to one side, listening to the council where Geronimo and the other warriors talked.

She-gha shook me awake with the toe of her moccasin and said, "You go make water. Wash. Drink much at pool. Long ride comes. You run off, I catch and beat you good if mountains no kill you first. Maybe Geronimo kill you. Comprende?" I nodded. I understood her very well. I crawled to my knees, found my shoes, and joined her at the fire, where she handed me a water bag and the coffeepot. "Fill bag. Bring water. Soon we leave."

CHAPTER 5
HIGH ON A MOUNTAIN

I filled the water sack and washed and filled the coffee pot before running back to the fire, not even taking time to make water or wash. She-gha looked at me, wrinkled her nose, and said, "You wash now. You stink. No good on trail. Go!"

A spring, its water sweet and cold, fed the tank we used. Looking around to see no one watched from nearby, I pulled up my sleeves and washed my arms, neck, and face, and—lifting my dress above my knees—washed my feet and legs as high up as I dared, still protecting my modesty.

When I returned, Geronimo sat speaking to a slowly nodding Naiche. I said to She-gha, "Why do we leave so soon?"

She crossed her arms and smiled. "Move all the time, except when we hide. Bluecoats about a day behind Geronimo and Naiche. Geronimo says to council what we should do, and council agrees. Soon we leave."

I didn't want to hear that. I was tired and needed to rest. "Where're we going?"

"Follow hard trail east to high Pinito Mountain. Geronimo thinks we might lose many horses on this trail, but so will Bluecoats who follow. They have to walk when they lose horses. Slows them down. Not as strong even as Apache women and children. We lose horses? Go to ranches, take more. Warriors go to canyon with steep cliffs. Fight Bluecoats when they come. Kill some, then they no follow while we take other trails."

I knew I couldn't run a long time like the Apache women

and children. I hoped they would let me ride, even if my pony slipped over the edge of the trail. "Where will the women and children go?"

"We stay on canyon rim above ambush. Maybe in one sun, Bluecoats come. Warriors make easy trail for Bluecoats to follow in canyon. Warriors hide high up in canyon cliffs. Wait. Women and children watch from canyon rim. Warriors know families watch, make them fight hard. Geronimo says Bluecoat chief who follows is strong warrior. Leads black-skinned soldiers. Good fighters, but place Geronimo chooses makes Bluecoats climb and fight. Easier to kill that way."

She saw me frown. I didn't think I had ever seen a black man in a blue coat. The flame of my curiosity was lighted and flaring up. I could only remember ever seeing a black vaquero once on a trip to a mercantile store in Nogales with Petra and Artisan, buying tools and other supplies for the ranch. I said, "I don't think I've ever seen a black man in a blue coat."

"Hmmph. We fight them before. Brave warriors. Eat now. Geronimo eat. Then we leave."

The trail leaving the camp was very rough for the women and children. Most of the women and children walked and ran. They let me ride on a mule pack, but even that left me breathless on the trail winding around and across the high mountain ridges. I marveled at the strength and speed of all the women and children, and I was very glad they understood that I wasn't strong enough to run with them.

We were on the trail all night. From the little moonlight we had, I saw enough narrow trails and deep plunges off cliffsides into the cold black air that I was glad I couldn't see them in full light all the way to the bottom. Early next morning, Geronimo and the warriors rested and camped at the mouth of a canyon leading up the side of the tallest mountain I could see in any direction. They had lost almost half of Geronimo's stolen ponies on the trail the night before.

We rested together for about a hand against the horizon, and then the warriors went up the canyon to the place they wanted to fight the Bluecoats. It was a canyon that led to a saddle between two high mountains. A rock shaped like a giant finger stuck out from the saddle and faced the canyon the soldiers would have to approach. Even the trail nearing the saddle wound among many boulders, making plenty of places where the warriors could hide for an ambush. It was easy, even for me, to see that the cliffs forming the saddle and lying in a semicircle above the canyon trail had the best places for the warriors to attack the Bluecoats.

Two men helped the women and children drive the cattle and horses to a place on top of the saddle near the canyon rim where the warriors waited for the Bluecoats. The women and children made a rough brush corral and cut brush for the livestock. Then She-gha and I, with the others, climbed among the rocks on the canyon rim, looking for places with clear views from which to watch the coming fight with the black-skinned Bluecoats.

In the camp on top of the saddle, things grew quiet except for the singing of insects and occasional bird calls as the women and children waited for the warriors to climb up to the top of the saddle from the spots they had picked for their ambush. I lay down in the soft, scented pine needles near She-gha and looked up through the junipers at the sky slowly changing to late-afternoon blue.

I thought of Artisan and wondered what he did when, barefoot and nearly naked, he found Petra and the baby in the ruins of his burned ranch. It was all I could do to keep from crying. I chewed my lip, listened to the breeze swishing through the trees, and watched a couple of great black birds floating above us. It all seemed so peaceful, away from the bloodshed and killing I had seen in the last week. I relaxed and drifted into sleep. I was weary, so very weary.

When my eyes crept open, it was nearly dark. Stars were filling the sky above the edges of the mountaintops. I saw men moving about the camp with women and children in tow and Geronimo and She-gha sitting together, drinking from cups. I sat up, yawned, and rubbed my eyes. She-gha motioned me to them.

As I approached, I saw a hole for a fire that had left cooking coals heating the coffeepot, and over the coals, a stick held roasting meat. She-gha said, "You sleep much. Not strong like Apache girls, who can run all day and then help their mothers. Work hard. Your strength grows. Sit down. I give you something to eat."

Geronimo took a swallow from his cup and said, "I told She-gha how you spoke to the grandfather snake in the Pajarito Mountains and how he crawled away and left you alone. Snakes, especially that tribe, have much evil power. They can make your skin red and scaly like his just by being near you. I didn't have time to do you a ceremony and make medicine to protect you from its power. Is your skin hurting, red, or scaly anywhere on your body? I will sing for you now if the snake's power has harmed you."

I shook my head. "My skin doesn't hurt anywhere. I don't think I need your medicine."

He looked at the pile of orange and yellow coals and sighed. "Nit'ééhi. You are no good to us sick."

I had never seen a battle between Apaches and cavalry before, and my curiosity and imagination had come to a full boil, especially about Bluecoats with black skins. I was thinking the Apaches had made that up as part of their religious beliefs. But what if they hadn't? What if there really were soldiers with black skins? Would they actually fight for people with white or brown skins like mine? "When will the Bluecoats come?"

Geronimo relaxed. He spoke to me like I was an adult. "I think they will be where we camped at the foot of the mountain around dawn at next sunrise. They will follow our trail up the canyon and be ready to fight a long rifle shot away, two or three hands after the time of shortest shadows. If we can kill a few before we leave, they'll stop following us."

"Why?"

"They've been on the trail a long time and are tired like a worn-out horse. They need to stop and wait for supplies on pack mules. That is the way they fight since Crook first comes to the Blue Mountains. In mountains, Apaches better off without a horse. Can go more places. Use horses to carry supplies and loot we take. Apaches strong in mountains. You not strong—yet. Work like She-gha says, you grow stronger. Maybe one day, good Apache man take you for his woman."

I nodded I understood, but inside I knew I'd never stand for serving one of these devils like a wife, if that's what Geronimo had in mind.

Naiche came to Geronimo's fire. He and his woman, named Haozinne, had a boy with them who looked ten or eleven, maybe a little younger than me. Haozinne was always smiling and seemed easy to be around. I couldn't understand a word they said, but while they visited with Geronimo and She-gha, the time was easy and casual. They laughed often and seemed to make jokes they all found funny. Their gathering around the low light from fire coals reminded me of times when ranching neighbors came and spent an evening visiting with Artisan and Petra. It seemed so strange to me that the Apaches could fight and raid one day and sit and talk together like everyday neighbors the next.

The boy who Naiche and Haozinne had with them said nothing as his large black eyes stared at me. Naiche said something to him. He nodded and looked away. Naiche smiled and glanced at me before saying in Spanish, "The boy's name is Garditha. He is very young, an orphan. He hasn't learned that Apaches don't stare at others. It's an insult to stare. He speaks only the language of his fathers. Maybe you help tell him how the Nakai-yes—hmmph, Mexicans—speak? Maybe he tells you Apache words?"

I nodded, feeling important that he would speak to me. "Sí. I teach Garditha to speak Spanish and learn all the Apache I can from him."

Naiche nodded and said, "Enjuh," as he turned back to the grown-ups.

I motioned Garditha over to me. He hesitated a moment, looked at Naiche and Haozinne, and then came and sat down beside me. Patting myself on the chest, I said, "Trinidad."

He grinned and pointed at me and said, "Towndead."

I had to shake my head several times and correct him before he could say my name so anyone would know it was me to whom he referred. When he had it right, I pointed at him and said, "Garta."

He shook his head and said slowly, emphasizing each syllable, "Gar-di-tha." I made sure I said it correctly, and he was all smiles. We spent the rest of the evening teaching each other the names for body parts, trees, and other plants. We had a good time teaching and learning from each other, and I forgot for a while the sorrow I carried.

The night grew long, and Naiche, Haozinne, and Garditha left for their blankets. She-gha gave me a blanket, and I rolled up in it near where she and Geronimo lay together by the coals that kept the coffeepot warm. The air was cold. I shivered, even wrapped in the good blanket She-gha had given me and sleeping close to the firepit. Looking up through windows to the sky formed by alignments of pine tree limbs, I thought the bright stars looked like they were burning holes in the night sky. Off to the south, so many stars were so close together in a streak across the sky that they looked like a great white river.

I was glad I had made a friend in Garditha. We had much to teach each other, and I hoped we would stay alive long enough to learn what we had to share. I was still very tired, even with a good nap that afternoon.

As my eyes were closing, I heard wolves howling below us, and the memory of the warriors in a circle like wolves around Artisan, ready to do whatever the head wolf wanted, filled my mind. The only voice in that memory was mine, filled with tears, telling Artisan his family was gone—the only image, Artisan's face twisted in pain and rage, surrounded by Apache warriors, coolly indifferent, ready to take his life or give it.

The memory disappeared, and I remembered Ahnandia telling me it was war. Kill a man or a woman with no quarter. Put a hurt child out of its misery. I felt a tear roll down my cheek, *Oh, God, when will this misery end for us all?*

CHAPTER 6
BLACK SOLDIER CAVALRY COMES

The sun was halfway down its arc toward the west, and shadows were beginning to grow long when the warriors saw the dust from the soldiers' horses far down the canyon's wash following the trail the warriors had left for them. Warriors aroused from napping or cleaning and repairing weapons jumped to their feet, snatched up their ammunition belts and rifles, and ran and slid from tree to tree as they edged down the side of the saddle, going to the cover they had found earlier in the rocks forming part of the cliff sticking out like a finger.

The women and children stayed on top of the saddle but moved down among the trees and brush from where the band camped so they could watch death in the afternoon come to the Bluecoats. She-gha, anxious not to miss the first shots between the warriors and black-skinned soldiers, headed for the place she and the other women had found earlier, where they could sit together as they watched the warriors ambush the Bluecoats trying to climb up the saddle toward them.

I started to follow She-gha, when I saw in her parfleches of supplies two or three pairs of Geronimo's soldier glasses she carried to replace those he lost during raids or battles like this one. I was so curious about what the black-skinned Bluecoats looked like that, with trembling hands, I took a pair of soldier glasses without asking and worked my way down through the trees to a place where I, too, hidden in the brush and shadows, had a good view of the fighting.

I watched the Bluecoats approach and heard the steel in horseshoes clink and scrape against rocks in the hot canyon wash as they climbed toward the cliffs where the warriors hid. A white captain followed by two white officers led the column of black soldiers. With the soldier glasses, I could see sweat on their black skin glistening in the hot sunlight, most men with hats shadowing faces with jaws set, and their rifles held vertical with butts resting against their thighs. The soldiers, rising slightly on their stirrups, tense and ready for a fight, rode up the wash, looking up the canyon walls and studying the saddle's rock cliffs. The squints in their eyes and scowls of concentration were those of hard, tough, experienced men. I wanted to run down the steep saddle, calling to them to take cover and hoping bullets from either side didn't kill me. But I decided to stay out of the way, proud they had come to rescue me and avenge the killing of Petra and Andy and what the Apaches had done to Artisan.

Half the column had ridden past the finger-of-rock cliffs when one of the soldiers raised up in his stirrups and pointed up at the rocks, yelling, "Cap'tin, they up there!"

The white captain held up his arm, barked a command, stopped the column, drew his field glasses to his eyes, and studied the finger of rock where Geronimo, Naiche, and the warriors waited. While he studied the rocks and cliffs, the white officer behind him pulled his glasses to study the saddle and soon pointed the captain to a place where a warrior was hiding. The captain and his lieutenants began yelling orders that echoed down the canyon sides. I heard the faint sounds of leather creaking and the occasional clink of iron on iron as the soldiers dismounted—keeping their rifles in hand while watching the saddle cliffs—and snapped ammunition belts and pouches in place, pulled canteens off saddles, and raised dust as their boots hit ground, relaying shouted commands to each other.

Every fourth man grabbed the reins of two soldiers on one side and one on the other, to pull and hold the horses back down the canyon out of the line of fire while the men formed a line with their rifles ready and ammunition belts and canteens slung across their bodies. The men looked up at the rocks the officers had studied but didn't seem to see anything. More shouted orders. All the soldiers hunched over to make smaller targets. Watching the cliff rocks, they began to move in a line across the bottom "V" shape of the saddle canyon.

Geronimo and Naiche watched them with their soldier glasses, talking and pointing as the soldiers came closer and closer. Geronimo shook his head and laughed. The soldiers moving up the saddle toward the rocks showed great courage despite the foolish officers who were sending them to fight a deadly, unseen enemy.

They climbed up the steep saddle and were within maybe two hundred yards of the finger-of-rock cliffs when one of the soldiers, yellow stripes on his shirtsleeves, yelled, "There's one!" He and the soldier next to him stood up, straight and tall, to fire their rifles, their bullets whining ricochets off the rocks in the finger cliff, the thunder of their rifles echoing down the canyons.

The returned fire from the hidden warriors was quick and deadly. The man firing the first shot, hit in his knee, his pant leg turning wet-black, flopped on his back, clenching his teeth in agony and moaning in pain. The soldier next to him—hit five or six times by the return volley, his pants and shirt suddenly showing red wet spots—fell back. His legs twitched a couple of times, and then he was still. The warriors kept up their fire, bullets raising little dust geysers around and near his body or pinging off nearby rocks.

The soldiers in the advancing line took quick cover in the rocks and juniper trees around them and sprayed the cliffs with many shots that did little harm but filled the canyon with a cacophony of echoing thunder and the high-pitched whines of ricochets. The white captain jumped up on a boulder and yelled directions for their movements. "Lucas, get down! Shoot in that shadow. Mose, move to that rock on the left! Johnson, shoot higher into the rocks on your right. Brown, don't raise up so high." Apache bullets swarmed and howled around him, but all somehow missed him.

The white officer who had ridden into the canyon behind the captain, showing great bravery, dashed from cover and grabbed the wounded soldier under the arms and began dragging him back to cover. Bullets whizzed past him, sending leaves and branches off brush and junipers around him flying to drift to earth in lazy spirals. In the heat of that fire, the officer didn't leave the wounded man. He kept pulling and struggling backward until a large boulder hid them from direct fire and rebounding bullets. I was just a prisoner and young girl watching the fight. But those Bluecoat soldiers and their officers strengthened my spirit and made me very proud.

Bullets from the soldiers' initial volley sprayed among the rock and boulders where the warriors had taken cover but did no damage. The shooting slowed as soldiers and warriors took more time studying the other side as they looked for targets—warriors or soldiers making the least mistake and showing themselves or body parts a few seconds too long.

Geronimo sent several warriors down a side canyon to overtake and run off the soldiers' horses, but the men soon returned. The white captain had anticipated the move and ordered the horse holders to move farther back down the canyon, making it too hard and risky to take or run off the soldier horses by surprise. I watched Geronimo when the warriors returned. He made a face and shook his head and then began yelling to the warriors under cover in the rocks below. As the shadows stretched across the cliff faces giving them cover, the warriors began to climb back up the saddle to where the women and children watched.

I saw She-gha and the women begin to stand and return to the top of the saddle. I left my place and ran up the saddle to She-gha's fire, where I returned the soldier glasses back to the others in the parfleche and then disappeared into the brush just before she returned.

Two or three warriors stayed behind to keep the soldiers pinned down until the warriors, women and children, and horses began moving up the saddle ridge to the top of the mountain and then down the ridges south until, under a fingernail moon, we turned down the ridges twisting northwest toward a canyon trail that led west, down and out of the mountains.

Coming down from the top of the Pinito Mountains, we rode carefully across canyon rim ridges and then hard and fast down canyon washes until we crossed the iron road south of Nogales to ride into a canyon, west, into the Cibuta Mountains.

As dawn was breaking, we came to a big spring burbling into a pool in the rocks and Geronimo and Naiche stopped to rest. The women made camp and prepared to cook while the men sat and smoked. I looked for and carried wood and brush to the fire She-gha had made in a hole she dug under some big piñons that would spread any smoke her fire made. She was careful to choose what to burn at her fire in order to make as little smoke as possible but still make a nice bed of coals.

Although I had ridden with the warriors going into the mountains, I had not ridden very far with the entire band including women and children. They surprised me by how quietly they were moving a long distance. I had watched the warriors pin down a large number of Bluecoats for a long afternoon of shooting that luckily, for both sides, produced few victims but stopped the soldiers in their tracks from chasing us. I began to understand why Artisan had once told Petra that the Bluecoats found it hard, some said nearly impossible, to catch or kill the warriors they chased, and I wondered if I would ever escape.

The next morning, Geronimo led us up a trail to another big spring high in the Cibuta Mountains, where he planned to make a camp from which he and the warriors could take some rest and raid when they wanted. The trail to the new camp followed a canyon most of the way. While it rose in altitude, its bottom was smooth and sandy, making for an easy ride that covered the distance before the time of shortest shadows.

In that high camp, I learned what it was like to work as an Apache woman, from the time she was up before the sun until she lay down with her husband. She-gha, always anxious to please Geronimo, worked hard and made me do the same.

That day, while the women made shelters and built cooking fires, Geronimo met with Naiche and the warriors. I watched them talk while I gathered brush for She-gha's fire. I knew little Apache, only what Garditha had taught me, but I could tell from the grins and frowns on their faces and sometimes raised voices that Geronimo and Naiche were arguing about something before Naiche shrugged his shoulders and threw up his hands, while Geronimo grinned and began to draw in the dirt with a piece of dry yucca stalk.

CHAPTER 7
MEXICAN SOLDIERS COME

"What will we do now, Geronimo?"

He slowly chewed on a piece of meat from his knife as he listened to She-gha's question and stared at the little fire where we took our warmth. He shook his head and said, "I don't know. Maybe we ride east and raid around Buena Vista and Santa Cruz. Bluecoats and Mexicans know we turned west by now, crossed the iron road, and camp somewhere in these mountains. Naiche agrees we go east. He wants to cross the border, go to Fort Apache, and learn about what happened to our families and what kind of terms we might get if we surrender. Bluecoats are everywhere along the border from Nogales to Columbus, watching and waiting for us to cross. Makes it hard to cross border without being seen or fighting Bluecoats."

A piece of gristle he tossed into the fire flared and crackled as he continued. "Soon we leave this camp and go east. Once Naiche sees the Bluecoat patrols, he'll decide how to get past them if he goes north. I won't leave the land of the Nakai-yes even if Naiche rides north. Bluecoats offer a big sack of *pesh klitso* (literally yellow iron, i.e. gold) for my head. I surrender? Bluecoats will kill me in the guardhouse in the middle of the night like they did the great chief, Mangas Coloradas, and like him, maybe cut off my head and boil it for my skull to send to the big chiefs in the east. I would rather die like Victorio, fight to my last bullet, and put my knife in my heart before I'm taken."

She-gha stared at the fire and shook her head, lines of of sorrow filling her face. She started to speak, when the sound of ponies coming up the big canyon southwest of where we camped made the camp grow quiet and the warriors check their weapons. I fantasized that it might be someone coming to rescue me, but it was warriors looking tired, covered in dust, and needing rest. They were scouts who had ridden the mountain ridges looking for signs of Bluecoat patrols. They rode directly to the flickering golden light of the little fire where Naiche, Haozinne, and the two children, Garditha and Leosanni, a little girl about six, camped. After hearing their report, Naiche sent Garditha to each fire to say he had called a council for all to hear what the scouts had learned.

I sat with Garditha and Leosanni close to She-gha and Haozinne and the other women in the cold dark behind the warriors, listening to the men who had returned. I didn't understand their language, but knew from frowns on the faces of the men and women that it was important.

The scouts told the council they had killed two vaqueros to the north early that morning and then ridden south to check our back trail. They found and watched a camp of Mexican soldiers who were following us to this camp on the same trail we had used, and the scouts believed they would be on the other side of the ridge from our camp by the time of the next sun's shortest shadows. She-gha told me later what the returning men had said and thought we had to move at first light, but Geronimo and Naiche had said no.

Geronimo and Naiche decided to ambush the Mexicans at a pond some rancher must have built on the other side of a high ridge from us to catch runoff where two canyons crossed. The pond, surrounded by high, rough ridges covered with scattered pines, was within two hundred yards of good cover for marksmen and had boulders even closer, where the warriors could take cover for easier shots during an ambush. It was a good setup for a deadly trap.

Later that night, wrapped in my blanket, I listened to the sounds of the little animals scrambling in the brush near our blankets and insects and frogs croaking around the camp's spring. I remembered the fight I had seen two days before, although it seemed years ago. I saw a black-skinned Bluecoat killed and another shot in the knee by hidden warriors. Most of the Bluecoats fled to cover while their captain stayed exposed, urging them to pick good targets. I thought it a miracle that he escaped unwounded. The black-skinned Bluecoats were brave men. I wondered how the Mexican soldiers would fight.

Geronimo was eager to ambush and kill as many as he could. But he wasn't nearly as eager to fight the Bluecoats as he was the Mexicans. The memories of Petra and Andy dead at the ranch-house door and Artisan in the hot desert swept across my mind and lingered for a moment, pushing water to my eyes, but the winds of survival blew those memories deeper into my mind for another time to grieve.

She-gha awakened me in the cold darkness, the stars still bright and blazing, to help her make ready to leave. I gathered more sticks and brush for our fire along with the others already lighted. She roasted meat and steamed baked-mescal slices for the morning meal. Geronimo had already disappeared from his blankets when she woke me up. She-gha saw me looking around in the dark for him and said, "Remember, Trinidad? He prays every sunrise to our great god *Ussen*. Geronimo is a powerful di-yen. Ussen shows him the way."

I nodded, shivering in the cold air, and said, "Yes, now I remember he prays every sunrise. Does he pray he will kill lots of Mexicans today?"

She shrugged. "Only Ussen and Geronimo know for what he prays."

After Geronimo returned to our fire, he put a little sage on it and bathed in the smoke while singing in Apache. Then She-gha served him a morning meal and promised to pray for his success in attacking the Mexican soldiers. Finished with his meal, he strapped on his revolver holster and ammunition belt, buckled an ammunition belt above that for his rifle, picked up his rifle, and said to She-gha, "I see you again, woman." She smiled and nodded. He disappeared into the darkness to meet the warriors on the other side of the ridge and place them where their bullets would be the most effective.

I helped She-gha gather her camp supplies, personal belongings, and loot Geronimo had brought her from raids and make them ready to load on a pack animal before we started for the winding trail up to the top of the ridge where the women and children could watch the fight. Garditha and Leosanni ran up and each took one of my hands. They said something to She-gha, who said to me, "They want to stay with you to watch the fight. Don't let them out of your sight or make noise when we get to the ridgetop." I nodded I understood, squeezed Leosanni's hand, and smiled at Garditha, and we headed for the ridgetop.

The trail to the top of the ridge was rough and steep, but the Apache children ran up the trail like it was flat and made a game of throwing pebbles at each other as they ran. The sun hadn't been up long, and the air was bright and clear and had a sweet, clean smell. Geronimo told the warriors that the soldiers would follow the same steep, winding trail we had followed down from the saddle to the pond.

From the top of the ridge, we could see most of the warriors waiting in hiding for the Mexicans to come down the trail.

There was no breeze, nothing to rattle the brush. Garditha and Leosanni sat with me and didn't move as they watched the trail, expecting Mexican soldiers to immediately appear. Even the birds were quiet. We waited.

We heard the unmistakable jingle of harness iron on mule pack-trains and then the occasional calls of men climbing up the saddle trail on the other side of the ridge we were watching. Three men wearing officer uniforms and riding fine-looking white horses appeared at the top of the saddle trail and began the descent down to the pond glimmering below. Men walked behind the officers. They weren't in perfect order, their columns a little ragged in places, but even I could tell they showed signs of training.

A third of the way down the trail to the pond, the lead officer held up his hand for the column to stop while he used his soldier glasses to study the trees and boulders around the bottom of the crossed canyons. It was the same thing the Bluecoat commander had done at the fight in the Pinito Mountains. Satisfied they were not walking into a trap, the commanding officer waved them forward.

They took a while to get to the canyon bottom and the pond. The officers dismounted and led their horses to water. The men rushed forward, followed by the pack mules, to get their drinks too. The soldiers and their livestock gathered around the pond, drinking in deep swallows, obviously thirsty.

The sharp, distinct crack of a rifle shot broke the stillness and made a cacophony of echoes down the canyons. The head of one of the officers exploded in a cloud of red as he mopped his brow with a wet bandana, and a thundering storm of bullets whining and ricocheting off rocks and raising little geysers in the sand flew around the soldiers while they scrambled to take cover. One man ran to grab the pack mules. Three shots hit his back before he fell to his knees and flopped facedown in the dust. A brave soldier ran from cover to grab a wounded man but died after a few steps in the deadly hail of lead. I saw two more soldiers fall wounded, but couldn't keep up with the number of fallen.

Geronimo was up on the ridge above the pond and had a commanding view of the soldiers and their cover. I saw a warrior run up and squat behind him as he spoke and pointed toward the trail down from the pond to the big canyon to the west on the far side of the mountains. When they finished talking, Geronimo raised his rifle and signaled for the warriors to stop their firing.

Soon commands from the surviving officers began echoing down the canyons. Men began to run from cover, headed for the trail up the saddle they had used to walk into the ambush. A few soldiers got to the trail and aimed their rifles to the ridges where they believed the Apaches must be hiding. The rest of the soldiers, followed by their officers, ran past them up the steep trail and disappeared over the top of the saddle. The marksmen who covered their brother soldiers soon backed up and followed the others over the top.

They left their dead, their horses, and their pack mules. The pack mules were a great resupply opportunity for the Apaches, who would take them and disappear, but Geronimo signaled again and no one ran out to get them. Naiche and two or three of the lead warriors came to talk with Geronimo. I thought I could hear them laughing before they left him. The women looked at each other, questions in the wrinkles of their foreheads. I decided that since Garditha and Leosanni were with me, I couldn't move, although we were thirsty and needed to visit the bushes.

She-gha left the women and went down the ridge to speak with Geronimo. She was smiling when she came to us with a

bag of the mixed stuff Ahnandia had given me to eat and a
soldier canteen of water. She told us to go to the bushes, drink
and eat, and watch—there would be more fighting before the
sun left.

The sun was two hands past the time of shortest shadows. It
was hot and still, the only sounds from buzzing insects. Soldiers
carrying big, long rifles suddenly appeared, running on the trail
crossing the saddle top and down toward the pond. Soldiers we
hadn't seen before came running up to the pond from the
canyon trail that connected to the big canyon, which ran all the
way back to the town of Imuris, to the west. Most of these
soldiers, and there were a lot of them, looked like they were
Indians. They were yelling and firing their rifles at any place
where a warrior might hide as they ran to join the soldiers coming down from the saddle top. The warriors watched and waited
on Geronimo's signal. Like two streams of brown water, the
columns rushed together, and men—in different uniforms,
which added to the confusion—made for the pond and moved
on farther toward the trail over the ridge to the water tank
where we camped. Geronimo waited.

The pack animals the soldiers had left after the first fight
grazed on the brush near the pond. The new column brought
up its horses and pack mules as the men spread out looking for
cover on both sides of the canyon trail over the ridge to the
Apache camp. As they began to climb the trail to the camp,
Geronimo stood, waved his rifle in a great arc, and then with a
whoop brought the rifle to his shoulder and shot a soldier on
the far side of the canyon.

Hidden Apache rifles roared. Mexican soldiers scattered along
the canyon bottom collapsed on the sand and gravel, dying or
wounded. Soldiers not under cover ran back down the canyon
toward the big one to the west.

Two or three officers swore at their men, yelling, "Damn it, don't run, *hombres*. Geronimo is on your land. Take it back. Geronimo, today you die! Kill Geronimo, you cowards! Kill all the Apaches!"

Even after most of the soldiers had run from the pond and down the canyon, with the rest pinned down, the Mexican officers still shouted insults at the Apaches.

Geronimo looked up the ridge at his audience and, seeing me sitting with Garditha and Leosanni, pointed and motioned for me to come to him. I was afraid he had decided to kill me in front of the Mexicans to show them his Power. I wanted to run in the other direction, but I knew if I did, the Apaches would catch and kill me for certain, or if I got away, I would die of thirst or from a wild animal attack in the mountains.

My feet felt like heavy stones as I approached him, but then I saw Naiche sitting with him and they were laughing. When he saw me, he patted the ground beside him and motioned for me to come sit down.

He said, "Trinidad, today we won two easy battles with the Mexicans and their Tohono O'odham Indians. A fool officer down by the water still yells insults and believes they will drive us off. I want you to stand between Naiche and me while I rub his nose in his own dirt. Maybe then he'll decide he's had enough for today and go away. Their pack animals have a great supply of ammunition and other supplies that will help us live well for a while. I want their supplies and horses."

He looked over at Naiche and then me, and we stood up together as he yelled down into the canyon. "Ho! General, where are all your soldiers? If you are so powerful, come take Trinidad from us. She is from the land of the Nakai-yes. We took her from Americanos north of the border. Now you can take her back from us. Come on, brave men! Don't leave her. Come take her from us. We will not harm her if you try. Come on, great

81

soldiers. Come and take Trinidad."

The Apaches stopped firing so the Mexicans would hear Geronimo. The taunting voice from the Mexican officer stopped as I stood there in the afternoon sun between the two warriors, the breeze blowing through our hair high on the ridge above the Mexicans.

Geronimo waited a little while, but we heard nothing. He yelled down into the canyon. "So you don't want to come take back Trinidad? Soon she will be a beautiful woman, *señores*. Come and take her. If not, then leave your supplies and go. We will not kill you."

I looked down into the canyons and saw men running down the canyon toward the big canyon to the west, one wearing a tan uniform—Geronimo told me later that he was the officer who had been shouting insults—and waving his arm for the men to follow him. I watched them run and heard Geronimo and Naiche laughing.

All these men—Geronimo said there were over two hundred, counting the ones in the first fight—were men of my own blood. They wouldn't fight to take me from fifteen Apaches? Why should they die for some girl they didn't know? It was a hard question to face because there was no good answer if they wanted to live. I knew then I would have to free myself. My captors were powerful people. For me to get away, I had to learn all I could from them, and be better than them at what I learned.

CHAPTER 8
EAST ACROSS THE MOUNTAINS

The warriors appeared from their hiding places like ghosts from tombs, and grabbed the reins and lines of the horses and pack animals wandering confused and shy with their precious loads of ammunition and supplies. Geronimo waved his hand toward the women disappearing back down the ridge and told me to go back to the camp with She-gha. I climbed back up the ridge, where Garditha and Leosanni awaited me with big smiles and threw out their arms, saying, "Enjuh. Enjuh."

We followed the women down the ridge trail back to our camp. The women harnessed the packhorses and mules, easily hoisting the pack frames up on the animals. We began loading them as the falling sun left a golden glow in the western sky, the last bright light of day resting on the mountaintops, and deep black shadows in the canyons and arroyos. The women and children, sweating in their labor even as the day became cooler, finished loading. A cloud of dust drifted down the ridge trail toward us. Out of it came men leading the pack animals on their way down to the spring. They watered the horses and mules and pulled water casks off pack frames to refill, making ready to ride with their plunder.

Geronimo led us up the north canyon wash in a gentle climb. It was a good time to ride, while the air was growing cooler and there was still a little light. I wondered how far we could go up the wash toward the top of the mountain before the night came and left us all in darkness. We weren't on the north canyon wash long before Geronimo turned east up a steep canyon that the horses, grunting and snorting, labored to climb.

I remembered listening to Artisan tell a visiting neighbor that Apaches didn't travel at night and waited until first light to attack unless the moon was full. He said they thought it was dangerous to travel at night. Maybe it was, but from what I saw, they welcomed the darkness as good cover.

The last two hundred yards of the climb up the east canyon to the saddle top between two mountains was the hardest part of that night's ride. We all had to dismount and pull our horses along as we climbed. The pack animals, led on a much longer, much easier but riskier climb—one slip and the animal and its pack of ammunition and needed supplies would go tumbling down the mountain in near darkness, never seen again—followed a switchback trail created through the brush and trees. Those who followed the short, steep trail all made it to the top of the saddle and stopped to wait and rest while the pack animals came up.

From the saddle top, I could see faraway lights, golden specks in a deep well, along the big canyon where the Río Magdalena and the iron road that we had followed south from near Nogales ran. I even recognized hills around the canyon where we had come out of the Pinito Mountains to cross the river and iron road to hide here in the Cibuta Mountains. I thought, *If we cross the iron road back into the Pinitos, I've got to either get away and follow the iron road back to Nogales before we get high in the mountains or wait a long time for another chance to escape.*

The mules and horses carrying loaded pack frames finally appeared out of the long shadows in the yellow light at the top of the saddle. The trail east down the other side of the saddle led into a canyon. As we started down, I saw the trail into the canyon was longer by half and about as steep as the side we had just climbed, but the trail along the canyon bottom was smooth and sandy with few boulders to maneuver around. The men with the pack animals led them on a switchback path for about three hundred yards down to where the wash widened out enough for two to ride side by side, and then it wasn't nearly as steep as the initial trail down from the saddle top. The rest of the band, leading their ponies, followed the pack mules and horses led by the men down the switchback trail. We were lucky. A handful of times, some horses, but none of the mules, came close to slipping and rolling head over heels down the mountain, but we made it down without losing any supplies, mules, or horses.

After the trail down from the steepest part of the saddle, the wash flattened out enough to ride our ponies, and the ride went much faster and easier, especially with a half-moon rising, making it clearer to see the white sand and gravel in the wash. The canyon we followed down from the mountains led into a much bigger one that soon opened to the river and iron-road canyon from Nogales.

Geronimo swung south down the river canyon and crossed the iron road near the wide canyon we had followed out of the Pinito Mountains. He rode a little south of the canyon opening and led us to a big iron water tank fed by a windmill where we could quench our thirsts and water and rest our animals. The moon was near the top of its arc south. We had come a long way but couldn't stop long. My friends Garditha and Leosanni came to sit with me, one on each side, in the new grass surrounding the big tank. We lay back in the grass to rest until it was time to go. I was so tired and sleepy. It was warm and comfortable there between them, and I closed my eyes for just a moment.

I awoke with a start. My friends, already mounted, looked barely awake. She-gha was looking into my eyes when they opened as she shook me awake. She told me to find a bush and then fill a canteen she gave me. Geronimo rode down from the water tank to the canyon entrance and, down the center of its wide wash, set a pace of walk, jog, gallop that didn't wear out the horses but covered a lot of distance as the canyon narrowed and began to rise, making us ride single file.

Riding in the wash meant we had to pay much more attention to where the ponies stepped to avoid them brushing us off against boulders or stepping into washed-out holes and throwing us off or breaking a leg. Despite all the opportunities to fall, I was determined to stay on the pony, no matter what, to show these people I was worth keeping even if two hundred Mexicans wouldn't fight fifteen of them for me.

As the bright horizon stars started to disappear, a ridge made the canyon we were in divide into a canyon running northeast, and another that ran southeast. A trickle of water flowed down the southeast branch, where we made a camp. I gathered brush for the fire She-gha made to give us a little warmth and coffee to drink with the food mix the Apaches seemed to live on when they were on the move. There was enough green brush for horse and mule grazing while we wrapped in our blankets for some rest. A couple of sentinels climbed up the ridge dividing the original canyon to a place high enough to watch both canyon branches and the canyon through which we had just passed.

Geronimo and She-gha slept on one side of her fire and I on the other. It was warm down in that canyon, and with the blanket around me, I was soon in a deep dreamless sleep.

The snorting of horses and mules, the "ummph" sounds of women hoisting saddles and pack frames on the animals, and light from a brilliant sun awoke me. I felt a strong need to find a privacy bush and walked up the south branch, which the women and children used. When I returned, the loads on the packhorses and mules, and saddles on the horses, signaled we were ready to ride. She-gha offered me trail food out of her bag. I ate a couple of handfuls and then filled my canteen to hang on my pony's saddle. Geronimo was in council with the warriors in the north branch of the canyon.

Back down the canyon we had followed up from the river, Garditha and Leosanni were practicing with their slings. I watched them for a little while and decided a sling was a weapon I might have good use for. After we made camp for a day or two and the men started raiding again, I would get them to show me how to make and use one.

The morning was still young and the air cool from a nice little breeze falling down from the high canyon places. Bushtits fluttered in the junipers and called from the brush on the canyon sides. The men left their council and began to gather their ponies.

She-gha said to me, "Soon we go." She motioned up the ridge that divided the canyon we had followed from the river and iron road. It was too steep to ride up from where we had rested. We would have to first climb about a hundred yards on foot, leading the horses and pack mules.

Geronimo came, looked us over, and nodded. Leading his pony up to She-gha, he said, "Woman, we go." She nodded as he walked past her and began climbing the faint trail we had followed coming down from the mountains. His face might look like that of an old man, but he had strength and agility to match much younger men. When he got to the top of the steep initial climb, he swung up on his pony and motioned for the rest of us to follow.

After I finally pulled my pony to the place where he could climb and carry me, She-gha helped me mount. She mounted her pony, and we began the long, winding climb back into the

Pinitos, following the ridge trails toward the mountaintop we had taken to get down to the river and iron-road canyon.

Two hands before midday, Geronimo stopped in the middle of a saddle between two low mountains and, using his soldier glasses, studied the mountains and ridges in front of us before looking down the canyon funneling up to where we sat. From the back of the line, Naiche rode up to him and they talked. I saw Geronimo nose point toward a distant ridge for Naiche to direct his soldier glasses. I looked in that direction and was surprised to see a line of tiny dark figures, looking like ants on the march, following the ridges north. I saw She-gha watching them, too, and frowning. She looked at me and shook her head. "Bluecoats." We were riding in their direction but were far behind them. Another chance to escape was vanishing in front of my eyes.

Geronimo turned his pony and rode down into the canyon he had studied. The first part of the trail was steep, but not so steep that we had to dismount. He created a switchback trail that made it easier for everyone to navigate. This was a new trail off the one we had ridden from the saddle top after the battle with the black-skinned Bluecoats.

We followed Geronimo down the canyon for the rest of the afternoon. On the way, we rode around much brush and many boulders until we came to a trail leading to a spring feeding a pool in the canyon where we had camped before climbing up the saddle to watch the black-skinned soldiers fight our warriors. We stopped. Women made cooking fires in deep little pits. The young men slaughtered a beef, and we ate well that evening.

CHAPTER 9
THE SLING

At first light, the band moved again. We went northeast down the canyon and out across llano foothills. We crossed a canyon with another iron road and a river nearby, which I later learned was the Santa Cruz River. The iron road ran from Nogales to Santa Cruz and the mines beyond. Far down the canyon, we could see the tops of houses and a church steeple. Soon after the time of shortest shadows we came to a large water tank some rancher must have dug out of a big wash that lay near scattered junipers. Naiche and Geronimo decided to make camp there for two or three days. They sent scouts out to look for any Bluecoat patrols they needed to avoid and for ranches to raid.

The women unloaded the pack animals, set up shelters, and began cooking an evening meal from leftovers of the meat we had eaten the night before. I helped She-gha all I could with putting up her shelter and by gathering brush and wood for her fire. She didn't want any help cooking and didn't make anything worth teaching me to cook. When Garditha and Leosanni came to her fire wanting me to go play with them, she waved us away.

We practiced what we had learned of the other's language. I spoke Apache as best I could, giving them many laughs at how tongue-tied I was in Apache, but we mostly spoke Spanish, because they often heard it around the wickiups and had learned many of its words. I finally signed to them to show me how to use a sling. They laughed with delight and clapped their hands when they understood what I wanted.

Garditha ran to Naiche's shelter and soon returned with a piece of soft tanned leather about the size of my hand and two long pieces of rawhide. He tied the rawhide to the opposite short sides of the leather, where he had punched holes with the point of his knife, and made loops at the ends of the rawhide thongs for holding on to the sling after the rock was thrown— one thong for looping around my wrist and one thong for holding the other end. Taking a small smooth stone from a leather bag hanging from his breechcloth belt, he showed me how to fold the leather over the stone, loop one piece of the rawhide thong around my throwing-arm wrist, and hold the second thong in my hand near where the first thong looped around my wrist.

Leosanni, three or four years younger than Garditha and me, had a sling too and knew how to use it. She showed me how to whirl the stone in vertical circles, or above my head or even at some angle in between. With whatever style I felt most comfortable and accurate, they motioned their approval with nods and grins. I signed to them that I wanted to practice with my sling.

Garditha led us to the wash that filled the big tank where we camped and showed me the places to find the best sling stones, which were about a third the size of my fist, rounded and smooth. I found some nice ones, for which he nodded approval, and I put them in my pockets. He and Leosanni found enough to refill the bag hanging on his belt.

Then he led us to a tall, nearly vertical, bank on a hill outside the camp, put a couple of crossed yucca stalks against it, walked back about thirty paces, put a stone in his sling, showed me how he held the thong and released it, and then in two hard whirls sent the stone flying toward the crossed yucca stalks. The stone slammed into the dirt beside the crossed stalks no more than a hand width from their cross point. He tried four more stones. Their strikes clustered around the first one, and one almost hit the cross point.

I studied Garditha's hand release point on the downward arc of the windup circle and decided I knew when to release the thong. He motioned for me to try. I took care to stand about where he had been, found one of the better stones in my pocket, loaded my sling, gave it two hard circles, and let the rock fly. Heat filled my face. I knew it was turning red. The stone had flown over the top of the bank and into the grass at the top of the hill.

Garditha didn't laugh. He acted like a grown teacher, and with a serious face took my throwing arm, made me point with my forefinger, brought it up and directed it to a spot about a foot above where the stalks crossed, and said in Spanish, "Throw there. You better by and by." He also gave me some tips about flexing my wrist for overhand throws and then motioned for me to try again. I came within two feet of the cross point. My sudden great improvement made me throw up my arms and jump with delight, which made Garditha and Leosanni laugh. He motioned for me to try again and then again, but neither stone was much closer than the second one.

Garditha said, "Throw many times, you more better."

I nodded, understanding that I would have to practice a lot to get good with a sling. I wondered how long it would take me to be as good as Garditha.

He motioned Leosanni up to where we stood and told her to take a turn. She cast four stones, and they were nearly as accurate as Garditha's, although she couldn't throw as hard. I thought, *If someone as young as Leosanni can be nearly as accurate as Garditha with a sling, then there's hope for me.*

Garditha made targets for Leosanni and me, and we practiced most of the rest of the afternoon, going back to the wash twice for more good stones. As the sun was falling into the mountains, we finally stopped and went back to the water tank. My shoulder was sore from all the throwing, but my stone strikes were starting to cluster and get closer to the cross point of the yucca stalks. I was getting better, but not as much or as fast as I'd have liked. Even so, my skill with a sling now might be enough to make a difference if I had to defend myself.

Naiche, Geronimo, and most of the warriors were in council all that afternoon. *No doubt,* I thought, *discussing where to strike and when.* That night, Geronimo had a lot to tell She-gha as we ate, little of which I understood, the complex tones of the Apache language not yet registering much meaning in my mind. I saw that he shook his head often as he talked and guessed he had a different opinion from the ones he had heard that day.

There was a long pause during their talk. She-gha smiled, nodded at me, and said in Spanish, "After Trinidad helped me gather brush for the fire and make a shelter, Garditha made her a sling and she threw stones at a target with it all afternoon. She has much to learn but works hard and has light behind her eyes."

Geronimo nodded. "Hmmph. Nit'ééhi. When you are a woman, maybe you take a good Apache man, eh, Trinidad?"

I smiled but thought, *Not in this lifetime, Grandfather.*

I helped She-gha clean up around her fire and gathered more brush for the night and morning fires. I felt dirty and went to wash. Near the tank, the noise of galloping horses sounded on the trail, and I moved into the darkest brush to watch. Soon they came over the hill, down to the tank. The riders, two scouts who had gone out when we first arrived, called into the camp for Garditha and Kanseah, a nearly grown boy who served as a novice warrior under Yahnozha, to come take care of their horses. The boys came running while the scouts walked over to visit with Naiche and Geronimo.

The horses were lathered, blowing hard, and thirsty, and the boys let them drink a little, wiped them down with dry grass, and then let them drink again more deeply before leaving them to graze, hobbled, with the other horses and mules. Careful to check that no others were around, I waited a little while after the boys left with the scouts' horses before emerging from the shadows to go to the tank. I pulled off my shoes and dress, now nearly in rags, waded into the warm water, feeling the sand ooze between my toes, and was surprised that even near the edge, the water came up to my waist. I grabbed handfuls of sand and gave my body a good scrub everywhere I could reach and rinsed my hair, but it still felt oily after I stepped out of the water and found a big stone in the darkest of shadows to sit and dry.

I quickly dried in the arid night air, put my dress back on, and returned to She-gha's fire, but she wasn't there. I saw a larger fire with the men gathered 'round it in council. At the edge of the light, the women sat and watched. I went to find She-gha and sit with her. She smiled when she saw me and nose pointed for me to sit beside her. Naiche was speaking, but she whispered, "You smell like you had a good bath." I nodded but pulled at my hair and made a face. She ran her fingers through it and whispered again, "I fix."

After the council, while Geronimo and Naiche still talked together, She-gha showed me a piece of dried yucca root from her parfleche box and said to chop it up, put it in a cup, and boil it until suds appeared. When it cooled, I could use it to wash my hair clean. She gave me a piece of the root to use, and I thanked her for her generosity and for instructing me how to use it.

Then she told me that while the men raided a horse ranch to the east, the women and children must move the camp up into the mountains to the north, where it would be harder for the

Bluecoats and Mexicans to find and reach us after the men took the horses. I thought of all the work the women and children did, packing and loading, and *Does run, run, pack, pack, and fight ever end for these people? Don't they ever get tired of it all?*

Geronimo returned to She-gha's fire and had a cup of the hot, bitter roasted-piñon-nut mixed coffee they seemed to like. Sitting across the fire from She-gha and me, he took a swallow of the brew and said, "Trinidad, many women are good with a sling. They have to defend the camp when the men are gone. A good weapon to use, it takes many rock throws in practice before you can use it to kill. You should use it often against many targets. Silent and deadly, one day it will be useful to you."

I nodded. "Yes, Grandfather. I want to defend myself and the camp."

"Nit'ééhi. I also think you must learn to speak in our tongue. She-gha will help you."

I had been thinking the same thing but was hesitant to ask She-gha to help me. Now that Geronimo wanted me to learn and speak Apache, I wasn't so sure that's what I wanted. "I will do this, Grandfather, but why do you think I should speak your tongue?"

"A woman who becomes part of the band needs to understand what is said in council, what she is told to do, and how to speak of the day with her husband."

At last I knew why he had saved my life. I was glad to have my life, but I would never serve those who murdered Petra and Andy and destroyed what she and Artisan had worked so hard to build. *Somehow,* I vowed in the deepest center of my soul, *I must get away.*

"You will be a good woman, Trinidad. Now we rest. Tomorrow, I think we take many horses." He threw the last few drops of coffee into the fire and lay down by She-gha. I wrapped in my blanket and stared at the dimming coals in the fire. I had learned much that day.

CHAPTER 10
THE BLUECOAT FIGHT

We left the camp at the big tank when the stars were still bright on the horizon and the rising sun was pouring a line of gold along the mountaintops. The men rode with the women and children back down the same trail the band had followed after crossing the Santa Cruz River and the iron road.

When we came to the river, we turned east and rode down the river canyon toward the outlines of rectangular adobe houses and the church steeple of a small village—I learned later it was named San Lázaro—that we could barely see in the distance with the dim, gray light. Soon we turned south out of the canyon and followed a dry wash for a short distance before again turning east across the rolling llano.

In front of us, the Cocóspera Mountains stood in deep black shadows as the sun floated up over their tops. We rode at a good jog that ate up the distance until we reached the mountain foothills, where we slowed down to follow a narrow wash single file through a canyon leading toward the mountains that appeared ever taller and more imposing as we drew closer to them in the cold morning air. We came to a canyon that crossed ours but ran straight south. Four of the men and the novitiate Kanseah led the women and children and stolen livestock up a canyon heading east, while the rest of the warriors passed down the canyon headed south and, as I later learned, rode for the Milpillas Rancho.

Our canyon crossed a few shallow south-running canyons,

and then the men found the eastern trail that crossed the Cocóspera Mountains. It went up the south side of the second-highest mountain. Although it was a good trail, it had stretches where the drop-offs on its edge were hundreds of feet down very steep sides, some nearly vertical. Just after the trail topped out and started east, down the mountain, the men turned northwest off the trail. They led us a short way up a wash and then began a climb up the side of a ridge through the junipers.

It was a hard climb, but we had climbed a much steeper one in the Cibuta Mountains three suns earlier. I was beginning to think I was as good as any Apache in the mountains until I saw Garditha and Leosanni racing each other again on foot to the top. I was fast learning how to stay on a horse in the mountains, but I knew it would be a long time before I had the strength and endurance to run up a ridge like an Apache child.

We followed a faint path on the top of the ridge, winding through scattered junipers and brush, until we came to a large flat place covered with green weeds and bushes the horses reached to nibble when we stopped. It had enough green brush to feed the animals with us and the ones the warriors might take at the Milpillas Rancho for several days.

Downslope from this place, at the edge of a steep drop-off, was a hollow shaped like the palm of a cupped hand that held a spring-fed pool of shimmering black water. It was easily large enough for the entire band to camp there if we left the horses in a rope corral up on the flat place, and I didn't doubt it was the site of our future camp. Camping down in the depression meant the glow from the evening cooking fires wouldn't be visible at night from the canyons below. It was a good place for a hidden camp.

I helped She-gha unload the packhorses, make a brush shelter, and gather wood for her fire. Before lighting the fire, she led me to the edge of the depression where we camped. The

97

W. Michael Farmer

drop to canyons below, almost straight down, looked breathtaking and scary. She nose pointed to the mountain slope on the north side from where we camped.

"See, the ridge slope is not so steep there to the north? We can work our way down that slope on foot to the foothills below us."

I looked where she pointed and nodded. Then she pointed west toward a low range of gray mountains in the far distance.

"We rode with the men at sunrise on a trail that runs across the llano in front of those mountains and came down to that trail from the pass there to the southwest. If you look closely, you can see the little village we rode past early, before sunrise. The trail we were on runs in front of us here." She pointed straight down. I recognized the wash we had been in just before the men left us. "Do you remember these trails, Trinidad?"

I nodded.

"Enjuh. For attacks on the camp, we always have a way to escape and a place and time to gather later. When you run during an attack, take nothing but your knife and blanket. They will help you live. Leave everything else. Taking things you don't need will only slow you down. Everything we need for comfort we can take in raids. Do you understand what I tell you?"

I nodded. "Where will we gather if the enemy scatters us?"

"Return to our last camp at the big tank. We wait four days at gathering places for all who can escape. Otherwise, we believe you are taken as a slave or ride the ghost pony to the Happy Land."

"I have no knife or blanket to take with me if we have to scatter."

She-gha smiled and nodded. "I know this, child. We have learned to trust you, and you have light behind your eyes. I give you a knife from Geronimo's last raid, and the blanket I give you tonight, you keep as yours."

I had learned it was not Apache custom to thank anyone for a gift. The thanks came when you could return the favor.

I said, "Can I help you now?"

She smiled. "Come. I'll show you how to make food for the trail. My supply grows small, and I need to renew Geronimo's. While we work, I help you learn our tongue."

I said, "Enjuh," and she laughed out loud at my try to show I had learned some of the Apache tongue. "You learn fast, child."

She-gha made a small fire. While we waited for it to burn down to coals, she gave me the long-desired knife she had promised. It looked like a knife Petra might have kept in her kitchen. It had a plain wooden handle, with a blade about five inches long, and was as sharp as Artisan liked to keep his razor. She also gave me a trade wool blanket patterned in red and black geometric designs, mine to keep, and a sheath for the knife so I could wear it stuffed in my dress waist behind me or in one of my pockets. Fearful of losing it by wearing it behind me, I carried it in a dress pocket.

We looked for and found two specially shaped stones we carried back to the fire—one stone big and heavy with a saucer-sized depression on a big flat side, and the other stone round and smooth, small enough to get my fingers around to lift it. She-gha pulled from her parfleche long, narrow sacks made from leather or cloth. From one, she poured bits of dried meat into the saucer-shaped depression of the big rock and told me to rub the round rock over them to grind them up into much smaller bits. As I worked, she added first a handful of dried berries, then acorn and walnut nutmeats, and finally dried light tan mesquite pods, all from other sacks, for me to grind together along with the dried meat. When the mixture was smooth and uniform enough for her, she held up her hand, palm out, to stop. We tasted a pinch. I thought it was tastier than what

Ahnandia had given me.

She-gha smiled and nodded when I said, "Enjuh." We filled her bag and a spare one for Geronimo, shook them down, and set the stones aside. She planned to also refill the bag Geronimo carried when he returned from the raid. Pointing toward the grinding stones, she told me to put the rest in a bag she gave me to carry on my belt.

When we had climbed up the ridge off the main trail, one of the warriors with us took a deer with his bow. The families in the band divided the meat up between them. She-gha decided to make a savory stew with her share.

I sat with her as we cut up the meat, herbs, and wild potatoes she kept in her parfleche and mixed them in a pot. While she worked, she began teaching me to speak Apache and named things around the fire and explained how to use the words in complete sentences. The words were hard to pronounce correctly. With different emphasis on its syllables, the word might mean something entirely different than what you meant. We worked on my Apache tongue most of the afternoon, and I slowly began to feel comfortable speaking the Apache she had taught me.

As the falling sun made the shadows long and filled our ridge with great pools of bright, yellow light, the warriors from the Milpillas Rancho raid came up the ridge off the main trail, driving a herd of thirty horses they had taken. It was good to see them return and made me feel safe—a strange feeling, I thought, for an Apache captive. The men watered the horses and led them to the roped-off corral for them to graze with the other livestock before going to their family fires.

The sun had fallen behind the far mountains, but a golden glow still filled the western sky when Geronimo came to our fire. He was in good spirits and laughed often and made jokes about She-gha and me. She-gha told him what she had taught

me that day as we sat eating from her venison stewpot. He ate
with hunger, saying often, "Hmmph, *gonit'éé* (it's fine)."

I didn't know if he meant the stew or what she said she had
taught me. Judging from the twinkle in her eyes, I supposed he
meant both. That night, I rolled in my new blanket and slept
next to the orange coals left from the fire. I was so tired I didn't
dream. I didn't dream, as I often did, of Petra, Andy, and
Artisan. I didn't dream of all the killing I had seen since I had
left their ranch.

After eating a morning meal out of She-gha's stewpot, gathering wood and brush for the fire, and doing a few other chores, I
went with Garditha and Leosanni to the top of the ridge beyond
the rope corral for the livestock. In another depression on top
of the ridge, we found a supply of small, rough stones for our
slings. They were not as easy to use, nor did they fly as true as
the smooth, rounded stones we found near the big tank at the
last camp, but they were good enough for practicing throwing
form against targets.

Garditha made us some targets, crossed sticks like we used at
the big tank, and we began to fill the air with flying rocks. I
could tell the day without practice had helped my muscle
memory and improved my accuracy. My throws were closer to
where the sticks crossed, but still had a long way to go before I
was consistently no more than a hand width away.

We threw for about a hand against the horizon, when Garditha stopped and looked down the ridge. He stared for a moment and then said, "Come on. Now!" He started running for
camp with Leosanni and me right behind him.

Garditha ran to Naiche, who saw him coming and frowned.
Garditha, breathless, said without raising his voice, "Bluecoats
are on the ridge."

Naiche reached for his rifle as he said, "Where? How do you

know this?"

"I saw a scout on a white horse a long rifle shot down the ridge from where we were slinging stones in a hollow near the horses."

"Go to Geronimo, tell him, and then find the rest of the warriors and tell them to meet me here. Tell their women they need to pack and then join us. Hurry!"

Leosanni stayed at Haozinne's fire, and I ran behind Garditha, quicker than a jackrabbit, to Geronimo at She-gha's fire. Not far behind Garditha, I passed Geronimo on his way to Naiche.

The men, like shadows growing out of the ground, and their women not far behind them quietly gathered around Naiche and Geronimo. Naiche said, "Bluecoats come up the ridge. The women and children must leave camp, stay out of sight, and be ready to go down the mountain to the place where we agreed to meet if the warriors cannot drive off the Bluecoats. Go now."

I ran to She-gha's shelter, grabbed my blanket, and looked around. It was hard to understand how she could just run off and leave all her things and the food we had worked hard to make and save. Not far behind me, she rushed to grab her blanket, open the parfleche for Geronimo's spare soldier glasses and trail food, loop them across her body, and then nod for me to follow.

We ran out the north side of the camp's depression on the path she had shown me the day before and down the ridge a little to a place where it wasn't too steep for us if we had to begin working our way down to the foothill canyons. We stopped to wait for the other women and children along with Garditha and Leosanni. Soon they came, and we found a place to sit and wait. The once-noisy birds in the brush were quiet. Even the breeze easily strumming through the junipers didn't make much sound. We waited.

My heart thudded as I thought, *Maybe today I can get away. Maybe today.*

I said to She-gha, "What do the men plan?"

She shrugged and lifted her hands. "I think they probably ambush the Bluecoats. Bluecoats have the advantage. There are probably more of them, and they are higher up the ridgetop than our men. Soon we know."

A distant sharp snap and crack of rifle fire from near the camp broke the silence. Horses squealed and men yelled. Then came a return volley from up the ridge, and another round of return fire from near the camp but in different places than before. Then the shots became scattered in time and place. A warrior appeared from around the edge of the camp hollow and waved for us to go. He followed us with others behind him. The rifle fire from the camp continued against heavy return from the Bluecoats as we helped each other down the ridge and across washes, through dense groves of tall pines, down to the brown-and-tan canyons and llano foothills.

Once, we rode on fine ponies with good saddles. Once, the women had all they needed for a comfortable shelter and to cook for their families. Once, we all had a few nice possessions. Now we had nothing. I didn't understand how these people could run off, leave it all, and never look back or worry about how they would replace it.

Down from the ridge, all the band, with the exception of a few warriors who stayed back to watch the Bluecoats, jogged in canyons and arroyos to keep out of sight. It might have been easy jogging for the adults and children like Garditha and Leosanni, but I was weary, scratched, and footsore just from sliding and half running from tree to tree on our way down off that ridge.

It was becoming harder and harder for me to keep up when

we finally stopped at a small spring. I had never been so thirsty and tired. The cool water surging down my throat was better than the best sweet drink from a mercantile store, and rest from running was an unexpected comfort to my sore muscles and heaving chest.

We waited, shadows in the brush. Then the men who had tracked and watched the Bluecoats after they raided our camp and took all our supplies and livestock appeared and spoke with Naiche and Geronimo. She-gha cocked her ear to one side and, after listening, nodded.

She turned to me and said, "The scouts say the Bluecoats follow the west trail down the mountain and take the canyon we used yesterday. Geronimo and Naiche think they go to the village of Santa Cruz a hand on the horizon's ride north of here with our horses and supplies. The horses need water. Geronimo thinks he knows the spring where they will stop before they go on to Santa Cruz. The men go now to set up an ambush. Maybe get the horses and supplies back."

CHAPTER 11
LONG RUN

The women and children in the band included Nohchlon, Chappo's wife, who was about six months' pregnant. Another, Nahbey's wife—I never learned her name—had a child about Andy's age that she carried effortlessly in a sling across her shoulders. There was a young boy about six, very shy, who had a long name, Estchinaeintonyah; and then me and my friends Garditha, about my age, and Leosanni, about six.

The other women, all married, were about Petra's age or older and in their years of greatest strength. One or two were near a grandmother's age. There was not one among that group, except me, who could not run all day and, when they stopped to camp, still have enough energy left to make a shelter and a hot meal for their warrior husbands and children.

I was already tired and worn out when the women and children left the spring to run down the wash toward a big canyon. Their running pace was fast for me. Like a running herd of antelope, the weak either kept up and grew stronger or dropped out, food for the wolves and coyotes waiting and watching. Only the strong survived. As we ran in the bright, glaring sun, I saw She-gha look back and wave her arm at me to come on, but she kept running. I fell farther and farther behind, and finally slowed to a walk.

I climbed the brush-filled arroyo the women and children running ahead of me took to the top of the low ridge that formed the west side of the canyon in which we had been running and saw them, the size of ants far in the distance. They were off to the side of a dusty wagon road that must go to the little village we had dimly seen on the way to make camp in the mountains. To bypass the village, I knew they must soon turn south to find the trail we had used two mornings earlier.

As I padded along in the road dust, trying to follow the women and children, I realized, as if seeing a flash of lightning, that if the women and other children couldn't see me and disappeared trying to avoid the village, this was my chance to escape them by running for the village. My heart fluttered like a butterfly as I walked along, not dallying but not running either, in order to let the women and children disappear.

In about half a hand against the horizon, I came to a curve in the road, and after walking a short distance, I could see where the road not far ahead dipped across a wide canyon headed south. I decided that was where they turned to avoid the village. If I followed that canyon north, I would come to the canyon where the Santa Cruz River and the iron road ran. If I followed that canyon west, I knew it would lead me straight to the village and freedom.

When I reached the canyon running north to south, I couldn't see the Apaches after its first turn to the west. I smiled. Maybe today I truly would gain my freedom after all my false hopes before. I turned to cross the road and head north up the canyon for the river and iron road. I hoped it was not too far to the river. I was desperately thirsty.

"Yi, yi, yi! Hey, hah!"

I jumped from fright and nearly fainted as Garditha ran out from behind some junipers, waving his arms and yelling like an attacking warrior. When he saw how I had jumped in surprise and fright, he nearly fell down, he was laughing so hard.

"Ho! Trinidad! You look like you've seen a witch. Did I scare you?"

I could feel the coolness of moisture on my legs and knew I had wet myself, but I wasn't about to tell him that. I held up my chin and said, "You surprised me, but I wasn't afraid. You don't look like any warrior I've ever seen."

His face fell as he tried to think of a good retort. "You're too weak and slow to ever be an Apache. If I had done that to an Apache girl, she would be winding up her sling to defend herself, but you just jumped and made a face."

"Yes, you surprised me. I ought to have had my sling ready. But I'm glad I didn't. I might have stoned you. I couldn't decide the way to go. Now a novitiate warrior can show me the way. I'm glad you're here." I hated to lie to my friend like that, but who knew what the women might do to me if they thought I wanted to run? "Why did you come after me?"

I could see I hadn't hurt his pride much when he stuck out his chest and said, "She-gha asked me to stay back, run with you, and show you the way. She thought you might get lost or captured by Mexican bandits who wouldn't be reluctant to abuse you, even as young as you are, especially if they knew you had been riding with Apaches. Come on. I know you're weak and tired, but we have to get back on our own before the men return from their ambush and look for another camp."

"I'm very thirsty. Do you have any water?"

He shook his head but reached into a small sack he carried on his belt and brought out a smooth pebble about the size of an old musket ball. Putting it in my hand, he said, "This will help until we can reach the river."

I stared at him like he was crazy. He grinned and said, "Put it in your mouth and suck on it. It'll bring spit. Your mouth won't feel so dry, and you won't be so thirsty. Just be careful not to choke on it."

We headed south down the canyon. I didn't know where that pebble had been. I didn't care. I put it in my mouth and liked the feel of its smooth, cool surface on my tongue as I worked it over to my cheek. He was right, spit soon took the dryness out of my mouth, but thirst, like a hot coal, still lingered.

We moved south down the canyon. Garditha kept wanting to run, and he got far ahead of me several times but always came back. I walked on, too weak to move any faster. The burning sun seemed to bring visions to my mind. I saw myself using my sling on Garditha, braining him with a stone, and then running back up the canyon to the village. I even considered trying to make the vision a reality but didn't believe I had enough strength to make it back up the canyon to the river and water.

In one vision, I saw a small skeleton lying in the wash and realized it was me, and in another, my face was bright red and my tongue swollen and protruding through my lips as I staggered forward. I thought, *It would be so nice to just lie down and rest to die without fighting it.* But then I remembered Petra and the baby lying in the blood-blackened sand near the ranch-house door. My determination to live grew. I would get away from these people who killed without mercy and now held me. I would live. It was the Apaches who would die. I walked on, brushing by mesquite and prickly pear, my now-ragged dress becoming even more torn, but I didn't care. Tear my clothes, tear me to naked, bleeding cuts turning black in the hot, glowing sunlight. These Apaches weren't going to have the pleasure of seeing me die.

I heard a voice. No, not a voice, a yell. I looked up through the burning, shimmering air and saw Garditha on a little rise, yelling and waving his arms for me to come, to hurry. *What was he saying? Water! Could he be saying "water"?* I ran for him as fast as my stumbling feet could carry me and my lungs could suck in the fiery air.

I reached him, gasping for breath. Grinning, he pointed to a small pool among the rocks down in a little arroyo, nearly hidden in brush, its dark surface a black mirror. Was it a mirage? Was he teasing me? "Is it safe to drink?"

"Yes, safe. Drink slow so you don't get sick. Give me my pebble now so you don't swallow it." I spit the pebble into my hand and gave it to him. In a few steps down the slope, I was on my belly, sucking in the warm water, trying to drink as much as I could swallow without choking. I nearly strangled myself with that lack of self-control. Garditha yelled, "Slow down! Don't make yourself sick!" I stopped drinking and plunged my head into the cool darkness, then pulled it out of the pool to shake from side to side, and then bent down to drink some more before I sat up, panting, to wipe the droplets from my face.

Garditha came down the bank, kneeled by the pool, and scooped up water to drink from his cupped hands while looking around the terrain as he no doubt had seen warriors do. His thirst satisfied, he sat down by the pool while I drank again, trying to hold enough water to see me through until we could drink again.

We ran on. At least for me, the gait was faster than a walk, but Garditha kept getting ahead and coming back. After a while, the little ridge we were on began to slope down, and before long, we were in the wash of the canyon we had first followed toward the mountains.

Garditha jumped high and waved both arms when he ran into the wash and headed west, waving me on to follow him. I didn't know whether to laugh or cry. I knew then I would make it back to the big tank, stay with the women and other children, and be as safe as an Apache group could be safe. But this time, despite the opportunity, I wouldn't be free of them.

In less than a hand above the horizon, our canyon fed into a wide one running north-south with a wagon road running down its middle. We hid in the brush and looked both ways up and down the road and saw no one. We could see a few adobes and the church steeple in the far distance toward the north and knew it must be the village. Once more checking the road for travelers and seeing none, we ran across the big, wide canyon to the much smaller one we had followed two mornings earlier before we crossed the river and iron road.

Clouds came and the air cooled. I felt stronger and began to run. I couldn't keep up with Garditha, but we passed up the canyon much faster than we would have had I been walking. In less than half a hand, we crossed the road running toward the village, drank again, waded the river, and soon crossed the iron road to run up into the hills toward the big tank.

When we came within sight of the big tank of water sparkling in the midafternoon sun, I was back to walking, so weary I don't think I could have made it if the tank had been another mile away. Garditha plunged forward. He knew the women must have made camp in the depression where we'd camped before. I pulled the last bit of strength from my body and ran toward the camp with my head held high, a White Eye–Mexican girl who had run all day with the Apaches and lived to tell about it.

CHAPTER 12
THE HEART OF AN APACHE

She-gha saw Garditha and me run into camp. A big smile filled her face as she waved me to her fire, where I slowly sat down, looking at the ground, afraid I would bring shame to her if I collapsed like my body wanted.

"Ho, Trinidad! I feared we had lost you, that you would make food for buzzards and coyotes. I knew if you were coming, Garditha could show you the way. You have the will of an Apache. Soon you will be as strong as one." She lifted my head with her leather-tough fingers under my chin and frowned when she saw my cracked and bleeding lips.

I croaked, "Water."

She gave me an army canteen, saying, "Not too much at once, mujercita. Your body may still be that of a child, but I call you woman because your will and courage are that of an Apache woman. Soon your body will call you woman too."

The cool canteen water restored me to life. She-gha gave me a salve to put on my lips and face, which, without a bonnet, had cooked to a bright red by the unrelenting sun. I remembered watching her one evening, making the salve from prickly pear and a couple of other herbs. After using it on my lips and face, I believed she had the best of restorative elixirs. She let me rest a little while and then nodded toward her axe. More wood for the fire. I had just picked up the axe when a rumble fell on our ears from galloping horses leaving the foothills northeast toward Santa Cruz and coming toward us.

The warriors were all business as they herded the horses and led pack animals loaded with the supplies we had left in the mountains, in addition to several new white horses and new supplies on mules. They drove the animals toward the large depression where the livestock had been kept before. I watched and counted the herd and men as they came down the ridge. All the warriors who left us at the spring to ambush the Bluecoats returned. I smiled in spite of myself. It was a very successful raid.

The warriors watered the livestock, drank deeply and washed away the trail dust at the tank, and then went to their women's fires. I had just returned with an armload of wood and brush when Geronimo, his hair wet and pulled back from his face, sat down in the shade of the wickiup at She-gha's fire, took a cup of coffee she wordlessly offered him, acknowledged me with a nod, and, smiling, began telling She-gha about the raid against the Bluecoats.

I spoke very little Apache then and could barely follow bits and pieces of what he said, but She-gha told me later that the warriors had surprised the Bluecoats at a spring in a deep ravine. Geronimo thought they had killed two Bluecoats and wounded two more. The warriors took back our livestock and supplies and four white horses, even one belonging to the officer who led the Bluecoats. Geronimo slapped his knee, laughing as he told the story while gesturing often with his hands. He thought tomorrow would be a good time to go after more horses on the east side of the Milpillas Rancho since the Bluecoats had gone on to Santa Cruz. That left the ranches to the south undefended except by Mexican soldiers the band had already defeated twice in the Cibuta Mountains fights.

"Yes," he said, "it's a good time to raid south." He nodded at me and said in Spanish so I understood him, "How did our girl do on the run back to camp?"

She-gha smiled. "She's still weak, not strong like an Apache child, and ran far behind us. I had to send Garditha to show her the way, but she didn't quit and came in running a little while before you appeared with the horses. She has a strong heart. I like her."

He nodded and said, "Nit'ééhi. Keep teaching her our tongue. She may be useful one day."

"This I do, husband. Now take some rest. The day has been long."

He finished his coffee in two quick swallows and then lay down on a blanket in the shade of the wickiup. Soon I heard a soft snore. The sun was halfway down its fall into the horizon, and the air was hot and still.

She-gha worked with little noise, putting an evening meal together and teaching me more Apache. She steamed slices of dried baked mescal and yucca tips. She mixed dried juniper berries with piñon nuts and some other kind of berry I didn't recognize that had a nice tart flavor, and she made some acorn bread. Later, she roasted pieces of dried meat on sticks over the fire. It was a meal any ranch house in Arizona or Sonora would have welcomed.

All the while we sat at the fire, she spoke in a low-throated voice, just above a whisper, telling me in Apache as she had done in the Cocóspera Mountains what she was doing and then having me repeat it back. Later, she asked the same thing again to learn if I remembered what she had taught me. When I spoke, she usually answered with a nod or "Enjuh." A scowl greeted me when it was wrong, and I had to repeat it until I got it right.

That night, after the men had eaten, they gathered in council with Naiche and Geronimo. The women and my friends and I listened. After smoking, they talked for a while about the day's raid and laughed at how they had beaten the Bluecoats to take back what was ours. Geronimo, with the shadows in the yellow firelight dancing on his old sculptured face, said, "The Blue-coats ran for Santa Cruz after the attack. There they'll wait for more supplies from packtrains coming across the border. I think they'll be there at least two, maybe three, days. Their wait makes tomorrow a good time for us to raid for more horses south of the Milpillas Rancho. When we have a large-enough herd, then we can swing west and trade it at the border near Nogales for more camp supplies, ammunition, and"—he smacked his lips and gave his head a little jerk—"good whiskey."

All the warriors, including the tall, young chief, shook their fists and nodded, saying, "Enjuh, Enjuh." They decided to leave before dawn while they still had a bright moon. That would allow them to take the horses early in the day and stay out of sight while riding the canyons as they returned to camp.

I gathered firewood and brush after the council broke up. I expected to leave my blanket early to help She-gha give Geronimo a hot meal before he rode south. Custom, training, and respect demanded it. Even so, if I gathered wood and brush before I slept, I wouldn't have to stumble around half asleep in the predawn darkness. I added wood to the pile already by She-gha's fire while she lay down in the blankets with Geronimo.

When I thought I had enough wood and brush for the morning fire, I went to the tank and washed as much as I could around my rags and my face, burned and uncomfortable despite She-gha's soothing salve. The night air was cold as I wrapped in my blanket and lay down by the fire. The moon full and bright, coyotes seemed nearer and more plentiful than usual as they yipped and called to each other. I even heard a couple of wolf calls mixed in with them, making the horses in the depression corral snort, shuffle around, and stamp their feet.

Images from the day swirled through my mind. I thought of the long walk down the ridge from the mountain camp and the missed chance to get away when the women and children ran off and left me, how Garditha had led me back to the tank, and how She-gha had shown me kindness. Still, the memory of Ahnandia killing Petra and the baby, and Artisan walking barefoot across the desert back to find his ranch in flames, drifted through the day's memories and left me teary-eyed with anger and frustration as I slipped into a deep sleep.

The men left the camp with stars still lighted on the eastern horizon and the bright moon floating near the horizon to the southwest. I ate a morning meal of roasted meat and steamed mescal with She-gha and then helped her clean up by her fire, filled her water bags at the tank, and gathered more wood for the fire. Geronimo had brought her parfleche back after the Bluecoats had taken it, and while I worked, she took some calico cloth from it and her leather sewing bag of needles, thread, and sinew, and started working on the calico.

The sun was rising and creating long shadows through the junipers and mesquite when I finished my wood gathering. She-gha motioned me over to stand by her, and she held up the piece of calico next to me. She grinned when she saw the surprise on my face.

"Little Woman, you have run past too many mesquites and cactus. Your dress is in rags. You live with Geronimo and his woman. You must keep your modesty and show his wealth. Let me see how good my eye is for the right size as I make you a new skirt."

Her guess as to length was perfect. She made the waist a little large, but with a belt and a few minor alterations, it fit perfectly. She also used some string to get the arm lengths for a shirt and the sizes around my chest and neck. Before I left to find Garditha and Leosanni, she looked at my shoes, over a year old and now coming apart at every seam, and shook her head. She brought a piece of thick leather—she said it was from a bull elk—out of the parfleche, told me to stand on one corner of the leather barefoot, and took a burnt stick to draw the outline of my feet before waving me away to my friends.

I found Garditha and Leosanni at the wickiup of Haozinne. Garditha had already gathered her wood, and we left to find pebbles to use for sling practice. We found all the stones we needed again near the wash at the tank and went back to the bank we had used for target practice before we left for the mountains. We made our targets and practiced until my arm was sore.

Garditha and Leosanni, who had been accurate when they showed me how to use the sling, were a little better at their targets. I did much better than I had earlier but was still not nearly as good as Garditha and Leosanni. I knew it would take me a long time to become as good as they were with a sling, but still, I was happy with my progress.

We stopped our target practice at about the time of shortest shadows and went for a drink at the tank. The women were sitting and working together in the shade of some nearby junipers. Some were sewing, others sharpening their knives, and a couple—one of them She-gha—were working on pieces of leather. They waved but otherwise didn't pay us any attention as they chatted and their nimble fingers flew through their work.

We walked through the brush toward the horse corral in a nearby depression. We heard the horses and mules snorting and stamping their hooves. Garditha frowned. A low, rumbling growl floated through the brush on the hot, still air. The hair on the back of my neck prickled and felt as if it were standing straight out.

We ran to the top of the depression to see the horses bunched together, facing a cougar not ten yards away, its tan coat shining in the sunlight and its tail, longer than its body, slowly swishing back and forth as it looked over the herd for an easy victim, unaware that we stood watching on the little rise above it. The cougar was a big one, bigger than the ones I had seen Artisan take after hunting them in the canyons and foothills around his ranch when he found two or three of his cows killed and partially eaten—at first, he thought a pack of wolves had killed the cattle until he found the tracks of two large cougars and looked at the claw and teeth marks on the carcasses. The cougar in front of us had its ears laid back on its head, one ear appearing to be nearly gone, and looked ready to take one of the horses.

Staying silent, we squatted down in the grass. Garditha whispered to Leosanni to run and tell the women a cougar was after the horses. Like smoke through the brush, she disappeared, quick and quiet. Garditha pulled his sling from his belt and nodded for me to do the same. We took a handful of pebbles from our pockets, loaded our slings with nice smooth stones, held the rest ready for fast reloading, and nodded ready at each other. Moving apart to have room for winding up good, hard throws, we slowly rose out of the weeds and grass.

The cat crouched, quivering, ready to make a run for its intended victim. Garditha yelled at the top of his lungs, "Hi ye!"

Startled, the cougar jerked from its crouch and turned to face us, its eyes yellow, giving its own roar of fury for interrupting its hunt. I screamed with all the anger building inside me and whipped my stone at the cat as hard as I could. At the same time, Garditha whipped his stone hard and grazed the top of its head to leave a red streak between its ears. My stone hit it in the chest and bounced off. The cougar screamed, showing its great curved teeth in defiance, and crouched, ready to run at us.

The horses and mules stood strangely still and quiet, watching us with their ears pricked up. Garditha and I were quick to reload our slings and whipped them in two or three loops to let fly as hard as we could at the trembling cat. Our stones hit on his muscular shoulders and chest, not seeming to do any damage.

Then the cougar ran straight for me. I dropped the sling and pulled my knife, thinking, *Come on, cat, today is a good time for one of us to die.* Garditha ran to help me with his knife drawn.

It was almost on me. I drew back my arm to stab him wherever I could, when ear-ripping thunder exploded behind me and a dark spot flashed on its chest. It rolled forward in midstride for the space of a breath and clawed at the spot turning red as it collapsed in front of me, not three paces away, the light leaving its eyes.

I turned to see She-gha gasping for breath behind me, levering another cartridge into the chamber of an old rifle Geronimo had left with her.

She huffed, "You were very brave to stand your ground, mujercita. You have the heart of an Apache."

CHAPTER 13
WIN SOME, LOSE SOME

The women ran up behind She-gha, most with old, worn-out rifles, two or three with revolvers. They stared at the cougar, mumbling, "Enjuh, Enjuh." Garditha stood looking at the cougar with his fists on his waist like he had killed it.

I looked at the great curved teeth and tongue hanging out of the cougar's mouth and realized they could have been pulling chunks of meat off my bones if She-gha hadn't gotten there in time. I trembled and wanted to puke, but like a cloud passing the sun, the sourness in my throat left as I turned to her while she kept her rifle pointed at the cat in case it wasn't dead after all.

I said, "I wasn't brave. I was filled with fear, but I wanted that cougar to pay a price for attacking me."

She-gha shook her head. "Bravery is being filled with fear and wanting to run, but you stand your ground and fight, regardless of what happens. You truly have the heart of an Apache. Geronimo will be very proud of you. The women and I carry it back to camp. The hide holds its Power. We must not ruin it by dragging it back to our wickiups. You can watch how we skin it and dress the meat."

With a woman on each leg and one on the tail, they lifted the huge cat with an "ummph" and carried it to shade near the tank and wickiups. The Apaches still carried their bows and arrows on some raids. The bow was a silent killer, and in a close fight, as fast and deadly as a revolver. They believed that a cougar, a quiet and deadly killer, had the best hide for making bow-and-quiver cases, and they often used the tail as a case decoration.

I watched the women, fast with their sharp knives, skin the cat from its button nose to its tail. They scraped the hide clean of flesh and salted it to keep it moist for when they would have time to work on it like they wanted. She-gha sent me to bring water for washing the meat after they dressed the carcass, and then to her parfleche for a big, flat basket to hold the meat they cut up into chunks and sections shared the around the camp.

"The men," She-gha said, letting her knife dangle in her fingers for a moment, "will be happy we have saved their horses and killed a cougar. Cook the meat all the way through or it can make you sick. Still, it has a good flavor. We'll eat well tonight. You children carry the cougar guts far out beyond the camp for the coyotes and buzzards. Trinidad, come back to my fire and help me cook when you return."

The women expected the men back before sunset and began cooking as the sun cast long shafts of yellow light through the trees and turned the evening clouds into a glory of oranges, reds, and purples. I carried water bags and watched while She-gha cooked. The smoke from the cooking cougar meat smelled good and made us all hungry.

The stars began to glow, scattered bright points of light on the horizon, as the sun's gold softened to nothing behind the mountains. I sat with She-gha as she taught me more of the Apache tongue while we waited for the men. There were many coyote yips and occasional snarls among the pack out where we had left the cougar guts. I wished the men would come. I was hungry. Even the face of She-gha, who had lived through many delays in the men coming, showed a pinch of concern in the flickering firelight as she scanned the darkness.

The moon, big and bright, floated up over the eastern mountains. We waited. She-gha handed me her axe and said, "Go and bring us a night's supply of wood and brush for the fire, and remember the talking lessons I gave you by the fire. There is much to learn. Come to me if you can't remember how to say the right word and say it correctly."

I took the axe and had to wander farther into the brush than I had the night before. I mumbled over and over the Apache words and phrases She-gha had taught me that day. The brilliant moon made it easy to find the wood and brush around the junipers. I gathered all we needed in three trips. Still, the men had not come. We waited, listening for hoofbeats in the cold air.

The moon rose to the top of its arc, and still no men had appeared. All the women were singing songs in low, melodious voices. From what She-gha had taught me, I understood enough of the words to know they were praying to their god, Ussen, for their men's safe return. The moon had long passed the top of its arc and headed southwest when we heard the distant rumble of horses. They were running from the same direction they had come from the day before. There were nickers of greeting from the horses in the depression used as a corral. She-gha raised her hands to the sky and sang loudly, "Hi ye! They come. Ussen is good."

The men drove the horses straight to the tank and let them drink before leading them to the corral. She-gha built up the fire for light and started warming what she had prepared for the evening meal. She told me not to let it burn and went with the other women to collect their men's saddles, blankets, and rifles. She-gha soon returned, humming a song of thanks to Ussen and carrying Geronimo's saddle and rifle. After leaving them near the wickiup's blanket door, she squatted by the fire to put the finishing touches on the meal, ready since sunset.

The men washed and then went to their wives for food and rest. Geronimo walked into the firelight. His hair wet and pulled back, his face pinched with lines of weariness, he sat down across the fire from She-gha and me, smiling a little as he said in Spanish, "Nish'ii', my woman and Trinidad. The spirits tell me you killed and have cooked the meat of a cougar today. The air is filled with its good smell."

She-gha smiled back and nodded. "Today Trinidad and I killed a cougar that went after the horses. She has a brave heart, the heart of an Apache. When you hear the story, you will swell with pride for her. Your meal, I made when I believed you come when the sun leaves. I have made it warm again. Eat and then rest." She handed him a gourd filled with her good things.

He held the meat with his fingers, cut off a piece with his knife, and took a bite. "Hmmph. She-gha is a wise and good woman who knows the ways of fire to make food better. The meat is good on my tongue. Eat! Don't wait on me."

She-gha filled two gourds and handed me one, and we ate. I didn't think I would eat cougar, but I was hungry and it was good. It reminded me of *carnitas* meat that Artisan bought in Nogales and Petra used to prepare for supper.

After Geronimo finished and rubbed his hands on his legs and moccasins, She-gha said in Spanish, "Husband, tell us of your day."

Geronimo, sitting with his legs crossed, set his gourd aside and leaned toward us to rest his elbows on his knees. "Ussen was with us, but it was a hard day. We found and took twenty fine horses and some mules and, at one ranch house, found a great box of ammunition and several fine rifles we took from the vaqueros. We had covered much ground and taken many supplies by the time of a hand before shortest shadows. We stopped to rest in an arroyo under the shade of bushes along its sides. We weren't there long when Bluecoats coming from the east attacked us. We had to scatter and leave what we had taken, and a few warriors even lost their ponies. I lost the fine white horse I had taken from the Bluecoats yesterday and had to jump on a white mule we had taken early this morning. Lucky for me, he knew how to run."

We heard a woman laugh two or three wickiups over, and then coyotes fighting where we had left the guts of the cougar. Geronimo paused and listened a moment and then went on.

"When we gathered in the canyon near the wagon road that leads up into the mountains where we stayed two days ago, it was certain we had lost much. Both white horses—one I had ridden, the other Naiche had taken—and three we had taken earlier today and all the rifles and ammunition we had taken earlier that day, all gone. One of the warriors, Naiche's good friend, Tah-ni-toe, was missing. He had no wounds. He badly wanted to see his wife, E-dood-lah. I know this is true. He had said so many times in the last moon. Naiche and I think he decided to return to Fort Apache to get her. We will learn if this is so one day, but I know he was tired of running and fighting.

"Our warriors were weary and had no spirit after losing so much to the Bluecoats. I said, 'Let's go to Santa Cruz. The Bluecoats we hit yesterday are waiting there for more supplies to pick up the chase for us again. There may be much for us to take there.' The warriors thought it over and decided we should go to Santa Cruz.

"We came to Santa Cruz while the sun still showed its face and waited until the village slept. In the meantime, we looked over the livestock in corrals and barns. Most of the good horses belonged to Bluecoats. They foolishly put them in one big corral. Those were the horses we took and brought back tonight. It was easy. The Bluecoats will follow our trail and find this camp. We must leave before the sun is high."

★ ★ ★ ★ ★

The People were up before the dawn. The women made a morning meal from leftovers from the night before and then made their things ready to travel. The men ate and then held council while the women, my friends, and I listened. Naiche spoke first. I understood a little of what he said, but She-gha later told me all his words.

"Although the Bluecoats surprised us yesterday with a second group we didn't know was nearby, and we lost horses and mules and rifles and ammunition, we still took twenty horses from the Bluecoats in Santa Cruz. The Bluecoats we fought yesterday are a sign of many who search for us on the border. A scout I spoke to in the shadows at Santa Cruz tells me Crook is no longer the *nantan* for the Bluecoats in this country. The new nantan is Miles. I think we must learn what kind of terms Miles will give us if we surrender, and we need to learn of our families at Fort Apache."

There were "hmmms" and nods from most of the warriors, but Geronimo and an old, fat, gray-haired man they called Natculbaye sat listening with crossed arms, their faces impassive masks.

"I want to go north to Fort Apache and learn what I can about the nantan, Miles, and our families. The Bluecoats watch the border with many soldier bands from Nogales east to the village of Columbus. If we tried to cross the border to go north, then they might trap us and we would lose men. We need them busy and looking for us in a different place from where we cross.

"My brother, Atelnietze, has agreed to lead four men north and cross the border near the San Jose Mountains. His raid will stir things up among the White Eyes so the Bluecoats leave the border to chase him away. Those who come with me and I will cross the border west of Nogales and meet Atelnietze and his warriors in the Dragoon Mountains near my father's reservation. There, we leave our women and children while we scout Fort Apache and learn what we can. Those who do not want to cross the border with me, I will meet at our camp in the Azul Mountains when we return."

There were nods of agreement and murmurs of "*Ch'ik'eh do-leel* (let it be so)."

Geronimo stood and said, "Naiche is chief. What he says, I will do, but I will not follow him across the border after stirring up the White Eyes and Bluecoats. When he crosses the border, those with me and I will turn toward the Azul Mountains there to wait for his return and to pray to Ussen. Who goes with me?"

A brilliant yellow glow was growing behind the mountains to the east. Birds in the brush were beginning to sing. Natculbaye stood and said, "I ride with Geronimo." A young warrior, Hunlona, also stood and said, "I, too, ride with Geronimo."

Naiche waited for more to speak up. When none did, he said, "Then the rest go with me. Atelnietze, choose the warriors you want to ride with you and ride for the border. Kill any White Eye or Mexican you meet, take what you can. Make the Bluecoats come after you. I'll meet you in the Dragoon Mountains in six or seven suns. The rest of us will ride for Buena Vista Rancho. I know a man near there who trades rifles, bullets, and whiskey for horses."

Chapter 14
The Vaqueros

Atelnietze called out the names of four warriors he wanted with him to draw Bluecoats away from their border patrol trails. He spoke privately with Naiche and Geronimo before he and his men leaped on their ponies and charged down the trail we had made going to the mountains across the Santa Cruz River within sight of San Lázaro.

The rest of us, following an arroyo north, rode in a formation the band used when it moved together. Two warriors herded the horses behind the women, me, and the other children led by Geronimo. Naiche and the warriors rode at the back of the group with two warriors at watch on the flanks. Everyone seemed to know what they were supposed to do and when. The entire camp had organized and was moving at a good pace in less than a finger width against the horizon (about fifteen minutes). The arroyo took us to a shallow twisting canyon, running east to west, where we turned west toward the distant ash-gray mountains in the dim early-morning light.

As soft flaxen-colored light spread over the land, we saw the iron road from Nogales and then the Santa Cruz River just beyond it in the Buena Vista Canyon. Crows roosting in the trees along the river flew croaking over us toward the foothills and mountains. The river was a source of green on the brown canyon floor. Down its length, it was rarely over twenty feet wide, sometimes disappearing into the sand only to reappear a few hundred yards farther along. It had long stretches where the water flowed smooth and easy but was no more than a foot deep, and then there were places where pools were waist deep but the flow was nearly at a standstill. We stayed east of the iron road, in the covering dark shadows from the foothills that made us hard to see by anyone on the far side of the river.

Geronimo set a comfortable pace north toward the Rancho Buena Vista. Smooth green fields covered the wide canyon. Scattered among them, workers stood up from their rows of vegetables to watch us, their faces invisible in the shade of their big hats. We rode by without any hurry, as if we were out on an easy Sunday ride to visit neighbors. Tempted, I decided not to run for my freedom. Some of those farmers might die for my lack of patience, and the Apaches would still catch me.

In the early afternoon, we stopped at a spot on a long shallow stretch of the river, wide and knee-deep on me, with tall green cottonwoods and willows that provided good shade and plenty of brush where it would be easy with a few ropes to make a corral for the horses, and for the women to make shelters and cook. We camped against a high bank in a curve on the river that would make us hard to see from the iron road, and by anyone upstream or downstream. Soon Naiche, with two warriors, headed north to look for the man who would trade supplies for horses. Geronimo told the other warriors to find places where they could hide and keep watch over the camp so Bluecoats or Mexican soldiers couldn't surprise us.

I helped She-gha make a shelter, gathered wood and brush for her fire, and watched her begin a meal. Geronimo sat crosslegged on his blanket nearby in the shade of a big cottonwood and cleaned his long-barreled rifle. His rifle, called a "trapdoor," looked old to me, kind of like those I had seen in drawings of American Revolutionary War battles. It didn't have even a lever for reloading. It had to be handloaded, cartridge by cartridge, by flipping up the "trapdoor" to flip out the used cartridge and insert another. Little did I know then how deadly and feared that old trapdoor was in the hands of Geronimo, who could load and fire about as fast as a man with a lever rifle.

She-gha gave me more lessons in speaking and understanding Apache while she taught me to steam the yucca tips I helped her gather earlier as we rode down the canyon. I learned fast to understand Apache, but I didn't do well making my mouth form the right tones for correct pronunciation. It infuriated me to speak slowly, especially since I had a lot to say. She-gha was a good teacher, patiently making me repeat over and over words and phrases she taught me until I spoke them correctly, and then making me say them in phrases that I might use every day.

Geronimo finished cleaning his rifle, running an oily rag in a final wipe down the rifle's fine-grained brown wood stock to make it shine. He took the rifle and his blanket to the shade of a big willow close by the river, spread the blanket under its limbs dragging the ground, and lay down, hidden from anyone who didn't know he was there, to take a nap. It wasn't long before I heard him snore, and She-gha looked at me and grinned.

Garditha came running up the river after gathering wood and brush for Haozinne's fire and asked, in Apache I actually understood, if I wanted to practice slings. When I looked toward She-gha, she flipped her hand, waving us on our way.

We ran upstream, jumping from rock to rock on the river's edge or hiding in the brush to ambush each other in a game of tag, until we found a place where a wash, now dry, flowed into the river and provided a wealth of small sling stones. I had learned the value of a smooth pebble with a rounded shape for sling accuracy. I filled my ragged dress pockets as I sorted through many stones, keeping only the ones with just the right size, shape, and smoothness. Garditha did the same to fill the leather bag hanging on his belt. The sun was hot but the air cool by the river. We played there for a while, seeing who could make flat stones skip the most times downstream. Garditha usually beat me by one or two skips. I just couldn't get my elbow cocked and my hand at an angle needed to throw for more bounces than him.

We soon tired of skipping rocks and followed the curve in the river south until we came to a high bank with a wide bench to the river on its east side. The bank, in deep shadows, was an ideal place for us to set up crossed-stick targets for our slings. The sun moved about a hand while we practiced. I was happy my stones were hitting closer to my crossed-sticks target than in earlier practices, and I was throwing harder. Garditha was throwing with such speed and accuracy that he destroyed his target and had to replace his target sticks twice.

I was waiting for him to replace his target a third time when I heard a horse snort upstream and, looking over my shoulder, saw three vaqueros, with amused looks on their faces, mounted on horses standing in the middle of the river a little upstream from us. The oldest, his face covered by a gray, scraggly beard and his sombrero hanging against his back, had a cigarette dangling from the crooked smile on his lips. The other two, a couple of steps behind him, seemed to be waiting for him to take the lead. The one to his left looked the youngest and didn't have any hair growing on his face. The one to his right looked about Artisan's age and moved as if there was little doubt what he would do next. They all wore holsters filled with big revolvers on full cartridge belts.

I had no idea how long they had been there and didn't think Garditha, working on his target against the bank, had seen them either or could see them now. I felt a surge of hope—perhaps today freedom—but as I looked at the Old One's narrowed eyes, his long and greasy salt-and-pepper hair hanging close to his brows, and the sneer on his lips, I heard warning bells ringing in the back of my mind. I didn't like the looks of the man, whom the others seemed to follow and who might save me.

He took a draw on his cigarette, blew the smoke up toward the trees, and said in Spanish, "So, *muchacha,* how is it you play with an Apache? Where is his *padre?* Maybe he has stolen you from your padre, eh? Apache hair, even from a muchacho, sells for good money in Nogales." He flipped his cigarette in the river and held a finger to his lips for silence before he motioned toward the young man on his left and pointed toward me. Young One grinned and rode across the river toward me.

I had frozen, uncertain what to do, until Old One spoke of Apache hair selling in Nogales. He was going to kill and scalp my friend Garditha—take his hair for money. I felt sick just thinking about it. The Apaches were no more brutal in killing Petra and Andy than the vaqueros would be in killing and scalping an Apache child, not to mention what they might do to me because my family wasn't rich enough to pay a ransom for me.

As Young One approached the riverbank, I shook my head and pointed for them to go away. Old One, grinning like a hungry wolf, again held his finger to his lips and drew a skinning knife from a sheath on his gun belt. He nodded to the man on his right, who drew his knife too. What they planned to do I could not let happen. I had left a nice smooth pebble in the pouch of my sling while I waited for Garditha to fix his target, and I started to whirl it as I took a step back. Young One's horse was nearly to the riverbank when I heard a smacking sound like a fist striking a palm.

Garditha's throw, straight and true, hit Young One in the right temple just above his eye. Young One's arms flew up as his head snapped back, a look of surprise frozen on his face, his eyes wide and losing their life. His reins slid from his fingers, and he rolled slowly off his horse to land facedown in the river. Garditha screamed his war cry, just as I threw as hard as I could to hit Old One. My stone struck his arm near where he was holding his skinning knife. He dropped the knife and bellowed, "Owwww! *Maldita puta!*" (Damn whore!) I was very lucky to hit him at all. I had been aiming for his head.

He dropped his reins and reflexively tried to reach his revolver while holding his wrist, but he couldn't make his hand close on it and lift it. There was a big knot on his arm, near his wrist, where my stone had hit. I knew then that the stone must have broken a bone.

While Old One tried to pull his revolver, I loaded another stone and started to whirl it, when a stone from Garditha whizzed past the third vaquero's face and took off most of his ear just as he threw his knife, which thudded into a tree a hand width from Garditha's head. The vaquero's hand flew to cover his bleeding ear. A grinning snarl filled his face, which was wrinkled in pain. He laughed, reached for his pistol, and had it halfway out of his holster but then glanced to where the riverbed's curve blocked his view of our camp and slammed it back in its holster.

Old One's horse spooked and pranced around, raising sprays of water with each hoof as it tried to decide which way to run. The Blood Ear vaquero managed to gather its reins and jerked it to attention, saying quietly, "Whoa, whoa, muchacho. Jose, stick your arm in your shirt for a sling. We ride!" He glanced at the young vaquero still facedown in the river, then me, and snarled, "Soon, *putajovencita* (whore, young and small), we come back and kill you all!"

My sling's throw whizzed across his horse's rump, leaving a streak of bright red and making it squeal and rear, nearly throwing him off. He yelled at the old man, "Grab your saddle and hold on." He put spurs to his horse and, leading Old Man's horse, charged straight for me. I waited until they were nearly upon me, so close I could see the blood from his ear trickling down the collar of his shirt, to jump out of the way as they thundered past. They spurred their horses unmercifully, their hooves leaving a dust cloud behind them as they raced up the river toward San Lázaro.

Garditha ran past me, pointing toward the young vaquero's horse, signaling for me to grab its reins. I waded into the river, holding my hand out and clicking to him, and he stood long enough for me to snatch the reins. He didn't try to run, but I held on to them like they were a lifeline.

When Garditha stopped splashing in his run to the vaquero, I turned to see him jump and land on the man's shoulders with his knees. His knife was out and, it seemed in one motion, he grabbed his black, greasy hair, pulled his face out of the water, and made a clean, fast slice across his throat before dropping his head to make the water around the vaquero's body slowly turn red. I felt sick and wanted to puke, but I swallowed it back.

Garditha, who told me later he had never killed a man, was pale and looked sick too. We stared at each other for a moment before I led the horse out of the water and tied it in the brush, out of sight from the river. Garditha and I tugged Young One's body out of the red water and onto the bank. We each took an arm and struggled to drag it into the brush where it would be hard to see.

I told Garditha to stay nearby while I ran to get Geronimo. He nodded, waved for me to go on, and ran to a towering cottonwood with big roots where he could slump between them and become practically invisible to anyone near the river's edge.

I ran down the river to She-gha's fire, where she still worked on her evening meal. I ran up to her out of breath. "Geronimo?"

"You run hard, mujercita." She cocked her head to one side. "Why Geronimo?"

I puffed, out of breath, "Because . . . Garditha and I . . . have killed a vaquero and driven two others off toward San Lázaro. They yelled they were coming back to kill us."

She-gha's jaw dropped, and then she was up and running over to the willow tree where Geronimo napped. When she pulled back the limbs where he snored, he was already up on his knees with his rifle cocked and ready to bring it to his shoulder.

His eyes glittering with excitement, he said, "What's happened, woman?"

CHAPTER 15
YOUNG WARRIORS

She-gha said in rapid-fire Spanish so I understood what she told him, "Geronimo! Trinidad and Garditha have killed a vaquero and run off two who say they will be back."

I trembled, fearful he would be angry that we had given away our camping place.

"Two children have killed a vaquero and driven off two more?" He laughed and slapped his thigh. "Ho, what mighty warriors we raise. Where was this great battle? Where is Garditha?"

Surprised and relieved he wasn't angry, I pointed upriver and said, "Not far around the bend there. Garditha stays to guard the dead vaquero and his horse until you come."

"Then we go. She-gha, tell Ahnandia to alert the others that trouble maybe comes soon. Be ready."

Without a word, she ran downriver toward Ahnandia's wickiup. Geronimo waved me to lead him upriver to where our fight with the vaqueros had been. We ran all the way, he in an easy lope that covered ground fast, my legs churning, trying to keep up. I was gasping for air, but Geronimo was barely puffing when we came to where Garditha and I had been practicing. The river moved so slowly that we could still see a patch of dark-red water in splashes of sunlight near the riverbank, and I heard Geronimo say under his breath, "Hi yeh."

Garditha sprang out of the cottonwood tree roots where he had been hiding and ran to us, his eyes big, pointing to the brush where we had dragged the vaquero. He yelled, "There! There! He's over there!"

Without missing a step, Geronimo ran straight to the body. He looked the vaquero over. "His throat is cut, but that's not how you killed him?"

"He was coming for Trinidad. The place on his forehead is where the stone from my sling hit him. He fell off his horse, facedown in the river. I thought I had killed him, but I made sure by cutting his throat. Did I do the right thing, Geronimo?"

Geronimo nodded. "Yes, Garditha, you did the right thing. You did it well, like a man full grown. We're all proud of you. What did you do, Trinidad?"

"I heard the old man, leader of the three, say he wanted to know who stole me and that they pay good money in Nogales for Apache hair, even from a child. I couldn't let happen, what they planned to do. They drew their knives, motioned this one to get me, and . . ."

Geronimo held up his hand for me to stop. "The old man, what did he look like?"

"He had black and gray hair on his face, bad teeth, a scar here near his mouth where the hair on his face wouldn't grow, and squinty, hateful eyes."

"Hi yeh. I think I know this one. I tried to kill him a time or two, but he got away. I get him someday. Tell me of the other vaquero."

"He was older than this one but younger than the old man. He followed the old man like he was chief. He didn't say much, but I could tell he was mean and wanted to kill Apaches. They kept making quick looks down the river like they were expecting to have to run from or attack someone. The man had smooth hair on his face, not as much as the old man, and there was a big white patch in the middle of his black hair. I remember his *pistola* was fancy. It had white handles."

"Ho. I think I know this one too. A hard, strong vaquero we call 'Badger.' I think he is the one who killed Zi-yeh's father three harvests ago. You don't know Zi-yeh yet. She is one of my wives taken prisoner a harvest ago. I tried to get her back, but Nantan Crook hid her from me. I never had a chance to avenge the death of her father. Now maybe I will. What happened when this one came for you?"

"He was nearly to the riverbank when Garditha's stone knocked him off his horse. About the same time Garditha's stone hit this vaquero, mine hit the arm of Old One, who was pulling his pistola. I think maybe he was going to shoot Garditha. When the stone hit his arm, Old One dropped the pistola back in its holster and yelled and cursed me. I saw a big bump on his arm where my stone hit. I think it broke his arm. He couldn't use it to pull his pistola."

Again, Geronimo held up his hand for me to stop. "Why didn't you kill him rather than break his arm?"

I bowed my head and said, "I . . . I missed. I was aiming for his head. I'm not very good with a sling yet, and his horse was shifting around."

Geronimo laughed. "Hah! You must practice more with your sling, Trinidad, but breaking his arm shows you throw hard. Then what happened?"

"Garditha slung another stone at Badger that took off most of his ear. He yelled and held his hand against his bloody ear. Starting to pull his pistola, he looked up the river toward our camp and changed his mind. He grabbed the old man's reins just as my next stone raised blood on his horse's rump, making him squeal and rear, nearly throwing the vaquero off. He cursed me, saying soon they come back to kill us, and tried to trample me with his horse, but I was quick enough to jump out of the way. Leading the old man's horse, he took off as fast as he could ride upriver."

Geronimo laughed again. "Ho! Even our children are great warriors. Garditha, take the pistola from this one—it is yours—and anything else on his body you want. Come. Let us look at his pony."

Garditha started to keep the pistola and walk away, but he went back to the body, slid the pistola back into its double-loop holster, unbuckled its belt, a nice one of soft leather with cartridge loops, and pulled the holster and belt off the body as Geronimo and I watched him. He wanted to wear it, but the belt was much too large for him, so he buckled it again and slipped it over one arm and his head so it hung from his shoulder, the holster and pistola near his waist. He looked at Geronimo and raised his brows as if to ask, "Is this good?"

Geronimo smiled and nodded. "Remember, don't leave a cartridge under the hammer. If the pistola falls out of the holster, it might go off and kill one of us. You don't want that, do you?"

Garditha, his eyes wide, shook his head. "No, Grandfather. I would never want that."

We led Geronimo back into the brush where we had tied the young vaquero's horse. He untied the reins and led it to bright light at the edge of the bank's shade. He looked him over carefully, ran his hands over its legs, and studied the mark on its rump for a moment.

He said, "Hmmph. I know the rancho that uses this mark. It's in the Cuitaca Mountain foothills. The vaqueros you stoned can call many riders to return with them and attack us. We have taken many horses from this rancho. Maybe now we have a good ambush and get more horses and cartridges when they come."

I looked at the saddle on the young one's horse for the first time and saw it was of very fine quality, the best of light-tan leather trimmed with silver. There was an embossed rifle holster on one side that held a big, fancy lever rifle, and saddlebags that contained extra cartridges, a shirt, pants, a cook pot, and a small sack of beans and one of coffee.

Geronimo nodded and said, "This is a good pony worth keeping. Garditha, you killed its owner. The rifle and saddle are yours, but I keep the rifle until you shoot it as a warrior. Do you know how to use the pistola?"

"I've seen it used many times, but I've never shot one myself."

"I teach you soon. Now we must make the camp ready for an ambush." Geronimo handed the reins over to Garditha. "Here, he is your pony. You lead him."

I had never seen a boy prouder than Garditha as he led his horse and trophies off to camp, and I was proud of him. He had saved our lives.

We were walking past the place where the bloody water had been when Geronimo stopped, stared at the water, and waded into the river. He stopped with the water up to his knees and reached down into the water. He brought out the knife the young vaquero had been holding when Garditha's stone killed him. Like the guns the young man carried, the knife was fancy, with a shiny blade and fine staghorn bone handle. Geronimo handed it to me and, smiling, said, "Trinidad, even though you killed no one, you helped drive the vaqueros away. You have much courage. This knife should be yours. Every woman needs a fine knife."

I was happy to get both the compliment and the knife.

Naiche had returned and waited with most of the warriors at She-gha's wickiup. As we approached, he stood and waved his hand parallel to the ground, the "all is good" sign. Geronimo waved back. He said, "Ho, Naiche. Our children make fine warriors. They kill one vaquero. Garditha leads his horse. They ran off two. One I think we call Badger, the one who killed Zi-yeh's father three harvests ago, the other an old one I may have missed killing a time or two. The pony's brand says they're from the big rancho we've raided often in the Cuitaca foothills. They'll return with many vaqueros to attack us."

Naiche frowned and looked at the ground, his arms held behind him. Soon he looked up and said, "My heart is filled with pride for our children. They grow strong, make good warriors. The trader comes with a wagon of supplies to trade for our horses and saddles. We need to leave soon if we escape the returning vaqueros and meet Atelnietze in five or six suns. What is your counsel?"

Geronimo pointed to the canyon across the river. "After trading, leave on the trail we often follow to the Magdalena River and Planches Canyon to the west. Two warriors stay here. Watch for the vaqueros. When vaqueros come, warriors warn us. We make ready an ambush. Kill them all. Let none escape. They bother us no more."

Naiche nodded. "Geronimo speaks wise words. Ahnandia and Yahechul, watch for the coming of the vaqueros. When the trader comes, we make quick trades. No mescal drinking. Then we go."

The warriors all nodded and murmured as one voice, "Ch'ik'eh doleel (Let it be so)."

Geronimo went to Naiche's fire, and they talked over coffee for a time after the council broke up. I helped She-gha pack. We were leading our horses to her fire when we saw the dust from a wagon and riders coming down the trail from the north. The men mounted their ponies and went to meet them.

The warriors mostly traded for new rifles, cartridges, or a small cask of mescal. The women traded for a few blankets, a pot or two, or canvas they could use for a wickiup covering. We were in a hurry. There was little haggling, and the trading didn't last long before the wagon was rolling south, followed by the horse herd surrounded by American cowboys and Mexican vaqueros. We finished packing and followed their trail south for a short time and then turned southwest up a canyon toward the western mountains, leaving Ahnandia and Yahechul hiding in Buena Vista Canyon to watch for the returning vaqueros.

We followed the long, winding canyon west up into the hills. The wash in the canyon bottom was dry, its rocks and gravel clicking and snapping as we passed over them. Groves of junipers lined reddish canyon walls, giving us shade and shelter as the trail climbed and twisted higher and higher. It would have been an easy ride, except Naiche and Geronimo were in a hurry to put as much distance between them and Buena Vista Canyon as they could before they had to stop to lay an ambush for the vaqueros who were following us.

The shadows were growing long and black. It was getting cold as the sky grew dark and the stars appeared above the eastern mountains. We stopped to rest and water our horses by a spring surrounded by boulders near the trail. I was listening to coyotes yip as the Apaches went about their business, quiet and sure, when I saw two dark figures on horses riding in the direction of Geronimo. He stood as Ahnandia and Yahechul approached. Warriors grabbed their rifles and watched.

Yahechul dismounted and, holding up two fingers, said to Geronimo, "Only two vaqueros come. They stay behind Lawton's Bluecoats. The Bluecoats have stopped and camp for the night."

Even in the low light, I saw Geronimo raise his brows in surprise. "So Lawton follows, but there are only two vaqueros? Hmmph. I tell Naiche we ought to move on while the Bluecoats sleep."

CHAPTER 16
PURSUED

A big yellow moon floated up from behind the eastern mountains, filling the canyon with brilliant white light and inky black shadows that stood out even in the background darkness. Naiche soon left the water tank and continued leading us up the canyon on firm sand lining its wash. The canyon narrowed and forced the band to ride strung out in a long, single-file line. I rode just behind She-gha and her packhorse.

Earlier in the afternoon, before the trader's wagon left, She-gha gave me the skirt and shirt she had sewn to replace the filthy rags I had been wearing since Geronimo took me from my aunt and uncle's ranch nearly three weeks prior. It was a bit of genuine kindness on her part, and I was happy at last to wear something besides my old clothes the cactus, mesquite thorns, and brush had torn to rags.

Hidden by green-leafed willows with limbs dragging in a river pool where we camped, I eagerly tore away my rags, bathed with soap She-gha had made from yucca root, and dressed in my fine new clothes. The shirt and skirt fit perfectly. A better seamstress couldn't have sewn them, and I was as proud of my new skirt and shirt as of anything I had ever owned. She had also given me a pair of Chiricahua-style moccasins with a big silver-dollar-sized button on the toes and shafts that reached above my knees. They felt much better than my worn-out shoes, and I was very grateful she had made these too.

The cold air down in the bright darkness filling the canyon

stung my face, and the steam from people breathing formed little clouds around their heads. All the women and my friends, Leosanni and Garditha, and I rode with our blankets over our shoulders, making the long, twisty line of riders look like a giant caterpillar. With my moccasins, new clothes, and blanket over my shoulders, I was comfortable.

The moon was approaching the top of its arc toward the southwest when we reached the summit of the canyon pass and stopped to let the horses rest. We dismounted, unloaded the pack frames, loosened cinches, and tied the horses where they could graze in the brush along the canyon's north wall before wrapping in our blankets and finding a soft, sandy spot to get a little rest. The canyon walls still blocked any views of the low mountains around us except for the deep black outline of distant peaks against the stars we saw through the notch made by the trail.

I was very tired and sleepy and sat down against a boulder near She-gha, who was lying wrapped in her blanket. Hugging my blanket tightly around me, I tilted my head up to look at the moonlight playing with the shadows on the rim of the canyon. I jerked to attention when I saw the dark outlines of two figures on horseback looking over the canyon's rim. My heart pounded, and my breath made a steam cloud around my head. I started to point them out to She-gha, but then they disappeared. The figures looked like they had big, round heads as if they wore sombreros, and I wondered, *Could they be the vaqueros Garditha and I stoned and Ahnandia and Yahechul saw? Maybe I'm just having a dream. If I see them again, I'll tell Geronimo.*

I shivered in my blanket, remembering how angry those two vaqueros were when they left. They were sure to come after Garditha and me and do evil to the band. Many Apache scalps meant a lot of money. I fought to stay awake and watch for them no matter how tired and sleepy I was, but I lost that battle.

She-gha gave me a little shake and motioned toward the line of horses ready to leave. She had already tightened cinches and loaded the packs. The moon had moved about two hands toward the southwestern horizon. I jumped up, ashamed I had fallen asleep, and rushed to join her at the horses. It had become colder, and standing near my pony's body while rolling my blanket around me made me grateful for its warmth. We watched up the line, and when Naiche swung up on his horse, we all mounted. The ripple down the line of rising bodies as they mounted the horses reminded me of a wave moving down a shaken rope.

As the moonlight began to fade and the darkness just before dawn grew deeper, we rode slowly and carefully down the canyon trail. Nearing the canyon holding the Río Magdalena and iron road that ran to Nogales, I could see the black outline of the tops of the Cibuta Mountains against the star-filled sky and the brushstroke of the milk river of stars soaring across their tops just barely lighted by the glow of the sun still below the mountains behind us.

We stopped to rest and eat in a small box canyon on the north side of the big canyon we had just come down. We gave the horses water from a small nearby iron tank fed by a windmill and fed them some grain we had taken in trade the afternoon before. Naiche wanted to put in a long, hard ride for the coming day and needed the horses to have their strength.

She-gha shared her trail food with Geronimo and me. After eating, we found a big juniper in the dark dawn shadows and crawled under its protective branches to sleep until Naiche and Geronimo were ready to move on.

★　★　★　★　★

The sun was maybe two hands above the horizon when She-gha shook me awake, saying, "Get ready to ride. Soon we move." The day was bright and warm, the details of canyons in the Cibuta Mountains easy to see. I watered my pony and waved at Garditha and Leosanni doing the same nearby. Garditha still wore his shoulder holster rig. I don't think he'd taken it off since he put it on. They both looked tired and sleepy. I knew I did too. She-gha helped me saddle my pony and tightened up the loads on her packhorses.

I asked if trouble was expected when we crossed the big canyon over to the Cibuta Mountains. She shrugged. "We hope not, but with Nogales not far north, we're more likely to run into trouble. You stay watchful." I remembered seeing the two dark figures on the canyon rim in the night and nodded. I wondered what had happened to them, for I had seen no more signs of them.

Naiche and Geronimo mounted and led us out of the side canyon and down the trail toward the big canyon that carried the iron road and Río Magdalena. Once in the big canyon, we turned north toward Nogales and rode at a steady jog, staying on the east side in the late-morning shadows next to the shining rails of the iron road.

Abruptly and unexpectedly, at least for me, we halted our line of march. I could see the entrance to a big canyon heading west across the way leading into the northern end of the Cibuta Mountains. Warriors galloped up to and grouped around Naiche and Geronimo. Soon three or four rode off and crossed the iron road and the wagon road nearby. We watched them a short time, but then the ground seemed to swallow them up and they disappeared. I learned later they had ridden into a dip among junipers by the iron road. The rest of the band moved into the trees and shadows and waited. I nudged my pony over to She-gha and, leaning forward, asked, "Why are we stopped? What's happening?"

She looked over her shoulder and said in Spanish, "Watch and see."

The air felt quiet and expectant, as if it were the lull before a hard storm. In a little while, I could hear men talking, and bridle and saddle leather creaking. Then two young vaqueros, talking and laughing and riding in an easy jog, came into view down the wagon road from Nogales toward us. I thought, *Oh no. I'm so sorry this is happening to you. I wish you weren't here.*

Sudden flashes of fire, smoke, and thunder came out of the junipers, where rifles shouted death and destruction. On the side closest to the junipers, four or five bullets slammed into a vaquero. Big, red wet spots suddenly appeared on his white shirt. He jerked from the near-simultaneous bullet strikes and fell backward off his frightened, running pony to land facedown in the dust. The other vaquero might have suffered a scratch or two in the first volley but didn't appear seriously wounded and, ducking low, furiously quirted his pony into some nearby trees, snatched his rifle out of its holster, and grabbed his saddlebags as the Apaches stormed out of the junipers after him. They took cover behind a nearby bank and poured their rifle fire around the cottonwood tree where the vaquero had hidden among its big roots extending out from the trunk like giant fingers.

Two warriors ran out from the shadows where we watched and stripped the fallen vaquero of his boots and weapons—a rifle, a fancy pistola, and a big skinning knife—and caught his horse, a nice roan with good conformation, carrying an old saddle and wearing a bridle trimmed in silver. They brought the loot to one of the women, who loaded it on a packhorse. These warriors then turned to join the fight with the other vaquero. He put up a good fight. I wanted to cry as I watched the Apache wolves close in on him, creeping closer and closer through the brush for a kill shot, but I knew to keep my feelings to myself. It took over a hand against the horizon before the warriors finally killed him. They respected his courage and took only his weapons after dragging the first vaquero off into the trees.

Naiche led us across the iron road and the wet sand of the river toward the canyon, heading west across the northern end of the Cibuta Mountains. After we crossed the big canyon, Naiche and Geronimo set a fast pace and drove the horses hard until the shadows grew long and dusk fast approached.

We came to a small spring surrounded by brush and a few junipers and stopped for the night. Except for what we had eaten in the side canyon where we rested earlier that day, I hadn't eaten anything and was very hungry. I helped She-gha with her fire and gathered wood and brush to keep it burning.

She disappeared for a little while and returned with a nice piece of meat. Mystified as to where she had gotten it, because we had no cattle with us, I realized a couple of horses had been nearly lame and couldn't go much farther when we stopped. She cut up and grilled the meat on sticks angled over the fire and sliced and boiled some kind of tuberous root she had found near the spring that looked and tasted like potatoes.

I wasn't sure I could eat horsemeat, but hunger drove me to it, and I liked the taste. A person will eat just about anything when they're hungry enough. Even so, there were things the Apaches wouldn't eat, even if they were starving, because their god, Ussen, told them not to. They wouldn't eat any kind of bug, but they would eat honey. They wouldn't eat snakes or anything that ate snakes, like hawks, eagles, roadrunners, or pigs. They wouldn't eat fish, because fish moved like snakes and ate insects and other nasty things. Sometimes, when I was especially hungry and wanted to eat some of the things they wouldn't, I thought the biggest item in their diet was their willpower not to eat forbidden things.

We ate the horsemeat, perfectly cooked, its juices dripping into the fire and making a smoke with a smell that made our mouths water, pulling it from the sticks on which it was cooked in bite-sized chunks, using our fingers or the knives we also used to spear the chopped-up roots She-gha had boiling over the fire in her pot. It was a good meal, and I felt much stronger after we ate.

Sitting next to the fire's warmth and watching its orange light dance on his old, hard face, I decided to go ahead and tell Geronimo what I had seen. "Geronimo, last night I saw something I think you ought to know about."

He raised his brows, looked at She-gha, who shrugged, and said, "Speak, mujercita. I will listen."

"Last night when we rested at the top of the pass, I was looking at the bright moonlight and shadows on the canyon rim. Two men on horses appeared on the rim and looked down on us. At first, I thought they were our sentries, but then I saw they were wearing sombreros. I thought I might be dreaming. They were only there a moment, but they didn't go away when I blinked my eyes. I'm sure they were real. I wasn't dreaming. I've waited to see them again to be sure before I told you. I have not seen them again, but the more I think about them, the more I'm sure they were two vaqueros. So I tell you now." I decided to end the way I had heard others end when they spoke in council. "That is all I have to say."

Geronimo grinned. "Mujercita listens to how Apaches speak. Nit'ééhi. You do well to see the vaqueros last night. Most did not. I watch them with my soldier glasses this sun as they follow us. They are far ahead of the Bluecoats who follow us. Let them come."

I frowned. "I know you are a wise leader, but why let them come? They might kill us while we sleep. You could send warriors to kill them like the ones this morning. Did you recognize who they were?"

He stared into the fire a few moments, scratched the side of his face, and then nodded. "I think they are the same ones you and Garditha stoned."

I swallowed and felt the hair on the back of my neck prickling. "Then why do you let them come?"

"Ussen gives me a plan, mujercita. They will not die a good death. I have waited to take them for a long time. Now you sleep. Next sun will be a long, hard day."

CHAPTER 17
SEPARATION

I slept without bad dreams after Geronimo told me he knew the vaqueros followed us and had a plan to take care of them. Before my eyes closed, I smiled and looked at the bright moon, and as I fell asleep with my thoughts drifting like a leaf looking for the ground, tried to imagine his plan. Despite their trying to kill Garditha and me, I didn't want the vaqueros tortured. Still, after Geronimo took them, regardless of torture, they would sell no more Apache hair to put gold in their pockets. I thought that was a good thing. Garditha and I had to watch out for them. They were enemies now. Soon after Geronimo took them, one way or the other, they would be no more. *Doo dat'éé da* (It's all right). A little startled, I realized I had begun to think and speak like an Apache.

We were up and moving again in the early dawn, the sun just a glow behind the mountains to the northwest, and the stars' bright points of light scattered across the sky in numbers beyond counting. As long as it was dark, Naiche rode at an easy pace. We were following a canyon stream due north that ran into a wide canyon running east to west. I learned later we were on the range of the Arizona Ranch.

At the east-to-west canyon, we turned east and had not gone far when the edge of the sun popped over the mountains, bringing us enough light for Naiche to pick up the pace in the cold morning air. We stayed single file, riding far away from lights, probably from ranch houses, scattered up and down the canyon.

A few warriors left the line to look for horses to replace the ones we had eaten the night before and maybe a beef or two for when we stopped at the end of the day.

We hadn't ridden far before the canyon began to narrow and make a gentle climb that twisted through the foothills, but its floor was smooth and easy enough for us to cover ground at a good pace. Near midmorning, we stopped to rest the horses. Off in the distance, we could see the smoke plumes from a small mining town.

Two warriors rode past us in a gallop just before we were ready to mount. They spoke to Naiche and Geronimo, who motioned for three more warriors to follow the other two back toward the end of the line. They all disappeared around a turn in the trail. Naiche motioned for us to mount, but he stayed in place.

It wasn't long before we heard the crack of rifle fire echoing across the canyon and then the thumps of galloping hooves coming toward us. Three lathered horses came running around the bend with no riders but with blood streaking from large spots on their saddles. A warrior was behind them. He stopped at Naiche and, waving his rifle at them, yelled in excitement to ask if he should catch them. Naiche shook his head and waved them back. He wanted to move on. The horses ran for the mining town. We wasted no time passing the town and heading into a canyon that climbed north toward the Pajarito Mountains.

By the time of shortest shadows, we found a big iron water tank and windmill, watered the horses, and let them rest while we ate from our sacks of warrior trail food. We were at the tank about a hand above the horizon before moving on in a wide, shallow canyon, steadily climbing toward a high, cliff-filled mountain standing above the others farther up the trail.

The trail turned west of the mountain with high cliffs and looped around it, back toward the east, still climbing in the warm midafternoon sunlight. Expecting at any time to see the vaqueros following us, I kept looking at the high places but saw nothing. We turned into an arroyo that I thought looked familiar and left the main canyon to ride up to a natural water pool that I recognized. We had camped there the first night after Geronimo took me captive.

We watered and rested the livestock for a while and then followed a trail—not the one I had ridden when I first saw the water pool—that twisted and turned along ridge trails with sheer three- or four-hundred-foot drop-offs, and the trail was no more than a man's height wide. I feared to look down, thinking I might faint and fall off my horse to land smashed, crumpled, and lifeless on boulders far below. The Apaches, paying little attention to the drop-off altitude, rode those trails as if they were on a road through the middle of Nogales.

We finally rode down into a deep canyon where there were many junipers on the east side but few on the west. The trail was narrow, and we had to stay in a single line as we did on the ridges, but we were able to ride faster until, late in the afternoon, we stopped at another place I recognized from the first day of my captivity. It was a place we had passed on the way south, with a small spring and a side box canyon where it would be easy to hold the livestock overnight.

I helped She-gha make her fire and gathered wood and brush, trying to avoid rattlesnakes I knew must be there, but no one heard or spoke of any big grandfather snakes like I had seen the first day that seemed so long ago.

As the shadows grew long, the air cooled, and the sun turned the clouds hugging the mountains into splashes of deep purple, orange, and blood red. A warrior stopped by our fire and gave She-gha a piece of fresh beef to cook for her family. She cooked it like she had the horsemeat, and the smell of its fat dripping into the fires gave us all a roaring hunger after facing the terrors of the ridge drop-offs. She boiled more of what I thought were wild potatoes after throwing some extra herbs in the pot and steamed some yucca tips and dried mescal slices she had in her parfleche.

I had watched all day for the vaqueros trailing us, but they never appeared. *Maybe,* I thought, *they decided to turn back.* But it didn't take long for me to decide that they still watched and waited. Whatever Geronimo's plan, I hoped it worked fast against them.

After we ate, Geronimo went to Naiche's council fire. She-gha and I hurried to clean up around her fire so we could join the other women and children to sit in the shadows and listen to what the men decided. When we took our places, the men had already smoked to Ussen and Naiche was speaking.

"Atelnietze and his warriors wait for us in the Dragoon Mountains near our old reservation. They should have raided enough by now to make the Bluecoats leave the border to chase them and give us a chance to get across the land unseen. I leave long before dawn and during next sun ride for the Dragoon Mountains. After meeting Atelnietze, we leave the women and children in the Dragoons, protected by a few warriors. We ride on to Fort Apache to learn what surrender terms the new nan-tan, Miles, will give us and the whereabouts of our families. We bring them back if we can. Geronimo will take a different group south into Sonora. He does not want exposure north of the border when there is no Bluecoat chief he knows he can trust. He has other plans for our enemies in Mexico. Speak, Geronimo. We listen."

Geronimo stood and looked at each warrior around the circle in the fire's flickering light and shadows. He nodded and said, "Every man must do what is best for him and his family. Na-iche wants to know what happened to our families and what

Miles wants from us to stop running and surrender. We need to know these things. We need to get our families back. I will not go with Naiche. I do not know a Bluecoat chief who keeps his word at Fort Apache. If the nantan catches me, he keeps me in chains in the guardhouse. I will never go to a guardhouse again. I say this many times. The White Eyes want to see me dancing in the air while hanging from rope around my neck. This, they will never see. Now I have other enemies to take care of south of the border while Naiche goes to Fort Apache."

Only Natculbaye and a young warrior, Hunlona, had stood earlier to ride south with Geronimo. He looked around the fire at the sitting warriors, waited a bit, and then smiled and nodded. "Natculbaye and Hunlona have chosen to ride south with me. Enjuh. They are strong fighters. We will do well. That is all I have to say." The rest of the warriors again sat looking at the ground as though they were ashamed.

Naiche, his arms crossed, stepped back into the yellow firelight and nodded. "Nit'ééhi. We leave this place before the sun comes. Within a moon, we meet again at the camp on top of the Azul Mountains."

Geronimo waved his right hand parallel to the ground. "It will be so. Ussen will help you, my chief." Naiche made the same sign and the council broke up.

Back at She-gha's fire, I helped her make ready for the ride south. Geronimo came and sat by the fire and watched us as he rolled a cigarette and smoked. She-gha and I finished, and she sat down beside him.

I wrapped a blanket around my shoulders, for it had grown cold down in the canyon. I said, "Grandfather, tell me of your plan for the vaqueros."

He took a long final pull on his cigarette and tossed the remains into the fire, studied me for a moment, and then said,

"I tell you. Listen close. I won't tell you again."

I nodded my understanding.

"Those vaqueros will be hard to kill. They have escaped ambushes before. This time they will not be so lucky. Their minds are clouded because they are eager for revenge, and I have what they are after—you and Garditha—and much money for Apache hair they sell in Nogales for gold."

I shivered when I realized that my friend and I were bait for two hard men who wanted revenge and scalps.

"Don't be afraid, mujercita. We protect you and Garditha. Next sun, we ride south toward the village Altar. We have to ride down a long canyon for many hands against the sun. Many chances for ambushes on that ride. If the vaqueros escape my ambush, they still follow. They want revenge. They want our hair, much money for our hair. Maybe much money if they sell you back to your family. West and north of Altar is a great llano, mostly desert with few watering holes. We will appear to wander into that desert. The vaqueros follow us. The llano always has many good places for an ambush. We take or kill their horses and leave them to walk for the nearest water. Vaqueros suffer much on long walk in sun's fire. Think only of their thirst. When they are weak, we take them."

Geronimo reached behind his back and pulled out his skinning knife, the firelight reflecting off its shiny razor edge and his glittering eyes. "Then they know the anger of Geronimo."

I nodded but trembled inside. I was glad I was not his enemy.

CHAPTER 18
VAQUERO AMBUSH

Tiny fires burned to drive away the cold and dark in the deep canyon camp. I shivered and wanted to stay wrapped in my blanket when She-gha shook me awake to help her saddle the horses and load the pack animals. But I unpeeled my blanket, jumped around a little to ward off the cold, and ran for the bushes before I helped her.

Geronimo was out of the blankets, but I didn't see him anywhere. The horses already brought to the little firepit seemed skittish and wanting to go. I heard low voices and saw dark outlines of men and women all around the camp shuffling blankets, saddles, and parfleches as they saddled and loaded the animals. I pulled the cinch tight on my pony saddle and then helped She-gha load the packhorse already mounted with the pack frame.

A bright glow was forming below the mountains to the east, and a few birds were beginning to call as Garditha, still wearing his pistola holster rig over his shoulder, walked up leading his pony. "*Nish'ii*' (I see you), mujercita."

We had not spoken since stoning and escaping the vaqueros. I said in the pidgin Apache we shared, "Nish'ii', Garditha. Who rides with you?"

"Oh, I ride with you. Geronimo asked that I come. He said if I were with his little group, the vaqueros he wants to take would be more likely to follow, and besides that, he always needs strong warriors."

I believed what Garditha said about Geronimo saying that if he were with us, the vaqueros would be more likely to try to come after us, but not the bit about needing a strong warrior. I started to say something ugly to let Garditha know I thought he lied about Geronimo saying he wanted him to come because he always needs strong warriors, but I stayed quiet. I'd wait until I needed to speak up.

I said, "I feel much safer. Help me load this pack."

Garditha grinned, not understanding I was being sarcastic, and helped me finish loading the packhorse before tying the pack frame load tight and snug. She-gha brought me a piece of meat that she cooked the evening before to pack. It was in its own parfleche to keep the sun from drying it out. She said, "We eat for our evening meal."

I saw a dark outline of a man descending from a nearby cliff. Once on the floor of the canyon, the figure seemed to float through the juniper trees toward our camp. Soon, Geronimo appeared in the dim light. He said, "Ussen spoke to me and said this is a good day to ride. Natculbaye and his wife come soon. I see Hunlona coming already."

Hunlona, a quiet young man and fine warrior, his face smooth but with piercing eagle's eyes under heavy brows, came leading a pinto with good conformation and a blanket thrown over a Bluecoat saddle. Hunlona didn't look like a killer, but I knew better, even if he was kind to me.

Wearing his gray hair tied back and walking with his rifle in the crook of his arm, Natculbaye—followed by his young wife, Juanita, leading a packhorse and two gray horses with saddles—was not far behind Hunlona.

Geronimo spoke to Natculbaye, motioning up the same trail we had followed to the camp the day before. Then he left to have a final word with Naiche. After he returned, we mounted and Natculbaye led us up out of the canyon. Following the trail back to the last water that we had used the day before, the high drop-offs didn't seem to bother me as they did then. I noticed Garditha, who liked to ride with his right hand resting on his pistola, loosened his reins and let his pony pick his way along the trail while he looked everywhere except down. I tried that approach and decided trusting my pony on those endlessly deep drop-off trails was a much easier way to ride than trying to choose his path.

We stopped at the water we had used the previous day and let the animals rest while we ate a few handfuls of warrior trail food before beginning the short ride down to the big canyon we had followed yesterday.

Geronimo and Natculbaye, looking around the pool, were like hounds sniffing a hot trail. I had no idea what they were looking for, and neither did Garditha, but it didn't take them long to find it. Geronimo ran the end of a yucca stalk through the dust in a little bare spot back under a nearby juniper. The trace of the stalk turned over bits of charcoal. Natculbaye picked up a piece and smelled it before holding his hand flat against the place. He said, "Not covered long, no more than two or three hands against the horizon."

They scouted around and found horse apples that had been covered with needles from junipers and places where the horses had stood for a while before being led to a place below the top of a high hill that must have given a good view of the canyons and trails we had used the day before. Standing where the horses were tied, Geronimo studied the top of the hill with his soldier glasses. He finally lowered them and, shaking his head, told Hunlona to run to the top and have a look around. Hunlona soon returned and said two men had been there for a while but had left two hands ago. The trail from where the horses stood appeared to be moving south toward the trail we had used earlier and not the trail Geronimo planned to take to Altar.

We passed where we had entered the north-south canyon the day before and turned west across rolling llano. We soon crossed a small alkali flat that had a big green pool off to one side with flat, nasty-tasting water. In less than a hand, we came to a little-used wagon road, where Geronimo picked up the pace. The sun was hot, but the ride smooth, and by alternating between walk, jog, and gallop, Geronimo didn't tire the horses while we covered a good distance as the twisting, dusty road turned southwest.

The road passed a large scattering of junipers, which we rode up into and stopped in their shade. The smell of their tart sap tickled my nose, but I dared not sneeze. Geronimo and Natculbaye rode up into the trees at the top of a high hill and used their soldier glasses to search for any sign of the vaqueros, leaving Garditha, She-gha, Juanita (I never learned her Apache name), and me with Hunlona.

After a hand against the sun, Geronimo and Natculbaye returned. Geronimo said he had seen a glint about a hand back up the road we followed. He had also seen a big water tank about a hand farther down the road and said we would stop there to water the horses and learn the source of that glint. I was glad to hear this. I was thirsty and my pony was tiring. I didn't want to eat her for supper that night.

The water tank formed among the boulders was big and shallow sitting at the bottom of high cliffs and lined on the south side with big boulders as though someone had started building a wall. After letting our horses drink, I watched how the Apaches, who must have been as thirsty as I, kneeled on one knee and drank with little handfuls of water while watching for attacks from enemies in all directions, including the cliffs above us. I had seen Garditha do the same thing at the little spring when we were running back to the big tank camp and decided that was the best way to drink. I copied them.

Geronimo, Natculbaye, and Hunlona stood off to one side and talked for a little while as the rest of us relaxed in the cliff shadows. Garditha sat on a small boulder back in the trees and practiced loading and unloading his pistola. Geronimo had shown him how to load it and eject spent shells and told him to practice often loading and unloading so his hands would become used to handling it. I wished I had a pistola. Maybe then I could get away from these people and still survive in the wilderness, but I knew the only weapons I'd probably ever get were a sling and a knife. I knew I would have to learn to be deadly with them if I had any chance of getting away.

The men finished their talk. Hunlona mounted and disappeared off into the trees along the foot of the cliffs.

I said to She-gha, "Where is Hunlona going?"

She shrugged her shoulders and, half smiling, said, "Geronimo knows. Probably he goes to watch the trail behind us."

Geronimo and Natculbaye sat down with us for a little rest. It was very quiet and peaceful. Sleep nearly had me when we heard a horse galloping toward us through the trees. Geronimo and Natculbaye jumped up and motioned for the rest of us to get behind some nearby boulders while they disappeared into the shadows.

The horse slid to a stop as Hunlona reined up to look around. Geronimo called to him out of the shadows, "What have you seen?"

Hunlona pointed back down the trail and said, "Seven vaqueros come. Maybe here in half a hand."

Geronimo frowned. "Hmmph. Garditha's vaqueros bring back more friends than we thought. Make strong enemies." He grinned and barked, "Ch'ik'eh doleel! (All right)." He nose pointed toward our boulders maybe fifty paces away from the water tank and in dark, concealing shade. "Lead the ponies up to the tank and then away down the trail, but bring them back and hold them there. We make the vaqueros think we watered our horses and then followed the canyon south. Tie the horses in the trees behind us so we get them fast when we run. Hurry. Now our fun begins."

The men brushed away the tracks of the ponies from the boulders to the water tank, retreated to where we hid, waved us farther back from the boulders, and picked out spots behind boulders along the water tank edge where they had a clear shot at the far side of the water tank. Hunlona returned with the ponies and hid them well before joining Geronimo and Natculbaye. I knew where they were, but looking over my shoulder, I couldn't see them. Soon the only sounds came from a breeze blowing through the tops of the trees, insects humming, and birds calling in the distance. Garditha, hunched over, ran to the men like he was avoiding making himself a target. I heard him say, "Geronimo, I want to watch from here so I can learn what great warriors do when they face their enemies."

Geronimo studied him a moment and nodded. "You stay here. Do nothing except watch. Hide behind these rocks. Only look out through cracks between the boulders. Stay out of the way and watch you don't show yourself or these vaqueros will kill you."

Garditha grinned and nodded. "I know, Grandfather. They tried to kill Trini and me five suns ago."

Geronimo motioned for Hunlona and Natculbaye to come close. I heard him say, "Maybe we have only one good shot each before those vaqueros run for cover. I want the vaquero who told Garditha they are coming back to kill him. I take the first shot. Shoot to kill everyone you can. Be ready if they want to fight rather than run." Hunlona and Natculbaye nodded and returned to their places among the boulders.

No one moved. I watched a shiny beetle half the size of my palm and with big horns on the front of his armor carrying a twig across a patch of sunlight filtering through the trees. Then I saw the men stretch to look out through the cracks between the boulders. I wished I had moved over by Garditha so I could see too. As we slumped down in the shadows, the heads of mounted men, their faces in the shade of their sombreros, seemed to float above the tops of the boulders as they approached the far side of the water tank. They had their rifles out and cocked, ready to shoot, as they looked around the tank before dismounting to water their horses. I heard my breath as if I were running and felt my heart racing. There were two of them for each of our men. I thought, *Geronimo's made a fool's choice, but that's good too. I might yet get away this day.*

I saw Geronimo motioning who was to shoot at whom and then his thumb pulling back the hammer all the way on his old rifle with a distinctive click. I faintly heard it from where I sat and was surprised the vaqueros didn't hear it. He shifted his position as he eased the rifle forward and took aim. The others made ready to fire, steadying their arms against the boulders and aiming like Geronimo but with their rifle barrels pointed toward different targets.

Geronimo's rifle roared, instantly joined by the shots from Natculbaye and Hunlona, sending the crack of doom echoing off the cliffs and rippling through the trees. The horses reared in surprise, bucked, and crow-hopped as the vaqueros put frantic spurs to them, making them race away from the water tank. They ran down the canyon in the direction we planned to go as Hunlona and Natculbaye fired several shots after them to ensure they kept going. One saddle was empty in the cloud of dust they created.

The vaqueros' sombreros flew to their backs. I recognized the two Garditha and I had stoned, but the others I didn't know. Several showed splotches of blood on their shirts and pants from minor wounds. I also saw one who had a little blood running down his cheek. The old man who had attacked us, showing no signs of wounds, had his forearm, where my stone had hit him, wrapped in a splint. A much younger man's left pant leg had a fresh bloodstain that started just below his knee. Seeing it, I understood what Geronimo was doing. The torture had begun. If Geronimo had hit where he wanted, he probably shattered the vaquero's leg bone so the man couldn't walk without help or could only ride in great pain. As they flew past, I saw that the man Geronimo had shot in the leg was not the one who had sworn to kill Garditha and me.

I remembered a story Artisan told me about how one of our neighbors came to get a peg leg. He had taken a leg wound in a battle with some French soldiers during the Juárez war. The wound turned green quickly and began to stink—a sure sign of infection. Splinters from his leg bone were sticking out of his skin everywhere around the wound and made it look awful. It hurt so bad he begged friends to shoot him and put him out of his misery. The army doctor told him that his leg had to come off or he would die from gangrene within two or three days. The man told the doctor to take it. He still had a lot of living to do, and he did. He was still working on a ranch near us twenty years later.

Geronimo was grinning like a coyote in a chicken coop. He had done exactly what he wanted. The only problem was that the vaqueros were in front and could ambush us now. Geronimo didn't think they'd try before we rode into the Altar desert. They were riding for help from villages downriver. Geronimo said that if they didn't stop at some village soon, their fast gallop would kill their ponies before they got halfway to Altar.

The vaquero horse with the empty saddle belonged to a young vaquero sprawled in the dust near the far bank of the water tank, a bright-red spot fast turning black in the center of his chest. Hunlona had shot him in the heart. He took the vaquero's holster and revolver, a fancy bandana, and smoke makings out of a shirt pocket.

Natculbaye rode on ahead as advance scout. We followed the road and then kept to a wash for a while and then back to the road until we left it and rode almost due south. As the sun started touching the clouds with orange and purple, we came to a line of trees following the scattered pools of the Río Altar between long stretches of damp sand. Although there was still good light left, Geronimo said we would camp on a bank above a pool of water. Natculbaye continued to follow the tracks of the running vaqueros.

She-gha and Juanita picked a sheltered spot back in the trees for their fire and sent Garditha and me off to gather brush and wood. Told to help me, Garditha made a face. He was nearly a novitiate warrior, not some little boy helping women do their usual work, but he knew better than to complain.

Chapter 19
Hit and Run at Sáric

Natculbaye had not returned by full dark. We had no idea when he might appear and didn't wait for him before we ate. Geronimo and Hunlona didn't seem concerned by his late return, but Juanita's eyes kept darting around, looking into the darkness and toward every little night sound.

During our supper, I said to Geronimo, "Why isn't Natculbaye back? Has something bad happened to him?"

He had a small piece of beef on the end of his knife and waved it at me. "Mujercita, a good advance scout doesn't return to his band until he sees what's ahead. Natculbaye returns when he has something to tell us."

The fire had only a few flickers left and I was nearly asleep, wrapped warm in my blanket and listening to the frogs, tree peepers, and insects, when Natculbaye rode into camp on his pinto pony. Juanita was out of her blankets and ran to him for a few words as he pulled the cinches to unsaddle. He hobbled the pinto, letting it graze with the other horses, and then came to the fire Juanita had built up to heat the meat and other good things she had kept for him from our earlier meal. Geronimo and Hunlona threw off their blankets and crabbed over to sit beside him.

Geronimo said, "Ho, Natculbaye, you come late in the night. Eat. Then we hear what you have to tell us."

Natculbaye nodded. "Hmmph. My belly is empty. I eat before

I talk. Maybe you want coffee. My woman has plenty."

Geronimo and Hunlona nodded, and She-gha brought their cups for Juanita to fill.

Juanita soon had the meat on a stick, again dripping grease into the fire, and the pots with potatoes and steamed mescal slices hot. She served her man his meal in a gourd while the rest of us sat back and waited for his news. At last he wiped his fingers on his legs and the shafts of his moccasins, looked around the fire, and nodded he was ready to talk.

Hunlona took the smoke fixings he had taken from the dead vaquero and handed them to Natculbaye, who made a cigarette. He lighted the cigarette with a twig from the fire, smoked to the four directions, and handed it to Geronimo, who smoked and then gave it to Hunlona. After Hunlona smoked, he passed it back to Natculbaye, who took another puff and then threw the remaining bit in the fire.

Geronimo said, "Speak, Natculbaye, we listen."

Natculbaye stared at the fire for a moment as if thinking, and then looked at the men and women who were watching his every move. He said, "I think you shot a vaquero good, Geronimo. I could follow their trail from the blood on the bushes by the trail. They stopped at a river pool to stop the wound's bleeding. There was much less blood on the bushes after that, and I found no grave or body, so I guess whatever they did worked. From the brush trimmings nearby, I think they also made a splint for his leg. The tracks said they got the vaquero back on his horse and rode on down the river."

The cold night breeze through the treetops seemed to pause as if it, too, waited to hear more. Three or four coyotes yipped nearby, making the horses snort and look out across the dark land with their ears up. I wondered why they paid any attention to coyotes. There were no colts or fillies in the band's horses that coyotes might attack, and very rarely did they go after the grown horses. Natculbaye paused and looked over at the horses, but saw no problem and continued.

"I followed the trail to Sáric, a Tohono O'odham village, an easy ride about two hands above the horizon from here. The vaqueros stopped at Sáric to find a Nakai-yi di-yen. One doesn't live there, but there was a woman, a Tohono O'odham, who did the work of a di-yen for her village. The villagers say she has strong medicine and sent them to the woman. She looked at the wound, gave the vaquero medicine he drank from a brown bottle. He went to sleep plenty quick. After he passed out, she pulled out all the bone splinters she could find around the wound—hah, you never miss, Geronimo—poured some good whiskey on the wound to drive evil spirits away, and asked Ussen that her work be good. She made a splint to hold the leg bone in line so maybe one day the vaquero can ride again. I think the others will stay with the Tohono O'odham and ride after they learn what happens to him. They have lost our trail. I think maybe they go back to the rancho from where they came."

Geronimo stared at Natculbaye. "Where did you get the Power to know all this?"

Natculbaye laughed hard, making his round belly shake. "From pants and a hat."

Geronimo frowned and, cocking his head to one side, looked at him like he was crazy. I thought he was crazy too, and from the looks of the others, so did they. Garditha, surprised that a great warrior would talk so crazy, looked at him with eyes the size of the twenty-five-centavo coins Artisan had kept at the rancho before the Apaches came.

Natculbaye said, "Most of the village crowded around the di-yen's door to watch her ceremonies and learn what had happened to the hombre. I found a place to hide my pony and was sneaking into the village to watch what happened when I found a pair of pants drying on a wash line and, close by, an old hat hanging on a *jacal* (small reed or adobe house) wall. I put them on and walked into the village like I belonged there. The way I looked, not one villager paid any attention to me. I think I use this trick again to learn about a village before I raid it. I joined the crowd around the door, listened, and learned all I could. When the di-yen put their *compadre* to sleep to pull out the bone splinters, the other two vaqueros came outside her jacal. The Tohono O'odham gave them something to eat, and the local padre talked to them. I heard it all."

Geronimo's grin would have outmatched any coyote that we heard howling. "Hi yeh, Natculbaye, nobody has more light behind their eyes than you. I say, early tomorrow we ride through Sáric. Shoot a few times. Make those people think the Apaches have come to get them, and then ride on. Then the vaqueros know we're heading south and will have a trail to follow if they still want money for our hair or revenge against our children, or for our ambush at the water tank. I think they must want us bad enough that they ride a long way for revenge, two of them for revenge against our children, the rest for our raids on ranchos and the good price for Apache scalps. They will follow us. If Ussen guides our weapons, they won't return. But we will return, and at Sáric deep in the night, the last vaquero knows my knife. What do you think? Should we do this or dodge away and disappear?"

Natculbaye squinted at Geronimo across the fire and shook his head. "These vaqueros must die. I have said all I will say."

Geronimo's grin grew bigger. "Enjuh."

We stopped in the bosque along the river just outside Sáric. The glow behind the mountains to the east said the sun was coming, and in the cold air, mists were slowly lifting off the standing pools of river water. Birds were beginning to call. Inside, I trembled. I didn't know what to expect. I wondered what

Geronimo was waiting for to begin the raid. He nudged his pony over to She-gha and Juanita and said, "Soon we go. You and the children ride on around the village and downstream. When you're past the village, wait until you hear shooting. Then ride your ponies hard until we catch up with you. We won't be far behind. Now go."

She-gha looked over at Garditha and me and jerked her head in a motion to follow her, Juanita, and the packhorses as we rode out of the bosque at a brisk trot along the river trail around Sáric. When we were south of Sáric, I heard a rooster crow followed by hair-raising Apache war yells and the cracks of rifle shots echoing among the adobes and jacals. She-gha and Juanita kicked their ponies and took off down the river trail, throwing clouds of sand into the air. Garditha and I raced behind them, eating their dust and dodging branches from the brush and trees whipping past us.

When we heard no more distant pops from rifles shooting, the women slowed down as the dawn brightened into day and the cold morning air began to warm. It wasn't long before Geronimo, Natculbaye, and Hunlona caught up with us. They were in high spirits after running up and down the streets of Sáric, yelling and firing their guns while the villagers shook in fright inside their jacals, dreading Apaches bursting through their doors. Geronimo was certain the village "attack" was enough to lure the vaqueros into following us.

He thought they might talk some of the villagers into coming with them but doubted it. The Tohono O'odham wouldn't risk fighting unless forced into it. But the vaqueros had scores to settle. From our tracks, they knew no more than six or seven Apaches had killed one of them and badly wounded another. "Yes," he said, "our little morning ride spurs them after us. Soon now they pay for all the trouble they have caused us."

★   ★   ★   ★   ★

Geronimo rode down the river trail, leading us in the walk, jog, gallop cycle he had used before to eat up the miles and keep the horses going a good distance between rests. The sun, like a big yellow-and-red egg, floated up over the far brown foothills, birds flashed from the bushes, and the cold night air grew warmer. When the sun was halfway to the time of shortest shadows, we stopped by a pool of water in the bosque. Geronimo told the women to make a nice fire and boil us some coffee. He wanted the vaqueros following us to think we believed we had escaped them.

The men and Garditha led the horses to a little ribbon of green grass in between a line of trees and the river, loosened the saddles and the packs, and hobbled the horses so they could graze and rest. I gathered brush and pieces of dead wood from along the riverbank to feed the fire, and soon a boiling pot of coffee was giving the air a mouthwatering smell. It brought me memories of Petra making her family's breakfast. I wanted to cry, remembering those times were gone forever, but I knew, as the Apaches said, now was not the time to make eyewater. I had to stay strong.

The women gave us each a little cup of coffee that lifted our spirits. Geronimo and Natculbaye stood in the road, drinking theirs, as they studied the land and the mountains to the south with their soldier glasses. Hunlona climbed to the top of a nearby hill to watch our back trail. The women reloaded packs and disappeared into the brush. Garditha and I practiced with our slings at targets across a river pool. Garditha still wore his pistola in its holster hung over his shoulder, but he quickly learned that wearing it got in the way of good, hard sling throws. He slipped it off over his head and his accuracy and throwing power were much better.

We had tossed maybe twenty stones when out of the stillness

came three whistles of a Gambel's quail, Hunlona's warning that we needed to ride. Garditha snatched up his revolver holster, slid the belt loop past his arm and over his head, and motioned for me to follow as he ran for the horses to tighten cinches. I saw Hunlona run down the hill to Geronimo and Natculbaye.

By the time we had the horses cinched, Geronimo had kicked dirt over the fire and the women had come running from the brush. Garditha and I mounted, and the women flew to their saddles, grabbed the lead ropes for the packhorses, and rode at a gallop down the road following Natculbaye, with Garditha and me right behind them, followed at a distance by Geronimo and Hunlona.

We weren't far when we heard a few rifle shots snap behind us. Natculbaye led us into the bosque, where it was almost impossible to see us from the road, and we waited there, letting the horses blow while we watched back up the road. Soon Geronimo and Hunlona came at a fast, deliberate jog. Natculbaye rode out of the bosque to meet them and, after a short talk, motioned for us to come on. We followed Natculbaye in a fast jog and, near the time of shortest shadows, passed by the little Tohono O'odham village of Cuauhtémoc, the Indians in their fields and gardens standing to watch us ride by.

In less than half a hand after passing Cuauhtémoc, Geronimo rode up to Natculbaye and pointed toward a big sandy wash that snaked off west toward a range of low, green mountains in the distance. The men occasionally stood in their stirrups, stretching to look at our back trail, but never saw anyone following us.

After we stopped to water the horses and gave them a little rest, we rode toward the wash around big fields with long rows of green corn nearly knee-high. Natculbaye, again advance scout, rode his pony into the big sandy wash and soon the women, Garditha, and I, followed by Geronimo and Hunlona, rode the wash's snakelike twists and turns toward the low, green mountains.

Geronimo stopped often to use his soldier glasses on the trail behind us. During one stop to rest the horses, he watched the back trail for a long time and finally lowered them, saying, "Nit'ééhi. They come."

CHAPTER 20
COUGAR BAIT

We rode up the wash toward the low, green mountains with only a couple of rests for the horses all that afternoon. Geronimo kept a close watch on our back trail, but the vaqueros seemed to draw no closer, and that pleased him. Near dark at the entrance to a big canyon leading into the mountains, we came to a windmill and big iron water tank for cattle. We let the horses drink and rest, and we filled all our canteens and water-skins. Hunlona found a cow in the brush, drove it up close to the water tank, and slaughtered it. The women partially skinned it, took choice cuts of meat, and, under Geronimo's direction, chopped off its head and threw it and the guts into the water tank to spoil the water after we had all washed and let the horses drink again.

Apaches don't like to ride at night. They think it's dangerous. A horse might take a wrong step and break a leg, leaving its rider stranded and hurt. Geronimo believed the vaqueros knew this about Apaches. He thought they would push on in the dark, hoping to catch us asleep like the Bluecoats had a few times in the past. But that only happened when the Apache scouts supported them and found our camps, something a Mexican tracker likely could not do. Geronimo knew the vaquero horses would be weak with thirst and the vaqueros would take time to drain and clean the tank, let their horses rest and drink, and begin to refill the tank before following us.

The moon was full and bright and the riding easy except in

occasional shadows blacker than the devil's heart. We left the spoiled water tank and rode up the dim trail at the bottom of the canyon that led across the mountains. We moved slowly, not in a hurry like we were running. We hadn't gone far when Geronimo spoke with Natculbaye and then rode up an arroyo, tied his pony, and—taking his soldier glasses, blanket, and rifle—found a place where he could easily watch the vaqueros when they got to the water tank.

We continued up the canyon for maybe a couple of miles until the trail turned behind a hill. Natculbaye led us off the trail and up the hill to a flat place below the ridgeline where we could unload the horses and get some rest ourselves. I was too excited about ambushing our pursuers to feel tired, but I was yawning a lot. Garditha and I gathered wood and brush for a fire and then wrapped in our blankets. I wondered what Geronimo had planned for the vaqueros, but sleep took me before I had any ideas.

It was dark. The moon had disappeared, and the river of stars swept across the black sky as I waited for the dawn. The air on my face was cold, but I was warm wrapped in my blanket. I raised up and rested on my elbow to see Geronimo, Natculbaye, Hunlona, and the women squatting around a small fire, eating and talking.

Behind me, I could hear the deep breathing of Garditha still asleep. I threw off my blanket, stood up, and went for a privacy bush. I saw She-gha stretch and twist to look where I slept. When she saw me, she smiled and motioned for me to come to the fire.

Juanita and She-gha had cooked pieces of the beef they had taken from the cow Hunlona had slaughtered for them the evening before. When I returned from the brush, She-gha motioned for me to sit beside her and gave me a gourd of coffee, a piece of meat on a stick, and a steam-heated slice of dried mescal. I wolfed them down as if I hadn't eaten in days. As I thought about it, it had been close to two days since my belly had been full.

Garditha appeared, wearing his holster rig over his shoulder and yawning in the circle of firelight. He sat down near Juanita, who gave him a morning meal like I had, and he, too, ate as if his stomach was rubbing his backbone.

The sky behind the eastern mountains had a soft glow, and the stars were fading. Geronimo left the fire. In a short time, I heard him up on top of the ridge above us singing toward the rising sun with his arms spread wide—his morning prayer to Ussen. When he returned, She-gha gave him another cup of coffee and I finished mine.

He said, "Trinidad, you know why we are on this trail. The vaqueros and their friends, the ones who tried to kill Garditha and take you, follow us into this desert to kill us all and take our hair, and maybe yours, or take you to ransom back to the White Eyes. This will never be. I let them follow us, show them our trail until we are ready to wipe them out. No more will they bother you or Garditha. No more will they take Apache scalps for gold. I prayed to Ussen this sun that one or two of them will live long enough after our ambush to know the sharpness of my knife before they ride the ghost pony. All this you understand?"

I nodded. I understood what he wanted to do, just not how he planned to do it.

He grinned. "Enjuh. I know you have much light behind your eyes. I need your help with this ambush."

I sat up a little straighter, proud he had asked. "I know how to shoot. Yes, I will help the People wipe out these men who tried to kill Garditha and take me."

The sun was fast bringing light to the shadows on the western side of the canyon where we camped. Geronimo nodded and, quietly sipping his steaming-hot coffee, smacking his lips, and looking at She-gha, said, "My woman makes fine coffee." Then he turned to me.

"The help I need takes much more courage than shooting at men from behind a big rock. I need you to bait the vaqueros, like a fawn draws in a hungry cougar, unthinking, to easy meat, into a side canyon I found last night where we can ambush them and none will live to ride away."

He looked at me through the cold, narrow slits of his black eyes. He wanted me to betray my own people. I felt a little sick just thinking about it. But these men were hard cases who killed and scalped not only warriors but also the very young and the very old and assaulted women of all ages before they killed them—for their hair. That was not right. How many of the People of any tribe had they killed? Their evil must end.

I looked into the shining black eyes behind the narrow slits and nodded. "Yes, Grandfather, I'll help you. I'll be your bait, like a fawn for a cougar."

He crossed his arms and leaned back as he said, "Trinidad has much courage. Truly, she is a mujercita, a little woman, not a child."

Geronimo told us his ambush plan and we made ready. Hunlona stayed on the ridge just above our camp to watch for the vaqueros. He would come warn us in the side canyon Geronimo planned to use that they were on the way. The ride up the big canyon was an easy climb to the side canyon. The trail up the side canyon wash passed through thick manzanita bushes and mesquite. The wash out of the side canyon looked like a short tunnel through the manzanitas, and it was easy to see up the canyon for two or three hundred yards. Geronimo told the women to go up the canyon, find a place where they might camp, and start a little fire that would give a small, easy-to-see smoke plume from the big canyon trail.

The women, taking Garditha to help them gather brush and wood, headed up the side canyon. Natculbaye sat on his pony in the middle of the big canyon trail watching for Hunlona, and Geronimo led me up the wash trail the women and Garditha had just taken. He stopped in the middle of a thicket of dry brush a long rifle shot from the big canyon trail.

A crafty little smile crossed his craggy old face as he said, "Yell, *'Ayúdame!'* (Help me!) as loud as you can. Let's see if Natculbaye can hear you."

I yelled, practically screaming, "Ayúdame! Ayúdame!"

Natculbaye jerked his pony around so he could look up the side canyon through the manzanita tunnel. Geronimo grinned and waved the "all is well" sign with the palm of his hand parallel to the ground. Natculbaye smiled and made the same sign before turning to watch the main trail for Hunlona.

Geronimo said, "When the vaqueros ride for you, run to hide behind that boulder there just behind us. I'll be there to bring them down with my rifle. She-gha and Juanita will be in those rocks on the other side. Natculbaye and Hunlona will be on the other side of the big canyon trail to take down those who try to run."

I nodded that I understood. He smiled and said, "Nit'ééhi," patted me on the shoulder, and pointed for me to go and wait behind the rocks where he would be until Natculbaye signaled the vaqueros were coming. The sun rose higher, and She-gha and Juanita's smoke plume rose straight up in the warm still air, but went just high enough that a rider would see it easily from the big canyon trail.

The women with Garditha came down the canyon wash to where Geronimo and I waited. Garditha sat down by me and began to practice loading and unloading his pistola. Geronimo showed the women where he wanted them in the rocks on the other side of the trail and made sure they had spare cartridges for the fully loaded lever rifles and pistolas they carried.

Geronimo led the horses a little way up the canyon and tied them out of sight to graze on the brush. Then he walked back down the wash toward the grove of manzanita trees, looking back to be sure the horses and women weren't visible. Satisfied we were all well hidden, he walked out to the main trail to talk with Natculbaye.

It was nearing the time of shortest shadows when I heard a horse running, looked over the top of the rocks where we hid, and saw Hunlona come riding up, speak to Geronimo and Natculbaye, and then lead his pony and Natculbaye's to the same place Geronimo had left the others.

I watched Garditha load and unload his pistola one more time, only this time he put a shell in every cylinder chamber. I said, "I thought Geronimo said for you to load only five chambers and to leave the empty one under the hammer."

Garditha shrugged and looked away. "In a fight, I might need every chamber filled. I'll be careful."

I said, "All right," and leaned back against the boulder, feeling the sun warm my face while my heart thumped with excitement. I looked across the wash to the rocks where She-gha and Juanita hid, but I couldn't see them, only flocks of chickadees in the brush fluttering from bush to bush.

Geronimo appeared at our boulders. To the right of Garditha he found a place where he could rest his rifle for clear shots up and down the wash trail. He said, "When Natculbaye sees the vaqueros coming, he'll whistle like a quail. You run out to the wash trail when you hear it, and when you see the vaqueros, throw up your hands and scream like you did this morning. You, Garditha, don't shoot that pistola until I use my rifle. Don't shoot unless you have a target. Comprende?"

Garditha was grinning. It would be his first chance to shoot his pistola in a fight. He said, "Yes, Grandfather, comprendo."

I was getting hot and thirsty, but the canteens were on the packhorses back up the trail. There were few shadows left in the canyon. A canyon wren squawked, *jeet, jeet,* at the women across the wash, who had invaded its territory. A quail whistled. I looked at Geronimo for confirmation and he nodded. Garditha shook his pistola for me and grinned.

I pushed myself up and, on trembling legs, walked to the edge of the wash. I waited, watching the edge of the hill from where the riders would appear, feeling the rivulets of sweat roll off my brow and neck, and thinking, *I'm fawn bait for a cougar. What if the old man or the other one sees me first and tries to kill me? Can I run fast enough to get to the rocks before they catch me?*

CHAPTER 21
THE SECOND VAQUERO AMBUSH

The vaqueros rode single file up the big canyon trail. The man in the lead wore a big sombrero pulled low for shade over most of his face and a full cartridge belt looped over his shoulder. He had a big pistola hanging on his hip and carried his rifle pointed toward the sky, ready for instant use, its butt resting on top of his thigh and his fingers coiled around the stock through the lever. The others following him rode with their rifles held the same way. They expected an ambush and rode slowly and cautiously, looking at the canyon walls and rims, and the ground all around them.

The trail they followed as they came into view rose a little on the opposite side of the canyon and crossed to my side, where it turned again before passing the manzanita entrance into the side canyon. As the leader approached the manzanita tunnel, I threw up my hands and screamed, "Ayúdame! Ayúdame! *Por favor* (please), ayúdame!"

The lead vaquero jerked back on the reins of his horse so hard it reared, almost throwing him off and causing a lot of prancing around by the others behind him as he came back down. The vaquero stared in my direction a moment, and again I threw up my arms and screamed, "Ayúdame!"

When he spurred his horse for the trail through the manzanita with two others following him, I ran for the rocks where Geronimo and Garditha hid. Geronimo had changed his position a little and was sighting his big old long rifle through a split between two boulders at the men who had stayed on the road.

The men on the road yelled, *"Espere! Espere!"* (Hold on! Hold on!) Long experienced with Apaches, they knew my plea for help might be a trap and wanted the men riding into it to use their heads before they had to use their guns.

Just as I reached the boulders, Garditha, whom Geronimo had told to leave his pistola in its holster until I was out of the line of fire, jerked it out of the holster. He didn't have a good grip on it, and it flew out of his hand and fired when it hit the ground just beyond my feet.

Past the manzanita tunnel into the side canyon, the vaquero horses had a short, steep climb. They had just got on the part of the trail where I had been when Garditha's pistola went off. Its bullet left a red stripe across the rump of the middle rider's horse. It reared, squealing and bucking in pain and throwing its surprised rider to the ground before it headed back for the manzanita tunnel. There were four or five shots from the women's side. The vaquero thrown off his horse collapsed, red bullet holes scattered across the front of his shirt.

Geronimo fired his old long rifle, its thunder echoing off the walls of the side canyon. With his sombrero hanging on his back, I recognized Old One, the old man I had stoned and saw the splint on his arm. The big bullet from Geronimo's long rifle hit Old One in the center of his chest. He seemed to jerk back and then slumped forward over his pony's neck, sliding out of his big silver-trimmed saddle to finally thump in the sand and stones in the wash, his eyes open but unblinking.

On the trail beyond the manzanita tunnel, I recognized Blood Ear, the vaquero who had waited with Old One in the Río Santa Cruz as the same man who had tried to run Garditha and me down and said they would take me after they took Garditha's scalp. He rolled to the side of his pony away from Geronimo's rifle sights and quirted it hard to run past the manzanitas and up the canyon trail toward the western pass through the mountains. The two vaqueros leaving the side canyon through the manzanita tunnel also rolled to Geronimo's side of the trail to follow the first vaquero up the canyon.

Natculbaye and Hunlona took shots at the escaping horses and brought down one, its rider crashing with a hard thump into the middle of the trail, but the one in the lead, Blood Ear, the one carrying the vaquero Geronimo most wanted and the one who had the best pony, charged around a hill and disappeared. Hunlona ran to the stunned vaquero, who was beginning to sit up, snatched up his rifle and pistola, pulled a cartridge belt from around his head, and motioned with his rifle for the vaquero to stand up and walk back to Natculbaye at the manzanita tunnel as he was busy stripping the old vaquero Geronimo had killed.

The women climbed down from their places in the boulders on the opposite side from where Geronimo, Garditha, and I had hidden, and walked over to the vaquero they had killed. They took everything he had except his hat, shirt, and pants. Juanita strapped on his holster holding his pistola. She-gha pulled a new set of boots off him. They looked about the size one of us might wear. She caught his pony but left the silver-trimmed saddle and bridle on it, waiting for the men to decide what to do with it.

Geronimo patted my shoulder. "You did good, Trinidad. Just like we needed you to do. Still, we missed the vaquero we most wanted, the one who meant to harm you and Garditha, but we will find and kill him."

I tried to smile but couldn't. My acting had gotten two men killed, and one likely tortured to death. They were men who might have saved me. But for Garditha's pistola, five might have died. I wanted to cry but dared not. Maybe one day, my eyewater might wash away the regret staining my soul.

Geronimo turned to Garditha, who stood with his head lowered, staring at the ground between his moccasins. "So, *guerrerocito* (Little Warrior), you still have much practice to do handling the pistola. You forget to leave the chamber empty under the hammer?"

Garditha slowly shook his head. "No, Grandfather, I didn't forget. I used all the chambers because a fight comes. I thought I might need to use all the bullets."

Geronimo grinned. "Hmmph. You will be a powerful warrior one day, guerrerocito. Don't forget the lessons you learn here today."

Looking relieved, Garditha sighed and said, "I won't forget, Grandfather."

As She-gha and Juanita approached, Geronimo waved toward them. "Powerful warrior women come. You also did well." The women smiled and nodded but said nothing.

Geronimo looked up the side canyon, saw the little smoke plume from the fire he had the women build, and said, "We have a fire already built. Let us eat and think about what to do about the vaqueros who got away. Maybe we have a little fun with the one we catch."

The women led the way up the canyon, followed by Geronimo, Garditha and me, and then Natculbaye and Hunlona leading the vaquero they had taken, who had his hands tied behind him and a rope around his neck like a cur dog. The vaquero, young but grown, showed fear in his eyes even I could see.

He knew what every Mexican must know. Geronimo enjoyed taking the blood of Mexicans of any age or sex and making them suffer horrifically in the process. But a grown man was a special opportunity for more revenge as he had taken against the Mexicans for over thirty years.

When we got to the fire and the women began making ready

to cook, Geronimo said, "Tie that dog to the tree down in the wash there." He pointed to a juniper off to one side of the wash about thirty paces away.

She-gha and Juanita cooked some more of the beef we had eaten from the night before. Geronimo, Natculbaye, and Hunlona sat off to one side, smoked, and talked, occasionally casting glances toward the vaquero or to the top of the ridge above us.

We were all hungry, and the smell of the juices dripping into the fire made our bellies rumble with hunger. At last She-gha and Juanita handed Geronimo, Natculbaye, and Hunlona their meat, and the rest of us took ours, all attacking it like starving dogs. When the men finished eating, Hunlona climbed to the top of the saddle ridge rising up from where we sat.

Geronimo and Natculbaye smoked and talked while the rest of us cleaned up the camp and saddled the horses. Hunlona soon returned and spoke to Geronimo and Natculbaye with much hand waving and nodding when they asked questions. Geronimo finally nodded and said, "*Gonit'éé* (A good place)."

He waved Garditha over to them from where he had been sitting with me and said to him, "Guerrerocito, I think you need target practice with your pistola. Have you ever shot a man before? I know you made sure the vaquero you hit and killed with a stone was dead, but have you ever shot and killed a man?"

Garditha looked solemn and distant when he slowly shook his head. "No, Geronimo. I kill no one with gun or bow."

The old man grinned and nodded. "Doo dat'éé da. I want you to take your pistola and shoot that vaquero tied to the tree down there. Kill him with one bullet if you can. Shoot him in the heart or head. Soon, we need to go."

Garditha's jaw dropped. He looked kind of the way I felt—sick and wanting to puke. "But, Grandfather, this is not fair. He has no weapon with which to fight back. It's not right that I kill him that way. There is no honor in that."

Geronimo's eyes narrowed as he said, "We test his courage and strength this way. There is no chance of him going free. Let his death teach you something so he has not lived for no reason. Shoot him. Or I will burn him—slow."

Garditha nodded he understood and pulled his pistola from it holster, held its grips with his right hand, pushed the hammer back to full cock with his left, and—resting its butt in the palm of his left hand—raised the gun toward the vaquero.

The vaquero had been watching Geronimo and Garditha and understood he was the subject of their talk. When he saw Garditha pull the pistola from its holster, the vaquero decided to die with dignity. He stood and faced them and raised his chin with pride.

Garditha held the pistola at arm's length, its weight hard for him to support, as he tried to aim the barrel wavering on and off the vaquero. The canyon grew quiet, no breeze through the brush, no birds calling. I watched with my hand over my mouth, afraid I might scream or vomit up the burning sickness I felt heaving in my chest.

The pistola thundered, hurting my ears. There was a groan of pain as the vaquero staggered back a step or two, a spreading blood spot showing on his right side just below his belt.

Geronimo slapped his thigh. "Hi yeh! Enjuh. Enjuh. Again, my son. Shoot again. Aim for his heart. Shoot! Shoot!"

I wanted to scream, "Stop! Stop it!" but knew it was too late now.

Garditha cocked the pistola, took aim, and fired, hitting the vaquero in his left shoulder. He must have hit the joint because his arm hung in his shirt, unmoving as blood poured out the sleeve cuff and off his fingertips. The vaquero clenched his teeth as he rocked back and forth, fighting to stand.

"Again! Shoot, boy! Shoot! You do well to make this one suffer like a man."

Garditha shot again. The bullet must have passed through the right lung. Blood suddenly appeared on the vaquero's lips, and he stumbled backward and collapsed. Blood filled with air bubbles flooded the wound over his chest.

Garditha looked at Geronimo with pleading eyes. Geronimo shook his head a little. "You are a guerrerocito but not ready to be a man." He touched the space between his eyes with his forefinger. "Go. Finish him."

Garditha walked down to the vaquero, who with the light slowly leaving his eyes watched him come. The vaquero saw him cock and point the pistola at his head. I heard him say just before Garditha fired, *"Gracias, amigo."*

I squatted down and buried my face in my arms, wanting to cry, but unable. I knew those vaqueros would have shown us no mercy, tortured the men, and taken the women, maybe even me, before scalping them. I knew the Apaches asked no quarter and gave none. I thought, *This has to end. Somehow, someway, this never-ending spilling of blood has to end.*

CHAPTER 22
THE LAST VAQUERO

Garditha holstered his pistola, turned—as if in a dream—from the body of the man he had just killed, and climbed back to where I sat. My face must have shown my despair and agony about what I had done to help kill the three men.

Garditha said, "It's all right, mujercita. This is war, and men die in war. Today I killed my first man using my pistola. I saw the light fading in his eyes, and he thanked me before I shot him to end his misery. Today I am a man. Geronimo let me do a good thing. Geronimo could have made me continue target practice on the vaquero, but I didn't want to, and I don't think he wanted to waste the bullets teaching me how to shoot. I would not want to be the one he's after. That man will suffer."

I puffed my cheeks, sighed, and nodded I understood, but truly, I didn't understand all the hate, fighting, and killing I had seen on both sides.

She-gha motioned to us and said, "The men have decided we camp near the top of the ridge, where they can watch the canyons for the vaqueros who got away. Help us load the horses. Then we go."

The climb to the top of the ridge was so steep we had to lead the horses, and Natculbaye warned us to let them go if they started to fall. Near the top, the ridge edge seemed to curl over on itself, leaving a depression about three houses high below the top, where we could camp with a small fire hidden from the world below. Garditha and I gathered wood and brush in the junipers and manzanitas below the camp and then made a firepit for the women to cook over. The men climbed to the top of the ridge, where they looked at the countryside while we worked. After we finished the firepit, Garditha and I climbed up there too.

The view made me feel as though I were standing on top of the world. The ridge was part of a chain of low mountains scattered over with junipers and connected by saddles. These ridges and mountains formed one side of the big canyon we had ridden into from the windmill. Standing there, we could see to the north a great brown desert from which grew a tall, black-topped mountain that seemed to be in the center of a great foreboding llano. We had a great view of the east and west sides of mountains and ridges below us streaked with tree- and brush-filled canyons and arroyos that drained down to big canyons. The canyon on the west side, which we had used, twisted up toward a notch in the mountains to the northwest. The men believed the notch was a pass that led down the north side of the mountains there and probably into the canyon on our east side, passing between where we stood and a range of low mountains and foothills to the east of our ridge.

Geronimo believed the vaqueros, thinking the windmill provided the only known water for many miles, would circle back toward us following the canyon on the east side. By knowing when they came down the canyon on the eastern side of the mountains, he could set a second ambush to wipe out the last two vaqueros in the east canyon and, as the Apaches said, make the world smooth again. Those vaqueros would pay for trying to scalp Garditha and trample me a few days ago.

A few days? I thought. *It seems more like months ago when we had practiced with our slings on the Santa Cruz River.*

★ ★ ★ ★ ★

The men decided that they would each take turns watching the canyons for riders for half a day or night. Since the moon was still bright, making it easy to see at night and increasing the possibility the vaqueros would ride the canyon in the dark, the men included Garditha to take a turn watching. I saw him smile and nod, swelling with pride when the men told him that he was to have a turn in watching and that he would be the first to watch for riders.

Geronimo let Garditha use his soldier glasses and went with him to the top of the ridge, where he found him the best place to sit while he watched the canyons. I asked to go watch with him, but Geronimo didn't think it was appropriate for two nearly grown children to be alone together. "Besides," he said, "you can watch the big canyon from near the camp and use the other pair of soldier glasses I have. You don't need to sit with Garditha."

Neither Garditha nor I had the faintest idea what he was talking about, except that we knew unmarried men and women didn't work together alone. We were both proud that the grown-up people now viewed us as being close enough to grown that we might act like grown-ups alone—whatever that meant.

I spent the rest of the day watching the big canyon trail, the western side of the mountains, from a place just above the camp while Garditha watched the canyon on the eastern side. We saw nothing. Although the air was cool up high where we were, the sun was hot enough to burn long-exposed skin.

It was dull work, monitoring the canyon trails, and with as little sleep as we'd had since we left Naiche's band, we had to fight to stay awake. Our camps had been dry, and our own water supply was going fast since we'd used a cow's guts and head at the windmill to poison the water and slow down the vaqueros following us. I heard She-gha tell Geronimo that, without more water, we could not stay in this camp more than another day or two. That didn't seem to bother Geronimo or Natculbaye, who believed we would probably see the vaqueros headed down the big canyon on the eastern side sometime tomorrow before the time of shortest shadows.

The long mountain shadows stretched into darkness as the sun disappeared behind the mountains. The women gave Hunlona a meal for the night before he went to relieve Garditha from his watch. They told me to come down from my lookout nest and eat, and not to worry about missing riders in the big canyon on the west side because Hunlona expected to watch both east and west canyons.

Garditha joined me in the early-evening dusk. The meal was good but not much different from what we had eaten earlier in the day after the vaquero ambush. My eyes were tired from staring through soldier glasses, and I had a hard time staying awake. Garditha, still excited and slow to calm down, chattered about not seeing the vaqueros all the time we ate. I tried to listen to the conversation Geronimo and Natculbaye had about the best way to take the last two vaqueros. Natculbaye suggested that they just shoot them and ride away. Geronimo wanted to make the one who wanted scalps and had tried to trample me suffer.

I helped She-gha and Juanita clean up after the meal and then wrapped in a blanket close to the fire near where She-gha and Geronimo slept. The last thought I remember before falling asleep whispered, *Tomorrow tells many tales.*

The night was disappearing into the glow stretching across the mountains, but the stars high above the horizon burned cold and bright in the shiny black of night. I heard others in the camp stirring, and off toward the top of the ridge, Geronimo stood, with his arms raised, facing the coming sun, praying and singing to Ussen. The air was cold, but I was warm enough wrapped in my blanket. I wondered how a man like Geronimo, who prayed and sang to Ussen every day, could be so casual about killing and torturing people. *Maybe sometime,* I thought, *I can ask him to tell me the ways of Ussen that led him to do this.*

Using dry brush on the coals blown to glowing orange, She-gha and Juanita brought the firepit back to life, adding light and a little warmth to the camp. I saw they would soon need more brush and wood for the fire, and with a sigh, I arose from my blanket and rubbed some warmth into my arms as I headed to scavenge for brush and wood. She-gha smiled when she saw me come with a load, poured me a cup of coffee, and held it out to me where I could drink it and warm myself by the fire. The coffee was hot and ground, roasted piñon nuts gave it a kind of chocolaty taste. I liked it, and its heat with that from the fire brought my body back from its sleepy lethargy.

Geronimo came to the fire after his prayers and singing and waited with his hands held toward the heat while She-gha filled his eating gourd with a little heated meat and sliced mescal to go with his coffee. Garditha came to the fire, bringing more brush and wood, and Juanita gave him a cup with coffee and a gourd with something to eat. Hunlona stepped into the circle of light and nodded to us around the fire. She-gha gave him his morning meal. Geronimo finished his meal and walked up the path to the ridgetop to replace Natculbaye.

The sun was a full hand above the mountains when Geronimo and Natculbaye returned to the fire. While Natculbaye ate, Geronimo talked with Hunlona while he oiled his rifle. When Natculbaye finished eating, he joined them and they talked more as Geronimo drew wiggles in the sand that I later recognized represented the trail down the eastern canyon and some arroyos on the western side. When their council broke up,

Geronimo and Natculbaye spoke briefly with She-gha and Juanita, and then strapped on their pistola holsters, put a bandolier of ammunition over a shoulder, checked their rifles, and headed for the ridgetop. Not having a wife, Hunlona was already fully armed and gone.

She-gha motioned for me to help her while Garditha helped Juanita. "We make ready to travel, then go to top of the ridge and watch for vaqueros."

My heart began to race. "Are the vaqueros coming?"

She nodded. "Hmmph. Maybe. Natculbaye thinks he sees glow from fire back up canyon on east side after sun hides. The men have picked out a place for ambush just below us. Now they go down to eastern canyon and wait for the vaqueros. We watch for them from ridgetop and tell the men when they come."

Juanita and Garditha finished with her packing about the same time She-gha and I finished hers, and then we all climbed up to the ridgetop. The men had already disappeared down a big arroyo that started where we stood and grew wider, filled with manzanitas and mesquite as it headed for the canyon bottom.

We all had soldier glasses the men had left behind. We were to watch the canyon trail and, when we saw the riders coming, flash a mirror signal that the vaqueros were on the way. Looking down into the canyon, I saw the eastern trail just below us had a straight stretch of about a hundred yards with very little of the brush or rock cover I thought they would need for an ambush. Near the middle of the straight stretch was the wash from a short arroyo, also with a little brush and no boulders for hiding. It led to a much larger arroyo that came up the mountainside toward us and ended where we sat.

She-gha pointed at the straight stretch of trail. "Ambush there."

Confused, I frowned. "But there's no place to hide there."

She-gha looked at me and grinned. "Best place for Apache ambush. Watch, you see."

I looked over at Garditha sitting nearby with Juanita, and he nodded.

Three, maybe four hands of the sun passed once we settled on the ridgetop to watch for the vaqueros and see their ambush. I studied the ambush area a long time and never saw any of our men. She-gha and Juanita took turns watching for the vaqueros on the canyon trail winding down out of the mountains like the path of some great snake. We waited. I fought dozing off while the sun climbed on its arc toward the top of the day. The air grew warmer as the insects buzzed in the brush around us and small blue-striped lizards soaked in the sun's heat on the large, flat stones scattered around the top.

Garditha cleaned and oiled his pistola after Hunlona showed him how following the morning meal, and then practiced loading and unloading his empty cartridges. The one live round left from yesterday was in a holster cartridge loop. Geronimo wouldn't give Garditha any replacement ammunition until he needed it, and we both believed he wouldn't need any more unless we were in desperate circumstances. It was the price he paid for not loading the pistola as Geronimo had told him.

Juanita, watching the canyon trail back into the mountains, pointed in that direction and said, "Ho. Vaqueros come." She-gha lifted her soldier glasses, and Garditha and I used ours to look where Juanita pointed. The vaqueros looked like ants creeping down the trail. They took their time, seeming to pause to look for attackers behind every mesquite, manzanita, big cactus, or boulder along the trail. Far in the distance, it was hard to tell much about them. There were two, and they dressed like men.

She-gha twisted her soldier glasses, caught the sun's reflection, and flashed it three times on the sand near the short arroyo on the straight stretch of trail in the canyon below. A single flash from the trail below signaled the men were ready. We waited.

As the vaqueros approached the ambush site, I studied them using the soldier glasses. Their sombreros shadowed their faces, but I could tell, from the way he sat his pony and the big pistola hanging on his hip, that the one in back was Blood Ear, the one who had wanted to scalp Garditha and kill me. I scanned up and down the sides of the trail in front of them but saw none of our men. The vaqueros entered the straight stretch of trail and appeared to relax. They didn't look around as much as when there was cover.

The first vaquero passed the side arroyo opening, and the second was just to its northern edge when Hunlona seemed to rise out of the ground with his rifle raised and shot the first vaquero in his throat. He jerked backward, dropping his rifle, and his pony reared up, threw him off, and then ran, leaving him lying in the trail, his eyes frozen open as a red bloom spread down across the front of his dirty white shirt. Hunlona was quick and caught the pony that ran toward him.

As soon as the second vaquero saw Hunlona, he brought up his rifle to shoot. Natculbaye—and I never saw where he had been hiding—stepped onto the trail and shot the second vaquero's sombrero from behind, sending it flying past his fallen compadre. The vaquero leaned over his pony's neck and, whacking his horse's rump with his rifle barrel, charged up the little arroyo. He saw Geronimo suddenly appear, standing on the arroyo's edge not more than fifty paces in front of him and sighting down the long, deadly barrel of his rifle. The vaquero rolled to the far side of his pony for cover like he had yesterday, but this time, he tried to bring his rifle up under his pony's neck for a shot at Geronimo. The thunder from Geronimo's rifle echoed off the canyon sides. Its big bullet hit the vaquero's leg just below his knee where it lay across his saddle.

The vaquero screamed, "Ayeeeee," as he fell off his pony and landed on his back in the arroyo rocks and sand washing into the big canyon. His horse raced on up the arroyo past Geronimo, giving him a clear shot at the vaquero lying on his back and trying to roll onto his good knee and crawl to cover, but he saw no cover.

He sat up to face Geronimo slowly edging down the arroyo bank and loading another cartridge. Then he saw Natculbaye advancing and holding him in his sights while Hunlona scrambled up the arroyo to fetch the horse that had stopped not far from its rider. The cartridge loaded, Geronimo pointed the rifle skyward and fired, and then, faster than most men can fire a lever rifle, he fired twice more, loaded again, and then squatted down with his rifle across his knees to face the vaquero.

She-gha turned to Garditha and me. "Now you go down to Geronimo. Hurry. He waits."

We gave our soldier glasses to Juanita and She-gha and ran off down the ridge. It was steep going, but we had played on steeper slopes and knew how to maneuver them. It took less than half a hand for us to zigzag down the slope, where we found the men sitting and smoking but silent as they studied the vaquero who sat clenching his teeth and frowning in pain. His eyes looked from one Apache face to the other but showed no fear. When we arrived, Geronimo stood up from where he squatted between Natculbaye and Hunlona and turned to us.

"Nish'ii', Garditha and Trinidad."

With one hand, he swung his rifle toward the man sitting with his left leg splayed out in front of him, drying blood turning black around a bullet hole near the knee of his pants. "Is this the man who said they should take you for ransom, Trinidad, and kill Garditha for scalp gold?"

I had seen that face in my sleep, and I always woke up sweating when I saw it. I nodded. "Yes, he is the man."

Garditha pointed at him. "See. Part of his right ear is missing. I took it off with my sling. That is the man who said my hair brings gold in Nogales."

Geronimo looked at the vaquero and grinned, shaking his head. "So, hombre, you chase Geronimo and his little people until we catch you."

The vaquero bowed his head and looked at his feet.

"Where are all your compadres who come with you?" Geronimo held up a finger as he had seen the White Eyes do when they motion they remember something. "Ah, yes. I think we killed them all but you. No. Wait. There is one left with the Tohono O'odham people in the village of Sáric, but soon he, too, goes to the Happy Place. Maybe you will be brothers there. I shot him in nearly the same place in the leg when I thought he was you."

The vaquero looked at me, grimaced, and spat. "*Puta jovencita* (whore, young and small), Apache puta." He spat again. "We could have saved her from you, but she chose you over her own people."

He must have hoped he could goad Geronimo into killing him quickly, but Geronimo was having none of it and just stared at him, letting him talk and rant. I stared at him too. I wasn't quite sure what a whore was, except Petra told me they were women who worked in saloons, wore short dresses, and used too much makeup. I didn't use makeup, my skirt reached to my ankles, and I had never been near a saloon. Why did he call me a whore?

"And that boy there," he said, pointing with his chin, "with my brother's pistol hung over his shoulder. He killed my brother and took off half my ear with his sling. I was determined to catch and kill him like the little snake he is. I didn't care how young he was. I owed him for the death of my brother. I came to get him and maybe have a taste of that puta." He shrugged his shoulders. "It wasn't to be. Now you have me."

Geronimo said through clenched teeth, "Yes we have you. You sound more like a witch after these young ones than a human being. Apaches know how to send a witch to the Happy Place."

He turned to Garditha and me. "Bring brush and wood here while we make ready to deal with this witch."

Garditha and I ran about and collected dead, dry brush and chunks of wood that had washed down the big canyon. We brought it to the men, and all the while thoughts were drifting through my head like clouds on a windy day. *I don't want to see this. Awful. Awful. Why couldn't they have left us alone? Why? He's right. They could have saved me from these people. Why didn't I go? They wanted to take Garditha for his hair. That wasn't right. Maybe they also would have kept me for ransom. Maybe I made the right choice. Maybe. Why did the Apaches have to kill Petra and the baby? Why did they do that?*

Geronimo had Hunlona and Natculbaye arrange the brush on the bottom and then the wood on top in a low, washed-out place in the arroyo. The vaquero watched with a raised chin, trying to appear proud and undefeated. After they packed the low place with wood and brush, Geronimo, smiling, walked over to the vaquero. In a smooth, unexpected motion, he cracked the vaquero's jaw with the butt of his rifle, knocking him senseless. Hunlona and Natculbaye dragged the vaquero over to our pile of wood and brush, laid him spread eagle on top of it, and, with pieces of rope cut from his *reata* (thin rawhide rope), stretched out and tied his arms and legs to pegs on the edge of the depression.

After they finished tying him down, they made a small fire nearby and waited while Geronimo made a long, limber switch from a tall weed stem and, sitting near the vaquero's head, began to slap his face with it. It wasn't long before his eyelids fluttered open and he licked his lips. Geronimo stopped with the switch and waited. The vaquero raised his head until his chin touched his chest, looked at where he lay, and then let his head flop back as he moaned from deep in his throat. The useless leg showed fresh blood, and his face twisted in pain.

In his low, rasping, old man's voice, Geronimo said, "Ah, señor. You are awake? Bueno. Five or six harvests ago, my brother-in-law Juh and I caught Juan Mata Ortiz, who with Terrazas led the attack on Victorio, killed him, and enslaved many of our people. We wiped out Ortiz's command in Chihuahua before we took him alive and burned him to test his true strength." The vaquero's eyes narrowed as he stared at Geronimo, but I could tell from how fast his belly moved up and down as he breathed that fear was on him. "Juan Mata Ortiz was a strong enemy. I pray to Ussen that you are as strong as Mata Ortiz, but I think you are not. You threaten children and chase my people no more. Let us see your strength, señor."

I wanted to be sick and look away, but I watched Natculbaye and Hunlona take scoops they made from sticks and rake up the fire and its coals to drop on the brush between the vaquero's legs. The brush under the wood was dry and thin, and the coals made big yellow and orange flames race up through the wood with a whoosh. The vaquero's mouth opened wide, his lips pulled tight over his teeth, and his eyes squeezed shut. His whole body seemed to tremble. He tilted his head back and strained against his ties, but he made no sound until his shirt and pants began to burn. The loudest, most awful yell turning into a scream I've ever heard roared past his lips. I clamped my hands over my ears and turned away, but I still heard the scream coming from the man's core, coming from his guts, giving voice to his agony. In my worst nightmares, I still dream about that horrific scream. It didn't take long for the heat and smoke to smother him and, mercifully for me, for the screaming to stop, but to him, I'm sure it felt like a lifetime.

As the body turned into black char and the flames began to die, sending stinking black smoke high into the sky, Geronimo turned to the others and said, "See, I told you he was no Juan Mata Ortiz. Now we go. There is another vaquero I need to visit."

CHAPTER 23
THE AZUL MOUNTAINS

Geronimo sent Hunlona down the east canyon with the vaqueros' horses, boots, weapons, and anything else they had worth saving. He was to water the horses at the windmill and stay out of sight until Geronimo and Natculbaye came down the big west canyon on the other side of the ridge with the rest of us. The ridge where we had camped was easier to climb up than go down with the horses, but we took a zigzag track down to the canyon where we'd killed the three vaqueros and didn't hurt anyone or any of the animals. Geronimo had left the bodies of the vaqueros where they fell, left them as food for the coyotes and buzzards. The bodies had started to smell, and we had seen the cloud of great black birds circling high above us as we left.

We were out of the side canyon and well down the big canyon trail as the sun hung low in the sky, painting the clouds dark purples, blood reds, and firelight oranges. I watched the colors and wondered, *How can there be such beauty in a world where today I watched such awful cruelty and brutality? I have no answer. The Catholic padres teach their followers how God loves each one of us. Geronimo's god, Ussen, speaks to Geronimo, but he rarely tells us what Ussen says. Are Ussen and God the same person? If they are, how can God or Ussen let things happen like I witnessed today? I don't understand.*

At moonrise, we came to the iron water tank. The water was warm, but good, cleaned up by the vaqueros after we left it, and we let the horses water while we, too, drank deeply before filling our canteens and waterskins. Hunlona soon appeared from a nearby arroyo with his horses and loot. Garditha and I rested for a while, wordlessly watching the stars in the shiny, flint-black sky.

The women, without complaint, pulled themselves up from their rest and loaded the loot taken from the vaqueros onto the packhorses. Geronimo, Natculbaye, and Hunlona sat and smoked and talked about what we should do next. Geronimo wanted to get a good bite out of the distance toward Sáric before the sun came and then make a hidden camp where we could rest during the day. The next night he planned to slip into Sáric and kill the last living vaquero who had been chasing us.

We followed the same trail out of the desert we had used to reach the windmill. Reaching the fields around the village of Cuauhtémoc, the trail north wound through the bosque of the Río Altar. We stopped to water and rest the horses after the stars traveled every two or three hands against the horizon. I was so tired. To keep from going to sleep and falling out of my saddle, I imagined struggling against weariness as if it were some warrior attacking me. Every time we stopped, I drank a little water and lay down for a minute of rest, and the next thing I knew, She-gha was shaking me awake to mount my pony.

The stars were still bright when we saw a lantern light in the little village of Nogalito sitting up above the planted fields on the west side of the river. We were about a hand's ride to Sáric. We crossed the canyon fields to the east side and rode to the top of a hill with a deep depression on its top that let us camp and keep our animals out of sight. We let the horses graze hobbled in the brush around us, ate some dried trail food, and put our blankets under manzanita trees, where their leaves would keep the rising sunlight out of our eyes and let us sleep through the day.

The night following that day, She-gha laughed when I appeared to help at the fire. She said, "You must have been snoring before your eyes closed when you crawled under the manzanita and stretched out on your blanket." I smiled and nodded. She spoke the truth.

The moon, wrapped in a dark blanket, showed only half of herself as we rode up the bosque trail toward Sáric. We came to the great fields under long, straight rows of corn, chilies, peppers, and other vegetables around Sáric and turned east into a big canyon that crossed the northern end of the Cibuta Mountains. Fields also covered the new canyon at its entrance, but these soon ended in trees scattered along the Río Altar. Determined to kill the wounded vaquero, Geronimo left us and rode into Sáric.

With half a moon shining among the stars, the trail up the canyon was an easy, fast ride, and Geronimo had to ride hard to catch up with us. He came just as we were stirring to ride again after letting the horses drink and rest. We had ridden under oaks and pine trees that filled the canyon for two or three miles, making it hard to see and were dark and scary in their inky black shadows.

We heard him coming long before he reached us. When the rider coming at a fast jog rode out of the shadows, the women, Hunlona, and Natculbaye all had their rifles resting across their saddles with their horses giving them cover. Garditha and I huddled together by a boulder sticking out of the sand like a big thumb. Garditha had his one good bullet loaded in his pistola and had it cocked, ready to shoot if the others did. I saw the rider pass by a small stand of oaks and willows and heard Natculbaye say to the others, *"Doo dat'éé da"* (He's okay). It's Geronimo." We were all glad to see him. I felt safer knowing he was there to protect me, even if I was just a piece of his property.

He rode up to our horses and swung off his saddle with an easy, graceful move. We all laughed in relief. She-gha gave him a canteen of water that he took several long pulls from before he gave it back to her. I looked him over in the moonlight but didn't see any blood splatters on his shirt or vest. Natculbaye said, "You settled with the vaquero?"

Geronimo nodded. "I did, but I didn't kill him. You would not have known he was a Mexican, as white as he grew when he awoke and saw me standing over him with my knife. I decided I wanted him to return and tell the vaqueros around the Milpillas Rancho and Cananea mining country what had happened to their compadres after chasing Geronimo and the other Apaches. I told him what we did to the last man and that they would be wise not to chase us again." Geronimo laughed and made the "all is good" sign. "I think this story will soon be told all over Sonora. Maybe for a time, it keeps the Mexicans off our trail. Let us ride. The Azul Mountains are far."

We continued the steady, easy climb up the canyon trail until a couple of hands before dawn, when the canyon broadened out on sides of the river, yielding big fields of crops and some fencing around herds of cattle. We avoided low campfires scattered up and down the river by riding far around them. The fires supported night-riding vaqueros who watched over the cattle in the fields. The vaqueros at their fires never knew we passed. Geronimo understood attacking any one fire would bring riders from the other fires thundering in to help their amigos and an unwanted chase would be on.

We rode into a large canyon opening into the south side of ours. I thought the area, even in the cold darkness and scattered over with junipers and oaks, looked or felt like I had been there before. I asked She-gha where we were. She said, "This place where the two canyons meet the White Eyes call Arizona Ranch.

Naiche led us past it on the way to the camp in the canyon of the Pajarito Mountains before he rode north and Geronimo rode south."

I remember, I thought. *It was also near dawn when he led us past here then. It's odd how a person can remember places they've passed and know little about them when the light is nearly the same.*

We rode for half a hand down the canyon we had used earlier and then turned up the southwest side for an easy climb into the foothills. At the top of the ridgeline, we followed one of several trails down the far side to a pool among scattered boulders and fed by spring.

We made camp on a low rise east of the pool, and She-gha and Juanita were soon cooking a morning meal. It was still dark, just before dawn. After I carried water to She-gha for her camp, she told me to go bathe. We all wanted to bathe before the day was over, and she thought I would be quickest before she sent Garditha.

I went to the water's edge, where a few junipers made a perfect screen against anyone seeing me when I bathed. I stepped into the water and was surprised to feel how much warmer it was than the cold desert-night air. The mud oozing between my toes felt so good after my feet had been in moccasin boots all night. I pulled off my shirt and skirt, tossed them on the bank, and waded deeper into the tank so I could squat with the water up to my chin. I scrubbed myself with the sandy mud under my feet, rinsed a few times, and felt like a new girl. I dressed and walked back to the fire. When Garditha saw me coming, he jumped up and ran for the water. The smells from the stewpot made my mouth water as I spread my blanket under a manzanita bush. The sun was just sending burning gold over the mountains. It was going to be a fine day.

The camp by the pool refreshed us all. As dusk came, we were back down in the canyon that ran across the northern end of the Cibuta Mountains. The half-moon was slow to rise. Even so, the trail was familiar and easy to ride. By the time the stars had reached the top of their arc, we came to the canyon that led north to Nogales but turned south, staying near the bosque of the Río Magdalena. Soon we crossed the river and took the same trail in the canyon we had used to head west from the Río Santa Cruz.

There were plenty of watering places on this trail. We didn't stop at every one to let the horses rest and drink, but even so, in the cold night air the horses were eager to go. We stopped that night's ride to camp beside the big spring and pool where we had first rested when we left the Río Santa Cruz camp to ride for the Pajarito Mountains. We were about two hands' ride from where we had camped on the Río Santa Cruz and where Garditha and I had faced the vaqueros who tried to kill us.

After we bathed and were eating our morning meal, I said to Garditha, "We're not far from the Río Santa Cruz camp where you killed your first man and Geronimo gave you the man's pistola. You only have one cartridge left for it. Do you think he'll give you more soon?"

Garditha shrugged his shoulders and thought for a few breaths. "I don't know. I'd like to have more, but I'm satisfied with what I have now. The pistola isn't just a heavy lump of *pesh* (iron). It's a weapon that can kill, and I need to handle it often if I want to be good with it. Someday a pistola might save my life."

He studied the golden light from the rising sun on the hillside opposite from where we sat and said, "The warriors tell me that, for up-close fighting, a bow is just as fast and, for night fighting, is probably better than a pistola because it doesn't make noise or make a flash of light. But bows and arrows have shorter ranges and are harder to carry and keep near at hand than a pistola. I keep my pistola and use it often to make my hands and mind smooth holding it. Do you understand this, Trinidad?"

I smiled. "Yes, I understand. In not too many harvests, you'll be a warrior all the chiefs will want with them."

He laughed. "I hope so. It is what I want. That and a fine wife and children. Maybe you'll be my wife, Trinidad. You're brave and work hard. I like you."

I laughed. "I like you too, Garditha, but we have to see what tomorrow brings. It will be many harvests before you can court a woman. Geronimo might trade me back to the Mexicans or Americans before then. Even if he doesn't, you might find someone else that you want more than me."

Neither of us were smiling then. He looked me in the eye and said, "Yes, see what tomorrow brings. If I have a chance for you, I'll ask for you. That is all I have to say."

I felt a little strange that a boy said he wanted me when we were older. I never thought I would marry. Life was too dangerous and filled with uncertainty.

That evening we left when the sun was low in the sky. Dusk was just turning the sky from dark royal blue to shiny black sprinkled with stars over the big canyon of the Río Santa Cruz when we turned south. Although Apaches don't like to ride at night, Geronimo was making good use of the darkness to pass through Sonora unseen. The risk of someone seeing us was much less at night than it was in daylight, and because it was much cooler than riding under the sun, the horses didn't tire out as fast. I thought it was a good thing for us that he did this, but it lessened my chances of somehow getting away—I could barely find my way in the daylight over rough country, much less so in the darkness.

We reached the canyon where we had left the fight with the

buffalo soldiers to go north. This time, we turned east toward the Cocóspera Mountains before turning south. I could see the mountains' main peak barely outlined against the night sky in the coming dawn. It was a long, dry, easy ride down a canyon that steadily widened until we came to a big natural pond used by a rancho. By then, it was good light and we would be easy to see, but we saw no one anywhere.

Geronimo and Natculbaye talked for a while about whether to risk riding on in the daylight or wait until dark. The trail into the Azul Mountains was about three hands' ride southwest down the canyon where we were resting. They decided to wait until dark because we had to ride past a big rancho that probably had many vaqueros able to chase us. We made a camp in a draw no more than a quarter mile from the pond.

Geronimo pointed me toward the Azul Mountains' peak we could see standing dark and tall in the distance. As high as it was, I wondered if we actually would ride to the top and how the world must look from that vantage point.

CHAPTER 24
TOP OF THE WORLD

To avoid vaqueros seeing us when we passed near the big rancho, we waited until full darkness to leave our little camp. We rode at a steady pace southwest down the big canyon, which had a smooth trail that weaved in and out of the bosque along a river, occasionally disappearing in sand and gravel only to resurface a few hundred yards farther downstream. The trail passed through groves of sycamores, cottonwoods, and willows, which for about three hands slowed us down a little. The canyon ended with a large field butting up against the foothills of tall, black mountains, their jagged high horizon outline blotting out stars. The blackness below the stars scared me. I dreaded moving into the unknown inky blackness but knew we would ride on. The Apaches knew the way, even in the dark, and believed they would be safe high on the mountains.

Small canyons ran southeast and southwest at the end of the big canyon field, where we stopped to rest and water the horses at a small river pool. The streambed, once mostly dry, turned into the southwest canyon, and the water, clear and sparkling in the moonlight, gurgled like a small river as it entered a dense, dark bosque. The dry southeast canyon, its sides covered with a scattering of mesquite, straggly creosotes, cholla, and Spanish dagger, held a dusty road that wagons must have used often, judging from its deep ruts. Geronimo led us into the southeast canyon. For a little while, it ran between the foothills and then turned into another canyon heading southwest. The new canyon bottom was wide and its shallow sides were mostly scattered over with junipers.

Again the bright moonlight made for a fast, easy ride. We came to another wide canyon that we followed southeast until, after about a hand, Geronimo rode up into a brush-filled, steep arroyo filled with junipers and yucca to reach the top of a hill, where we found a trail that wound through the hills, crossing ridges and climbing up their sides in a few places. The trail was mostly downhill and was wide and easy, but where it followed the sides of the ridges, the drop-offs were deep and there would be no coming back if we slid off.

After about a hand's ride, we turned and rode up a narrow arroyo to the top of a low ridge. It startled me to see a big natural spring-fed pool spread out before us. The horses were thirsty and so were we. Geronimo and Natculbaye had decided to rest there until the sun came. It looked to me, as I stared at the black outline of the peak in front of us, that we faced a hard climb in the coming morning. Geronimo and the other men sat and smoked while they waited for She-gha, Juanita, Garditha, and me to take care of the horses and wash before we went to our blankets.

In the time I had been with the Apaches, it had become clear that they had, in nearly all situations, a clear division of who did what jobs. Apache women didn't normally hunt, fight, or raid. Apache men, while they would die defending their women and children and keep them in supplies, weren't about to help the women do their work. We finished taking care of the horses, had a quick wash, and grabbed our blankets, shivering, our breath turning to steam in the cold air lying like a blanket over the foothills. I was glad to wrap in the heavy wool blanket She-gha had given me and quickly fell asleep under a manzanita.

The morning came filled with life. The sun was a good hand

above the horizon formed by the high foothills. Crows called from high overhead as they passed toward the mountains. The air, filled with steam from our breath, smelled of early-morning flowers and good boiling coffee. Our side of the foothills and mountains were still in deep shadows that had kept the sun from disturbing our sleep. Geronimo's morning prayer and song to Ussen while he stood facing the sun on the little hill above the pool had awakened me.

She-gha and Juanita sat hunkered down by a small fire, wrapped in their blankets and watching their coffeepots boil. She-gha saw me sit up and rub the sleep from my eyes. She motioned me over for a cup of coffee and the mix of dried meats, nuts, and berries for the warrior trail everyone ate when there was no cooking.

While I ate, I stared at the tall mountain covered in deep shadow in front of us and wondered how we would ever get to the top and how we would take care of water and grass for the animals once we were there. The Apaches had all been there before and knew the way. Yet I knew from our mountain trips in the past month that with just one slip in the wrong place at the wrong time, one wasn't likely to come back from the mountain. I wondered, *Is all this daring and effort worth it to be free of Mexicans and White Eyes? I don't know, but I do know, as they've taught me, that it's their choice to make.*

We finished the morning meal watching the sun rise higher and then saddled and loaded the horses and rode back to the big canyon the way we had come. Reentering it, we turned southeast toward the big, black mountain we planned to climb. The canyon walls seemed to grow higher and the canyon became narrower the closer we came to the big mountain. Soon we had to ride single file and work through brush that continually pulled at our clothes as the canyon walls grew higher and we climbed the narrow, twisting path. The climb wasn't that hard, but the higher we climbed, the harder it was to breathe. We seemed to be going in a circle around the base of the mountain before dropping down through a small pass between a foothill and the mountain. At the bottom of the pass, we began to climb toward the top of the Azul Mountains.

The ride to the mountaintop was the hardest, scariest ride I've ever had. At first, the trail was a wagon-road wide that, while steep, was easy to follow. It soon crossed the rim of a high canyon, and a little farther along became so steep I thought we would have to get off and lead our ponies. It felt like we were going straight up. The thin air made it hard to breathe, even for my pony. I puffed and blew as if I were running hard. Then came a series of switchbacks through scattered junipers. Sometimes there was only grass and rock in steeply slanted mountain meadows, but always climbing, climbing, gasping-for-air climbing—never-ending, hard climbing. At last we saw the top edge of the mountain a hundred feet above us and pushed on for two or three hundred yards more to reach the top of the world.

We sat our horses and let them blow when we reached the top. I stared in disbelief at the desert's green and tan foothills, chaotic in their wave-like display. We could see in the mid-distance the Cuitaca Mountains, just to the north Cananea, and in the far distance and beyond it the San Jose Mountains. As I turned to look in all directions, I saw foothills that looked like unwashed, wrinkled sheets, great desert valleys, and long ranges of mountains running north to south.

Looking west, I saw the Cibuta Mountains, where I'd watched many Mexicans die in the sights of Geronimo's rifle and those of his warrior brothers, and across a wide valley rose the Pinito Mountains, where the Apaches had hidden their women and children while they raided to the north. Of course,

I didn't recognize those things then—not until I was freed and shown a map did I understand why Geronimo liked this mountaintop as his primary camp. He could see virtually all the major places where he had camped and, with good soldier glasses, could sometimes see the movement of soldiers across a great range.

On the mountaintop, plenty of trees offered firewood, and there were low places with firepits without making them a virtual beacon that could be seen from other high places for miles. Most importantly, there was a good spring, and hand-dug water tanks that held plenty of water from the rain clouds that passed by, and there were one or two springs that burbled out of the rocks just below the summit. Near the firepits, I saw a wickiup frame, then another and another, scattered under the trees. Altogether, there might have been frames for twenty lodges. A little farther on was a rope corral that kept the horses from wandering off the edge to their doom, and there was enough grass to keep them satisfied for at least a couple of weeks.

I helped She-gha unload the packhorses and cover and organize her wickiup before I went off to look for brush and firewood. I was slow moving and felt a little dizzy sometimes from shortness of breath and wondered if I had caught some kind of disease. She-gha grinned when I told her what was happening to me and said it had happened to her. She had learned through a White Eye di-yen that as you went higher above the lowlands of the earth, there was less air and your body had to adjust to it. Unless you were a runner, as most Apaches were, and worked hard to stay in great physical shape, it would take a while to develop the stamina to work hard up high where the air was in short supply.

After She-gha had her things in place and we had gathered all the wood she and Juanita needed for a fire, Garditha showed me the important places on the mountaintop, such as where men took turns watching the canyons and valleys for soldiers, where all the water was, and where food and other supplies were cached in the little caves in the rocks just down from the top. We found a place where we could practice using our slings. Not having practiced since facing the vaqueros, we decided that after he left his pistola rig with his blanket, we needed practice with our slings.

We weren't far from where the men sat smoking and talking. They watched us for a while and nodded. Geronimo called down to us. "We need to find some more vaqueros for you to practice on. Keep working. You get better, Trinidad. Soon, I think."

I was pleased he thought so and tried to throw harder, but I was much wilder and missed my target too often. I decided it was better to throw for accuracy, and I could learn to throw harder as my aim improved. That's what I told Garditha as we quit practice to lead the horses to water. He smiled and nodded. "Trinidad learns quick."

As the sun was about a hand above the horizon, we watched it falling into the mountains. The stars in the high royal-blue sky were already out, but not near the bright golden ball hanging above the glowing horizon. It was a beautiful sunset. I was glad we were up high and safe from unexpected attack by the American or Mexican soldiers and could see the great spread of the star-filled sky and most of the places we had been.

She-gha and Juanita went to a small cave below the camp and dug into a cache of food supplies they had brought the first time they had come to the mountain. That night, we ate dried beef they had cooked in a very tasty stew that included wild potatoes, onions, and herbs I didn't know grew in the desert or were edible. They also had juniper berries, steamed slices of baked and dried mescal that was sweet and syrupy tasting like I remembered molasses, and bread, crunchy and delicious, made from mesquite pods. I ate until I could eat no more. I hadn't realized how hungry I was.

CHAPTER 25
THE REVELATION

We filled our bellies from the big meal the women had made and sat back at ease, holding cups of hot coffee, feeling the warmth of the fire on our legs and faces, and the cold night air on our necks. Geronimo set his coffee to one side and pulled a tobacco pouch beaded in blue and white from his vest pocket. He had White Eye smoking papers too, which he didn't use often. He rolled a cigarette clean and quick with nimble fingers and, putting the rolled paper between his thin lips, lit it with a twig coal from the edge of the fire. He blew smoke to the four directions and then passed it to Natculbaye and Hunlona. Smoking to the four directions always meant discussion of serious business. I leaned forward, watching the shadows dancing on Geronimo's face, and pulled my hair away from my ears, trying to miss nothing he said.

Geronimo finished the cigarette, tossed the remains into the blue and yellow flames surviving in the firepit, spit a bit of tobacco off his lips, and said, "Trinidad, you and Garditha practice your slings well together. We watched you two throw as the sun fell into the mountains. Your accuracy improves by the throw, and Garditha throws as hard as a man. These are good things."

I was surprised and flattered and felt my face turning warm. "I try hard to learn, Grandfather. Garditha is a good teacher. I have learned much from him."

He nodded and his thin lips made a crooked smile. "Are

214

there other things you want to do with Garditha?"

I saw She-gha cast a sharp glance at Geronimo and cover her mouth as if she wanted to speak but wouldn't.

I said, "Garditha is a good friend. His harvests are close to mine. He teaches me Chiricahua ways and helps me learn Apache, and I help him with his Spanish. We work together gathering brush and wood for the fires and sometimes play games he shows me, or we race each other. Sometimes I win, but it is hard to run in a skirt."

Geronimo listened and poked at the fire coals with a yucca stalk while I spoke. I wondered where this talk was going and why it was supposed to be serious business.

"You know, Trinidad, soon Garditha will become a novitiate warrior and you a woman ready to marry. In the times before the reservations, children of your age no longer played together. Girls stayed together with girls, learning what women do, and boys with boys, learning work men do. The Apaches say after her womanhood ceremony, a girl is ready to marry. After a boy serves successfully as a novitiate on at least four raids, other warriors may accept him as a warrior and he is ready to accumulate enough wealth through raiding and war to marry. Do you understand this?"

"Yes, Grandfather, I understand the customs as you describe them. But what have they to do with Garditha and me?"

Geronimo continued to pick at the fire with his yucca stalk and thought for a short time. "If after being courted, a woman agrees to marry, the man offers the family of the woman a good gift for her. If they accept the gift as being worthy of their daughter, then she and her man live together and help support her mother's family. Do you understand all this, Trinidad?"

I wondered why he was telling me all this. It wasn't the way marriage and courtship happened with Mexicans or Anglos, but I didn't see anything wrong with it except they didn't have a padre to say the marriage words to them. I said, "Yes, Grandfather, I understand."

He nodded. "Bueno. Now I tell you something you may not know. The value of the bride gift depends on her value. Many things determine a woman's value—the skills she has, the strength she has, her honesty, how sweet tempered she is, the possibility of her becoming a mother, and . . ." She-gha, her hand still over her mouth, looked at Geronimo and gave a tiny shake of her head, but he ignored her. "And her chastity. Do you understand what I mean by the word 'chastity'?"

I didn't know what the word meant and slowly shook my head. Garditha sat on the other side of the fire, his head bowed, looking at the ground. He knew what Geronimo might say.

Geronimo smiled and nodded. "I thought so, but many times, White Eye women lose their chastity young and unmarried. They are weak women. If you have chastity, it means you have never been in a private place with a man or a boy, doing what married men and women do to make babies. Unmarried Apache women won't even speak to men who talk about such things. Nit'ééhi. They should not. For a girl who is ready to marry, her bride gift is much greater for the family if she is chaste. Even if she is chaste but the People think she is not, her value to her family is less. This is important for both you and Garditha to know and understand. No one around this fire thinks you and Garditha have done or will do anything that makes you less valuable as a woman. But what you do in the future, especially when Naiche and the rest of the band return from Fort Apache, the People will see and talk about. You must do nothing to make the People think less of you and make your value to your family less when a man asks for you. Do you understand my words?"

I nodded, but I was very confused. I didn't yet know exactly what a man and his wife did to make a baby. I remembered Petra had promised to tell me soon what made women have babies. I had never really thought about it. I had seen Petra with her baby and knew she had expected another not long before the Apaches killed her. How did a girl suddenly decide to become a woman and have a womanhood ceremony? I didn't know. *Maybe,* I thought, *She-gha will tell me when we're alone.* Far down the mountain, I heard a wolf howl and I wanted to howl in confusion myself.

Geronimo said, "Nit'ééhi. Now hear me, all. Trinidad and Garditha are good children, nearly grown. They must understand and obey my words. They must not go off by themselves to practice with their slings or play. Let them practice with someone watching like they did today. Let them stay within sight of the camp when they gather wood and brush for fires. For their own good, they must not be alone together anymore. I have said all I have to say."

Everyone around the fire, including me, said, "Nit'ééhi," but I was determined now to learn about how a girl became a woman and what a man and woman did to make a baby. I was a little angry that my friend, even if he was a boy, and I couldn't play without company or others watching because the People might talk. Geronimo spoke like I was already an Apache. I was not an Apache—yet—and I had no idea when I would become one.

My bed was near the blanket-covered door of She-gha's wickiup and close to the fire. I had a good blanket, one that She-gha had given me, but it was cold on the mountaintop, and after all I had heard that night, I had a hard time going to sleep. Lying in my blanket, I listened to the little night animals scurrying among the twigs from the trees over us, the occasional squawk of a night bird, the almost-silent swish of bats darting about to take insects, and yips of coyotes on the south side of the mountain. I was nearly asleep when I decided I needed to talk to She-gha and Garditha about what Geronimo had said.

The rising sun brought life to the camp. Garditha and I gathered wood and brush from within easy sight of the camp and then took the horses to water. I looked at him and smiled a time or two while we worked, but he just looked away. At the morning meal, She-gha seemed to laugh and smile more than usual and Geronimo had little to say except that Natculbaye, Hunlona, and he were going to watch in all directions. "Soon," he said, "I think Naiche and the others come."

She-gha nodded and said, "Juanita, Trinidad, and I will go down the trail to the meadow just below us. I saw a patch of sunflowers ready to gather, and it looked like the tuna in a big prickly pear patch might be ready to harvest. We'll know when we get there. I'll take a pony in case we find a big harvest."

Geronimo, staring off toward the east, drew a deep breath, sighed, nodded, and mumbled, "Ch'ik'eh doleel (Let it be so). Good luck with your gathering. I know we will eat well again when the sun leaves us." He slid a big cartridge into his rifle, and walked toward a spot on the other side of a small grove of trees where he could see north and east through the cold, still air.

I helped Juanita and She-gha straighten up around the fire. Then She-gha took a packhorse out of the corral, brought it to the fire, mounted a pack frame on it, and hung a big carry basket on each side. She strapped on her holstered pistola rig, checked the load with a practiced spin of the chambers, and then led the horse switchbacking down the trail we had climbed to get to the top. We soon came to the large spot covered with sunflowers filled with ripening seeds and, a little farther along, a large patch of prickly pear that showed many ruby-red tuna ripening on the big pads covered with sharp little thorns.

I walked with She-gha through the steep meadow of sunflowers and watched as she looked at the big brown eyes with the spiraling rows of seeds to pick out the ones mature enough for cutting and drying a few days in the sun before they were ready to eat. As we wandered back and forth through the sunflowers and tall grasses, I said, "I want to ask you a question."

She smiled. "Speak. I'll answer if I know."

The breeze came often and in puffs there on the high mountain, making the grass and sunflowers wave up and down as though they were on the surface of big water. I hoped She-gha didn't think I was stupid and ignorant for asking her about what Geronimo said the night before.

"Well, you know how Geronimo said last night that soon I would be a woman and have a womanhood ceremony and be available for marriage."

She-gha frowned a little. "Yes, I heard. I wish he had not spoken of that. You are still young, still a child who should not even worry about such things." She reached and sliced off the tall stem of a flower head nearly ready to drop its seeds and tossed it in the basket I carried.

"But how will I know that I've become a woman? Is there some ceremony done to make a girl a woman? When is it done for girls?"

The sun was warm on our faces, and a puff of breeze grabbed our skirts and whipped them about our legs. She smiled and motioned toward a couple of boulders sitting at the edge of some junipers. "Come, let us sit awhile and speak of how you become a woman." Calling to Juanita, she waved her arm to come join us at the boulder.

We sat side by side and leaned back against the warm stone in the bright sunlight and looked west across the crumpled foothills and lines of mountains in the distance. She-gha turned to Juanita and said, "We all heard what Geronimo said to Trinidad last night. She is young, a good girl who works hard, but she wants to know when she is woman. Today we tell her."

Juanita smiled. "Nit'ééhi. It is only right that she knows."

She-gha said, "So, Trinidad, today I tell the answer to your question. I know you will have many more as you think about what I tell you now. The answer to your question is simple. A girl knows she is a woman when her body is ready to make babies."

I looked from She-gha to Juanita, who was still smiling, and back again. "But . . . but how does a girl know when her body is ready to make babies?"

"There will be blood. And it will come once every moon until you are an old woman, when it decides to come no more. When there is blood, your breasts will grow, and hips fill out. You won't be able to run as you do now, but your body will be ready to make babies with a man of your choosing."

I stared at She-gha, my mind in turmoil. Was she teasing me or telling me the truth? She had never treated me badly or spoken in an evil way. I believed her.

"Where does this blood appear?"

"In your nether parts. You may need to stay in a special woman's house for two or three days when it first comes, but soon it disappears until the next time. You may feel weak and sick when it comes, but you must work if you can, and there are herbs and ceremonies di-yen women know that will help you. When you have blood, you must stay away from men. If they get it on them, their joints will ache and they will suffer. Men know this and will stay away from you at your moon time.

"When you first find your blood, it is a happy time for the People. It shows Ussen has made them a woman from a child. Women have children. Children we always want and need to make us stronger. Her parents tell all a new woman has come. They make her a special dress from the finest of doeskin and celebrate by giving her a great womanhood ceremony that lasts four days. On the fourth day, the new woman's spirit visits with Ussen in the sky, and she becomes White Painted Woman whose gifts and blessings uplift all who ask for them."

Amazed at what I had just learned, my mind no longer registered the great buzzard I had been watching as it wheeled in the air currents below us. I had never imagined such an answer to what I thought was a simple question.

I said, "I would never have thought what you've told me. You're right. I know I'll have many more questions after my mind has taken in all you've told me now. Can we talk again after I think on what you've told me?"

She-gha made the "all is well" sign, swinging her palm in an arc parallel to the ground. "We will speak again when your mind is smooth. Come, we have more food to gather."

CHAPTER 26
GARDITHA SPEAKS

Hunlona took Garditha with him to hunt for deer on the steep, green tree-covered western slopes of the mountain. Geronimo and Natculbaye went to their sentinel nests smelling of tart pine needles they had made for throwing a blanket over to sit or recline on under the trees. It was a comfortable way to keep an eye on far mountains for smoke signals and winding canyon trails leading to the mountain, and for cleaning their weapons.

I helped She-gha and Juanita lay out the sunflower heads we gathered in a sunny spot to dry for a few days. Once dry, pushing the seeds out of the big brown center of the flower was easy. Most of our work after our first gathering day was in preparing the prickly pear fruit, the tuna, for eating as a sweet after a meal. We spent most of the time burning the stickers on the fruit by putting it on a stick and rotating it over the flames. There is an art to roasting tuna to remove the stickers, because the fruit may become burned and ruined if held too long over the fire. Too little time over the flames and the little, hard-to-see thorns are tedious to pick out of your fingers.

After She-gha had told me about becoming a woman, my mind stayed in turmoil, trying to understand what all this meant for me. I knew now, at least, that I couldn't have babies until I became a woman, and I began to understand why Geronimo didn't want Garditha and me playing together and maybe somehow becoming too familiar. There was so much to learn and know. I wondered if Garditha understood what made a girl into a woman or how babies came into a woman's belly.

Hunlona and Garditha came up the trail to the camp in a slow, steady pace soon after the time of shortest shadows. Sweat made big, black damp places on their shirts as they carried a fat, field-dressed doe hung between them on a pole into camp. I was surprised Garditha could carry that much weight up the mountain, but he was strong and getting bigger every day. Hunlona had taken the doe with a bow and arrow to avoid alerting anyone we were nearby with the sound of gunfire. After finishing our tuna work, She-gha and Juanita finished dressing the doe and I helped scrape the hide clean and salt it before rolling it up for tanning later after we left or to cache it in a cave with the food supplies for winter work.

I took a rest after scraping the deer hide and saw Garditha look in my direction. I made an "all is well" sign with my hand close to my skirt so it wasn't obvious. He smiled a little and waved back. I felt better then. My best Apache friend wasn't mad or too embarrassed by Geronimo the night before to acknowledge me. I said to She-gha, "Can Garditha and I go practice with our slings where we were yesterday? You know, where Geronimo, Natculbaye, and Hunlona were watching the trails?"

She-gha smiled, a knowing look in her eyes. "Yes, go. You worked hard today and learned much. Be sure Geronimo sees you when you get there."

I called over to Garditha, "Do you want to practice slings? She-gha says we can go where we were yesterday. Geronimo and Natculbaye are there to watch us."

Garditha, with a big grin, pulled his sling off his belt and waved it. "We go."

★ ★ ★ ★ ★

I grabbed my sling and ran to catch up with him as he walked toward the trees. It was a short walk and climb to where Geronimo and Natculbaye sat in their nests. By walking slowly, Garditha and I would have a little time to talk.

I caught up with him and said, "I learned today how I become a woman. Do you know?"

"You become a woman when you bleed once a moon."

My jaw dropped. "How did you learn that?"

"I asked my uncle two or three harvests ago when we were on the reservation, going to a womanhood ceremony for a girl who had just become a woman. This is a very important ceremony for all Apaches, but especially for the family and girl who becomes a woman. It means for her People that when she marries, her family gets a new man, and when she has a child, new life will come and the band grows stronger. It means for the girl, she can marry when she finds a man she wants. Some girls have no choice in who they marry. Their fathers give them to rich old men for a big bride gift. They don't have to accept the one their father picks, but they usually do because it means their family is given good things by the man who wants her."

"Did you also ask your uncle how babies are made?"

Garditha made a little grin on one side of his face. "Yes, I asked him. I asked him that same day."

"And what did he say?"

"He said babies are made when a man sleeps with his woman."

"I don't understand. How can a woman sleeping with a man give her a baby? Is there some kind of spirit that comes from him when they're asleep? Married people sleep together all the time and don't have babies, just once in a while does a woman have a baby grow in her. Maybe it's because they're so close together under the same blanket? Maybe that's why Apaches don't hug each other in public? The woman will make a baby?"

"I think that's right."

"But White Eyes hug their women a lot in public. So do Mexicans. They don't have babies that often. Why not? Maybe Apaches make babies in a different way than White Eyes."

Garditha shrugged his shoulders. "I don't know, and I don't plan to find out until I get through my novitiate and start thinking about taking a wife."

The new information confused and shocked me. It didn't make a lot of sense to me that babies came just by a man sleeping with a woman. How did that happen? I knew I had to talk to She-gha again. She knew.

We came out of the grove of trees above the camp and walked to the trees where Geronimo and Natculbaye sat. They had cleaned their pistols and rifles and had them gleaming with a thin coat of oil, lying on a blanket between them. Geronimo looked up, squinting against the bright blue of the sky when he saw us, and raised his brows. "Nish'ii', Trinidad and Garditha. You come to sling more stones?"

"Yes, Grandfather, we come to sling where we practiced yesterday. May we do this?"

He nodded. "Stay near where you were yesterday so we see you."

"This we do. Have you seen anyone in the canyons this sun?"

He stuck out his lower lip and shook his head. "No one comes. Maybe too soon for the business Naiche wanted to do.

"Practice hard. Kill many enemies. One day you may need your slings and skills to help the People."

Garditha grinned and said, "Can I use my pistola, then, Grandfather?"

The wrinkles around Geronimo's narrow eye slits crinkled as he said, "Yes, you can use your pistola if you have bullets for it. How many bullets now you have?"

Garditha looked at the ground. "Just one."

"Hmmph. You have many more stones than bullets. Be ready with your stones until you find more bullets."

"This I do, Grandfather."

"Hmmph. Go practice. Show us what you can do."

We left him in a run for the place where we found good smooth stones and could practice with our slings.

Two or three suns drifted by, and Geronimo's little camp was developing a heartbeat's regularity in routine. One of the men hunted with Garditha, and the other two kept watch, mostly north but all around the mountain, for anyone approaching. She-gha, Juanita, and I collected food that grew naturally on the mountain. At first, I didn't care for some of the things the Apaches ate but learned to eat or go hungry.

In the evenings, we gathered around the fire to eat what the women had prepared, the men would smoke, and then Geronimo would tell Garditha and me a Coyote story or two before we wrapped in our blankets. I liked the Coyote stories. They always had a good lesson worth learning. And of course, I thought often of the business about becoming a woman and how women had babies.

The day after Garditha told me how women and their husbands have babies, I was with She-gha and Juanita, picking juniper berries a little down the west side of the mountain where the trees grew close together.

I said, "I asked and Garditha told me how women and their husbands have babies, but it doesn't make sense to me."

She-gha looked at Juanita, who had a crooked little smile and looked away. She-gha said, "What did Garditha say?"

"He said his uncle told him women and their men have babies by sleeping together. That doesn't make sense to me. Men sleep with their wives all the time but don't have babies very often."

She-gha grinned. "What Garditha's uncle told him is true. But you have much light behind your eyes. It is what they do in the blankets before they sleep that makes babies, not when they are asleep."

"That's what I want to know. What do they do?"

"You are still a child and have much to learn about your body. I tell you in a simple way, but you have to understand there is still much to learn. Comprende?"

I nodded, my heart pounding, excited about what I was about to learn, fearful of hearing the unknown.

"Think of it this way. A man carries in his body the seeds for your children. Your body is like the earth. Your man plants his seed in your body, and if the seed is perfect and your body ready, you will make a baby. Comprende?"

I nodded. This certainly made more sense than just sleeping together but was still mysterious. "But how does he put his seed in his wife's body?"

She-gha frowned, thought a moment, and looked at Juanita, who grinned, shook her head, and again looked away. "Have you ever seen horses or cattle mating?"

I had seen horses mating, but I didn't know what it was at the time and was afraid the stallion was trying to hurt the mare until Petra told me that they were just trying to make babies and that the mare was fine. I nodded. "Yes, I've seen a stallion with a mare."

"Nit'ééhi. A man and his wife do something like that or use a different way than the horses use, but the end result is the same. The man plants his seed in his woman to make a baby. As you grow older, you'll learn just how and when this is done. I think you know enough now. Don't you think so?"

I nodded. I knew enough to keep me thinking for a long

time. We went back to picking the juniper berries while I tried to remember the details of how horses mated.

A few more days passed, until one afternoon as the shadows began to grow long, Garditha ran to the fire. He practically yelled, "Ho! Women of the camp. Geronimo and Natculbaye have seen a column of smoke in the Pinito Mountains. They think it is a signal from Naiche. The People come. Two, maybe three suns, they are here."

She-gha said, "I will speak with Geronimo tonight and learn what feasts we should do to welcome Naiche and the People."

We all said, "Nit'ééhi." Good times were coming.

Garditha said, "Trini, you can see the smoke pillar without soldier glasses. Come and see. Bring your sling and we can throw more rocks before dark."

I looked at She-gha and she nodded. We raced to Geronimo's nest. He was using his soldier glasses to study a little white column rising into the sky near the top of the Pinito Mountains. He heard us running up to him, turned, and held out the glasses for me to look where he pointed. With the soldier glasses, what looked no more than a long white dot became a definite column of smoke. He crossed his arms and said, "Naiche comes."

CHAPTER 27
GERONIMO'S TALK WITH TRINIDAD

The day after Naiche's smoke column appeared in the Pinito Mountains, Natculbaye, Hunlona, and Garditha went hunting. The men hunted for deer, and Garditha for small game. We needed the meat to give a feast for Naiche and the fourteen men, twenty women, and four children with him, assuming he had taken none from the reservations. She-gha, Juanita, and I started to leave to gather more berries and nuts and other good things, when Geronimo, who stayed behind to watch the camp and check canyon trails for Mexican and American soldiers, said, "She-gha, I want Trinidad to sit a while and talk with me."

She-gha smiled and motioned with her head for me to go back to the fire where Geronimo sat. My heart raced a little. I had no idea what he wanted to talk about, but I knew I had worked hard and done what they told me. There was no reason for him to beat me or tell me I must do more if I wanted to live with them.

Geronimo motioned for me to sit on his left, which I knew Apaches understood as a place of honor. He took out his tobacco pouch and papers, rolled a cigarette and, after lighting it with splinter from the fire, smoked to the four directions but never offered it to me. After he smoked, he gestured toward the blackened and dented coffeepot and said, "Pour me some more coffee in this old blue and white speckled cup, and you have some too if you want."

I poured our cups of coffee and then took my seat beside him.

He said, "Mujercita, I'm glad I spared you from Yahechul's knife. I thought then maybe I could use you as part of a trade to get my wife, Chee-hash-kish, out of Mexican slavery, or if I couldn't save her, you looked smart enough to be a good slave. It seemed useless to waste a promising child. After I took you, Ussen told me that Chee-hash-kish would never return to me, even though I have tried many times to get her back. I thought then maybe I could trade you back to your family or some other Mexicans for guns and ammunition and other supplies. Soldiers press us hard. We need many bullets.

"You work hard without being beaten, work to learn our tongue, do what we tell you. She-gha is glad you help at her fire. You show courage and spirit. I call you Mujercita, Little Woman, because you are not yet a woman but show strength, courage, and determination like a fine grown woman. You learned to defend yourself and the People with a sling and work to get better with it. You do well playing with and learning from Apache children, and you learn our lifeways. Enjuh."

A puff of wind rolled through the tops of the trees, making the puddles of yellow light on the ground shimmer and wiggle in myriad shapes, before, like a sigh going away, collapsing into the shapes they were before the breeze. I listened with care to the old man, hoping to find some hint of my destiny as he took a long swallow from the battered cup of coffee fast cooling in his small, gnarled hands. I also sipped some coffee, but it was still much hotter than I liked to drink.

Geronimo said, "I don't know where the rest of my family are. Perhaps Naiche will find my wives and children and bring them to me, but probably not. She-gha lost the child we had together, a daughter who seemed sick all the time. She wants to keep and raise you as her daughter. This we have spoken about during our alone time in the blankets. She-gha is a wise woman. I agreed to keep you as our child. When your woman time comes, we will give you a big womanhood ceremony. Then you will be free to choose the man you want. The way you and Garditha play together, maybe you choose him. Maybe not. He is an orphan and has no one to help him, but I see him coming to manhood with great courage and skill."

I didn't know whether to laugh or cry. Geronimo was offering me a great personal honor: to adopt me as a daughter, a member of his family. He expected to treat me well. But I didn't want to run, run, run from soldiers all the time in perpetual war. I didn't want to worry about dodging soldier bullets or being under the ugly, arbitrary control of soldiers. I knew I had to be careful how I answered, and I needed more time to think about what to do.

I said, "Geronimo does me great honor to take me into his family. You already teach me Apache ways and, as a girl and future woman, how I should act around boys and men. She-gha treats me well and we work well together. She already sews me clothes and teaches me skills every Apache woman needs. It's hard to think about forever leaving the kind of life I had with my Aunt Petra and her baby, who the warriors killed, and her husband, who you let live. I'm grateful you spared me and that I'm treated well by the People. You live a life of freedom. I value being free." I thought, *Yes, Grandfather, I want freedom. I haven't lied, but I haven't said I would be your adopted daughter either. I want to live with my own people.*

He smiled, threw out his coffee now grown cold on the pine needles, and said, "Bueno. Pour me more coffee—my daughter. So we begin. First, I tell you the story of how the Apaches began, who your ancestors were in the long-ago times."

I poured his coffee, changed mine, and sat down with him again. "Speak, Father, you know I listen."

An eagle screamed its mastery of the air as it passed just over the treetops above us and then, spiraling in low swoops, hunted down the dark-green mountainside. A small breeze shook the tree limbs throughout the camp and they were still again.

Geronimo took a short swallow of coffee and looked out over the rippling brown and green foothills lying like waves on a big water below us and gray and brown mountains in the far distance. He turned to me and said, "There are many stories you need to hear to learn about the Apaches. Now I tell you only about the very beginning, about Ussen and White Painted Woman, who all women become for a time on the fourth day of their womanhood ceremony. She-gha tells me she has told you of becoming a woman, and when you are no longer a girl?"

I nodded. Geronimo had all my attention.[1]

"In the beginning, only White Painted Woman was with Ussen. His Power created her. She had no mother or father. Ussen sent her to this world, where she lived in a cave. It was a hard life here then. Some say there were no other people—some say there had to be a few other people and that's what the monsters lived on. I think that makes sense. There were four monsters who killed and ate people. There was Owl-man Giant, then Buffalo Monster, the Eagle Monster Family, and Antelope Monster. Owl-man Giant was the worst of the monsters, but once in a while, people got away before he could eat them.

"With White Painted Woman in those days was a boy named Killer of Enemies. He was either her brother or her son. Some stories say one thing, some another. Owl-man Giant liked to torment Killer of Enemies. He liked to be mean to him. He would watch him go hunting and take the meat away from him or mess up anything the boy might be trying to do. But Killer of

1 [Ed. Note. Geronimo's story of White Painted Woman and Child of the Water is based on James L. Haley's story in *Apaches: A Historical and Cultural Portrait.*]

Enemies never fought back at Owl-man Giant. He just cried and let his trophy go. He wasn't much of a fighter, I guess. Times were really hard.

"One day, White Painted Woman was praying to Ussen about it. She heard a Spirit say, 'When it rains, you have to go lie under the place where the rain makes a little waterfall over there. Open your legs and let the water run in on you.' She did that. Lightning struck her four times and she was pregnant."

I thought, *Maybe motherhood isn't for me if that's how you get a baby.*

"The Spirit said, 'You must call the baby Child of the Water,' and she did. After the baby was born, the Spirit came back and said to her, 'If Owl-man Giant finds this baby, he will kill and eat him. He'll look everywhere every day for him. Hide the baby under your fire. Owl-man Giant won't look there. If you can keep this baby till he's old enough to shoot a bow, he'll kill all the monsters. When he asks for a bow, you make him one. Don't worry how young and little he is.'

"White Painted Woman spent a lot of time crying and praying how to keep the baby alive. Like the Spirit told her, she kept him in a hole under the fireplace. Everyday, she took him out to nurse him, clean him up, and play with him. One day, a Spirit told her, 'Hide the baby. Owl-man Giant is coming.' She had just enough time to get Child of the Water under the fire before Owl-man Giant came stomping into camp.

"He said, 'I heard a baby crying. You give him to me so I can eat him.'

"She looked very sad. 'There's no baby here. I made the noise. I'm lonely for a little baby, so I cried like one.'

" 'I don't believe you!' he roared. 'You make that noise for me.' White Painted Woman tried hard, and the noise she made sounded just like the baby. Owl-man Giant said, 'I still don't believe you.' But he left her camp anyway. There are many of these stories. Listen at the fire for them. You will hear all about Owl-man Giant trying to catch her with the baby, but White Painted Woman was always too fast and too smart for him."

Geronimo knew how to tell a good story. I hung on every word. There was a stillness in the air like everything else was listening too. He took a big swallow of coffee, finished his cup, and let it dangle from his finger as he continued the story of Child of the Water.

"As Child of the Water grew into a little boy, he became too big to keep under the fire, so White Painted Woman kept him at the back of her cave. One day, a big thunderstorm came with great lightning and the boom of thunder. Child of the Water ran out to the cave entrance, saw it, and said, 'I want to go kill Owl-man Giant and those other monsters now.' White Painted Woman took him away from the cave entrance and said, 'No. It's too dangerous out there now. Wait longer, till you are bigger.' But Child of the Water went back.

"This happened four times. On the fourth time, Child of the Water pointed outside and said, 'That is my father speaking out there.' When he said that, White Painted Woman took him outside. She said to Lightning, 'Your son knows you.'

"Lightning said, 'How do I know this is my son?'

"She said, 'Test him.'

"Lightning had him stand over to the east, facing west, and black lightning struck him. He stood to the south and blue lightning struck him. In the west, yellow lightning struck him, and white lightning on the north. The lightning did not hurt or frighten Child of the Water at all.

"After he had tested him, Lightning said, 'My son.' Then he told White Painted Woman, 'Let him do what he wants.'

"Soon White Painted Woman made Child of the Water four little arrows of grama grass and a bow. I don't know what kind of wood the bow was, but they still use grama-grass arrows in ceremonies now because that's what White Painted Woman used.

"Child of the Water said, 'I'm going hunting.'

"Until then, Killer of Enemies had killed many deer, but Owl-man Giant had taken the meat of all of them. Child of the Water didn't want Killer of Enemies to hunt with him, but he went anyway.

"Killer of Enemies killed a deer, and they started to cook the meat. Soon they heard Owl-man Giant coming, and Killer of Enemies, afraid, started to cry. Owl-man Giant came and said, 'Ho! You have killed a deer for me. I'm going to eat it.' He took the meat off the fire and put it where he was standing.

"Child of the Water took it back and said, 'You're not going to eat our meat anymore.'

"Owl-man Giant said, 'I ought to kill you right here.' He took the meat back and said, 'I'm going to eat your meat and turn it into dirt.'

"Child of the Water took it back again. He said, 'You've eaten our meat for the last time.'

"The meat changed hands four times with Killer of Enemies sitting there crying."

Geronimo paused a moment, seeming to see the story in his mind. I picked up the coffeepot and raised my brows to ask if he wanted more. He smiled and, flipping his cup up, nodded. I poured him some more and he drank it down. He motioned for me to take more, but I had drunk all I wanted and shook my head. He took another small swallow and continued, waving the cup aggressively like he was Owl-man Giant.

" 'Who do you think you are?' said Owl-man Giant. 'What can you fight with? Show me your arrows.'

"Child of the Water held out his four little grama-grass arrows. Owl-man Giant laughed and took the arrows, looked them over, wiped himself with them, and threw them as far away as he could.

"Child of the Water had to go find them and clean them up. When he returned, he said, 'Let me see your arrows.'

"Owl-man Giant laughed and pointed to a stack of four big logs with sharp points. 'Those are my arrows.' Child of the Water walked over and looked at them. They were too big for him to lift. To get even, he lifted the back of his breechcloth and rubbed his backside on them.

"He said, 'I'm Child of the Water. I'm going to kill all you monsters, beginning with you, right now. We each shoot four times.'

"Owl-man Giant roared with laughter. He said, 'All right, but you have to let me shoot first.'

"Child of the Water said, 'All right.'

"Killer of Enemies was still sitting there, scared and crying.

"Child of the Water stood on the east side, facing west. There was thunder and lightning in the distance. Where he stopped, there was a blue stone at his feet. It said, 'Pick me up. Your father sent me.' Child of the Water picked the blue stone up and held it.

"Owl-man Giant said, 'Get ready now.'

"Child of the Water saw the first big log arrow coming. He waved the blue stone and said, 'Let it pass over my head.' The log passed over his head and shattered on the ground behind him. The next log, he waved the stone and said, 'Let it strike in front of me.' The log shattered on the ground in front of him. When the third log came, he waved the stone and said, 'Let it land on this side,' and it was so. When the fourth arrow came, he waved the stone once more and said, 'Let it land on the other side,' and it happened.

"Then Child of the Water got his bow and little grama-grass arrows. He said to Owl-man Giant, 'Now you hold still.'

"Owl-man Giant answered, 'I'm not afraid.' He was wearing four coats of solid white flint.

"Child of the Water shot his first arrow. Owl-man Giant picked up a stone and said, 'Let it pass over my head.' The arrow hit him right over where his heart was. It blasted one of the flint coats and knocked him over a little hill.

"Child of the Water shot his second arrow. The same thing happened on the second and third arrows as with the first arrow. Now Owl-man Giant had only one more flint coat left. You could see his heart beating under it.

"Child of the Water shot his fourth arrow. Owl-man Giant waved his rock and said, 'Let it pass to the side.' But the arrow shattered the flint coat and went into his heart. It knocked him over a fourth hill, and there he lay dead. You can still see the place today. There are four little hills and piles of flint. We get power from that place."

I said, "Child of the Water's father must have put some great power in those little arrows. Where is the place with the four little hills and piles of flint? I want to see it if you'll let me."

Geronimo smiled and nodded. "Someday Trinidad, I'll show you. It's a sacred place for the Apaches. Now let's see, where was I? Oh yes . . .

"Killer of Enemies stopped crying and was happy. He started to sing:

> We have killed the Giant.
> It will be good now.
> Owl-man Giant, dead he lies there,
> For we have killed him.

"He put some of the meat back on the fire and sat there eating, happy.

"Child of the Water cut off Owl-man Giant's head. It seemed too heavy to lift, but he feinted three times and lifted it on the fourth. He put it on Killer of Enemies' back, and they went home. They took some meat too.

"White Painted Woman had been crying for the two boys, afraid that Owl-man Giant would kill them. When she saw what they brought back, she danced and sang, and gave the woman's trill of approval, the same sound women make today at the Womanhood Ceremonies. It's a loud high cry, like this."

He tilted his head back and trilled in a high tone I didn't know he could make. I tried it, and it sounded a little like his. He grinned and nodded approval.

"Yes, that's right, daughter. You will learn it good. It is a way of celebrating. White Painted Woman's trill was the first time it was done on earth."

I had enjoyed hearing the story about White Painted Woman and thinking I would become like her on the fourth day of my womanhood ceremony. I said, "What happened to the other monsters when Child of the Water went after them?"

"They are good stories. You'll hear them soon enough."

Geronimo tossed his coffee away, looked up the path through the trees where his nest was, and said, "Come, daughter, let us go watch the canyons for a while. Soon She-gha and Juanita and the hunters return."

CHAPTER 28
NAICHE COMES

We had gathered enough food for a feast when Naiche returned with his people, slumped on their horses, faces lined and drawn as if they hadn't slept in a long time. They came in the middle of the afternoon on the day after Geronimo had spoken with me. Naiche rode up to Geronimo, threw a leg over his saddle to slide off his pony, and silently locked arms with the old man in greeting.

She-gha and Juanita passed by the line of dismounting, haggard women, greeting each one with a smile and welcoming words. Garditha welcomed Kanseah, a friend a couple of years older than him but already an advanced novitiate. He helped Kanseah unload the horses as he asked questions about what happened in Arizona. I gave the "all good" sign to Leosanni, who laughed with delight. She was about six and had always been friendly. We ran to help Naiche's wife, Haozinne. Leosanni was staying with their family. Her parents were in the group that had surrendered three months earlier. I never learned how she became separated from them.

Natculbaye and Hunlona passed among the men, greeting them as brothers and offering to take their ponies to the corral nearby. The women unloaded the pack ponies and covered the sapling and branch wickiup frameworks scattered among the trees with canvas to make them comfortable and ready to use.

The feast that night was a good, relaxed time, with the people mixing, laughing, and sharing food and stories of their adventures. Good-natured grumbling and comments about the women not having the corn or time to make a good batch of tizwin passed between the warriors and their leaders. The leaders agreed that some corn taken on the next raid must go for tizwin making, or at least they had to find some good White Eye whiskey.

After eating, the men sat in council around a fire in the middle of the wickiups. The women had cleaned up around their fires and sat listening in the cold darkness wrapped in blankets behind the men. Garditha and I sat there too. Nappi, a warrior who rode with Naiche, and his wife had the youngest child in camp, a two-year old baby. Their baby and Leosanni were both asleep on blankets in wickiups.

Stepping forward, Naiche stood tall in the amber light and dancing shadows and said, "Ho, brothers! We gather here on the mountain where we can see the earth around us, see when enemies come and friends go. We are together again with the great di-yen and my counselor Geronimo and those who ride with him. Let us smoke, and Geronimo will speak to Ussen for us."

They made cigarettes and smoked, and Geronimo stood in the dancing shadows at the edge of the fire's circle of light. He raised his arms and prayed to Ussen, thanking him for the Power that had brought us back together again. When he finished praying, he said, "Hi ye, brothers, our little band had a journey of Power. Shall I tell you of it?"

Naiche said, "Speak, Geronimo. We will listen."

Geronimo said, "When we all left the last camp on Río Santa Cruz, you know that the boy Garditha and the girl Trinidad, one I now call daughter, had used their slings against three vaqueros who would have taken her for ransom and him for his scalp."

There were "hmmms" of acknowledgment among the warriors. I looked up into the star-filled sky to see a cloud drifting across the moon and, not far down the mountain, heard a night bird squawk and a wolf howl.

"Garditha killed one with his sling, and he and Trinidad drove the other two away with hard-thrown stones. Riding away after they tried to attack our children, the two vaqueros who survived their stones swore to come back with their brothers and attack us.

"When the children showed me the vaquero's body and told of the other two who had run away, I recognized one from their descriptions, and the brand on the dead vaquero's horse told me the rancho from where they came in the Cuitaca Mountains. I believed then they would gather their amigos and come after us. On the way to the Pajarito Mountains, we saw two vaqueros watching us and knew they must be following us with more vaqueros behind them."

Geronimo told how the vaqueros followed us out of the Pajarito Mountains, how we ambushed seven of them, killed one and wounded one, and followed them to a Tohono O'odham village, where they left the wounded vaquero, and then how Geronimo had fooled them into following us out into the desert mountains north of Altar.

He described how brave I was when they used me as bait to ambush and kill three. Two vaqueros got away, but the next day, we killed one and captured and burned the one who was a scalp hunter trying to take Garditha and me. There were "hmmms" of approval and shaking fists all around the fire as Geronimo described the burning of the scalp hunter. Then he said, "It took us three suns from the camp in the Altar desert country to reach this camp, and we have waited a few suns watching for our brothers to hear of their journey. Now you are here. Speak. We will listen."

Naiche rose to stand at the edge of the firelight circle. Tall and lanky, almost swaybacked, with high cheekbones and long hair, he was an imposing man. "I speak for those who journeyed north with me to learn of our families who had disappeared. Even now, some of our People we hid from the Bluecoats don't know all we did.

"We left the canyon where we last camped together and raced for the place where I planned to meet Atelnietze in the Dragoon Mountains. Anyone we found on the way, we killed to hide our path. And we raided ranchos and mines for supplies and ammunition. A White Eye posse surprised us at an evening meal in the Rincon Mountains and took back a young boy—of maybe seven harvests—we had taken in a raid earlier that day. I took five warriors with me to meet Atelnietze and sent the rest to take the women and children back toward the border and protect them."

Nearly everyone in the group, including me, leaned forward to listen closely to the soft-spoken Naiche as he described hiding out near the junction of Bonito Creek with Río Negro.

"That night, we left our horses in a meadow and hid our saddles and supplies in nearby trees and bushes next to a canyon ridge. Then we ran the rest of the way to the Chiricahua camps at Fort Apache. I managed to get in the camp alone and saw the people of my wife, Haozinne, my mother, Dos-teh-seh, and other relatives. I spoke with one of the men and learned Nant'an Lpah had sent our close families away. He said it was true the big Bluecoat chief sent Nant'an Lpah away and that Nant'an Miles is leader now. Miles does not use Chiricahua scouts, only a few Apaches for trailing. I was glad to hear this, but he also said the new nantan was offering much money for Geronimo's scalp and less for warriors with him. I left the Chiricahua camps. I was not happy no one knew where our families had been sent and that the new nantan, like a Mexican *jefe*, was offering money for scalps to catch us."

The fire was growing low, and a woman came forward to feed it more brush and wood. It flared up in orange and yellow light, making deep shadows on Naiche's face. He stepped back from the flames' heat and continued.

"The next night, Dos-teh-seh and Et-tso-hnn, the mother of Yahechul, who was with me, brought me a message from Nantan Miles. He said he would treat us justly if we came in. I don't know what this 'treat us justly' means. We spoke of camp news, and then I sent them back to their camp.

"The next morning, we went to take our saddles and supplies out of the trees and brush where we left them, but Bluecoats had found them and nearly ambushed us. We got away and came back to try to learn more and maybe take back some of our equipment. The nantan sent Dos-teh-seh and Et-tso-hnn out to find us again. He gave them other terms for us to consider if we agreed to come in and surrender. We saw Dos-teh-seh and Et-tso-hnn coming that night even though there was little moonlight.

"I spoke to them from the shadows where they could not see me. I told Dos-teh-seh we narrowly missed a Bluecoat ambush and were then very careful to avoid the Bluecoats. I heard the nantan's new terms and thought he was playing with us. I did not trust him or my mother. We disappeared, raided some ranches for horses and supplies, and went back to the Rincon Mountains for our women and children, but they had already headed for the border. The men in charge of our women and children feared the many Bluecoats crossing the land might find them before we returned.

"Before we crossed the border and as the sun disappeared, we spotted Bluecoats at the same time they saw us near the Mowry Mine. We left the livestock and supplies we had taken and headed south, rested at our old camp on Río Santa Cruz, and then came on here, where we are happy to see our brothers. That is all I have to say."

Again, there were "hmmms" of approval among the men, but the women looked at each other with sad, weary eyes. I remembered visiting the women with She-gha and how they spoke of how tired they were of doing without, running at a moment's notice, and having little time to make a comfortable place for their families or how long it would be before they could plant their gardens or even when they had more food or could mend clothes or plan to have babies. Run, hide, fight, rest a little and do it all again was wearing them down.

I thought, *Is this the life a daughter of Geronimo can expect?* When the council broke up, I was yawning and didn't stare long at the stars through the black fingers of the tree branches over us before I fell into a sleep with no dreams.

The next day, some of the men helped the women bring in supplies they had cached in caves just below the mountaintop, and some went hunting down the heavily wooded western side of the mountain. Naiche studied the canyon trails with Geronimo and Natculbaye, looking for signs of Bluecoat soldiers he believed were not more than a day or two behind him. But they saw nothing. They strained their eyes the next sunrise, using soldier glasses most of the morning to watch the area of the Pinito Mountains where Naiche had been.

Near the time of shortest shadows, Naiche pointed a little east of the Pinito Mountains. There, the dust from horses rising high in the air seemed to hang there for a while like Naiche's smoke we had seen a few days earlier. Then they saw dust from two more columns that seemed to move toward the one near where Naiche had sent his smoke. Three columns? Nantan Miles must have thought he had enough experienced men and supplies now to catch us.

I went with She-gha as she wandered about the camp and talked to the women. Many wanted to quit the fighting and go back to Fort Apache. Others admitted that they had lost valuable supplies in their last encounter with the Bluecoats and now the men needed to raid to get more. However, a raid now might lead the Bluecoats to the camp on top of the mountain with only a very steep way down for escape. As the sun moved farther away from the time of shortest shadows, Geronimo and Naiche spoke together under Geronimo's tree, from where they watched.

The People gathered near Geronimo and Natculbaye's nests as the sun hung low over the horizon. A small fire lighted in a deep firepit produced very little smoke or light. The men rolled their cigarettes and smoked. Geronimo prayed to Ussen, and the second council in less than two days began.

Naiche said, "We see signs of three Bluecoat columns in the Pinito Mountains where we were not four days ago. If they have scouts, they will surely find this place. It will take them a few days to follow my band's trail to where we are. The women say our supplies run low and the men need to raid for more. Shall we move on or fight them here? What do the warriors think we should we do?"

The face of every warrior and those of most of the women wrinkled in thought. Geronimo waited and looked at every face before he spoke. He said, "The Bluecoats with their turncoat scouts will not be here for maybe another three or four suns. We are running out of supplies and will be trapped if we fight from here."

He pointed to the range of foothills and tall, brown and green mountains to the southwest. "The Madera Mountains yonder have good cover and water and easy access to ranches that can be raided in the valley of the Río Magdalena. I think we need to move over there. A camp in those mountains will have many more ways to escape."

I saw the men weren't frowning anymore and the women were slowly nodding agreement. Naiche looked around the group and said, "Geronimo speaks wise words." He pointed in the same direction Geronimo had. "I think we must move to a camp yonder in the Madera Mountains. I say we leave this mountain next dawn, when we will be in the shadows of the rising sun, where the Bluecoats and their scouts can't see us even if they are nearby. If they come up this mountain after us, it will give us an extra day to disappear into the Madera Mountains."

The men all nodded and, as if with one voice, said, "*Ch'ik'eh doleel* (let it be so)."

CHAPTER 29
THE MADERA MOUNTAINS

She-gha shook me awake deep in the night and motioned it was time to go. I shivered while I pulled on my moccasins in the warmth of my blanket under an endless spread of brilliant stars and the milk river that swept across the sky. She told me to drink some coffee at the little fire she had built for us and to stay warm. We were leaving soon. There would be little to eat until we reached the Madera Mountains, west down this mountain and across the foothills to a wide canyon running between the Madera and Azul Mountains.

The People led their horses down from the top of the mountain to the end of the trail we had followed coming up, and there we waited for the dawn. Slow and sure, the gray light came, and then there was sunlight on the Madera Mountains and deep shadows on the trail down our mountains and on the foothills below.

At Naiche's signal, the men leaped on their ponies, and women and children mounted and followed him and Geronimo down the north ridge. The steep trail led down through thick stands of junipers and a few scattered piñons. The horses had secure footing on this trail and moved through the trees without hesitating. We kept a sharp lookout to avoid boughs hanging hidden in the inky black shadows slapping us in the face. In the mix of shadows and gray light, it was scary and strange to ride in darkness on our mountain but to see the places of golden sunlight on the far Madera ones.

Down in the foothills, with the sun above the horizon, we followed twisting canyons still in the shadows of the morning. The canyons fell toward the west and grew progressively wider until we were in a wide canyon that led directly into a much wider, shallow canyon running north to south next to the Madera Mountains. We turned south in the big shallow canyon and then in a few hundred yards turned west to climb a Madera Mountains canyon, filled with trees, that led toward the top of the mountain. It was before the time of smallest shadows, and the trail we followed to get there was much easier than the one we had followed to get up to the Azul Mountains camp.

We followed a dry streambed through thick stands of junipers until about a hand after the time of shortest shadows and stopped at a spring leaking out of the rocks on a flat place where the trees gave good cover but weren't too thick for a camp. The women began making small fires to cook, and the men roped in a place for the horses to graze in a little meadow in an open place the trees had not yet captured.

I was quick to gather wood and brush for She-gha's fire and helped her roast a piece of venison she had saved from the night before. The fires, built under the trees, ensured we didn't generate easy-to-see smoke. She-gha laid out prickly pear tunas for us to nibble while the meat cooked over the fire. I liked venison but wished we had a piece of beef. Beef had a better flavor and seemed to give me strength longer than venison.

Geronimo came to the fire before the venison was ready. He sat and ate the tunas, not saying much, his eyes focused far away. After She-gha gave him meat in a gourd, his attention returned to the camp and he ate, looking around at those gathered by other fires. It was a quiet, peaceful time, almost easy to forget soldiers were hunting us.

Once more, my curiosity overcame my natural shyness. I

said, "Grandfather, what do you think we should do?"

He squinted his eyes, adding even more wrinkles to his bold, unforgiving face, as if saying he didn't know. At our fire, we had a clear view back down the canyon and out across the foothills to the mountain towering in the distance where we had camped the night before.

Sucking a piece of meat out of his teeth, he said, "I don't know. I must ask my Power to show us." Geronimo stood and began to sing a ceremonial song that made everyone look in our direction. He held his arms out straight with the palms of his hands out and slowly started to turn as he sang. He made two full circles this way. He stopped when facing the north end of the slope up the mountain we had just come down and, holding his palms up in that direction, waited and then nodded. Lowering his arms, he showed me his palms. They were red, as if he had been holding something hot.

I saw people around their fires lean forward to stare at his hands and then look at each other after they saw them. He said, "Daughter, this is a gift of Power that I have. My hands grow warm when they pass the direction from which enemies come. My Power says enemies approach the north slope of our mountain camp. I have seen them with my Power. They are many. Forty Bluecoats and twenty scouts—three times the men we have. They come to this place next sun."

She-gha had her hand over her mouth, frowning. She had no doubt what was coming. I didn't doubt that what I had just witnessed was some kind of supernatural event. Geronimo was a di-yen of great Power, after all. Still, the only thing I had seen with my own eyes was how red his palms got when he held them in the direction he claimed for the soldiers and scouts.

He left our fire and spoke with Naiche, who then sent Garditha and Kanseah to call the warriors to a council. Naiche's wife and mother-in-law moved back from the fire to make room for the men to gather in council. Soon the warriors were sitting together in a big circle around Haozinne's little fire, and the women and children sat as a group behind them.

They smoked and then Naiche stood, crossed his arms, and swept a look around the circle, meeting the eyes of each warrior. He said, "Geronimo's Power has spoken. Speak to us of what your Power says, Geronimo. We listen."

Geronimo also looked at each face around the circle before he said, "My Power says the Bluecoats—forty soldiers, twenty scouts—are on the north slope of the mountain we left yesterday. They will be in this place late next sun."

The warriors looked at each other, frowns of concern beginning to form. A cool breeze filled with the tart smell of pines blew down the canyon through the trees. I poked with a twig at a big blue-colored beetle making its way to a dusty, sunny spot on the other side of the council circle. It had a big curved horn on the armor behind its head and staggered through the pine straw covering the ground where the women sat. I wished I had protection like that beetle. It didn't fear rising up on its back legs to fight as I toyed with it using a twig.

I remembered a beetle like this one when we waited to ambush the vaqueros at the water tank on the way to Altar and thought, *Perhaps beetles like this are my messengers. But what's the message?*

Naiche said, "Brothers! We know the Bluecoats and their Apache scouts are not more than a day or two behind us. What should we do? Fight, run, hide?"

Atelnietze stood and crossed his arms, his voice filled with thunder and lightning. "I have fought the Bluecoats with a few men and driven them off, fooled them often, and killed a few in ambushes. Now Geronimo says they have the help of many scouts, not just trailers.

"I say we should fight. Take the women and children to a

high camp in the mountains here and return to ambush the Bluecoats and their scouts in this place. Maybe we wipe them out, maybe not, but if not, wound them so they return across the border for more soldiers and resupply for ammunition. We can take their supply train that carries more than we need now and disappear in this country where they can never find us. Maybe we go to one of Juh's old strongholds. I say fight and then hide. That is all I have to say."

As Atelnietze sat down, there were nods and "hmmms" around the circle, but a few of the older warriors shook their heads.

Geronimo spread his arms, palms up. "Atelnietze is a great war leader and does well fighting the Bluecoats. I ask him to consider what my Power says and if he still wants this fight. The Bluecoats have nearly as many scouts as we have warriors. The Bluecoat soldiers are twice as many as their scouts. They have fought us before. We will be lucky if we surprise them with an ambush. If we do surprise them, there are so many that we will surely lose warriors. Even if it is only one warrior—I think there will be many more killed or wounded—that is one less warrior we have to help us fight in the future, one less to protect our women and children. I have fought the White Eyes and Mexicans many harvests. I say we are better off not to risk the lives of our men now and live to fight another sun."

Atelnietze shrugged his shoulders. "Geronimo is a wise warrior. What does he say we do? Will Naiche agree? What do the rest of the warriors say?"

An old man, but looking younger than Geronimo—his name was Beshe, and he was the father of Naiche's wife, Haozinne—stood and said, "Let us hear what Geronimo has to say before we lose more time talking."

Naiche said, "As chief, I have given my war powers to

Geronimo. He speaks for me. Let him tell us what he thinks we should do."

There were mutters of "Doo dat'éé da" (It's okay) around the circle, and Atelnietze nodded.

Geronimo said, "Warriors, hear me. Let us divide into three groups. Either the Bluecoats will divide to follow each group and thus become weaker, or they will stay together and two of the three groups will have room and time to disappear. Smaller bands are much harder to follow, and we will not have to make big raids to feed ourselves that draw the attention of the Bluecoats. In a moon, let us meet at the camp near where the Río Aros meets the Río Yaqui.

"If Natculbaye and Hunlona agree, I will take them, our wives, and the children Trinidad and Garditha with me. We rode well together, and we proved our strength killing vaqueros who followed us into the desert north of Altar.

"I think Atelnietze should take eight warriors and their women, and Naiche take six warriors and their women, the novitiate Kanseah, the child Leosanni, and Nappi with his baby. Maybe there is a better division than what I suggest. If you think there is, then say so."

It was quiet around the circle of warriors as each man thought over what Geronimo had proposed. Most nodded to themselves right away. Others looked toward Atelnietze, who said, "Geronimo is a wise warrior. I say follow what he says."

A sigh of relief seemed to flow from every man and woman at the council.

Naiche said, "Nit'ééhi. We will follow Geronimo's way. I will make camp to the south of here in the Cucurpé Mountains."

Geronimo nodded and said, "Then I will go with Naiche as far as Cucurpé, then go east before turning north and then south toward the Ríos Aros and Yaqui. Naiche can continue on southeast from the mountains. Naiche and I together will look like the largest band to the scouts, and they will follow us. Atelnietze can lead his band northeast from here and watch for a few scouts following them. In a canyon somewhere, he can put an end to them."

Atelnietze nodded and said, "Enjuh. We go."

The beetle I had played with during the council had managed to disappear into the brush. With the decision to move on and break into three groups, I knew a lot of riding and work were in front of us if we were also to disappear.

The women were quick to repack and load the horses. I had no reluctance to ride with Geronimo's group. We had worked well together in the Altar desert country. I knew Geronimo and Shegha wanted me to stay with them, and I was glad to ride with Garditha again. But my life with Geronimo had become one of run, run, run. I was beginning to understand why the women had grown tired of it. It was a hard life, one I wanted to get away from but didn't know how.

After watering the horses and loading pack animals, we began the trek back down the canyon. At the big canyon, the eastern edge of the Madera Mountains, we turned south, staying on the east side next to the foothills we had left early in the day. We soon came to another wide canyon running east, and Atelnietze and his group left us to ride up this canyon that headed across the foothills that appeared to lead to the south of our mountaintop camp.

Naiche and Geronimo continued on down the big canyon filled with large green fields far from being harvest-ready. I could tell from occasional long, wide swaths of sand and pebbles where the water had run that this canyon probably carried a lot of water during the monsoons. I didn't see any standing water pools as we rode into the evening dusk. We avoided ranchos where vaqueros might see us. It was strange to be with so many people and to hear so little noise. We were like a cloud of ghosts.

CHAPTER 30
ACROSS THE RANCHO AGUA FRÍA

After the band led by Atelnietze left, we rode south in the wide, shallow canyon down the edge of the Madera Mountains toward the village of Cucurpé. As falling sunlight painted the clouds over the mountains in brilliant oranges, golds, and reds, and turned canyons around us deep purple, we began to find pools of standing water like pearls on a common thread. She-gha told me this was the beginning of the río the Mexicans called San Miguel.

Since we hadn't seen anyone as the sun began hiding behind the mountains, we stopped to rest the horses and let them water by one of the biggest pools we had yet found. It was nearly dark, and the frogs and insects made a loud chorus as cool air came from the mountains and found us. A more peaceful time I couldn't remember. Geronimo and Naiche waited until the full moon floated above mountains to the northeast before we moved on.

The moon, with its bright white light, and the cool mountain air let us ride faster than we would have under the sun. Soon we saw distant twinkles of lights from the village Cucurpé. By now, the Río San Miguel ran as a continuous stream. Geronimo and Naiche kept riding toward Cucurpé until a second river flowing from the east joined Río San Miguel. I heard one of the men say the Mexicans called this river Río Dolores, and that it flowed past the Agua Fría hacienda.

We followed Río Dolores up a winding canyon with high

255

walls and many arroyo trails leading south or north slicing into them. We rode for maybe two hands in the bright moonlight shadows, staying in or close to the river's flow, making us practically impossible to track.

After a hand more of riding, the canyon spread out and became rolling llano to the south, and foothills surrounding a tall mountain were black and outlined against the stars to the north. Far down the river, we saw a flickering light or two. I knew there must be a village or a great hacienda there. I considered trying to ride away in the dark but knew I'd never make it to the hacienda at this distance before the Apaches caught and killed or punished me. If we continued on down the river, I might yet be able to make a dash for the hacienda. I just had to be patient, but then we left the river and rode south across a high plateau, a part of the rolling llano.

From the plateau, we had a spectacular view of the llano drenched in moonlight all the way to the hacienda and beyond. I could even see moonlight sparkling on the river near the lights of the hacienda or village. Scattered across the llano, we could see little flickering fires like orange stars and herds of cattle, looking like dark clouds on a ground-borne sky. The vaqueros were riding night watches on small groups of the great hacienda herd on both sides of the river.

I might have been able to reach one of those fires if I had tried to escape, but again my mind warned, *Patience, patience.* I knew the Apaches might wipe out every man around that fire if I ran to it. The taste of disappointment soured in my mouth as I realized my escape was so near but so far away.

Naiche and Geronimo studied where the fires were and then decided on their best paths. They would travel east past the cattle and the vaqueros at which point Naiche would turn south and follow one of many trails across the llano toward far, high mountains, while Geronimo would cross the Río Dolores to the east and then head north up the river before turning back south. They thought the apparent reversal of directions would confuse the Bluecoat scouts behind us. Naiche and Geronimo decided to rest the band on top of the plateau where we had stopped and then leave separately near dawn so they could easily see and avoid the vaqueros and cattle near the smoke plumes from the little night fires.

She-gha helped me unsaddle our ponies and hobble them to graze before I found a juniper tree to sleep under, wrapped in my blanket. She and Geronimo soon joined me. Very tired, I was practically asleep as soon as I lay down. I was lucky we stopped when we did. Coming down the river, I had a hard time staying awake and had to concentrate, knowing that if I went to sleep, I'd fall off and land in the cold river water. Then I'd ride in freezing wet clothes, the People would tease me for days, and maybe I'd get sick.

When gold and brilliant white started to light the mountains to the east, She-gha tapped me awake with the toe of her moccasin. We rode south down off the plateau to the rolling llano hills, avoiding vaqueros watching over cattle, but still close enough to hear the occasional bellows of cattle being herded on the other side of the hills.

It was much warmer out on the morning foothills of the llano than on the high mountain where we had been two nights before. Riding slowly and carefully during a couple of hands against the horizon, I was almost asleep in the saddle when my pony stopped and snorted, jerking me awake. I realized Naiche and Geronimo had stopped, and there were men off their ponies looking around the nearby ground.

Naiche made an arm signal to stop and rest horses for a while, and the band moved over to a stand of pines along a low, steep ridge. After telling me there was a pond nearby if I wanted to wash, She-gha found a comfortable grassy spot for our blankets, and Natculbaye and Juanita, Hunlona, and Garditha lay down nearby on theirs. I could see the horses drinking around the pond but decided I would sleep first and wash before we left. I lay back on a heavy blanket in the dry grass, feeling and hearing it crunch as my body pushed it flat. Sleep had been stalking me since we had ridden down on to the llano, and it came quickly.

The rising sun was bright in my eyes when She-gha nudged me awake after the short respite, and the rest of the band began stirring. The horses had been unhobbled and brought in for their saddles. I found my way to the little pond and, squatting at the edge of the pool, washed my face and lower arms. The water was cool and bracing and snapped me fully awake. Women were filling up their water bags and washing too.

When I returned to where we napped, She-gha had finished saddling her horse and was ready to help me with mine. Our routine had developed naturally. I wasn't tall enough to easily put the blanket and saddle on my pony. She-gha put them in place for me and then left it to me to tighten cinches, which I was strong enough to do. The first two or three times we did this, she showed me tricks on how to get the cinches good and snug so that my saddle always rode well with no complaints from my pony.

She handed me her bag of warrior food and nodded that I should eat. There were no fires, and I missed my cup of coffee, but the mix of good things out of the desert's pantry woke me up and I was soon ready to go.

Off to one side of the camp, Geronimo, Naiche, and the warriors talked and drew lines in the dirt that I guessed must be map-like drawings of the routes they would take. She-gha brought me out of my curious stare at what the men were doing when she said, "Go over in the brush on the other side of the water tank and do your personal business before we go. You know Geronimo won't stop once we're on the trail. Go, and make it quick."

There was a brush thicket on the far side of the water tank that the women had been using. The men had been going on the other side of the little ridge from where we rested. I found a place, did what I needed to do, and walked out of the brush to discover I was face-to-face with a big cow that had wandered up to the pond. Her ears were up, and she swung her head from side to side as she watched me. She had a big set of long horns, together more than half again longer than I was tall. I thought, *God help anybody who's spiked by one of those horns.*

A calf—brown and shiny from where she had been licking him, wanting his breakfast, his tail swishing back and forth— stood nearby making noises like I might make if I held my nose and went, "Maaauh, maaauh." I had been around Artisan's cattle enough to know the cow was angry and ready to use those horns. She stamped the ground in front of her and bellowed at me as she lowered her head in warning feints a couple of times. I knew she could easily outrun me and was in no mood for negotiations. Nor would she be easy to run off.

What happened next unfolded slowly, like in a dream, but I know it actually happened in a flash. With an angry bellow that made my ears ring, tilting her head from side to side, intending to use one of those huge horns, she trotted toward me. I didn't move, trying to decide which way to jump when she reached me. Jumping to the wrong side meant I would be dead, an enormous horn spiking me. Bellowing again, she picked up speed into a full-blown charge, forty paces away, thirty, twenty. She dipped and seemed to favor her right horn. I waited until the last second to jump to the left.

The sharp crack of a rifle tore the air. The cow's knees

buckled, and her head hit the ground in a cloud of dust. Her forward motion would have carried her much closer, maybe even over the top of me, had her horn on the right side not dug into the ground and made an efficient brake. When she came to a stop, she was within four or five paces of me. My knees felt like water. I tasted stuff from my stomach, and I needed to run back to my private place in the brush. But I couldn't move. The calf, calling to its mother, ran up nosing around her udder, trying to nurse.

The Apaches, shaking their arms high, gave a low shout of "Hi yeh!"

I looked to see who had saved my life. Geronimo was loading a new cartridge into his old rifle, smoke still curling from its barrel. Three times the old man had saved me: once from having my throat cut; once from vaqueros who might ransom, rape, or scalp me; and now from an angry cow.

He said, "Ho! Brothers. Did you see how brave my daughter was?" I wanted to run away. I hadn't been brave, just frozen with fear, almost afraid to jump. Men and women came up to touch me and nod. They wanted some of my Power, but I had none to give. A warrior stepped up and, in a swift, strong swing with his war club, struck the calf between the eyes, forever ending its need to nurse. The same warrior stabbed the cow through the throat and then the calf to let them bleed out and motioned toward the women, saying, "Meat is here, come take what you need."

The butchering was ugly. The women, in a hurry to get some cuts of meat, used an axe. She-gha and Juanita got some rib meat, washed it, wrapped it in a wet cloth and squeezed red water from it, and loaded it on their packhorses so it wouldn't drain and leave an easy-to-follow trail. When the hacienda vaqueros found the cow and its calf, if any remained after the buzzards and coyotes came, we needed to be long gone.

The last time I saw Naiche's band, they were riding toward a southeast canyon into the mountains east of Cucurpé. Staying low in the arroyos winding through the foothills, always watchful against surprise by vaqueros, Natculbaye led Geronimo's little band toward the eastern mountains. Behind a high hill, we came to another water tank surrounded by paloverdes and stopped to water the horses. Geronimo and Natculbaye climbed to the top of the hill to use their soldier glasses. They could see the Agua Fría hacienda far to the north and the wide canyon nearby that probably took the Río Dolores runoff. They came back and told us to rest the horses. The remainder of the day would be a long ride with little water.

I found a place in the brush to lie down, when I felt someone touch my arm. I turned and saw Garditha. He grinned and said, "Let me have a little of your Power, mujercita. I need it."

I made a face, squinting like I had heard an insult, and we both laughed. He had his pistola with one good bullet hanging over his shoulder and his sling handy, hanging from his breechcloth belt. I pulled my sling out of my dress pocket and shook it at him.

He said, "Gonit'éé (That's fine)," as he walked away to find a good resting place under the trees.

I lay on my blanket a little while, watching the shadows grow short and listening to the insects as the sun marched toward its midday high. The next thing I knew, She-gha was again tapping me on the foot and saying it was time to travel. Natculbaye led us down a well-used trail toward the canyon he and Geronimo had studied from the top of the hill. They had not seen any hacienda vaqueros, but still took care that we would be hard to see passing through the brush near the trail we paralleled.

We came to the wide, shallow canyon where the river ran and paused to rest the horses. Hunlona made sure no one saw us crossing by riding up and down the river to find anyone nearby. He was soon back, saying he hadn't even seen any cattle.

Natculbaye led us across the canyon and up a trail into the rolling foothills on the other side.

CHAPTER 31
THE LAST CAMP

Natculbaye led us east after crossing the Río Dolores and up across what seemed like giant stairsteps, each step a small plateau that led to another step, all crossed by arroyos draining into the Río Dolores going south. Natculbaye and Geronimo seemed to be in no hurry, taking their time to stay out of sight of vaqueros. By midday, Natculbaye entered a wide, shallow canyon running northwest to southeast and turned northwest almost in a straight line toward the big mountain across the Río Dolores. The top of the mountain we had left the day before was easy to see in the far distance.

As the sun fell into the southern mountains, we came to the Río Dolores again and followed it north. We could see great rippling slabs of white rock that seemed to float on the llano like lumps of wood floating in a river, covering the land up the río. I had never seen anything like it. As the long shadows of dusk reached us, we came to a small canyon entering Río Dolores from the east. We turned up this canyon and, in a few hundred yards, found a good place to camp under trees with a small creek running through them draining down to the river.

We hurried to dig a little firepit and make a fire while there was still some light. Garditha and I moved up and down the creek, gathering wood and brush for the fire, while Juanita and She-gha unloaded the horses and began preparing the meat we had carried all day, cut from the cow Geronimo had killed.

The men climbed to the rim of the canyon to use their soldier glasses to learn where we were in terms of the hacienda. When they climbed back down, they said they could see its lights far down the river. Geronimo said he thought we would be safe here unless a vaquero, riding downriver at night, found us. When he saw Garditha and me frowning with concern, he laughed. "We are safe this night."

Juanita and She-gha hung the meat they had sliced into chunks to cook over the fire, made mesquite bread, steamed dried-mescal slices, and boiled wild potatoes together with some green leafy plants they had picked along the trail. They also dug out a bag of sunflower seeds to nibble on, and there was fine black coffee mixed with ground roasted piñon nuts. It was a great meal, none better. I helped the women straighten up after we had eaten. The men rolled cigarettes and smoked and waited for us to listen in on their council.

When we sat down in the circle of firelight, Geronimo said, "We have good wives and children here with us. The meal tonight was good and filling. Very tasty.

"I worry that vaqueros may attack us when they find the cow I had to kill. They hang their own men who take cattle not of their brand. I think it foolish that Mexicans and Americans would make war over such things." Nodding toward Hunlona and Natculbaye, he said, "What do you think we should do to stand against vaqueros who might come after us?"

Natculbaye said, "Geronimo's Power gives him eyes to see. We are too few to stand and fight if there are many vaqueros. They are afraid to send only a few fighting men against a few Apaches. They will send many. We need to stay out of their way if we can. If we must fight many, then I say let us carry full bullet belts and wait for them in ambush."

Hunlona said, "Geronimo and Natculbaye are wise and full of years. I follow what they say we should do."

Geronimo looked at the women and said, "What does She-gha say? What does Juanita say?"

Juanita, her eyes bright and shining, nodded and said, "Women always want to help their men. I want to help in the fight. When their men are away, women guard and protect their camps. We can fight. I say She-gha and I will wear our pistolas all the time now. I have mine in my things but need ammunition for it. That is all I have to say."

She-gha crossed her arms and nodded. "Yes, I also want to fight. Geronimo knows I shoot well with rifle and pistola. He showed me how. I will fight, but I say we need to avoid fighting or expect to see our people after riding the ghost pony to the Happy Place. Don't give the children weapons. If the vaqueros see them, they are happy for any reason to kill those who are young. That is all I have to say."

Geronimo nodded and shook his fist. "Our women speak wise words. Enjuh. We are few but have great Power from Ussen. The women should wear their pistolas all the time when the sun comes tomorrow. I will give them bullets from my sack. Let the children use their slings. Garditha must hide his pistola. He is a target using it.

"Trinidad has no pistola, but she is a mujercita, like a full-grown woman, very brave, and speaks the Spanish tongue. A stray bullet in a fight might kill her—otherwise, she lives. She does not know how to use a pistola. I will protect her. Soon I think she has a womanhood ceremony. This my Power tells me."

I bowed my head and said, "Thank you, Grandfather. You honor me." Inside, I trembled. Geronimo already thought of me as an Apache girl. I owed him my life three times over. I wondered, *Must I become an Apache because he kept me alive? It seems the right thing to do. But it's my life. It's my choice. I thought after they killed Petra and Andy, even if sparing me, that I had to escape. Now I'm not so sure it's the right thing to do.*

Geronimo spoke of the trails he planned to use to reach the camping place where the Río Aros and Río Yaqui meet. He said that he hoped Naiche and his band would go on fighting by our sides after we met them there—although he knew many of the women were tired of running from soldiers and the hard life in Mexico and might push their husbands to surrender. I knew what Geronimo said was true. I'd heard the Naiche women say so. Did they think life under the Americans would be easier? Would they push for surrender? I don't think anyone on Geronimo's side knew what Naiche's people would do. I knew Geronimo would never surrender.

After the council, there was a brief flurry of activity as the women found their pistolas and Geronimo found them bullets. Garditha handed his pistola over to Hunlona for safekeeping and went with me to the creek to fill the water bags and Blue-coat canteens.

As we squatted side by side to get the water, Garditha said, "Geronimo says you are very brave and act more like a mujercita, a little woman, than a girl. He believes you soon have your womanhood ceremony. Of this, I am glad. I told you when we were going to the Azul Mountains, you will make a warrior a fine woman, a good wife."

I looked at the creek rippling in the moonlight sliding through the tree branches above us and shook my head. "I'm not brave. All those times he saved my life, I was scared to death. Who knows when my womanhood time comes? Maybe tomorrow, maybe many harvests from now. Who will be a warrior then? Will the Americans and Mexicans have killed them all and made the women and children slaves? I hear the women in Naiche's band talk about this every sun. I don't know."

Garditha puffed his cheeks and shook his head as I pulled a filled water bag out of the creek to tie it off. "You are right. Who knows what the next sun brings? Still, I think you always speak true. I think you will be a fine *mujer* (woman). You're a fighter. I like you very much. If we live until I am a warrior and you a woman, I ask again, would you take me as your man?"

I looked at his serious face in the moonlight and felt like a hand had squeezed my heart. I liked and admired Garditha. He was fearless and always kind to me. He would be a strong warrior, maybe a leader in the future. But I knew anything to do with me becoming a warrior's woman, a wife, was far in the future. Who indeed even knows what the next sun brings?

I said, "I like you very much. You're kind and fearless. But truly, we don't know what the next sun brings. Yes, if we are alive and still together then, I will be your woman when the time comes."

He grinned and nodded, looking over his shoulder at me. "Enjuh! Enjuh! You make me happy in my heart. I'll always provide and care for you when you are my woman." He reached in a sack tied to his belt and brought out a smooth rounded pebble and handed it to me. I looked at it in the moonlight shining through the trees. It was the same pebble he had given me to ease my thirst when we were running back to the big tank camp. "For you, Trinidad. To always ease your thirst and to remember me by in the suns to come."

I smiled and nodded, my heart touched by his kindness, and wished I had something to give him but my pockets were empty. I could only say, "Enjuh."

I had just filled my last Bluecoat canteen when I heard She-gha call, "Stop playing in the creek and bring the water."

When we returned to the fire, the men were drinking coffee and talking about where to camp at the end of the next sun. Juanita and She-gha, blankets spread out in front of them, were cleaning their pistolas and loading ammunition belts. Both women handled their pistolas with the ease and confidence of a man, whirling cylinders to hear the clicks against the trigger advance, working them in their hands to get a feel again for the balance, and loading and unloading the cylinder several times so they wouldn't fumble while loading cartridges under fire.

I poured Garditha a cup of coffee. He smiled when I did, glancing at me with eyes that glowed with our shared secret. I poured myself a cup and sat back against a boulder. The camp grew quiet except for the gurgle of the creek and choruses of tree peepers, frogs, and insects. A horse snorted, and not far upriver, coyotes yipped.

The women finished their loading practice, put the pistolas in their holsters, and laid them by their saddles. The fire was burning down, and She-gha set the coffeepot off to one side on a flat rock, banked the fire, and rolled in her blanket next to her saddle. The men scattered to the bushes and soon returned to wrap in their blankets and lie next to their wives.

As usual, I slept near She-gha, and Garditha slept near Hunlona. I looked over at the dark outline of Garditha in his blanket and smiled. I thought, *Tonight, I heard my first serious marriage proposal and it was in the dark, from an Apache boy at a little creek in Mexico who gave me a stone to think of him when I was thirsty. I never expected it. Life has so many unexpected twists and turns and connections. Strange we never think about them, but maybe we should. The coyotes are calling again, this time from farther away than before. I wonder if dogs and coyotes are related.*

Too much thinking set me adrift in deep sleep as images of coyotes and dogs trotted side by side through my mind.

It was hot and bright outside. The dog, down by the corral, wouldn't stop barking. Petra had the baby laid across her belly nearly asleep as she rocked in the ancient rocker Artisan had found at a trading post in Nogales. She said, "Trinidad, go see what that dog is barkin' at. Might be that coyote after the chickens we ran off yesterday." I put the broom aside and said, "Be right back."

Running out the door of the cool darkness inside the adobe house was like running into a wall of fiery-white, bright heat outside. I saw the hair on the dog's back standing straight up. The dog stood planted in a semi-crouch, looking and barking through the corral poles. I stayed out of sight behind a garden fence of bushes and raised my eye up to a hole through the brush to see what the dog was so furious about.

As soon as I saw the corral, I wanted to scream, but no sound came out. Squatting in the corral dust was an Apache studying the horses as they nervously stomped their hooves and gathered in a tight little group. I knew the Apache. It was Ahnandia. He looked at the brush where I was and waved. I tried to run back to the house. I had to warn Petra but strained to put one foot in front of the other. I yelled for her to lock the door, but no sound came out of my mouth. The dog stopped barking. I looked over my shoulder and saw it lying in the dust, two arrows in its chest and one in its right eye.

Petra came to the door. Then thunder and darkness and bright-red blood appeared on the adobe-house wall. She and the baby were dead, and from far away, I heard Ahnandia calling me, "Trinidad . . . Trinidad, wake up. The night spirits fill you with dreams . . . Trinidad, wake up."

My eyes opened to see the face of She-gha. She had been shaking and calling me. It was still dark, but I could see the moon off to the southwest. She-gha said, "Ghosts speak to you. You moan much. Take water and go back to sleep."

I nodded and took a sip from a cold canteen. "I was having a bad vision. I'm all right now. Thank you for driving the vision away."

She-gha nodded and returned to her blanket.

I rolled over to get comfortable. I expected tomorrow would be another long day.

CHAPTER 32
CAUTIVA

I heard the camp stirring in the chill of dawn fast running from the light of the rising sun. She-gha and Juanita, their pistolas in holsters belted to their waists, had brought the fire back to life and were busy cooking the morning meal. Coffee boiled in the ancient, beat-up, blackened pot, and meat cooked on sticks angled over low, flickering, yellow and red flames occasionally flaring with melted fat dripping.

The smells of the coffee and meat fat dripping into the fire made my mouth water and my stomach rumble. I slid out of my blanket, folded and rolled it, and washed at the creek, its water cold and startling, making my blood rush as it touched my skin. Bushtits fluttered from bush to bush in little flocks, twittering about the coming day, and there was bright sunlight on the top of the big mountain west of us. Looking at the last fading stars, I saw the dark outline of Geronimo standing on the canyon rim with his arms raised and heard him singing his morning prayer to Ussen. All was well.

Natculbaye, Hunlona, and Garditha had gone up the canyon, caught the horses, and brought them to the edge of camp, where they tied them to the trees to await their saddles or pack frames. Geronimo climbed down from the canyon rim and took the coffee She-gha offered him. We all gathered around the fire to finish off the hot meat and desert food left from the night before.

While we ate, the horses watched us with raised ears, curious, stamping impatiently to be on the way. It wasn't long before we were wiping greasy hands on our moccasins and legs and then saddling the horses and mounting the pack frames. It hadn't seemed like much to me before, but I noticed She-gha's and Juanita's pack animals actually carried a lot of supplies and loot. It was a credit to them that they had held on to it, and a credit to the men who had taken it back from the Bluecoats and kept them safe and secure while so many Americans and Mexicans pursued them.

We mounted the horses where the creek ran into the river. A good trail ran beside the river, but Natculbaye led us up into and across the great wavy slabs of white rock that pushed out of the earth above the river canyon. In this way, we avoided leaving a trail or letting someone see us on the river trail. We rode slow and easy so the horses had good footing to avoid the green-and-purple thistle, prickly pear, and cholla growing in the stone crevices. The glare from the rocks made me tightly squint my eyes, but the air was pleasant and the mountains in the distance beautiful.

Maybe, I thought, *living with the Apaches isn't so bad.* I squeezed the bag that held the stone Garditha had given me and felt it round and smooth like the man he was growing into. *He's a good young man. I could enjoy life with him rather than being passed aunt to aunt. But what a hard life it would be. Would I be strong enough to survive living as an Apache?*

We came down out of the rocks two or three times to water the animals at the river, but since we were so slow on the trail, we didn't stop long to give the horses any rest. Geronimo told She-gha we would rest the animals and ourselves at the deep pool where the river turned northeast. There would be plenty of water, shade, and grass, a good place to rest and to eat a little something.

By the time of shortest shadows, the glare from the bright-white slabs of rock and their heat were making the trail much harder to ride than the nice one running through the bosque by the river. Natculbaye and Geronimo talked and decided we were far enough away from the village and hacienda to ride safely along the river, and that's where Natculbaye led us. It was cool there, and the shadows from the trees kept the hot air from the sun much easier to endure.

We came to a long stretch that had a few paloverdes and pines scattered over a narrow, green grass field. On either side of this stretch were cliffs cut through the great white slabs of stone upon which we had ridden all morning. The cliffs on the east side cast cooling shadows over the river's flow.

At the end of the grass upriver were trees on the west side that the trail went around, passing by the edge of a long, deep pool. The trees there had good shade and grass for the horses and easy access to the river. We unsaddled the horses and let them drink and graze while we ate. It was a very good place, cool and peaceful. I sat against a tree and wished we could stay there the rest of the day. She-gha sat nearby, and Geronimo stretched out in the grass, his rifle by his side, always under his hand. Natculbaye sat eating next to Juanita in the trees close to the trail. Hunlona and Garditha watched the horses to keep them from wandering off.

I was very comfortable and relaxed in the shade of my tree, slumping down on my side with my hand under my head, and was close to sleep when a tremble in the ground and a low, distant rumble in my ear jerked me awake. I sat up and looked around. Geronimo was on his knees, head cocked to one side, listening and staring down the trail with Natculbaye. Riders, Mexican vaqueros and soldiers in uniforms, appeared at the far end of the narrow field in a cloud of dust.

Geronimo bellowed, "Vaqueros! Leave everything! Run!" The Mexicans must have seen us at about the same time Geronimo saw them. They paused for an instant as they pulled pistolas and readied their rifles. The man in the center yelled, "Apaches! *Ataque!*" (Attack), and began charging forward, wildly firing his pistola into the trees as we scrambled for our horses. The men behind him began firing too. Bullets whistled and slashed through the trees. Twigs and small limbs and leaves filled the air. Never having been shot at before, I froze, trying to decide what to do.

I looked for my pony and saw the Apaches jumping onto the bare backs of their horses held for them in the dark shadows by Hunlona and Garditha. Geronimo was on his horse first and, seeing me hesitate, charged back into the hail of bullets. He leaned low over his pony, held out his arm, and yelled, "Take my arm, Trini!" Instinctively, I grabbed his arm and swung up behind him as he galloped, swerving side to side through the trees. The others in our band raced on in front of us. He rode up out of the trees and on to the sloping west side of the canyon, firing his pistola at the cloud of dust filled with shooting, yelling Mexicans.

Looking back, I saw Juanita hit and knocked off her horse. A bloodstain spread over one side of her shirt as she staggered to her feet. Dazed and disoriented for an instant, she found the Mexicans and screamed defiance as she pulled her pistola to shoot into their dust cloud. Natculbaye charged up and offered her his arm, but she was determined to make a stand and waved him on.

Geronimo's pony stumbled in the scattered rocks on the sloping side rising above the canyon and threw us off. I landed on my back, the wind knocked out of me, and sprawled there trying to suck in air and seeing silver stars floating and blinking against the deep-blue sky. Geronimo waved the others toward the back of a tree-filled box canyon that opened into the river canyon. I came to my senses and, rising to my knees, saw Juanita stand, firing into the charging Mexicans' bullets whistling around her. Hit again, this time in her upper left shoulder, she staggered backward. For an instant, she seemed to draw all the Mexican gunfire, her shirt showing new red blooms with black centers.

In the roar of the gunfire and whine of ricochets on the rocks around us, I stood and looked toward Geronimo, who had started for the canyon edge but stopped and waved for me, yelling, "Trini! Come!"

I stared at him for a moment, and again in a pleading voice, he yelled, "Trini! Come!" My mind filled with questions, *Where am I going? To more fighting and running? Hiding and running. Run. Run.* Something clicked in my brain. *Freedom!*

I ran toward the Mexicans, screaming and waving my arms, "*Cautiva!* (Captive!) Cautiva!" as I heard again, "Trini! Come!" Two or three shots whistled past me, but nothing very close before Geronimo disappeared into the canyon with the others.

I looked at Juanita. Hit many times, she was on her knees, fighting to stay up, her shirt soaked in blood. She fired once more. Then, hit in the temple, her head jerked back, and she collapsed, unmoving in the dust. All the Apaches had disappeared, but I knew Geronimo was in the canyon. The snap of gunfire and whine of nearby bullets stopped as if on command.

The leader of the Mexicans rode up to me as I stood in the middle of the trail. He looked like a strong, tough man, but he had kind eyes and I liked him.

He dismounted and bent over to look me square in the face, saying, "You were a captive of these Apaches, muchacha?" I nodded like I had no sense at all. "This is great news that you're free. Very, very few get away from them alive. Come, let us go sit in the shade and we will talk." He took me by the hand and led me to shade in the trees where the band had been resting.

He tossed his sombrero to one side and, with a groan, sat down against a tree and motioned for me to sit in front of him.

"And what is your name, please?"

"My name is Trinidad Verdín. I was taken from the ranch of my aunt and uncle, Petra and Artisan Peck, six miles southwest of Calabasas in Arizona about two moons ago."

"You have a fine name, Trinidad Verdín. My name is Don Patricio Valenzuela. I would be pleased and proud for you to think of me as your friend and call me Patricio. I own the Agua Fría hacienda near the village of Saracachi. The Apaches killed one of my cows and an ox yesterday. I will not let them steal from me, so I came after them. It is my great pleasure to meet and save you from these *Indios*. You must be very strong and very brave to have survived two months on the run with Geronimo and his Apaches. I will make sure you are returned to your family."

The men riding with Don Patricio had dismounted under the trees and were looking over the saddles and through the things She-gha and Juanita had carried on packhorses. One walked over to the body of Juanita, cocked his pistola, and kept it aimed at her while he toed her with his boot. When he was satisfied that she was dead or too weak to resist, he holstered his pistola, pulled a skinning knife from a sheath on his ammunition belt, and, grabbing her hair, jerked her head up and scalped her. Her scalp made a sucking pop when he pulled it free, and it was all I could do to keep from puking. Juanita had been kind to me and had died fighting with courage. It was a disgrace to scalp her. Two weeks earlier, a vaquero might have been taking my scalp.

Soldiers searching through the pack frame contents wrinkled their noses at the food supplies and threw them in the river. Booty like a couple of silver pitchers, ammunition, fancy cloth, and even a cartridge reloading rig Geronimo had traded for but had not yet learned to use, they admired as if part of some great treasure.

Don Patricio called one of the men over and told him to send men up the rims of both sides of the canyon where Geronimo had disappeared and look for where the Apaches might hide or try to escape. He warned him that these Indians were part of Geronimo's band, all deadly fighters, and that the men had to be very careful when they searched the canyon for the Apaches who expected to die and who wanted to kill as many as they could while they could. "I will join you soon to flush this Indio and his followers out and bring peace to us all."

The man nodded. "As you wish, Don Valenzuela."

Don Patricio's *segundo* (number two) made the vaqueros and the military men put aside the band's saddles and loot and deploy along both rims of the canyon while we continued to talk.

"May I call you Trinidad, muchacha?" I smiled and nodded. It was good to hear a kind voice who spoke without hesitation in my own tongue. "Can you tell me where you've been with these Indios?"

"After they took me, I know we crossed into Mexico through the Pajarito Mountains and then went southeast. I don't know much about the country except it had many high mountains and canyons, and our trail crossed the railroad tracks and a river next to it. I think I heard Geronimo say the Mexicans call it Río Magdalena, and I think once, we saw the lights of Nogales behind the mountains before we got to the Río Magdalena canyon. There was another river and train tracks we crossed and followed several times. I think the Apaches call it Río Santa Cruz."

Don Patricio was smiling and nodding. "Sí, sí. That would be right."

"We rode into the Pinito Mountains, where the men had hid-

277

den their women and children, and reclaimed them. They had a big battle with black American soldiers farther on in the mountains. The Apaches escaped without anyone wounded, but maybe one or two soldiers died. They were very brave, even Geronimo said so. We crossed back over the railroad tracks and river and went into the Cibuta Mountains, where they had a big battle with Mexican soldiers. No Apaches suffered wounds, but I think many soldiers died.

"Geronimo and Naiche split up for about a moon. Naiche, the chief, went into Arizona to look for his family, and Geronimo went south."

I started to tell about the vaqueros that Geronimo's band had wiped out in the Altar desert country. But I decided I wouldn't tell the Altar story. Someone might blame me for murder. Don Patricio lighted a small cigarro and waved his hand for me to continue when I paused and he lit up.

"We met a few suns ago with Naiche and his band at a camp on top of the Azul Mountains. They knew the American soldiers were close and coming. They decided to go over to the Madera Mountains to the west and then break into three groups. Geronimo kept me with his group."

"Hmmph, muchacha. It sounds as though Geronimo liked you."

"He saved my life three times. The last time, he killed one of your big longhorn cows when she charged me and I was too scared to run."

"Good for him. I'm glad he killed the cow, but why did he kill an ox?"

I frowned in confusion. "I didn't see him kill an ox. Maybe someone in Naiche's band killed it. They split yesterday, and Naiche went south."

"This Naiche. Who is he?"

"He's chief of the Chiricahuas. Geronimo advises him. He's

tall and thin. I think he wants to surrender to the Americans but listens to Geronimo, who would rather die than surrender."

"Hmmph. Well today we take Geronimo—dead or alive. He cannot get away. This Naiche can make up his own mind, then, eh?"

"Perhaps so, Don Patricio. Many have tried to kill Geronimo. He's a powerful warrior, and there are two other warriors with him."

Don Patricio grinned. "Trapped in a canyon with only two others? Surrounded by thirty men with good rifles? I think we will have him pretty quick now."

"Be careful, Don Patricio. I know many men thought they had captured Geronimo before they died."

"Ah, sí, sí, muchacha. This I will do. Stay here in the shade and rest from your ordeal while I go and direct his capture."

CHAPTER 33
GERONIMO'S BATTLE

As Don Patricio walked away toward the canyon where Geronimo had disappeared, I found a tree for shade as close to the canyon entrance as I dared. I wanted to hear what Don Patricio said and planned. I wondered if they'd bring Geronimo out dead or alive, but I wanted to, had to, see once more the man who had wiped out my family and taken me, but also saved my life three times in the last two moons, and called me daughter. I never dreamed on the morning of that day that I would be free, my days with the Apaches over. I had accepted that I'd probably be on the run with them the rest of my life and become the woman of someone like Garditha, who was fast becoming a fearless Apache warrior.

When the Mexicans attacked, Garditha disappeared with the others but showed great courage holding the horses until the others mounted and charged in front of Geronimo, with me hanging on behind him. It had all happened so quickly, in the blink of an eye.

I wanted to cry for Juanita when I saw her cut down like green grass before a scythe. I wondered if the Mexicans who had attacked us were more savage than the Apaches. The image of Artisan stripped of his clothes, standing barefooted on the hot sand, and looking toward the smoke rising behind the hills from his burning ranch house where his pregnant wife and little son lay in a pool of blackening blood came to me.

Who was worse? I didn't know. Ahnandia had told me after

he killed Petra that she had a gun. It was war—kill or die. Was there no mercy anywhere in this hard, unforgiving land?

I heard the yells back and forth across the canyon rims from the men who were looking for Geronimo. Don Patricio went to the mouth of the canyon and stood not far from me. I watched and heard him calling to his men. He studied the dark, shadowed depths of the canyon with a brass telescope that had a front lens twice the size of soldier glasses. I guessed that made it easier to see things in the dark shadows.

After a while, he shouted to his men that he thought there was a cave near the end of the canyon. He told me later that, for a while, he thought the opening was just a shadow among a jumble of boulders, but after looking up and down the canyon, he realized the shadow never moved with the sun.

He called to his men under the trees where Geronimo's band had stopped to rest, "Come over here, muchachos, and bring your rifles," and he yelled to the men on the rims, "Muchachos! I think we have the great Geronimo trapped in there. Be careful when you look over the edge into that canyon. He can kill you."

Don Patricio took a rifle from one of his men, aimed toward the dark place, and fired. He told me later he saw a streak of light in the dark spot, and we all heard the ringing zings of ricochets off rock. Grinning, he handed the rifle back to its owner. "Now we have him, muchachos! He is in some kind of cave—maybe nothing more than a depression at the bottom of the cliffs. He cannot escape. Fill that dark place you saw me hit with your bullets. A ricochet can be as deadly as a direct hit. Geronimo will not leave that place alive." He shook his fist. "Make him dance, muchachos. Make him suffer."

Nine vaqueros stood nearly shoulder to shoulder and shot bullet after bullet into the dark place down the canyon, raising many sparks in the dark place. The roar of the guns and scratching zings of the ricochets so hurt my ears that I covered them with my hands, and the smoke from their guns burned my nose. Soon Don Patricio, nodding, said, "Sí, that ought to do it," and signaled for them to stop with a short wave of his arm. The men lowered their rifles and waited for the breeze to carry away the last thin cloud of gun smoke.

Don Patricio pulled out his telescope and stared down the canyon. He watched without moving for what seemed like a long time and then closed his telescope. He yelled up to the men on the canyon rim, "Munguía! Check if you can see anything in that cave, but don't show yourself if you can avoid it."

A big man up on the canyon rim pushed his sombrero onto his back and ran to the rocks just above the cave. Holding his rifle in his right hand, he leaned around a boulder and looked down into the canyon. A breeze rolled through the tops of the canyon trees, ruffling the stillness with the sound of branches shaking, and passed on. Circling high in the deep-blue sky, an eagle screamed. Then silence. Munguía stretched his body out a little farther for a better view of the cave.

A rifle snapped with cracking, sudden thunder. I knew that thunder, had heard it before. Geronimo's old long rifle made it. Munguía's head snapped back. His rifle fell out of his hand and, bouncing and tumbling off the rocks supporting the boulder, sailed into the trees below while Munguía slowly twisted around the boulder, smearing a bloody streak down its side as he slid off the edge headfirst and followed his rifle cart-wheeling through the air to crash into the trees below, the sound of their snapping branches welcoming him to his final rest.

Don Patricio threw up his hands in fists, stomped his foot, and yelled, "Damn it, Munguía, I told you to be careful!"

From down the canyon, I heard the dry, rasping voice I knew well shout in Spanish at Don Patricio and his men, "Ho! Jefe, your vaqueros, their angry bees did not sting me. Señor, the vaqueros look good flying through the air, but they don't land so good in these trees. Send another. I help him fly like this last man. Come to my lodge. I help you fly too."

Don Patricio clenched his teeth and shook his fist as he paced about, thinking. After a while, he called the men to him and told some of them to advance up the canyon on foot but to stay behind the oaks and big boulders as much as possible. Others, he told to go up the rim of the canyon and, when they found a good place, to ease into the canyon, staying on or behind trees and rocks to screen them from that deadly dark place that had killed Señor Munguía. Don Patricio pounded his fist in his palm as he talked to them to emphasize that they had to be careful, that they were running out of time. If they didn't catch Geronimo before dark, he would slip away again, and that would mean more death, robbery, and destruction for Sonora and Chihuahua.

The men moved into the canyon carefully and quietly. Those up on the rim of the canyon began descending, a few trying to hurry by somehow getting in the top branches of big trees and climbing down, keeping the tree between them and the shooter hidden in the cave darkness.

Geronimo, hearing them in the trees and brush, taunted, "Hey, muchachos. Come and get me. I wait for you. Are you afraid of the man in the dark? Come on. Catch me if you can. Make your women proud of you, or are you all cowards?"

Don Patricio kept his eye to his telescope, pulled it down, paced in the heat, and then stared through it again. He saw one of the trees near the cave tremble a little and then saw one of his men climbing down through the branches, occasionally stopping to look through the branches toward the cave. I heard Don Patricio mutter, "Careful, Francisco. He's already killed Munguía. Don't let that miserable Indio kill you too."

I was very tired and leaned back against the tree, listening to the buzz of insects and watching dragonflies darting about and resting before zipping to a new place in the brush, looking for a new meal. Sleep was fast closing my eyes when the thunder from Geronimo's rifle cracked again, followed by the sound of breaking branches as a body bounced through them to catch on a bottom limb and hang there suspended, unmoving.

Don Patricio, staring through his telescope, said in a loud voice sick with despair, "I told you! I told you! Damn it, Francisco, I told you to be careful. Now you ride back to Santa Cruz across your saddle. Your wife will spit on the ground whenever she hears my name."

Any thought of sleep left me as I watched Don Patricio pace and then watch through his telescope down the canyon toward that deadly cave, all the while muttering, "Come on, muchachos. We're running out of daylight. You've got to move faster."

The men who had started at the mouth of the canyon crept from tree to tree, moving closer and closer to the cave. I walked down to a standing pool of water, found a handful of small stones, and, squatting by the edge, used my thumb to flip the stones at particular weeds growing in the shadows on the opposite side and then insects skating on the surface. The sun and its glare from the white rocks surrounding us made the day even hotter than I would have guessed it might have been if we were on the llano.

One man on the opposite rim from where Munguía fell had almost crawled into position to take a shot. Don Patricio was grinning again. He waved me over and said, "Do you want to see the man who is about to take Geronimo from that black hole where he hides?"

I made some quick nods. He kneeled on one knee behind me, gave me the telescope, and, pointing up the north rim, showed me where to aim it. I saw the vaquero lying behind two boulders with his rifle poked out through the crack between them. It looked like he was trying to adjust the rifle so it pointed down a little more.

Don Patricio said, "Do you see him?"

I nodded, handed the telescope back to him, and said, "Soon I think he takes a shot."

His telescope stayed on his eye as if there was some kind of unseen attraction holding it there. He puffed his cheeks and shook his head. "Careful, Tomás. Don't show yourself."

We both jerked a little when the sound of Geronimo's rifle again rolled down the canyon. Don Patricio, staring through the telescope, sighed and said, "Tomás is wounded but still conscious. Thank God! Now we have to get someone up there with a horse to get him back." He waved toward the packer who had come with them, bringing ammunition and supplies. When the man joined him, Don Patricio gave him the telescope and pointed toward the spot where Tomás lay. They talked a little while, the packer nodding and occasionally slapping his pistola holster.

The packer went back to his mule, threw a blanket across its back, and led it up the rim but far out of sight of anyone in the canyon. He got even with where Tomás was lying and crabbed over to him carrying the blanket. The packer slipped the blanket under him and pulled him back until he could stand and carry him on his shoulder to the mule. Tomás was conscious and able to sit upright on the mule. I could see the big, dried blood spot on his shirt as they worked their way back down to the little camp the packer had set up. At the camp, the packer eased Tomás off the mule and helped him stretch out on a blanket.

Don Patricio knelt by Tomás and examined the wound. After gently feeling around it while Tomás clenched his teeth and groaned in pain, he shook his head and said, "Tomás, you're very lucky. No bones hit and the bullet went all the way through. One of the men here knows how to take care of bullet wounds. I'll have him take a look at you after supper. You'll be in good hands soon."

I went looking for prickly pear, cut a few pads, and, after scraping the needles off, carried them back to where Tomás lay. He was still conscious and, when he saw me, said, "You're the muchacha who got away from the Apaches."

I nodded. "Geronimo's wife taught me to use prickly pear pads on wounds like yours. I think the juice helps stop infection and increase healing. Can I help you with them?"

He smiled a crooked little smile and nodded. I cut the pad covers off and put the pulp from one on the entrance wound and some on the exit, cut some of the cloth the Apaches had left behind into a long bandage, and wrapped and tied the pulp in place.

When I finished, Tomás murmured, "Mil gracias, mujercita. It feels better already."

I thought, *Well, maybe I'll be a nurse someday.*

The shadows were growing long, but the canyon ran northwest, and until the sun set, there would be good light on the northeast wall, giving the Mexicans more opportunities to take Geronimo, who shouted down the canyon, "Ho! Muchachos! I'm still here. Don't you want to come visit? We have a good talk, I think. You die. I walk away. End of talk. Come on. Let us see if it's my time or yours."

Don Patricio took another look down the canyon with his telescope. He told me later that he saw three men who had crawled close enough to take a shot into the cave but, looking west, saw the sun close to falling behind the mountains and ending the good light. He shook his head and said to himself, "So the old Apache gets away again after killing or wounding my men."

The sun fell behind the mountains in a golden glow, leaving the cooling air calm and peaceful. There was a sudden crack and boom of a rifle, and instantly Geronimo's rifle answered back. There were the sounds of men scrambling down the canyon, brush breaking, and rocks rolling. Soon in dusk's fading light, they appeared like ghosts at the canyon's entrance, grim and haggard, but nearly grinning to be alive. They all went over to the water pool and drank deeply, and then washed before going to the packer's fire for supper.

The last two men out of the canyon went to Don Patricio and told him that Geronimo had killed another of his men, Antonio Romero. They thought Geronimo had shot him in the head but couldn't tell for certain.

The jefe looked at the ground and shook his head. "A sad day to lose three men dead and one wounded when we had the Indio surrounded. At least we took one of his women and rescued the child. He and the others will go away tonight. They won't stay here to fight again. Let us eat and rest. We will find our dead in the morning and then return to Agua Fría."

CHAPTER 34
BATTLE'S END

Don Patricio and his men ate their supper with little conversation. Somewhere out in the dark of the canyon were the bodies of three of their friends, and one in camp lying wounded. The man who knew how to doctor bullet wounds said Tomás was lucky to be alive. If the bullet had been about an inch more to the right, it would have hit a major blood vessel and he would have bled out before they could get to him. Six inches higher and the bullet would have hit him in the head like the others. The man doing the doctoring was glad to see the prickly pear pulp pads over the wounds and asked if I could get more tomorrow. I said if someone would carry a torch for me, I would get more that night, and I did.

I spent a while talking to Don Patricio about my life with the Apaches. He had many questions about their fighting style. I had few answers. I told him I spent most of my time with the women and children, hidden from the raids and fighting, which was true when men went out to raid, but near their camps, I had seen some hard fighting. I had little to say about the fighting near the camps except that the Apaches were great fighters and usually won when they were prepared.

Dust and dirt covered me from head to toe, so I slipped past a sentry and went to a pool a little upriver from the one the Mexicans were using. I pulled off my shirt, skirt, and moccasins and slid into the dark water deep enough that when I squatted on my heels, my head was just above the surface. I scrubbed all over with soap the packer had given me and felt much better. The night air was cold. It took longer to dry than I expected, and I was shivering when I finally put my clothes on.

When I returned to the fire, the packer asked me which saddle in the collected loot had been mine and said to help myself if I recognized anything that I wanted or was mine in the loot the vaqueros had collected. I found my blanket and, with my saddle, moved to the edge of the fire's circle of light to make my bed. I spread and folded the blanket and lay down, listening to the smooth strumming on a guitar by one of the vaqueros and the low voices singing with him.

The fire's flames burned down to little ones of orange and blue, and coyotes yipped everywhere. My mind filled with a tumble of images and memories of my days with the Apaches, the long morning ride up the Río Dolores and then trying to get away with Geronimo when Don Patricio attacked before I escaped. Feeling very lucky that neither the Mexicans nor Geronimo had killed me, I had a lot to think about.

I already missed my friend Garditha. I reached for the bag on my belt and felt the stone he had given me. The thought that I would probably never see him again made me sad to the point of tears, but I was glad he had gotten away. I was exhausted. The only thoughts I could conjure up weren't any better than dim images in a fog, and it didn't take long for me to spiral into unconsciousness and a deep sleep.

The smell of steak frying, the morning calls of birds, the snorting of horses, and talk from men down by the water pool brought me awake to the new day. Gray dawn was fast fading into bright yellow light. I sat up, shook my moccasins to dump critters claiming them for a new home, and hurried to find a privacy bush. I washed at the main pool used by everyone and took the plate of steak, tortillas, and beans with green chilies, and a cup of coffee the packer offered me.

Don Patricio was just finishing his meal when I started eating, and he grinned and nodded when he saw me. I waved back and started stuffing my face. I was hungry. I'd eaten better meals but couldn't remember when. Crows high overhead came cawing downriver, probably headed for the tall trees around Agua Fría.

Don Patricio waved his arm for the men to gather 'round him.

He said, "Muchachos, this morning we collect our amigos the Apache killed and take them home for a proper burial. I have no doubt that the Apaches have gone, and we will not have to do this sad thing fearful of being targets ourselves. To make certain this is so, I send four of our best shots up the canyon to look in the cave where Geronimo hid. Guillermo, Miguel, Jose, and Pedro, take your rifles and walk the canyon, check the cave, and come back to us pronto, eh?"

Four men left the group crowded around Don Patricio and headed for the canyon's entrance. Don Patricio said to the rest of the men around him, "They will be a little while, muchachos. Let us go to the fire and drink our coffee until they return."

They all took their cups and drank up the rest of the packer's coffee while speaking in low, respectful voices and keeping an eye on the trail into the canyon, watching for the men to return.

I sat on my blanket where I had slept, relaxed against my saddle, and slurped the thick black coffee. Flocks of gnatcatchers flew up out of the brush and, after making a few zigzag turns like a little black cloud looking for a home, settled in brush farther up the river. An eagle began a slow, lazy circle high above us as the sun began cooking the air. There was little or no breeze as dragonflies began prowling the tops of weeds and open flowers for their insect breakfasts.

★　★　★　★　★

In less than a hand against the horizon, the men returned from the canyon and went to speak with Don Patricio, who stood to meet them and pour them the last of the coffee. They all looked grim and angry.

Don Patricio said, "What did you see, muchachos?"

The others looked at Jose as if they had chosen him to speak for them. He said, "We found Munguía broken against boulders not fifty meters from the cave. There was a bullet wound under his right eye and not much left of the back of his head. Francisco was hanging over the bottom limb of a big oak by the east wall of the canyon maybe thirty meters from the cave, shot near the middle of his forehead. Antonio was on the ground about ten meters from the cave, shot through his left eye."

Don Patricio looked at the ground and shook his head, mumbling, "I told them. I told them."

Jose said, "We also looked in the cave, jefe. You were right. He's long gone. It's just a deep pocket, maybe no more than six or seven meters deep into the side wall on the west side. There were bullet strikes all over its top side and a few bullet remains on the floor. I think what saved him from the ricochets was a low place in the floor where he could lie and most would miss him. There were several bloody patches on the floor and a streak against one wall. He was hit, probably more than once, but I don't think seriously."

Don Patricio frowned. "Gracias, señores. I think you are right about Geronimo's wounds. I have much sorrow that he got away. The packer will give you blankets to wrap the bodies in."

He turned to Tomás lying on his blanket, listening to the meeting. "Can you ride, Tomás?"

"Sí, jefe. I feel better today after my doctor and nurse fixed me up. I can ride without help."

Don Patricio smiled. "Bueno. Let's get to work, muchachos, and return home with our sad burdens."

The packer's mule carried the bodies of the men Geronimo killed out of the canyon. It had been through enough battles and skirmishes with the militia that it wasn't skittish at the smell of blood and death. It was a sad and solemn moment when the mule appeared, following the men out of the canyon. I didn't know the men killed and felt much sadness for their families, but I had seen so much death and destruction in my time with the Apaches that I then accepted it as a normal part of life.

The men left the covered bodies in the shade. They planned to leave Juanita's body out for the coyotes and buzzards. When I heard this, anger and shame made me clench my teeth. I went to Don Patricio. He could tell I was angry before I opened my mouth.

"Mujercita, your face is red and covered with an angry frown. Has one of my men been bad to you? Tell me."

"Sí, Don Patricio. I'm very angry. Your men scalped the Apache woman who helped keep me alive these past two moons. Now they want to leave her body out in the open for coyotes and buzzards? Your men rode over her, breaking her body while she tried to defend her band. I want her put in a grave as she deserves. If you won't dig her one, then I'll stay here and make a grave for her using my hands and a digging stick. I'll come back to your hacienda when I'm through here."

Don Patricio studied my face and body trembling with anger. He said, "Sí, I understand how you feel, but you must understand these men, their fathers, and many grandfathers back in their history lost many loved ones to the Apaches. They don't want to give the Apaches anything, not even the courtesy of a burial. It is their way of avenging themselves when they cannot find those who have destroyed their families."

I expected such an answer, and I said, "All right. Then I'll stay here, dig her grave myself, and ride my pony to your hacienda when I'm finished."

He shook his head and smiled. "No, child. I cannot leave you here in the wilderness by yourself. If anything happened to you, I would never forgive myself after all you've been through. I'll tell the men to dig her a grave back in the canyon and give her a proper burial. This will please you?"

"Muchas, muchas gracias, Don Patricio. It pleases me very much. I'll go with them and put stones over her to protect her from the animals who might try to dig her up."

Don Patricio ordered some men to wrap Juanita in a blanket and dig a grave for her up the canyon while the rest made ready to go. I followed four men up the canyon as they carried the body of Juanita. We hadn't gone far when I saw a shelf in the canyon wall about the height of my head where they could lay her and put stones around the ledge and over her to protect the site. I ran up to Paco, in charge of her burial detail, and told him what I thought we could do. He was happy with an idea that meant not having the men work and sweat using a pick and shovel to bury a smelly Apache corpse in the growing heat of the day.

Juanita's body fit easily on the little shelf of the canyon wall, and it didn't take long to cover her and stack rocks over her. After we finished, the men sat down to have a smoke and I stood in front of Juanita's burial site with a bowed head and, in the rough Apache I had learned to speak with Garditha's help, asked Ussen to speed her ghost pony on the way to the Happy Land.

The men watched in curiosity as I did this, a couple of them frowning. When I finished, Paco asked how I had learned to speak Apache. I told him about Garditha and me trading Apache and Spanish lessons and then said, "Juanita was a big reason I was able to survive for the two moons. I asked their god to bring her quickly to their Happy Place."

Paco took a deep draw from his cigarette, blew the smoke into the hot, humid air, and nodded, grinning. "You have been raised well, child. Juanita will get her justice in the Happy Place. Come on, soon el jefe will be ready to go."

We walked down the shady trail to the canyon mouth. Just as we came to the river trail and our camp, Paco stepped back, pulled and cocked his big pistola, and exclaimed, *"Dios mío!"* The other men pulled their guns too and crept back in the dark shadows. They kneeled by boulders for cover, but I was curious to see what had caused the commotion and looked at the camp and then downriver before Paco pulled me behind him.

What I saw made me understand why Paco had called on God. Every man in camp stood with his rifle pointed downriver. Not a hundred yards away were ten or twelve mounted Apaches with the butts of army carbines resting on their thighs, ready for instant use.

CHAPTER 35
CAPTAIN LAWTON

The Apaches and Mexicans eyed each other, waiting for the other side to make the first move. The tension in the air was like the stillness in the wind before a thunderstorm begins. I saw the thumbs of some Mexicans cocking the hammers of their rifles. Don Patricio stood in front of his men, both hands on his rifle held ready to go to his shoulder, studying each Apache, his brow wrinkled and eyes narrowed. The low rumble of a herd of horses galloping toward us filled our ears.

The Mexicans, uncertain of attack, seemed to draw a little closer together. Stretching to look from around my tree, far down the trail, I saw a dust cloud with figures in blue mixed in it—Bluecoats, American soldiers. Why were the Apaches waiting on them? Then I remembered Geronimo had said in the Madera Mountains that his Power had told him there were Apache scouts with the Bluecoats chasing us.

A Bluecoat burst from the dust cloud and charged toward the Apaches, facing the Mexicans and yelling, *"No dispares! No dispares!"* (Don't shoot! Don't shoot!) I saw Don Patricio's shoulders sag a little as he relaxed and lowered his rifle as tension in both groups began to evaporate. The group of Apaches parted to let the Bluecoat ride through to Don Patricio.

The Bluecoat was a young American officer who spoke illiterate Spanish and saluted. He said, "Señor, I'm Lieutenant Leighton Finley. These Apache scouts are part of Captain Lawton's command looking to capture or destroy Geronimo. They have no harm for you. My commander, Captain Lawton, sends his respects and requests a meeting with you."

Don Patricio nodded. "Buenas tardes, *Teniente* (Lieutenant). I am Don Patricio Valenzuela, owner of the Agua Fría hacienda and today comandante of these men, who include my vaqueros, volunteers from the village of Saracachi, and militia sent from Cucurpé. Please, ask Capitan Lawton to bring his command in for water and a rest in the shade of these fine trees. I assume your Apaches will mind their own business and there will be no trouble?"

The teniente said, "Sí, Don Valenzuela. There'll be no trouble with our scouts, and I'll bring my commander pronto."

The Apaches began to relax, and one who appeared to be in charge listened as Teniente Finley stopped, spoke to him, and rode on to the Bluecoats waiting down the river trail. The leader of the scouts turned toward Don Patricio and waved his arm toward the water.

Don Patricio nodded and waved toward it. They came in slow, watchful in all directions, like a new dog creeping up to a pan of food someone has just offered it. The men also started to relax and move to sit in the shade and smoke, realizing they would be there while the Bluecoats and their jefe swapped information. The Apaches watered their horses and found themselves a shady spot, where they sat or squatted, their dark eyes studying everything and everyone in the camp. Their jefe sent four of them to scout up the canyon and around its rims for signs of the Apaches they were following.

Along with the men who had buried Juanita, I left our hiding spot in the canyon and went to Don Patricio. He nodded when we told him what we had done but seemed a little distracted and kept glancing toward the Apache scouts as if unsure whether he could trust them.

Captain Lawton and Lieutenant Finley rode at the head of

their column of soldiers and, upon reaching the Mexicans, had the soldiers dismount, water their mounts and themselves, and take a little rest. The Mexicans stared at the soldiers, apparently the first company of black troopers they had ever seen. They didn't appear at all odd to me. I had watched them fight the Apaches in the battle in the Pinito Mountains and had seen the great courage they showed against the Apaches who were firing down on them from practically inaccessible positions in the cliffs above.

Captain Lawton and Lieutenant Finley were light-skinned, sunburned, unshaven, and tall, and moved with the easy grace of natural athletes. Lawton pulled off his felt hat, slapped the dust out of it, and, pulling off his gloves, walked over to Don Patricio to hold out his right hand.

"Captain Henry Lawton, United States Army, señor. Thank you for accepting us into your camp."

Don Patricio shook Lawton's hand and smiled. "With much pleasure, Capitan Lawton. I am Don Patricio Valenzuela, co-mandante of these volunteers, vaqueros, and militia. I am also the owner and jefe of the Agua Fría hacienda."

I had not had time to get out of the way when Lawton came up and was standing mute beside Don Patricio, who, being the gentleman he was, moved his hand toward me and said with pride in his voice, "And it is my pleasure to introduce you to Señorita Trinidad Verdín. We rescued her from the Apaches yesterday. They had taken her from the Peck Rancho in Arizona two months ago after killing her aunt and little cousin. She has been all over Sonora with the Apaches since then and I'm sure will have many interesting stories to tell. She shows maturity and courage far beyond her years. She is a little woman, a mujer-cita, not a child."

Lawton's eyes grew round, and he smiled as I did the best curtsy I knew how to and said in my rough English, "With much pleasure, Capitan."

Lawton said, "I heard about your abduction by the Apaches. Forgive me for saying so, but most people who told me about you thought the Apaches had killed you. Seeing you alive has made this a fine day. You are very brave and smart to have gotten away alive. Where was Geronimo while you were with the band?"

"I rode with Geronimo and his wife, She-gha, and helped her with chores. He seemed to take a liking to me and saved my life several times. He often raids with a tall, thin Apache who acted like he was chief. His name is Naiche."

"It sounds like you are an epic survivor, señorita. When there is a little free time and you are agreeable, I ask Don Valenzuela if we can talk about your life and time with Geronimo and his band."

Don Patricio said, "Of course, Capitan. Anytime Trinidad agrees to talk with you is acceptable to me. Now please, let us get out of this sun and sit in the shade and drink cool water while we talk."

I sat listening to Don Patricio, Captain Lawton, and Lieutenant Finley discuss their experiences and the lessons they'd learned chasing Geronimo. Captain Lawton told how he and his company always seemed to be about a day behind Geronimo and perfectly described the trails they had followed that had led to the camp in the Azul Mountains and then up this canyon where we sat. He said he expected that Geronimo and Naiche would meet soon someplace in the Sierra Madre, probably on the west side of the Río Bavispe. I knew where they would meet in the Sierra Madre, but I said nothing. Geronimo had saved my life. I wasn't going to betray him.

Don Patricio told the captain how his men had surprised the Apaches who left everything to get away, how I'd made my

escape, and how Geronimo, despite being trapped in a canyon wall cave and surrounded by thirty men, had managed to kill three, wound one, and escape in the darkness with possible minor wounds. As Don Patricio spoke, Lieutenant Finley kept notes, writing furiously to keep up.

Captain Lawton listened and nodded often, saying a time or two, "Yes, I know. Always unpredictable. That's how he does it." He told us how he and his scouts had been on Geronimo's trail for weeks. I remembered seeing an occasional small dust cloud in the distance when we were up high but always thought it was just the wind. Maybe it had been the Bluecoats. Geronimo always seemed to know where they were and knew where to go to stay ahead of them.

Don Patricio said, "It is too bad you weren't here yesterday, Capitan, when we had him cornered. With the help of you and your soldiers, Geronimo now would be either dead or in chains, ready for the hangman."

The captain bowed his head and nodded. "I wish we had been here too, Don Valenzuela. Geronimo delayed us by splitting off from a group with two or three times as many people and horses. They headed southeast. It took my scouts a while to find the trail of this group and to recognize the tracks of a horse Geronimo had ridden when we followed him along the Río Altar. Were you with him then, Señorita Trinidad?"

Caught! I decided to answer truthfully but not to volunteer any more information about the vaqueros than I had to. "Sí, Capitan. I was with Geronimo and five others. The tall, thin chief, Naiche, wanted to go north. Geronimo didn't want to risk Bluecoats catching him north of the border and rode south. We spent a few days in the desert country north of Altar and then traveled to mountains he said the Mexicans called Azul."

"That's what my scouts say he did. You have a very good

memory, Trinidad. Do you know why he went into that desert country?"

I felt the noose around my neck getting tighter. What if the scouts had gone into that country and discovered the vaquero bodies, especially the one we burned? One little lie might get me hung or save me. I said, "He said he had never been in that country before and wanted to look it over."

"My scouts never followed his trail into the desert country north of Altar because they found the return tracks and followed them to the Azul Mountains when you came back out. You're a very brave young woman. I much admire your courage. I see a bruise on your forehead. Is that because Geronimo beat you or abused you?"

I smiled and noticed Don Patricio was staring and frowning at my face like he had not seen the bruise before. "No, Capitan. None of the Apache men ever hit me. Geronimo's wife, Shegha, might have wanted to cuff me a time or two when I first came to her because I was slow learning Apache words until an orphan boy about my age helped me with the language in return for me helping him with Spanish. Before long, I understood much of what they said, and Geronimo, who speaks good Spanish, usually spoke to me in Spanish."

"Hmmph. This Geronimo is a strange one. He won't hesitate to rip the guts out of a man but pets the head of a child." He looked up and saw his scouts returning from the rims of the canyon. "Please excuse us for a moment."

The captain, with Lieutenant Finley, walked over and spoke to the returning scouts for a few minutes and then followed them to water. While they were gone, Don Patricio leaned over and said, "Mujercita, if you are tired of the capitan's questions, just say so and I will tell him that is enough."

I shook my head. "Oh no, Don Patricio. I'm not tired. He seems like a nice capitan."

He smiled. "Bueno." He offered me a canteen, but I wasn't thirsty, so he took a couple of long swallows.

The capitan and lieutenant returned to our spot in the shade. The capitan said, "The scouts say the Apaches who got away had set up an ambush on the far end of the canyon and that's where Geronimo must have joined them. They're headed northeast. My guess is that they're going back to their Sierra Madre camps, and that's where I'll look next. I think, Don Valenzuela, your Apache attacks are over for a while."

Don Patricio smiled and said, "That is very good news, capitan. Please, return with us to my hacienda and refresh yourself and your soldiers for a day or two before you ride east. My men and I have the sad business of returning our dead to their families. I must also find Trinidad's family and make her whole again after all she has endured. Eh, mujercita?"

CHAPTER 36
AGUA FRÍA HACIENDA

The ride through the canyon to Don Patricio's Agua Fría hacienda was an easy jog down the trail by Río Dolores and took no more than a couple of hands against the horizon. We passed through the village of Saracachi, the villagers quietly watching us and taking off their sombreros in respect for the bodies lying across the horses of their owners. When we jogged up to the Agua Fría hacienda, Don Patricio's servants, three middle-aged women and two old men, came out the casa door and made a big show of welcoming him back.

Don Patricio asked one of the men to show Captain Lawton, Lieutenant Finley, and their men where they could camp, get wood for their fires, and be close to water for drinking, cooking, and bathing on the river just to the east of Saracachi.

Before they left, he said to Captain Lawton, "Capitan, my men and I are very grateful that you stopped to support us. Please accept my invitation for you and Teniente Finley to join me in a modest *cena* (supper) tonight, about sunset. As I said when we met, take two or three days and let your men rest and refit. Whatever supplies you need, I will be happy to provide them."

Captain Lawton said, "With much pleasure, Don Valenzuela. Lieutenant Finley and I will join you at your table this evening. I'll send a rider to find my packtrain and bring them here, and we'll take your kind offer to rest and take two or three days to refit before we take up the Apache trail again."

Don Patricio turned to me still mounted on my pony. He said, "Trini Verdín, mujercita, there is a room for you in my casa. I'll have one of my mujeres bring you hot water for a bath and a fresh change of clothes. After you rest a little, come and have supper with Capitan Lawton, Teniente Finley, and me. What do you say?"

I thought my smile might touch my ears. I said, "With much pleasure, I accept your kindness, Don Patricio."

He motioned to the other old servant to come take my pony while Capitan Lawton and Teniente Finley led their troops and followed the white-haired old man who gestured to them to come. He had the weight of years on his back and walked bent over with a little stagger from side to side, chattering all the while about the horror of facing Apaches as he led the Americans to a good camping place on the river outside of Saracachi.

After I dismounted, a short, middle-aged woman with a big bosom came to me, smiling. She gave a little bow and said, "Buenas tardes, señorita. My name is Francisca."

"Buenas tardes, Francisca. I am Trinidad Verdín."

She held out her hand. "Come, *mija* (*mi hija*—dear child), I'll show you your room and bring you hot water for your bath."

I took her hand, thinking, *A hot bath? I haven't had one of those since I was with Petra.* I said, "Many thanks, señora. A hot bath is a pleasure I have not had in a long time."

My room was bigger and finer than any I had ever slept in. The bed was big and covered with a mattress and down pillows easy to disappear in. Two windows with lacy curtains and tied-back *cortinas* (drapes) gave light from the east wall, and there was a stone fireplace on the wall facing the bed. A tall, fine-grained dark-wood armoire for storing clothes stood in a corner, and in an adjoining room was a white bathtub, each corner supported on a lion's foot—I had expected a big washtub like Petra had. A vanity dresser with a big pitcher of cool water sat in a washbowl on one side, and a mirror hung on the wall behind the dresser for ladies to use when brushing their hair and arranging themselves. I know I must have looked an idiot as I stared at each object in the two rooms, but I had never seen such fine things.

Francisca said, "Undress and leave your clothes on the bed. I'll wash them for you. There is a robe that should fit you in the armoire. I'll be back soon with hot water for your bath, and there are toilet facilities for you in the little room behind the door next to the bathtub."

I looked out a window and could see the mountains to the east in the glow of a sun not far from setting and knew I would have to hurry. I pulled a short robe out of the armoire, sat on the bed, and pulled off my moccasins, and then my skirt and shirt. As Francisca had told me, I left them there and pulled on the robe, which was several sizes too big and too long but felt smooth and comforting as I went to the room with the bathtub. I looked in the room with toilet facilities and was amazed to see a night bucket sitting under what looked like a fancy chair with a seat that had a big hole in the middle, and nearby stacks of little squares of soft paper.

When Francisca returned, I told her I had never seen such a thing. All the facilities I had known were outdoors in a little house or kept in a corner for dumping during the morning cleanup. She thought it was a true luxury invention, and I agreed with her. It was a great invention.

The warm bathwater was a delight, as were the big sponge and soap I used to wash. Although I had bathed as often as I could when the Apaches were around big water tanks or pools catching spring water, and She-gha had shown me how to make soap out of yucca root, I had little time to enjoy it. As a result, my hair needed a good washing, and a few places needed extra scrubbing. I had never felt such a soft towel, and it smoothly pulled the water right off my skin and wet hair. I was beginning to understand why so many marriageable girls were interested in rich old men.

Francisca brought me a freshly washed and ironed deep-blue fine muslin dress that was nearly a perfect fit. She smiled when she saw me in it. I said, "This is very strange that you have a dress that would fit me."

"One of the other women, Rosa, who also works here in the house, has a daughter, married now with only sons, who once wore this dress to Mass. She gives it to you. I have a few dresses this size from my daughters too, but they are calico and not as nice as this one."

"Please give her my thanks. The nicest dresses I ever had were calico."

Francisca smiled and nodded. "You look very good in that dress, my child. I'm sure Rosa will be proud to see you in it. Come sit over by the mirror and let me fix your hair. Cena will be ready soon."

Francisca fixed my hair in two short braids and arranged them on top of my head like I was a grown woman. I loved the arrangement and happily walked with her down long halls to a room with walls covered with shelves of books and a great desk and a couple of sofas with wingback chairs. There Don Patricio was already talking with Capitan Lawton and Teniente Finley over fancy glasses of amber-colored liquid I guessed was whiskey.

When Francisca came to the open doors with me, Don Patricio saw us, stood up smiling, and motioned for me to join them sitting at a big round table in the middle of the room. He said,

"How nice you look, mujercita. Come join us. Francisca will bring you a refreshment. Gracias, Francisca." Francisca smiled and left through a side door.

I sat down in a big chair between the two American officers, my legs just long enough for my feet to touch the floor. Don Patricio said, "These gentlemen were just telling me of their adventures and frustrations in trying to capture the Apaches they track now. They think the Apaches have broken into two or three groups and gone in different directions to confuse the scouts, and that the Apache groups plan to meet somewhere in their old range, the Sierra Madre. Do you have any idea where they might be planning to meet?"

I slowly shook my head, lying with a straight face, all the while knowing where they planned to unite. I said, with my heart racing, trying to outrun being caught in a lie, "No, Don Patricio. I know only that they spoke of many places, places they said even the scouts would not know, where they could hide in the Sierra Madre."

The men exchanged glances and took sips of whiskey, and Don Patricio puffed his cheeks and said, "Sí, mujercita, we asked you this before. It's not that we think you would lie for the murderous Apaches, but the Sierra Madre is a big, wild place. Every bit of information the Americanos can find might help them shorten their search and bring these renegades to justice. We were only hoping you might remember something more besides what you've already told us."

I shook my head. "No, Don Patricio, I can think of nothing else."

Francisca came back carrying a glass like the others but filled with a clear liquid. The glass was cold to the touch. I was surprised to see what looked like chunks of ice floating in it, and when I raised my brows at it, she said, "*Limonada,* señorita. I think you like it." I tasted it, and tart, sweet, and cold, it brought a smile to my face. I had never tasted such a drink, or one with ice floating in it.

Francisca turned to Don Patricio and said, "Cena is ready. We are ready to serve it at the big table in your dining hall whenever you want to eat."

"Bueno, Francisca. We will come soon."

She nodded and disappeared again out the side door.

I had another swallow of my limonada while the men sipped their whiskey. Captain Lawton said, "Trini, it would be very helpful for you to tell us your story and have Lieutenant Finley write it for the record so perhaps we can learn from it. Can you do that sometime before we leave in the next two or three days?"

I thought, *Capitan Lawton must be anxious to know what I know. He mentioned this when I first met him.*

"Of course, Capitan. Anything I can do to help your fight against the Apaches, I will do."

I knew my lying might catch up with me. I just had to run a little faster than it did.

Don Patricio said, "I believe you told me your padre and madre have passed away and an aunt, Señora María Cuen, left you with another aunt, Señora Petra Peck, to help her because she had a small child and was expecting another?" I nodded. He continued. "I'm trying to find your aunt, Señora María Cuen, for you, mujercita. I have made inquiries in Nogales and Calabasas. I think you also told me that you were from Minas Prietas, where I'm also looking. You, of course, are welcome to stay here as long as you like. I'm happy to have you here, but I thought you would want to go back to your family."

I wanted to see María, but I felt an even stronger bond with Petra's husband, Artisan, and hoped he had survived going through the desert nearly naked and had stayed sane after seeing his wife and child lying in a black pool of blood. I said, "Muchas gracias, Don Patricio. Will you also make inquiries about Petra's husband, Artisan? The last time I saw him, he was walking toward the smoke from his burning rancho, where his wife and child were lying killed by the Apaches. I often wonder if he managed to survive while I was with the Apaches."

Don Patricio took another sip of his whiskey, sighed, and said, "Sí, mujercita. This I have already done. Is there anyone else?"

I slowly shook my head, "No, señor, no one."

Our cena was very good—beef and chicken enchiladas in hot sauces, tamales, corn tortillas, beans and chilies, empanadas with honey, cooked apples, and hot coffee. As we ate, Captain Lawton asked that I tell about the morning the Apaches came and what happened to Artisan and me. I'd had enough bad dreams about that day to remember as if it had happened yesterday, and I told it that way.

When I described Artisan walking in the desert—wearing red long handles through goat's head stickers, with burning sand in his bare feet—toward the smoke behind the ridge where his destroyed home and family were lying, the men sat shaking their heads and clenching their teeth, with their forks and knives paused halfway to their plates. When I finished the story, it was as quiet as midnight on a mountaintop.

Lieutenant Finley put down his silverware, folded his hands as though in prayer, and leaned forward on his elbows. "So you don't know what happened to your uncle?"

"No, Teniente, I don't know. I can only hope he survived."

Captain Lawton said, "As do we, and that he heals in his soul and body. He's suffered much. I know Don Valenzuela is trying to find him, and I, too, will use all the sources I have at my disposal to help find him for you."

Their goodwill made me feel even worse for not telling where the Apaches were meeting. I nodded and whispered, "Muchas gracias, Capitan."

After cena, we returned to Don Patricio's office and library, the men for brandy and cigarros, while Francisca brought me a cup of hot chocolate. The chocolate had a light piñon nut taste that I liked very much. I listened to the men talk ranching and the countryside until I yawned.

Lieutenant Finley saw me and said, "I know Trinidad must be weary, but if I could take her statement now, then we wouldn't have to worry about it tomorrow or the next day, in case she has to leave soon. If she's willing, is this acceptable to you, Don Valenzuela?"

Don Patricio looked at me and I nodded. It would be good to do my duty and then not worry about it tomorrow or the day after. He said with a smile, "I think our señorita is happy to do that, Teniente. Please, use my desk while Capitan Lawton and I talk."

Lieutenant Finley nodded and pulled a leather-bound journal and writing pen from a pocket inside his jacket. He slid my chair to the desk, where he sat down in its big, high-backed, leather-covered chair. He explained that his jefe would want my description of what happened to me for army historical records, that he would write down what I told him and write a formal report that he would bring for my review and approval sometime before midday tomorrow. He asked if that was acceptable, and I assured him it was.

I told him my story in English, since it was better than his Spanish, but neither of us was very good in the other's language. I was sleepy and kept forgetting timeline details and then remembering them and telling them out of sequence. He asked many questions about the number of Apaches who had attacked Artisan's ranch, how many were in the band, whether the

Apaches had met with other Indians, Mexicans, or Anglos, and how many other Mexican and Anglo men I had seen them kill. I tried to answer all his questions, but I think my need for sleep slowed and confused my memory and his record became a little mixed up.

After I finished, he thanked me, looked over at Captain Lawton and Don Patricio, and said, "I think this young lady needs her rest. She's given me enough for a good report, and Captain Lawton and I thank her."

Don Patricio smiled and said, "Bueno. Mujercita, are you ready for bed?" I nodded, barely able to keep my eyes open. He motioned toward the open door Francisca used and she immediately appeared. He said, "Francisca, I think our brave mujercita is ready for some rest. Show her to her room and make her comfortable. Sleep well, Trinidad."

I slid out of my chair, bowed to the men, and said, "Buenas noches, caballeros." They all gave me a smile and a little salute. I followed Francisca to my bedroom, where she helped me undress and climb into that deep, soft down mattress. I lay back on the pillows, and as she pulled the cover over me, she said, "Buenas noches, *hija* (my dear child)."

"Buenas noches, Francisca."

I remember her turning down the bedroom oil lamp but not closing the door.

Chapter 37
Waiting

The canyon was dark, filled with trees and their shadows. A few shafts of sunlight passing through the trees cut toward a big, dark smudge among boulders scattered along the cliff wall. Men with big rifles darted from tree to tree, drawing closer to the dark place among the boulders, where a voice called over and over, "Trini? Trini? Come, Trini. Time to go."

There was a sudden flash of light. Startled, I jerked up in the soft down bed as a beam of sunlight poured through a crack in the window curtains and hit my pillow. My heart thumped against my chest as I looked around and then remembered where I was.

I got out of bed, went to the window, and squinted outside at the bright light in the curtain crack. It was a beautiful day. Laborers were busy in the surrounding yard and nearby fields. I could see vaquero horses tied to a hitching rail at the front of the casa. Several vaqueros stood around smoking cigarettes as if they waited for someone inside. It was later in the day than when I usually left the blankets.

The water I poured into the big washbowl was cold and refreshing, which made washing my hands and face a pleasure. Looking in the mirror, I saw my hair still in the nice braids Francisca had made for me the night before. After using a towel folded by the washbowl, I saw my skirt and shirt Francisca had taken yesterday. Cleaned and pressed, they were lying on a chair near the vanity, where she must have left them last evening after

I went to bed. I hung the beautiful muslin dress Rosa had given me in the armoire and then dressed in my freshly washed clothes.

I was just pulling on my moccasins when there was a gentle knock at the door. Before I could answer, the door opened and Francisca peeked around its edge into the room. "Ah, bueno, hija, you are up already. I hope you slept well after your long day?"

"Very well, gracias, Francisca. Muchas gracias for washing and pressing my clothes. I knew they were very dirty. Now they feel new and fresh. I hung the fine dress you brought me to wear to cena last night in the armoire for you."

"Oh no, hija. Rosa gave you that dress. She was very happy to see you in it last night when she peeked through the door at those eating her cena. I think you may need it again soon. She and I are proud for you to have it. That reminds me, I think Don Valenzuela may have good news for you."

"Then I owe you much, Francisca. Do you know the news?"

"No, I know only that a rider came in early this morning with a telegram for Don Valenzuela from Cucurpé. He said 'bueno' several times as he read it. I think it is good news for you because of the telegrams he sent out soon after you arrived yesterday."

My heart was palpitating as I finished pulling on my moccasins and took her outstretched hand. She said, "Don Valenzuela is out with some vaqueros. Come to the kitchen and I'll give you breakfast. He'll be back soon and tell you his news. I understand the packtrain carrying supplies for the Americano *soldados* (soldiers) arrived last night and they are busy sorting supplies."

"I'm hungry. I can smell the coffee and good baking things in the kitchen from here."

"Then let's hurry. The skillet waits on the stovetop getting hot."

I was just finishing Francisca's chorizo, scrambled eggs with chilies, tortillas, and fine coffee when Don Patricio came in the kitchen door. His face lit up with a big grin. "Ah, mujercita, buenos días. I trust you slept well last night?"

"I slept very well. Muchas gracias, Don Patricio."

"Bueno, bueno. I sent word to the *alcalde* (mayor) in Cucurpé when we returned yesterday to ask that he inquire as to the whereabouts of your aunt, Señora María Cuen. A rider brought me word this morning from the alcalde that he has sent inquiries to the alcaldes at Hermosillo, Nogales, Calabasas, and towns along the border all the way to Agua Prieta. He will send word to us as soon as she is found—and her travel schedule." I had been hoping for more and must have looked disappointed. "Smile, mujercita. Soon you'll see your *tía* (aunt). It won't take long to find her. In the meantime, you always have a place here in my casa."

"You are a very kind *hacendado* (wealthy man), Don Patricio. It's just that I hoped to see her sooner rather than later. What if she is hard to find?"

Don Patricio laughed out loud. "Why, we'll search until we find her. Finished with your *desayuno* (breakfast)? I'll take you over to see Teniente Finley. After you verify his report is correct, I'll show you a little of my rancho."

I smiled and turned to Francisca. "Sí, I've had a very good desayuno, gracias, Francisca. I'm happy to visit the camp of Capitan Lawton and see the report of Teniente Finley."

Don Patricio smiled and motioned toward the door.

I sat under a tree, the river gurgling by, as Teniente Finley read me his report on my captivity and escape from Geronimo. I heard mistakes in what he read, but since it was just for the record and no one else would read it, except perhaps his superior officers, who would then forget it, I nodded it was correct so he wouldn't have to rewrite it. He signed it and put it in a bag for the next rider to take to General Miles in Arizona. All around us, men worked in the shade of a few scattered trees, sorting supplies for each man or filling bandoliers with cartridges. Some had already finished their refitting chores and were rubbing down freshly washed pack mules and horses. The mules and horses had been through some rough days trying to keep up with Captain Lawton.

Don Patricio sat in the porch shade of a tent, pointing out places with a yucca stalk on a big map spread on the ground and telling the captain and two other officers I had not seen before about the country south and east in the Sierra Madre. Teniente Finley and I walked over to the tent. The officers stood as we arrived as though I was some kind of lady.

Captain Lawton said, "Gentlemen, allow me to introduce you to the bravest lady I've ever met, Señorita Trinidad Verdín. Three days ago, she escaped from Geronimo while caught in a cross fire between Geronimo's Apaches and the command of comandante Don Valenzuela. She's given Lieutenant Finley her story, which I'll send to General Miles in the next dispatch. Señorita Verdín, allow me to introduce First Lieutenant Walsh and soon-to-be First Lieutenant Doctor Leonard Wood." As Capitan Lawton introduced them, the officers smiled, bowed a little, and offered me their hands. They all said it was a great pleasure and honor to meet me.

I didn't understand why the officers were impressed with my getting away from Geronimo. His horse had stumbled and we were both thrown off, he to one side, I to the other. Don Patricio and his vaqueros were charging at us. I ran to them rather than Geronimo. I had wanted to run from Geronimo since he had taken me. I was just lucky Don Patricio's men hadn't taken me for an Apache and killed and scalped me like they did Juanita.

The officers resumed listening to Don Patricio describing the Sierra Madre country. I saw the Río Aros and Río Yaqui and where they met on the map. I only had to put my finger on the place and tell the soldiers to go there. I couldn't do it. Something in the back of my mind, as often as I could have spoken up, kept saying, *This isn't right. Be quiet.*

After Don Patricio finished talking about the map, Doctor Leonard Wood started asking me about the day Geronimo took me. He even made up scenarios, as though I might have forgotten some details, and asked if it might have happened that way. I told him all I knew, and that it was the way I remembered it. He didn't push it when he saw Captain Lawton and Don Patricio frowning at him, but I could tell he didn't quite believe me.

After a while, Don Patricio and I rode back to the big casa. At the midday meal, I met Rosa for the first time and thanked her for the gift of the beautiful dress. She had a kind smile and a soft voice and said she was happy for me to have it. Rosa and Francisca served us a delicious meal of chicken pozole and tostadas. I had never eaten so well as I had the last two meals with Don Patricio.

After we finished the midday meal, Don Patricio said he had work to do at his desk and suggested I might want to take an afternoon siesta until he finished, and then he would be glad to show me around the rancho. I wasn't sleepy and asked if I might look at books in his library. He smiled and nodded and said he was glad I had an interest in his books. He told me I could look at any book I liked. But then he pulled one off the shelves titled *Aesop's Fables* and said I might enjoy that one. The book was a collection of short stories a Greek slave had told about twenty-six hundred years ago, filled with pictures of talking animals and the old slave Aesop. Each story, short and easy to read, taught a valuable lesson. I liked all the fables. But the ones about the hare and tortoise and the cat-maiden were the best.

Don Patricio's work at his desk took longer than he had expected, and we didn't go out the rest of the afternoon. I didn't care. I had a fine time reading Aesop and looking at its pictures.

For cena, Rosa and Francisca served us chili colorado, with rice, tortillas, and empanadas, and again I ate more of their fine meal than I should have. After the sun disappeared, Don Patricio and I sat in his courtyard patio and listened to the night choruses of frogs and tree peepers down by the river while he smoked a cigarro and drank a little whiskey. Off in the distance, a bull bellowed.

Don Patricio said, "Hear that bull, Trini? He's my biggest and best. His horns stretch nearly four meters from tip to tip, about twelve feet by Americano measure. He has made many cows mothers, and with a few other bulls scattered over the rancho, they have made my herd grow to a great size, filled with strong, powerful animals."

"My Uncle Artisan had been rounding up wild cattle near where we lived. I think he had built up a herd of about three hundred and fifty and was finding two or three a day before the Apaches came. How large is your herd?"

"About four thousand head. I also have flocks of sheep and goats. My vaqueros stay very busy looking after them. Apaches will wipe out entire flocks just for the pleasure of killing the animals when they don't even need the meat. That is why I go after them so hard as soon as I learn they have taken only a cow or two for meat. Didn't you tell me you were with them when they killed one of my cows?"

"Sí, Don Patricio, I was there. I was the reason Geronimo shot the cow. She had a calf, and I surprised her when I walked out of the bushes. She was coming after me, and Geronimo shot to stop her. I'm sorry it was your cow."

"Hmmph. Your life is worth much more than a cow, mujercita. I'm glad in that case Geronimo was such a good shot, but I hated to bury those men he killed after you escaped. You said he saved your life three times before you escaped. How did he do that?"

"Well, the first time was when the Apaches came to Artisan's rancho casa and killed my Aunt Petra and her baby. When I saw her shot, I ran and hid under the bed she and Artisan used. But when the warriors came inside and tore the place up, they found me under the bed and dragged me out. The one who had caught me grabbed my hair and jerked my head back to cut my throat. I expected to see God in the next minute, when Geronimo came in and said, 'Wait!' He thought that I might be useful and let me live. He told his men to put me up behind his son Chappo to ride off with them."

I was afraid to tell Don Patricio the details about how Geronimo had saved me from the vaqueros and twisted the story a little. "The second time, some vaqueros were ready to kill me when he shot one and I got away. The third time, here on your rancho, he killed the cow that was going to run me down."

"I can see how you must think you owe Geronimo much, mujercita. But you must remember that he attacked your uncle's rancho in the first place and killed your aunt and little cousin. He probably saved you to use as a slave for his wife or something to bargain with in a trade with Mexicans in Chihuahua."

Don Patricio crushed his cigarro in an ashtray next to his chair and spat into a flower bed. He said, "The Apaches have been stealing from us here in Sonora and selling or trading things they steal from us to the fool merchants in Janos or Casas Grandes in Chihuahua. I have begged the governors in Chihuahua and Sonora to stop this practice and force the

Apaches on to a reservation somewhere around Ojinaga on the Río Grande about a hundred miles east of Ciudad Chihuahua. There, they are far, far away from Sonora. It is too bad the governors would rather kill all the Apaches or turn them into slaves in Mexico City than keep them on a reservation. In this, I think, they always fail."

I told Don Patricio it seemed to me that the Apaches just wanted their freedom and independence more than anything else.

He laughed and said, "I guess so, Trini, especially since their whole lives they have been little more than pirates roaming the land. Someday, I think, they will just fade away. I hope so."

We talked about the Apaches through another glass of his whiskey until I couldn't help yawning, and he called to Francisca through a screen door to come help me to bed. I told him "Buenas noches," walked down the long hall with Francisca to my bedroom where I washed my face, climbed into bed, and soon fell asleep.

Chapter 38
Magdalena

During their resupply and refit, the troopers had taken full advantage of the river to bathe, and to wash their clothes and animals. They all looked refreshed and ready to go when Don Patricio and I rode down to their camp the next morning to tell them goodbye and to wish them well. The sooner the fighting with the Apaches was over, the better I'd like it, and I knew the soldiers felt the same way.

It has always thrilled me to see men and animals working in unison under an officer's commands. When Captain Lawton gave his first sergeant the order for the men to mount and they all swung into their saddles at the same time, it was a thing of beauty. Don Patricio and I, smiling, saluted them as they rode past us in the early-morning light. The sun was just coming over the mountains, giving them long, wavering shadows toward the west as they jogged south downriver.

I wished I could have warned them and told them where to go in the Sierra Madre, but I knew Geronimo would avoid them unless they got careless and set themselves up for an ambush. I didn't think the scouts would let them do that.

Don Patricio and I rode back to the hacienda to have our desayuno. A vaquero's lathered horse was blowing, tied to the hitching post in front of the casa. The vaquero sat near a flower bed on a boulder, with a saddlebag made for carrying papers lying over his shoulder, smoking a corn-shuck cigarette. As soon as

319

he saw us, he hopped up, crushed his cigarette, and came to hold our horses while we dismounted.

He said, "As you directed, Don Valenzuela, I rode to Cucurpé this morning to check with the alcalde for any papers he had for you and have returned with ones he said you had been expecting."

Don Patricio smiled. "Ah, gracias, Pablo. Maybe now with this Apache business done, life will get back to normal." He took the saddlebag, waved adios to Pablo, and started to follow me into the hacienda, when Pablo said, "Oh, Don Valenzuela. I almost forgot the telegrams I picked up for you."

Telegrams? I thought as my heart quickened and I hoped one might have news about my aunt, María Cuen.

Don Patricio thanked Pablo again and put the telegrams in his vest pocket. When we reached the courtyard, he told me to go on to the kitchen, where Rosa had desayuno waiting for us, while he left the saddlebag in his study and would soon follow.

As always, Rosa's desayuno was a delight, but I could hardly eat any of it until Don Patricio joined me. He soon sat down at the table but said nothing about the telegrams. After eating a few tasteless bites, I couldn't stand it.

"Don Patricio, I don't mean to be nosy, but was there good news in the telegrams?"

He took a bite of his huevos rancheros and nodded. "Oh, sí, mujercita. My family is visiting relatives in Mexico City. Soon they will return."

The look of sad disappointment on my face must have been evident. He laid down his fork and, laughing, said, "Forgive me, mujercita. I tease you too much and too well. There was also a telegram from your aunt, María Cuen." My mouth dropped open, and I felt my eyes grow big and round. "She is very happy you have escaped the terrible Geronimo and wants to know if she can meet you the evening of June twenty-fourth at the Magdalena train station sometime after seven o'clock. She is now in Nogales, and that is the closest and fastest she can get near where you are now without more delay."

I was so happy I didn't know whether to laugh or cry. "Thank you so much for finding her, Don Patricio. Can you send someone to guide me to Magdalena? I won't be any trouble on the trail. I promise I can take care of myself."

He laughed again. "No, mujercita, I cannot send someone to guide you to Magdalena Station. I will take Francisca with us as your *dueña* (guardian) and see you safely in the care of your Aunt María Cuen. We leave tomorrow and go to Cucurpé, where the alcalde wants to meet you. You have become famous in this country for getting away from Geronimo before he could kill you. The Apaches have killed or kidnapped so many children never seen again. I also have a little business to do with Don Gritto, my neighbor to the north who is interested in a couple of my bulls.

"We'll stay in Cucurpé overnight and then take the wagon road over the mountains to Magdalena and stay overnight there. I have business the next day with a shipper of my cattle. We'll go to the train station that evening to meet your aunt. The next day, the secretary for the prefect wants to take your statement like the one Teniente Finley took for the Americano soldiers, and then you and your aunt can leave for wherever you want to go. Does this suit you?"

I was so excited my hands trembled when I held my coffee cup to take a sip. "Oh yes, Don Patricio. Your generosity knows no bounds. I am very grateful. When will we leave?"

He rubbed his chin, thinking for moment, while I set down my trembling cup, hot and nearly burning my hands, its steam filled with the smell of its thick black flavor.

He said, "Hmmph. I think since there is no hurry, we'll take

the long way around on the wagon road that goes through Cucurpé on the way to Magdalena. We'll leave after desayuno
tomorrow and should be in Cucurpé before midday. Is this
good for you?"

I grinned and quietly clapped my hands. I could see Rosa
working at the big iron stove, and she, too, had a smile filling
her face.

Leaving the hacienda, I hugged Rosa and thanked her for all
the kind things she had done for me and said that I would never
forget them. Francisca wore a new dress and was all smiles as
Don Patricio motioned for her to sit in the front seat of the
two-horse buggy with him and me. He wore a pistola, carried a
dress coat, and brought two of his best vaqueros with us.

We took a southwest trail out across the llano and passed
several small herds of quietly grazing cattle that raised their
heads with the tips of their long, pointed horns shining in the
morning light and bellowed at us before returning to the thin
llano grass. It wasn't long before we came to the dusty Cucurpé-
to-Magdalena wagon road and turned west.

Don Patricio was right. We reached Cucurpé well before what
the Apaches called the time of shortest shadows. He drove to a
big, fine casa on the edge of town, where the lady answering the
door smiled when she recognized him, Francisca, and the two
vaqueros. Don Patricio introduced me as the señorita who had
escaped the Apaches.

The lady made a little bow and said, "It is my pleasure to
meet such a beautiful and brave señorita."

The vaqueros waited while smoking their cigarettes in the
courtyard as Don Patricio, Francisca, and I went in to visit with
the alcalde and his treasurer, Señor Gabriel Sinohui. I
recognized Señor Sinohui, who had been with Don Patricio
when their men had attacked Geronimo and knew he must

have seen me get away.

Don Patricio described the battle in detail for the old alcalde, who said he had never heard of a child escaping the Apaches during a battle and wanted to meet me. The alcalde scolded Don Patricio and Señor Sinohui for three men killed and one wounded when even a fine young girl managed a getaway.

The two men looked at the floor and said nothing until the alcalde's rant blew away like a summer storm and he became sunny again. He invited us to stay for a midday meal with him and Señor Sinohui, but Don Patricio politely declined, saying he had other appointments he had to keep, and promised to return the next time he was in Cucurpé.

We went to another big house that served as the local hotel. Although it looked a little shabby, its paint peeling and weeds cluttering the flower bed on the outside, it was clean and polished inside and had very nice, dark, heavy furniture. Don Patricio took three rooms for the night, one for Francisca and me, one for the vaqueros, and the other for himself.

He told the vaqueros to take our horses to the livery stable and then to join us at the El Gallo Rojo Cantina, where we would have our *comida* (lunch) before he discussed the sale of a couple of his bulls with a hacendado who owned a rancho a two-hour ride north up the Río San Miguel. It was a big, fine rancho. I had seen gate signs, fences, herds of cattle, and wagon roads for it when the Apaches were on the trail to Cucurpé.

The green chili chicken enchiladas and tamales we had at the cantina were very good, and we were just finishing our last cup of coffee when Don Gritto, who wanted to buy the bulls, came through the door with a couple of his vaqueros and immediately walked to our table. Don Patricio stood and made introductions. Don Gritto, like the alcalde, also expressed pleasure in meeting me, the girl who had escaped Geronimo. I didn't understand why everyone I met knew about my escape or why it had been such a major event.

Watching the two hacendados negotiate the price of a couple of prize bulls was like watching a dance with all the moves carefully choreographed. First was talk of the old days and how hard it was to grow herds of any size and keep them when the Apaches came to steal and destroy. Then they drank a round of tequila and talked about what made a bull good breeding stock. Don Gritto described his herd bulls and how close they were to giving him what he wanted. Don Patricio then described his bulls and claimed there were no finer ones in Mexico. They had another round of tequila while again speaking of their families and their ranchos.

At last they got down to price. From the face Don Gritto made, Don Patricio seemed to be asking a very high price for his animals, but as they haggled back and forth, his price came down a little, and he offered to buy them back if Don Gritto's cows didn't have many calves in the spring. That seemed to be the warranty Don Gritto wanted, and they soon made the deal, with Don Patricio promising to send the bulls to Don Gritto's rancho as soon as he returned from taking me to Magdalena.

By the time the sale was complete, the sun was falling behind the mountains. Don Patricio asked Don Gritto to join us for cena at the hotel where we had taken rooms, but he declined, saying he and his vaqueros needed to get back to his hacienda. He was expecting a flock of sheep he had recently bought and wanted to be there when they arrived.

We were on the way to Magdalena soon after the sun rose, casting bright spots of light on the mountain shadows along the wagon road. Soon after we left Cucurpé, we began a long, gentle climb up through rust-colored foothills with scattered thickets of mesquites and large patches of bare, brown, sandy earth scattered over with creosote bushes, prickly pear, mesquite, and gourd vines with blue and yellow flowers opening to the sunlight.

Chirping flocks of titmouses and their morning songs were everywhere, rising like gray clouds out of one tree and into another. Crows flying high passed over us, cawing and croaking, after staying overnight in the trees along the river. The road carried us closer to the highest mountain overlooking Cucurpé, before the road, still rising, went through a pass that Don Patricio said was over three hundred meters higher than Cucurpé, down on the Río San Miguel, but seemed at the bottom of the great mountain it went around.

A little farther along, we began climbing a ridge. The road to the top of the ridge was so steep we got out of the buggy and walked to the top to keep from tiring the horses. From the top of that ridge, it was downhill the rest of the way into Magdalena. We stopped two or three times to rest the horses and give them a drink at nearby water tanks filled by windmills.

Magdalena spread out before us in the late-afternoon sun, and its buildings, mostly white-painted adobe, seemed to glow. Wagons and men on horseback filled the streets, and women of all shapes, ages, and sizes walked while carrying big loads on their heads or backs, while some in fancy-patterned bright-red skirts were laughing and dancing around the doors of cantinas on every street.

Don Patricio drove by the prefect's big building with a red tile roof and then, a few blocks farther south, turned another block west to a great hacienda, now used as a hotel, where only wealthy hacendados could afford to stay. The vaqueros took the buggy and horses to a livery stable while the proprietor showed us to our rooms.

Before they left, the vaqueros asked Don Patricio for permission to enjoy themselves in a cantina after the long ride over the mountains. He was glad to let them go as long as they agreed—

and this they promised—to be in the courtyard the next morning, where they could hear his talks with the shipper.

Francisca and I had a cozy room with a large bed. After washing away the trail dust and combing the kinks out of my windblown hair, we joined Don Patricio for a wonderful cena of roast beef in green chili sauce, rice, salad, fried vegetables, tortillas, and caramel flan for dessert.

I was able only to sit and talk with Don Patricio for a little while before my eyes grew heavy. Francisca and I bade him "buenas noches," and walked down the long dark hallway to our bed.

CHAPTER 39
REUNION

Two sets of rails passed in front of the Magdalena Station. West across the tracks was a wide sandy field where the Río Magdalena flowed, looking like a brown, narrow, twisting rope across the white sand. A little farther west, just beyond the river, were low, tan, barely lifeless but imposing mountains that ended here, far south of where the Cibuta Mountains began. The sun beginning to set behind the mountains left their eastern side that we faced in darkening shadows.

Casting dreamy ocher colored light, oil lamps lighted the station inside and out on the long platform used by people awaiting the train. Crates ready for shipping sat on one end of the platform. Vaqueros waiting on the train sat on these, smoked their corn-shuck cigarettes, and talked about cattle, bear hunting, and women they liked at the cantinas.

I sat on a bench between Don Patricio and Francisca as we waited on the platform for the southbound train from Nogales. It had been nearly two years since I last saw María, when she took me to help Petra. I wondered if she had room for me at her place, or if some other cousin or aunt needed my help. I didn't care as long as I was not running, running, always running, like the Apaches who had taken me captive.

I thought about the day the Apaches took me. I remembered Ahnandia killing Petra and her little son, and Artisan wearing his red long johns and walking barefooted across the burning sand toward the ridge with ugly black smoke rising from behind.

I had asked Don Patricio to learn whether Artisan had survived, but there was no word yet. Maybe Artisan had not made it back to Calabasas and died on the way. Maybe the Apaches came back and murdered him like they threatened if he went to the ranch. The more I thought about it, the more I wiggled around. Don Patricio smiled and pulled out his pocket watch but then frowned when he looked at it.

He said, "The train from Nogales is nearly an hour late. I wonder what the holdup is. I'll go ask the stationmaster."

I saw Don Patricio and the stationmaster talking. The stationmaster shrugged his shoulders and thumbed at the big pendulum clock hanging on the wall behind him.

Don Patricio nodded and returned to sit down beside me with a grunt. "The stationmaster said he doesn't know why, but the telegraph said the train was about an hour and a half late leaving Nogales. It's made up some time and should be here in a short while."

Francisca shrugged. "Trains. I've never known them to be on time. It's always something." Don Patricio made a half smile on his face and nodded he agreed with her. I got up and paced around the platform, wishing the train would hurry up.

I had made my third circuit of the platform when I heard the long, low moan of the train's whistle warning of its approach. I leaned out from the edge of the platform and looked north down the tracks. A point of light like a fallen star was slowly growing larger far in the distance. Vaqueros started climbing off the crates and gathering their bags, saddles, and rifles as a man driving a freight wagon with three others to help him pulled up to the crates and began sliding them onto the wagon bed.

I clapped my hands and ran over to Don Patricio and Francisca, who both had big, broad grins. "She's coming! She's coming!" I squealed and hugged them both.

They stood and walked with me as I whirled round and round

in excitement to the edge of the platform. The light from the train was much brighter and, when its whistle blew again, it was much louder and nearer, and I could faintly hear the engine puffing. The men with the wagon hauling the crates drove it out toward the edge of the station light, where they expected the freight cars to stop.

Don Patricio took my right hand, and with Francisca taking my left, we walked to the stairs leading down to the ground. Pausing on the platform, Don Patricio waited, and we watched as the big black engine slowly entered the lights, its bell ringing, the couplings rumbling, and the brakes squeaking and squealing as it stopped down the line under the water tower to take on more water while a wagon loaded with coal came to fill the tender behind the engine.

When the engine stopped, Don Patricio led us down the steps and toward the passenger cars, where a man in a fancy uniform stepped down from the first passenger car and put a box even with the train-car steps. It had a few more steps to make a continuation of the train-car steps down to the ground.

I stretched and stood on my toes, trying to see María through the windows, but there were too many passengers standing in the aisle and too much glare on the windows for me to see much. Ten or fifteen people stepped down from the train, and then there were none, but there was no María with them. Where was she? Why hadn't she come? What was I going to do?

Then she seemed to magically appear on the stairs, with her long black hair up in a twist on her head, a magenta *rebozo* around her neck and over her shoulders, a white blouse embroidered down the front, and an indigo skirt with a white print pattern that looked like twigs with small leaves. She looked up and down the tracks, saw us, laughed, and seemed to fly off the steps and run down the tracks toward us.

I ran to her, yelling, "María. María. I thought I would never see you again."

She ran to me, picked me up in her strong arms, hugged me, and gave me three quick kisses. "Nor I you, child. God has blessed us all." She set me on the ground and held me at arm's length. "Let me look at you. You look so thin. Are you feeling well? Nothing hurts or is broken?"

I laughed and shook my head. "Oh no, señora. I am fine. The Apaches were always on the run, but they never left me hungry. The men never bothered me, but the women might have cuffed me a little when I was slow to understand. I'm bruised and a little sore here and there from falling off Geronimo's pony a few days ago, but Don Patricio Valenzuela, who led the men who saved me and who owns the great Agua Fría hacienda near Cucurpé, and his servant ladies have taken very good care of me."

She bowed her head and I heard her whisper, "Gracias a Dios. Gracias a Dios."

I started to lead her to Don Patricio and Francisca and introduce them, when I looked up and saw the last passenger get off the train. He was a big, broad-shouldered man in canvas pants, a white shirt with sleeves rolled up to just above his elbows, red long-john sleeves showing to the wrists, and a silver-colored hat with the brim turned down in front that shadowed most of his face. I saw those red sleeves and remembered that was the way Artisan dressed, and my heart pounded again. The man walked toward us with a slight limp. When he saw me looking toward him, he stopped, smiled, and tilted his hat back on his head to reveal his face.

I squealed with delight and ran for him, sobbing. "Artisan! Artisan, you're alive! Gracias a Dios!"

His grin was as bright as the sun, and he swooped me up and held me high like I was a little child. Then he kissed me on my forehead and cheek as he hugged me and said, "Sí! Gracias a

Dios, you have come back to us, child. Now I take you back home."

CHAPTER 40
THE QUESTION

The men who had filled the grave moved wreathes and bouquets of flowers to cover the mound of soft, sandy earth and then quietly slipped away. The sun had disappeared and myriad stars took its place. Somewhere in the garden of stone a whip-poor-will called, and far outside the fence a coyote yipped. The once warm earth was cooling as the golden glow of the moon bloomed behind the mountains and grew brighter.

Trinidad, her story ended, said no more. Wandering in her memories, ghosts never leaving her had spoken. She opened a small wooden box she carried in her purse and returned the pebble it held to its original resting place in a little bed of cotton. The girl crossed her arms against the chill and stared into the darkness.

"Grandma, can I ask you a question?"

The old lady turned to her and answered in foreign words the girl had never heard before.

She frowned and said, "What? I didn't understand a thing you said."

"It's Apache for 'Speak. I will answer.' "

They both laughed, knowing that bit of her story was their secret to share.

"Did you ever regret leaving the Apaches?"

Trinidad was quiet for so long, the girl thought she hadn't heard the question and started to ask it again when her grandmother said, "That's a perceptive question, child. I was an orphan passed around among my aunts. The Apaches survived in a hard land with thousands of soldiers after them on both sides of the border. They asked no quarter and gave none. If you crossed their path you died. It didn't bother them to torture enemies to death. They lived by taking everything they needed. For reasons I never knew, Geronimo spared me after his men killed my aunt and her baby. I wanted to live. I worked hard and lived with Geronimo and his wife, who came to accept me as one of their own. A few days before I escaped, Geronimo and his wife had decided to adopt me as their daughter. The last day before I escaped, a boy who had become my best friend, said he wanted me for his woman when we were grown.

"Before I was taken, I didn't even know the difference between a girl and a woman, but She-gha taught me in a good way and expected me to live a chaste life. She was kind and I felt attached to her. She made me clothes and taught me many things I needed to know to survive. The entire band accepted me, and I've never felt being more a part of something bigger than me or more protected.

"Even when they were under attack by Don Patricio and bullets were flying, Geronimo did his best to protect me. I knew all this after falling off Geronimo's horse and lying stunned on the ground seeing stars floating in a sunlit sky, but I didn't think about it then. I ran to people of my blood by instinct and left those I knew wanted me. Would they have become my blood? History says no. Their time had run out."

Her granddaughter waited in the silence that seemed to settle on them like a warm blanket, then asked, "But, did you regret leaving them?"

"I escaped, but I've kept my memories, dreams, and warm heart for them. I stayed with them as I could. I've never forgotten them."

"Grandma, is that pebble you just put away the one Garditha gave you?"

Surprised at how closely her granddaughter had listened to her story, she smiled and nodded and, looking out across the night to distant lights twinkling in the darkness, saw the headlights of a car bouncing down the road toward the cemetery gate. It was time to go.

AFTERWORD

Despite Geronimo warning him not to return to his ranch house, Artisan Peck walked barefoot two miles across desert ridges back to his ranch. He found his pregnant wife, Petra, and his two-year-old son, Andy, killed by the marauding Apaches, and everything he had of value taken or destroyed, including livestock, firearms, six months of just-purchased supplies, and a thousand dollars from his mining days hidden in a trunk. He managed to walk another six miles to Calabasas, where— exhausted, torn, and bleeding—he was taken in by friends, who sent a wagon to collect the bodies of his family and neighbor and supported him while he recovered. He never returned to the ranch site where he and Petra had tried to make a life. He rarely spoke of the Apache raid.

In late June 1886, Artisan went to Magdalena, Mexico, and brought Trinidad Verdín back to Nogales after she gave her story to J.A. Rivera for the Magdalena Prefect. To make a living, Artisan started a livery stable in Nogales and did well. He married a lady named Carmen Canez, thirteen years younger than he, and had two more children, Delores Quinn and Arthur Leslie. After a long, full life, Artisan Peck died on August 30, 1939, in Nogales, Santa Cruz County, Arizona.

A few years after Trinidad returned to Nogales, she married Luis Margaillan, one of the brothers who owned the cave that became the famous La Caverna Restaurant in Nogales. In 1995, her great-great-granddaughter, Cynthia Margaillan, wrote a

Junior Historian article for the Cochise County Historical Society about her great-great-grandmother and Geronimo.

In late August 1886, two months after Trinidad ran to Don Patricio's militia, the Geronimo–Naiche band was found in the Teres Mountains in the great bend of the Bavispe River, by scouts and relatives, Martine and Kayihtah, who came carrying a white flag on a yucca stick. Geronimo wanted to shoot them because he believed they had betrayed their people by serving as scouts, but two of Geronimo's best warriors who were related to them demanded with cocked rifles that they be heard.

Geronimo relented and called them to a council. They asked the band to hear General Nelson Miles's surrender terms from his representative, Lieutenant Charles B. Gatewood, a former chief of scouts and a man the Apaches knew they could trust to speak the truth.

After two days of talks with Gatewood, the Apaches surrendered to General Nelson Appleton Miles in Skeleton Canyon, Arizona, on September 4, 1886. They had been on the run for over five months, pursued by five thousand American soldiers (one quarter of the total United States Army), three thousand Mexican soldiers, and hundreds of civilians in posses. They had not lost a single warrior to capture, wounding, or killing. Geronimo would remain a prisoner of war for the rest of his life. He died from pneumonia in the Apache Hospital at Fort Sill, Oklahoma, February 17, 1909, after sleeping drunk all night in a cold rain.

She-gha, shipped to Fort Marion (St. Augustine, Florida) from Fort Sam Houston, Texas, in late October 1886, is said to have shown signs of a prolonged illness. All of Geronimo's wives—Zi-yeh, Ih-tedda (who had been at Fort Marion for over a year), and She-gha—and two children (Fenton and Lenna) joined him at Fort Pickens on Santa Rosa Island in Pensacola Bay in May 1887. She-gha passed away in September 1887 and was buried at the Fort Barrancas Cemetery at Pensacola, Florida.

Geronimo took his best warriors with him to her funeral across the bay so they could scope out the possibilities of escape if they left Santa Rosa Island. They concluded escape that way was impossible. Nine months later, the Naiche–Geronimo men and their families were shipped to Mount Vernon Barracks, thirty miles from Mobile, Alabama, where they lived for over seven years with the other prisoner-of-war Chiricahuas, before they were sent to Fort Sill in October 1894.

During his years at Fort Sill, Geronimo became a nationally known figure, participating in three world expositions, riding in numerous parades in new Oklahoma towns, and riding in Theodore Roosevelt's inaugural parade in 1905.

Garditha surrendered with the Naiche–Geronimo band in September 1886, when he was about ten years old. He and the band's women and other children were sent to Fort Marion in late October of 1886. Little is known about him after Geronimo surrendered. He is likely to have died in his late teens or early twenties at Mount Vernon Barracks, Alabama.

ADDITIONAL READING

Ball, Eve, Nora Henn, and Lynda A. Sánchez. *Indeh: An Apache Odyssey,* University of Oklahoma Press, Norman, OK, 1988.

Barrett, S. M. *Geronimo, His Own Story: The Autobiography of a Great Patriot Warrior,* Meridian, Penguin Books USA, New York, NY, 1996.

Burrows, Jack. "Geronimo's Last Hurrah in Arizona Territory," *Wild West Magazine,* August 2001, pp. 38–45.

Debo, Angie. *Geronimo: The Man, His Time, His Place,* University of Oklahoma Press, Norman, OK, 1976.

Delgadillo, Alicia, with Miriam A. Perrett. *Fort Marion to Fort Sill: A Documentary History of the Chiricahua Prisoner of War, 1886–1913,* University of Nebraska Press, Lincoln, NE, 2013.

Haley, James L. *Apaches: A History and Culture Portrait,* University of Oklahoma Press, Norman, OK, 1981.

Holden, Walter. "Geronimo's Last Captive, Trini Verdín, Has Been Draped in Discrepancies and Wrapped in Contradictions," *Wild West Magazine,* August 2001, pp. 16, 62.

Hutton, Paul Andrew. *The Apache Wars,* Crown Publishing Group, New York, NY, 2016.

McCarty, Kieran, and C. L. Sonnichsen. "Trini Verdín and the 'Truth' of History," *The Journal of Arizona History,* Vol. 14, No. 2, pp. 149–64.

Robinson, Sherry, *Apache Voices: Their Stories of Survival as Told to Eve Ball,* University of New Mexico Press, Albuquerque, NM, 2003.

Sánchez, Lynda A. *Apache Legends and Lore of Southern New Mexico,* History Press, Charleston, SC, 2014.

Sweeny, Edwin. *From Cochise to Geronimo: The Chiricahua Apaches, 1874–1886,* University of Oklahoma Press, Norman, OK, 2010.

Utley, Robert M. *Geronimo,* Yale University Press, New Haven, CT, 2012.

ABOUT THE AUTHOR

W. Michael Farmer combines fifteen-plus years of research into nineteenth-century Apache history and culture with Southwest-living experience to fill his stories with a genuine sense of time and place. A retired Ph.D. physicist, his scientific research has included measurement of atmospheric aerosols with laser-based instruments. He has published a two-volume reference book on atmospheric effects on remote sensing as well as fiction in anthologies and essays. His novels have won numerous awards including three Will Rogers Gold and five Silver Medallions, New Mexico-Arizona Book Awards for Adventure, Historical Fiction, Literary Fiction, a Non-Fiction New Mexico Book of the Year, and a Spur Finalist Award for Best First Novel. His book series includes The Life and Times of Yellow Boy, Mescalero Apache and Legends of the Desert.

The employees of Five Star Publishing hope you have enjoyed this book.

Our Five Star novels explore little-known chapters from America's history, stories told from unique perspectives that will entertain a broad range of readers.

Other Five Star books are available at your local library, bookstore, all major book distributors, and directly from Five Star/Gale.

Connect with Five Star Publishing

Website:
  gale.com/five-star

Facebook:
  facebook.com/FiveStarCengage

Twitter:
  twitter.com/FiveStarCengage

Email:
  FiveStar@cengage.com

For information about titles and placing orders:
  (800) 223-1244
  gale.orders@cengage.com

To share your comments, write to us:
  Five Star Publishing
  Attn: Publisher
  10 Water St., Suite 310
  Waterville, ME 04901